A SURG

-Prequel to the novel Surgical Heights

By Paul E. Hardy, MD

Paul Hardy

Also by Paul E. Hardy - Surgical Heights, 2010

Edited by - Dania Sheldon

Note for Librarians: A cataloguing record for this book is available from Library
and Archives Canada at www.collectionscanada.ca/amicus/index-e.html

To Contact Paul E. Hardy write to him at:
Paul E. Hardy
#400 3939 – 50A Ave.
Red Deer, AB T4N 4E6
403-304-9290

Or email him at:
info@surgicalheights.com

www.surgicalplight.com

ISBN – 978-1-77084-239-7

Printed in Canada
on recycled paper

FIRST CHOICE BOOKS
DEMAND PUBLISHING & BINDING

www.firstchoicebooks.ca
Victoria, BC
10 9

For Barbara and Eric

"Worry retards reaction and makes clear-cut decisions impossible."

- Amelia Earhart 1897 - disappeared 1937

Table of Contents

Preface

This novel took place in Canada as evidenced by the characteristic spelling throughout the book. It is however, a story that could have occurred any place in the world with a relatively advanced society and medical system.

This is a work of fiction. Any resemblance to real events or people, living or dead, is purely coincidental.

I would like to thank friends, relatives and colleagues who took the time to read early manuscripts and to provide feedback. These helpers include Bryan Caddy, Janet Hardy, Sylvia Gillespie, John Moffat, Joanne Glen, Nancy Moffat, Bill Harris, Penny Harris, Nancy Hardy, John Ritchie, Lawrence Farries, Elizabeth Julian, Trevor Theman and John A. Ross. Ralph George, John Brennan, Julie Stevens, Blair Goranson, Clarke Hardy and Hilary Hardy provided additional support, which is much appreciated. Special thanks to Tilda Shalof, who prompted me to write again when I was least interested and who has been an invaluable source of advice along the way.

I appreciate the staff at First Choice Books including Sol Terlson Kennedy and Patrick O'Connor, whose quality of work was exemplary.

I would also like to give special thanks Dania Sheldon, once again, for her excellent editorial work, which put finishing touches on the novel, making it significantly better.

One of my early readers of the manuscript asked me, "If you had read a book like '*A Surgical Plight*' prior to choosing your career, would you still have chosen surgery?"

My response is simple: "*Absolutely!*"

A Surgical Plight

Prologue: March 1992

"PRIVATE AND CONFIDENTIAL". His heart raced as the boldfaced type leapt off the envelope. Standing in the front hallway, he saw Amanda in the mirror as she approached from behind. Jim clutched the letter as he smiled and turned to hug her. She looked up at him and smoothed his blond hair away from his eyes.

Jim gazed fondly at his beautiful wife. Her silky brown hair was in a ponytail, pulled back from her glistening forehead. Her green eyes crinkled at the corners as she smiled. *She looks happy*, he thought. As he stood back, he noticed blotches of sweat on the light blue tracksuit that accentuated the curves of her fit body.

"Open it! I've been wanting to tear into that letter all day," she exclaimed.

What a difference a few years have made, thought Jim. Six years ago, when he'd lost a parent for the second time, he could see no purpose in life. Now, he felt like the luckiest man alive. At twenty-six, he'd graduated with his medical degree and was now over eight months through his internship. He'd applied to several five-year residency programs in general surgery and was eagerly awaiting acceptance, hoping to get his first choice. He had the wife of his dreams. He could envision nothing but good fortune in his future.

He looked at the letter again, confirming it was from the Resident Matching Service. Although fairly certain he'd be accepted into general surgery, he was by no means a shoe-in to get his first choice, since it was one of the most competitive programs in the country.

"Hold on, let's sit down first."

"Hurry, my shift at the hospital starts in a less than an hour," she said excitedly. "I still have to shower. You know I can't be late."

Jim led Amanda by the hand to the kitchen table, where they sat down next to each other.

“Your hands are shaking, Jim. If you can’t open it, I will!”

“I’ll do it,” he said, pulling the letter tight to his chest. Hesitating, he added, “I’m just hoping to get my top pick.”

Amanda shrugged her shoulders and gestured with her hand for Jim to go ahead. He nervously tore open the envelope, taking care not to rip the contents. Then he held the paper up in front of his face so only he could read it. He paused.

“Well?”

Exhaling the breath he had been unaware of holding, Jim beamed. “I’m in.”

Chapter 1 ~ Edna

Thursday, September 26, 1996

"I'm not happy about this patient—at all." Jim Smythe ran a hand through his blond hair as he leaned his lanky frame against the wall while talking into the telephone. He spoke firmly to his supervisor, Dr. Herman Baker, whose silence on the other end of the phone was unnerving and frustrating. "I think something is going on and even though I can't put my finger on it, I'm worried. She might need to come into hospital."

"Look here, Jim," Baker's nasal voice was finally audible. "You either admit the patient with a proper surgical diagnosis or the patient can go anywhere else—but not to a surgical bed. What makes you think she needs to be admitted?" Before Jim could answer, Baker added, "How old did you say she was?"

"Seventy. She's had belly pain for two days. Worse today. She had an ultrasound yesterday that didn't show much—just some sludge in her gallbladder. I'm not going to lie to you. I'm not exactly sure what's going on with her. I know her X-rays don't show a heck of a lot, but I wonder if we should admit her. Could be her gallbladder or an ulcer. Something's going on."

"The ultrasound showed sludge? Only sludge? No actual gallstones?" Baker's voice escalated, creeping under Jim's skin.

"No—no stones."

"How was her aorta?"

"Fine," Jim responded. He couldn't recall the exact wording of the ultrasound report but surely he would have noticed if the radiologist had identified an aortic aneurysm.

"Blood work?"

"Nothing. Hemoglobin's a bit low at 102, but nothing else. I don't know what the problem is but I'm just not happy sending her home."

"I'll tell you what. I'll wander by in the next hour and see her myself, if that'll make you happy."

"Thanks, Dr. Baker." Jim exhaled with relief. He fumbled through the patient chart, reassured to find that the ultrasound report clearly stated the aorta was normal. "Edna Doyle—she's in Section E Observation."

"Section E Observation? That's an oxymoron if I've ever heard one! I told them," Baker raised his voice, "I never want my patients in E! Just because they're not sick doesn't mean they can be ignored. Sometimes you couldn't find a nurse in E if your life depended on it! One of these days I'm going to walk right out of E with one of their microwaves under my arm, just to prove I can do it."

Always the complainer, thought Jim. At least Baker wasn't whining about him this time. "Okay, Dr. Baker, I'll remind them to put your patients anywhere but E, at least D as a minimum. Let me know what you think of her."

The last person Jim Smythe wanted to emulate was Herman Baker. Yet here he was, in his fifth and final year of surgical residency, having to take call with Dr. Baker. As one of six chief residents dispersed to hospitals throughout the city, Jim ran the surgical service at St. Joseph's Hospital. On the first day of July every year, a new batch of residents populated the university-affiliated hospitals, providing a significant service to the medical system while learning in the process. Early July was always a little shaky, but within weeks each cog in the machine was functioning smoothly. Having started his final and chief year the first day of July, Jim was now hitting his stride in September. At the end of June, after twelve exhilarating months as chief resident, Jim was expecting to complete his oral exams. Passing them would thrust him into the real world as a full-fledged general surgeon.

At a time when most medical specialties were benefiting from an increasing proportion of female practitioners, general surgery remained a specialty steadfastly dominated by men. Long working hours were likely a considerable factor. A significant increase in female trainees was occurring only recently.

During his chief year, if Jim's team of junior residents and medical students cared adequately for the forty-odd patients on the surgical ward, the eight staff surgeons would be happy. And as long as they were content, Jim's reward was to do as much operating as he could for them. Now in September, over two months into his final year of surgical training, Jim had done most of the operations that a general surgeon in practice would typically perform. At thirty years of age, he had the advantages of stamina and enthusiasm. He was allowed to pick the best operations each week. Surgeons would provide interesting cases for their hungry chief resident, in exchange for him running a seamless surgical service, free of hassles or controversy. Jim was operating under minimal supervision except in the most difficult surgeries—he was having the time of his life.

As he hung up the telephone, Jim couldn't help but think how much he disliked Herman Baker. The silver-haired surgeon in his midfifties had a habit of relentlessly badgering his residents, a sign of Baker's own insecurity, Jim thought. He pictured Baker stretching his short, pudgy frame on the couch at home, clutching the TV remote in his left hand and scratching his protuberant potbelly with his right, while his long-suffering wife chastised him about changing channels too often. He smirked as he contemplated Baker on the receiving end of someone else's malice for a change.

Jim ran through a mental list of a few minor tasks to do before going home. At 10:10 in the evening, it was looking like a quiet Thursday night for him—nothing booked for the operating room so far. He hoped it would stay that way, as he looked forward to a weekend off at home with Amanda. Tonight had been unusual for Jim, seeing a patient with abdominal pain and calling his staff surgeon about it. Normally a junior resident would see such a patient first and call the attending surgeon directly. In the case of something simple, such as appendicitis, the junior resident would usually do the surgery with Jim supervising. The staff surgeon would be close at hand in the surgeons' lounge.

But tonight was a little different. The new junior resident, Hank Forsberg, particularly lacked confidence. Since Hank was busy on the ward, Jim had decided to see the emergency patient himself and interact directly with Baker, figuring it would be simpler than being the recipient of Baker's wrath for delegating duties to "some bozo junior who couldn't be trusted to make decisions commensurate with his level of training". Jim's own recollection of first-year residency, with all the difficulties of newfound responsibility, did not permit him to judge the current junior resident so harshly, but Herman Baker was not your typical staff surgeon. Jim had experienced his own run-ins with Baker and it was sometimes easier to provide a buffer between the junior resident and the staff surgeon. Feeling satisfied he had fully assessed Mrs. Doyle and had confirmed that Baker would drop by the Emergency Department to see her, Jim was looking forward to heading home for bed.

After completing some paperwork and doing a few minor checks on the ward, and with little traffic, Jim took his usual eight-minute drive home. Amanda would be sleeping at that hour, unless Emily was awake. Jim tiptoed into their bedroom and quietly slipped into their warm bed next to Amanda. Exhausted, he fell asleep within minutes.

The pager's shrill beep suddenly roused Jim from sleep after what seemed like many hours of deep slumber. As he groped for the pager to silence it, he glanced at the red numbers on the clock: 1:45. He'd been sleeping for less than two hours. He picked up the phone and dialed the number—the Emergency Department. *Shit, they shouldn't be calling me at this hour.* Usually the junior resident, staying overnight in the hospital, would be called first. Unless, of course, the problem was big. A motor vehicle accident, for example. Jim always found a multiple trauma situation to be an exciting challenge. After dialing, Jim counted seven exasperating rings.

"Emergency Department."

"It's Dr. Smythe, general surgery, did you page?"

"Oh yes, Dr. Smythe. I think you'd better come in. That lady you saw earlier—she's had a cardiac arrest."

"What?" Jim asked incredulously as he sat up in bed.

"Edna Doyle. She's in Section A. Trauma Bay One. She left but she's now back. They're coding her right now. Dr. Wong asked me to call—she's too busy to come to the phone—but she asked me to let you know. Can you come in?"

"I'll be right there," Jim responded quietly, now standing by the bedside. The phone was tucked under his chin and as he balanced on his left leg, he slid his right leg into his trousers. Then he put the phone back into the cradle on the bedside table. Trying not to wake Amanda, he pulled on his socks, grabbed a shirt and quietly closed the bedroom door behind him.

As he retraced his route back to the hospital, his Honda Civic hurtled at nearly twice the speed he had been travelling only hours previously. Jim's mind was also in overdrive. *What the hell could have happened to her that she's coding? She seemed fine—she can't be arresting, I was just speaking to her!* He gripped the steering wheel tightly and recalled his conversation with Dr. Baker. At least Baker had promised to see her and decide what to do. As Jim's anxiety softened slightly, he began to experience feelings of guilt, realizing he was caring more about his own role in this whole set of horrible circumstances than he was about the well-being of Mrs. Edna Doyle.

Jim turned his vehicle sharply into one of the physician-only parking spots next to the Emergency Department entrance. Before the car fully stopped, he reefed up on the parking brake, halting the Civic with a jolt. He sprinted through the doors straight to Trauma Bay One, to find a crowd of workers huddled around an apparently lifeless Edna Doyle.

Chapter 2 ~ Code Edna

Jim stared, wide-eyed and open-mouthed, as he watched an emergency nurse perform CPR with rhythmic consistency while a respiratory technician pumped oxygen through the patient's endotracheal tube by regularly squeezing on a delivery bag. A rotund nurse, masked, gowned and gloved, darted a suction wand in and around Edna's mouth, evacuating green vomit. Gastric contents were being expelled by the forceful compressions of CPR. Fortunately, Edna's airway was protected by the breathing tube, which was firmly taped at the corner of her mouth and extended into her trachea. Dr. Wong, a petite emergency doctor, was barking orders loudly enough to supersede the background noise of machines, monitors and incessant chatter. "Epinephrine! Give one more ampule now, then an amp of bicarb." Dr. Wong glanced over at Jim, who was making his way through the crowded room, trying to get closer to the patient. "Jim, I think you saw this lady earlier. She went home but they brought her back by ambulance after she fell unconscious in front of her husband. She must be bleeding internally. Look at her belly!"

As he looked at her bloated white abdomen, he couldn't help but notice her skinny arms and legs, bluish and mottled, a precursor of death. He couldn't comprehend why a seemingly healthy woman would bleed enough to cause a cardiac arrest. If it were a ruptured aortic aneurysm, they easily would have seen the ballooning aorta on ultrasound a day and a half ago. He looked over at the cardiac monitor. All he could see was electromechanical noise—artificial, wide, irregular spikes from the effect of CPR on the heart muscle. Jim looked over at Dr. Wong and said, "Does she have any underlying cardiac rhythm?"

"I don't think so now, Jim. When she was brought back in she was in extremis. Barely had a blood pressure. She arrested less than ten minutes ago so we started CPR. We've given her lots of I.V. fluids, epinephrine and bicarb. Now we're starting unmatched blood. So if she is bleeding, we've done what we can here." She then paused, her eyes focused on the emergency nurse who was rhythmically compressing the patient's chest. "Stop CPR." All eyes went to the cardiac monitor. A smatter of irregular blips superimposed on a flat line confirmed there were no intrinsic heart beats. "Shock her, 300 joules!" Dr. Wong hollered.

Everyone stood back from the patient, avoiding contact with the gurney. Another nurse applied two paddles to Edna's chest and yelled, "All clear!" A sudden loud, biphasic thud sounded as Edna's lifeless body jerked upwards, then slammed back on the bed. Heads turned to the cardiac monitor; this time some intrinsic cardiac activity was undoubtedly visible.

Another nurse, her hand firmly planted in the crease of Edna's upper thigh, shouted, "I can feel a femoral pulse!"

"Jim," Dr. Wong pleaded, "is there anything you can do for her here, or in the O.R.?"

Jim watched the rhythmic spikes on the monitor. He could feel his sense of despair receding. *Where there is life, there's hope.* With a viable heartbeat, there might be a chance of treating Edna's mysterious case. Jim gazed at the monitor and then at the patient. "All we can do here is open her chest to cross-clamp the aorta. That might reduce blood flow to the abdomen and buy us some time. But if she's bleeding somewhere in the abdomen and we can get her to the O.R. quickly, then we should take her there—now!"

"Okay, let's get the next two units of blood in as fast as possible and get ready to transfer," Dr. Wong yelled. "You give the word, Jim, and we'll get her up there right away." She glanced sternly at the patient, who was now maintaining a heartbeat of two hundred beats per minute—steady but far too rapid. Edna's skin was ghostly pale, her arms and legs still bluish, indicating her tenuous grip on life. Dr. Wong's brow furrowed as she said, "Until the O.R. calls, we'll do what we can." Her voice trailed off.

Jim swiftly snatched the wall phone receiver and punched the operating room phone number into the keypad. As he listened, waiting for someone—anyone—in the operating room to pick up, Jim observed the commotion unfolding in front of him. People were crowded around Edna, each one busily attending to the patient's needs. The pace seemed frenetic, underlining the severity of this woman's condition and the uncertainty of the outcome. The bright lights, pungent stench of vomit and cacophony of voices flooded Jim's senses. The pit of his stomach gnawed as he awaited a response on the other end of the phone. It crossed his mind that if the O.R. couldn't take Edna right away, then perhaps they should be opening her chest right there in the Emergency Department. If they had to resort to that, she'd likely not survive. The only hope for success with an emergency thoracotomy was in treating penetrating trauma to the chest, such as a knife wound. And that only succeeded in the rarest of circumstances. The voice on the phone brought Jim back to reality.

"Operating room," the calm voice answered.

"Stella. Glad it's you. It's Dr. Smythe. Can we bring up a stat laparotomy?"

"You're in luck, Jim. They've just finished an ankle fracture in Room One. If you have to bring it up right away, we can open up Room Two for you. Who is the patient?"

"Edna Doyle. Stat laparotomy...for bleeding," Jim said, faltering slightly. "Seventy-year-old. From emerg." He hoped he wasn't yelling.

"That doesn't sound good. And who is your staff?"

"Dr. Baker. He doesn't know about it yet but I'll call him right away. Tell anesthesia that I can give them details in a few minutes, but I need to do some things here first. We'll have the patient up there in less than five minutes."

"Okay. I'll call you if we have questions, but will expect you any moment."

He hung up the phone and waved his right hand across the room at Dr. Wong, who was still intently directing Edna's treatment. When she didn't immediately notice him, Jim yelled, "We can take her to the O.R. straight away. Get another two units of blood. Someone call the lab to get two units of fresh frozen plasma ready. She'll need all the help she can get to keep her blood volume up."

Jim paused briefly as he watched a nurse carefully wrap tape around Edna's left fourth finger, securing her wedding ring as the team began transporting her to the O.R.

Jim always hated phoning Baker, even about the simplest of cases. This, of course, was no simple case and Baker couldn't argue with him or put him off. But he still despised having to make the call. *Why couldn't it have been Steinberg on call tonight*? It was always easier to phone Steinberg.

Rushing out of the trauma room and around the corner, Jim looked for a quieter area to phone Dr. Baker. He strode across the hall to a desk at the nursing station and sat down by the telephone. Then he took a deep breath, picked up the receiver and made the call. *No beating around the bush here*, he thought. He wasn't going to ask—he'd simply inform Dr. Baker about the stat laparotomy—and then get the hell up to the operating room to see what they could do for Edna Doyle.

"Hello?"

"Dr. Baker, it's Jim." Before waiting for the usual painful pause, he continued. "I've got a stat laparotomy. No idea why, but I think she's got intra-abdominal bleeding. She arrested briefly in ER but they got her back. Can you come in? We're taking her up to the O.R. right away."

“Okay. I’ll be as quick as I can. Start without me if you have to.” Jim heard a muffled curse, then silence. The line was dead.

Well, that wasn’t so bad, Jim thought. He looked up from the desk and saw a group of nurses and others around Edna Doyle’s stretcher, hurriedly wheeling her down the corridor toward the elevator to the operating room.

He’d almost forgotten about his junior resident, Hank Forsberg, who should have been here all along but had been left out of the loop on this one. Jim quickly asked the unit secretary to page Dr. Forsberg and tell him to meet Jim in the operating room right away.

Jim jogged down the hallway, hoping to catch up with Edna and her throng of caregivers. In the distance, they disappeared into the elevator. Jim contemplated calling for them to wait but thought better of it. *Safer to get this unstable patient into the O.R. as quickly as possible. There’s nothing easy about delivering emergency medical care while in transit.* When Jim reached the elevator, the numbered display indicated Edna was already on the second floor and probably on her way into the operating room. Jim decided to take the stairs.

Chapter 3 ~ Operation Edna

As Jim exited the stairwell on the second floor, he nearly smacked into a bleary-eyed Hank Forsberg heading down the hall from the surgical on-call room. Hank's dark brown matted hair, thick glasses, and white lab coat inadvertently tucked into one side of his O.R. greens did not project an air of confidence. Jim hoped Herman Baker was not far away. He couldn't imagine starting a complex case like this with Hank as his first and only surgical assistant.

"Sorry, Hank. I meant to call you sooner. But this is a complicated case. I kind of got distracted and didn't call. Next thing I knew, they were calling me back from ER saying she was coding. I think she's got internal bleeding and we've got to get her belly opened up *now* so we can fix her."

"It's okay, Jim," Hank snorted, wiping his nose with his sleeve. "I was busy on the wards 'til about forty-five minutes ago. Just fell asleep before you called." He pressed the button to open the operating room doors. The two marched side by side through the locker room, hung up their white coats and put on surgical caps and shoe covers.

From there they made a beeline for Room Two, where Edna was being slid from her stretcher onto the narrow operating room bed. Dr. Renée Gossett stood at Edna's head, directing several nurses to gently position the patient. As chief resident in anesthesia, Dr. Gossett was now in control of this patient, with her staff anesthetist close at hand in the corner of the room, thumbing through the patient chart. Dr. Gossett adjusted the tilt of Edna's head, looking for landmarks in the neck to guide the insertion of an internal jugular intravenous line. In the narrow gap between Renée's cap and mask, Jim could see her creased forehead. She looked over at the cardiac monitor and squinted as Edna's heart pounded at two hundred and ten beats per minute. Jim knew Dr. Gossett from medical school and various encounters through residency. When she was worried, she squinted. They glanced at Edna's abdomen simultaneously. She was more distended than ten minutes ago.

"Jim, I'm worried that when I induce her under anesthesia, she could drop her pressure significantly. It's already low—80 over 40—do you think I have time to put in a line and catch up with some blood before you open her? I'd like to get her heart rate below two hundred before we start. And where's your staff surgeon? Is Baker coming along anytime soon?"

"He'll be here any minute." Jim paused, then looked at Renée steadily. "I don't think waiting is going to do a lot of good. I think we need to get right in there and find out what's bleeding and stop it. When you say 'induce her', it's not like you need to give her much anesthetic. I say we just open her now."

Unexpectedly, the rhythmic chirping of the cardiac monitor slowed to an irregular forty-five beats per minute, a sign of impending cardiac arrest. Two nurses were hanging more blood. Jim stopped pacing and firmly stated, "Prep the patient. Hank and I are going for a very quick scrub. We have to start before she arrests!"

"Okay, Jim. I guess you'd better start. She's not getting *any* anesthetic drugs in this condition."

Jim and Hank slipped out the door to wash up at the scrub sink.

Renée fumbled with the IV line. She turned to the nurses. "Get these next two units of blood in as quickly as possible." She then pushed a syringe of phenylephrine, in an attempt to raise Edna's blood pressure and heart rate. After staring briefly at the monitor, Renée waved at Jim and Hank through the windowed doorway. "Get in here Jim," she yelled.

Renée's attempt to improve Edna's pulse rate and blood pressure was to no avail as useful cardiac function ceased. The monitor showed ventricular fibrillation. The staff anesthetist emerged from the corner of the room and began hastily filling several syringes with medications. Renée shouted, "Start CPR and get ready to shock her," just as Jim and Hank burst back into the room with their forearms and hands pointing upward, water dripping from their elbows. One nurse was standing next to the patient's left arm, performing cardiac compressions. Another was at Jim's back, tying his gown as he thrust his hands into surgical gloves held out in front of him by the scrub nurse. A second scrub nurse was carefully placing surgical drapes on Edna's ballooned abdomen, which now appeared twice the size it had only twenty minutes ago in the Emergency Department. Jim stood at the patient's right side. He stared straight across Edna into Hank's wide eyes, which reflected terror back at Jim. They looked down at Edna's abdomen, brown from iodine solution and windowed by sterile drapes.

Jim exhaled audibly. "It's now or never, we're ready to start!"

"Wait!" Renée exclaimed. "Let's try shocking her first, then you go." Jim and Hank stood back one step as the nurse stopped CPR and applied paddles to

Edna's bare chest, which was partially hidden from Jim by a vertical curtain of surgical drapes.

"Ready to shock! Three hundred joules!" The instant jolt did not improve Edna's condition.

"No good," Renée stated. "Restart CPR. Jim, you gotta open her now."

The scrub nurse held out a scalpel to Jim before he had a chance to request it. He swiftly took the scalpel in his right hand and slashed a vertical midline incision from Edna's upper abdomen toward her pubic bone. The skin gaped open. Using his left hand, he applied pressure to the abdominal wall with Hank's help, pulling the wound gently apart, as Jim deepened the cut through the fatty layer to the linea alba, the final substantial layer before the abdominal cavity. Slicing through the fat, Jim expected to see the usual bright yellow, glistening layer with an occasional tiny spurting blood vessel. But it was like cutting through feta cheese rather than living tissue. The hopelessness Jim began to feel caused searing pain in his upper abdomen. He tried to ignore the discomfort and what it was telling him. As Jim was about to enter Edna's abdominal cavity, Dr. Baker stormed through the doors, hands elevated and arms dripping from his surgical scrub.

"What's up, Jim?" Baker asked, surveying the bustling activity throughout the room.

"Like I said on the phone, Dr. Baker, this lady's almost certainly bled out from something in her belly. I'm just about to open the peritoneal cavity. I can hold off until you're gloved and gowned."

Dr. Baker stood squarely facing Jim as the circulating nurse tied his gown from behind. "CPR, Jim? In the middle of an operation?" Dr. Baker slid his hand downward into the sterile glove held in front of him by the scrub nurse. His pitch escalated as he continued, "Aren't we a bit late to be stopping bleeding?"

"I—I know, Dr. Baker. But it's her only chance. We have to see if there's something we can do for her."

"I sure as hell hope it's not her aorta, Jim, because if it is, she hasn't got a chance. No matter what it is, things aren't looking too good for her at the moment." Baker secured the final tie at the side of his gown and sidled up to Hank on the patient's left, opposite Jim. "Move a step to the left, Hank. I think Jim is going to need all the help he can get."

Using a pencil-shaped electrocautery, Jim made an opening through the final layer into the abdomen at the upper part of the incision. As dark blood welled up, he slid two fingers through the hole and elevated the abdominal wall. Baker inserted two suction devices to minimize blood from overflowing into the wound. Keeping the wound free from blood allowed the cautery to work more efficiently, so Jim could burn through the entire length of the incision and enter the abdomen. As Jim cut toward the pubic bone, Baker and Hank stuffed surgical sponges into Edna's abdomen in an attempt to contain the bleeding and identify its source. Like absorbent dishcloths, surgical sponges were invaluable in cases like this. Jim had never seen so much blood at one time. He packed more into the seemingly unending pools of blood. Jim asked the scrub nurse, "Gina, how many sponges are inside now?"

"I counted twenty-five going in."

"Here, I'll trade you," Jim passed Gina a handful of dripping, blood-drenched sponges and snatched a packet of five more, firmly placing them inside as Baker and Hank continued to suck up the diminishing pockets of blood pooled in the abdomen. There was no ongoing bleeding, no telltale spurt or ooze to lead them to the source of the problem.

Baker impatiently shifted his weight from one foot to the other. "Any idea where it came from, Jim?"

"To be honest, no." His voice trailed off as he reached into Edna's upper abdomen up to his elbow. As he felt with his hand, trying to distinguish organs from blood-soaked sponges, he continued, "I think it's coming from the upper abdomen. But the liver and spleen feel fine to me. I'm not sure."

"What do you mean *coming* from, Jim? No blood is *coming*. This is old blood. I haven't seen a drop of fresh blood since I came in the room." Baker then turned to Renée and asked, "How long have you guys been doing CPR?"

"At least five minutes. And that doesn't include CPR in the Emergency Department," Renée said.

"CPR in emerg? You didn't tell me that, Jim. What's the chance of survival after CPR for hemorrhagic shock, Jim? What is it?"

I did mention she was coding in emerg, Jim thought, and then he said, "Small, I know but—"

"Stop CPR!" Baker bellowed, looking at the nurse doing cardiac compressions. She continued, but turned her head inquiringly toward Renée, who nodded. The nurse stopped CPR and everyone watched the flat line on the cardiac monitor.

"There's nothing here," Baker said. "She's dead! Jim, she's already dead! Why are we operating on a dead woman?"

"She was fine a few hours ago," Jim retorted. "Can we continue CPR and just see if we can find the bleeding source?"

"Fine," Baker huffed. "Continue CPR for now. But not for long, I suspect."

As Jim pulled out dripping wet sponges one by one, he realized Baker was probably right. Although there was still a lot of blood, there really was no new bleeding. He grabbed a suction from Hank and swept it around the abdominal cavity, starting from the lower half. "Doesn't seem to be coming from the pelvis." As he pulled all the remaining sponges from the mid-abdomen, he added, "Doesn't look like it's the aorta. I can't feel anything there."

"Look here, Jim, if you can't even feel pulsations of the aorta when someone is doing CPR, then this lady is long gone. She's got no blood volume left!"

"I didn't say that, Dr. Baker. What I meant was, she doesn't have an aortic aneurysm."

"Oh, so I suppose you can feel pulsations," Baker responded sarcastically. "Let me feel." He grabbed Jim's wrist and pulled it out of the abdomen, then inserted his hand and felt for himself. His tone softened slightly. "I'm sorry, but I just don't think there's much point."

Jim adjusted Hank's right hand, which was pulling on a retractor, holding the abdomen open. Jim pushed down on the stomach in the upper abdomen and felt resistance, indicating pressure coming from behind the stomach. "Can we just check the lesser sac? I think the bleeding was coming from behind the stomach."

"Okay Jim," Baker said reluctantly, "but make it snappy!" He then turned to Hank and asked, "How do we get into the lesser sac, Hank?"

"Well—but—gee," Hank stammered. "I'm not sure what's the best way in this particular case, but—"

"Hank, there are three ways to get into the lesser sac. You should know them!"

Hank winced.

Baker continued, "In this case, Jim is separating the transverse colon from the greater omentum in the avascular plane. He's in quick. And look, I think Jim's right, there's a helluva lot of blood in behind the stomach." Jim was now scooping large clots of blood from the lesser sac with his hand.

"What's behind the stomach, Hank?"

"The pancreas?" Hank stated tentatively.

"Yes, of course the pancreas. Any major blood vessels?"

"Splenic artery," Hank said, this time with more confidence.

"And where does it go, Hank?"

"From right to left, along the upper border of the pancreas, to supply arterial blood to the spleen."

Baker then looked directly across as Jim sucked the remaining pools of blood out from the lesser sac. "Jim, there's no fresh blood here. She probably died from a ruptured splenic artery aneurysm. It's just too damn late. We don't do autopsies in the O.R. if we can help it."

Jim was feeling attacked, from Baker on one side and the burden of this lost patient on the other.

Then Baker shouted, "Stop CPR! We're done here! I'm serious. We are done."

As the nurse stopped CPR, Renée disconnected the ventilator and the cardiac monitor. The room fell silent. Jim looked over at the scrub nurse, Gina, whose eyes, framed by her cap above and her mask below, welled up with tears. She looked away just as their eyes met.

After an awkward moment of quiet in the room, the nurses began counting instruments while Renée and her staff anesthetist began talking solemnly about the patient.

Jim leaned forward close to Dr. Baker, cleared his throat and in a hushed toned said, "Well, what did you think?"

"What do you mean, what did I think?" Baker responded softly.

"When you saw her in Emergency, what did you think of her?"

"I didn't see her in Emergency, Jim. I just met this lady twenty minutes ago when I walked in the room."

"No," Jim pleaded, "she was the one I talked to you about on the phone earlier this evening. You said you'd swing by emerg and see what you thought of her."

"Oh, this is the same lady?"

"Yes," Jim responded, his voice still low but now fuelled with desperation. "What did you think when you saw her?"

"I didn't see her, Jim. I came by to see her an hour after we talked on the phone, but she was gone. I thought you'd sent her home. I thought this lady here was someone completely new."

"No! No, I didn't send her home. I thought you did!" Jim could feel his heart racing and sweat accumulating under his surgical gown.

"No, Jim, I'm afraid you're the only one from surgery who saw this lady. Until now, of course."

Jim stared down at the lifeless body of Edna Doyle, her abdomen wide open. Edna's blood was all over the surgical drapes, the floor and his shoes. And his hands. *Shit!* He thought, *Holy shit!*

Chapter 4 ~ Mentor

As he stood in the empty waiting room, Jim quietly read the framed diplomas on the wall opposite the reception window. Dr. Maurice Steinberg had an impressive collection of credentials, many accumulated far from his current practice in western Canada. Jim gently rubbed his right eyelid and then blinked, trying to settle his contact lens into place. Since Edna Doyle's demise three days ago, he had not slept well. Even though he'd had the weekend off, he kept reviewing the events, wondering what he might have done differently. His anxiety was accentuated when the surgery program director, Dr. Steinberg, had hurriedly caught him at the end of the day Friday, suggesting they meet to discuss the situation on Monday. Steinberg had obviously heard about the case from either the nurses or possibly even Herman Baker. The fact that Steinberg had arranged a meeting was significant and it worried Jim. Over the weekend, Amanda had repeatedly tried to reassure Jim, but to no avail. Intellectually, Jim knew he had done what he could when Edna presented to the Emergency Department with vague abdominal pain. It wasn't his fault she had an obscure diagnosis, combined with relatively soft symptoms. He'd read about splenic artery aneurysms and he'd heard of a case a couple of years ago, but he'd never actually seen a case. Jim knew that splenic artery aneurysm was a rare condition, a ballooning of the artery that traverses from the midline across the left side of the back of the abdomen to supply blood to the spleen. He was aware that such an aneurysm can occasionally leak and then suddenly rupture, causing life-threatening hemorrhage. But in Edna's case, he had not been aware she was silently bleeding, and even if he had known, splenic artery aneurysm would not have come first to mind. And Jim hadn't sent her home. He couldn't understand why she would have gone home. He was sure he'd told Edna that Dr. Baker would be along soon to assess her. So Jim finally told the whole story to Amanda, hoping for some of the reassurance and comfort that she often so adeptly provided.

Amanda, his wife for over four years now, had worked part-time as a nurse until shortly before Emily was born. She was highly intelligent and possessed extensive insight into medical problems. She'd often been Jim's sounding board and usually knew how to ameliorate Jim's daily stresses. But this situation was different, and despite Amanda's attempts to help, he couldn't stop the case from lingering, like a note repeatedly played on an out-of-tune piano.

Looking at Dr. Steinberg's specialty diploma in general surgery, Jim was reminded that he and Amanda had met in Dr. Steinberg's operating room six years ago. A confident scrub nurse, she had taken Jim to task several times that day. It seemed everything he did required a reprimand, but he couldn't help but notice her soft green eyes and a stray tuft of brown hair peeking out from between her surgical cap and mask. He couldn't see Amanda's smile under her mask, but Jim knew the scolding was playful by the crinkling at the corners of her eyes. Jim found her assured manner part of her appeal. All the while, Dr. Steinberg appeared to be amused by Amanda's rule over his brand new medical student.

Jim sat down as he continued to await Dr. Steinberg. He glanced at the digital readout on his pager and blinked. Five o'clock. Steinberg was not usually late. Jim scratched his head, then rubbed the short blond hair over his temples. As he shifted in his seat, he smelled his own sweat as it wicked through his surgical greens inside his white lab coat.

Suddenly, Dr. Steinberg whisked from the hospital hallway into the waiting room. "Well, what are you waiting for, Jimmy, let's get this done and out of the way!"

Jim felt a flood of relief, hearing Steinberg's familiar gregarious tone. Perhaps this meeting wasn't going to be quite so bad after all. Jim stood up and leapt forward to keep up with Steinberg, who was heading through a doorway for his office at the end of the hall. Although Steinberg hunched slightly, his wiry frame sprung forward with each step. His thinning grey hair was always held firmly in place—the residents speculated by some kind of semi-solid hydrocarbon that smelled like a hair salon. Steinberg burst through his office door and maneuvered in behind his desk to sit facing Jim, who sat down in one of the two vacant chairs. Dr. Steinberg slipped off his bifocals and positioned them inside his wide-open mouth before moistening them with a couple of vigorous puffs. He then wiped them clean with a handkerchief, put them back on, stared intently at Jim and spoke first.

"I don't think we should have done a barium enema on that guy."

"Wh—I beg your pardon, sir?"

"It would've made sense just to operate," Steinberg said.

"Why do you say that?" Jim queried, his expression blank. Steinberg's habit of connecting conversations over periods of weeks, without warning, had been both puzzling and amusing to Jim over the years.

Steinberg continued, "Barium enemas may help with appendicitis when it's not clear-cut, but this—"

"I…I don't mean to interrupt," Jim interjected, perplexed, "but I'm not sure which guy you're—"

"Well, we thought he had appendicitis."

Exasperated, Jim raised his eyebrows expectantly, hoping the guy with appendicitis might crystallize in his memory.

"So why did we do the barium enema? We would've operated anyway. It didn't show much, but even if it had, the X-ray really didn't change our management in this case."

"Okay! Yes! Of course," Jim replied as he remembered a scrawny, white-haired, fifty-five-year-old man from three weeks ago. "I was thinking the same thing too. We should have just operated. Would have saved us some time and him some grief. Although, you know, I read an article about diagnosing appendicitis with a CAT scan."

"Ha! That's a good one, Jimmy. That'll be the day when we get a radiologist to do a CAT scan at ten at night for appendicitis! There'd be some evenings the scanner would be tied up for hours."

"I know, I thought it seemed a little far-fetched." Jim stiffened in his chair as he observed Steinberg's expression become serious.

Dr. Steinberg leaned forward. "Of course, Jimmy, you know that's not why I requested this meeting today."

"Yes, I know," said Jim, staring at his shoes.

Dr. Steinberg had been like a father to Jim over the last six years. Losing his father suddenly at age thirteen had been difficult enough. But when his mother passed away after a six-month battle with cancer when Jim was twenty, he was devastated. It took about a year to get back to the old carefree Jim. He figured it was his decision to try for medical school that had finally elevated him out of his funk. A few years later, he met Dr. Steinberg and ever since, his mentor had been a source of knowledge and inspiration both in and out of the operating room. Rarely one to raise his voice, Steinberg could still make tough decisions when required as the surgery program director. A common theme amongst residents, patients and other health care workers was a high level of respect for Dr. Steinberg.

Jim's trance was truncated as Steinberg continued, "Dr. Baker had a word with me Friday morning. He said you'd had a tough case the night before. Do you want to tell me about it?"

"I'm sure you've heard everything. This lady, she just didn't look too bad and yet I couldn't send her home. She had belly pain. I'm not going to lie to you; I couldn't put my finger on it. And Hank was the junior on call that night, so I thought it was better if I dealt directly with Dr. Baker, myself."

"Yes." Steinberg nodded.

"So Dr. Baker agreed to go see her. I took care of a few minor things and headed home. I forgot about her until they called a few hours later. She was coding. After that, there wasn't much else I could do to help her. We got a heartbeat back for a while, but it wasn't good enough. Dr. Baker thinks she had a ruptured splenic artery aneurysm. I haven't heard anything yet from pathology, but whatever it was, it was a horrendous bleed. And the funny—the surprising thing was, she went home before Dr. Baker had a chance to see her—left AMA."

"Well, Jim, not exactly *against medical advice*; she would have had to sign a form. She just left!"

"You've reviewed the chart?" Jim was looking at the ceiling, trying not to let Steinberg know the depth of his despair.

"Yes, briefly. And it looks like you did all the right things. Except it does concern me."

"What?"

"We have a dead patient and you were the last and only one from surgery to assess her before she coded. Look, Jim, I know you well enough to know you wouldn't take shortcuts, or shirk responsibility. You're a top-notch resident. But there's a chance this could get bigger—turn into a complaint of some kind. And I don't want you to be made to take the blame."

"What are you saying, Dr. Steinberg?"

"It's a serious case. And I know you and Dr. Baker, well…"

"Have a bit of a history together?"

"Yes," Steinberg continued. "I don't want this to turn into a conflict between you two to see who can cover his butt better than the other guy."

"Do you think it will come to that? A complaint? Or worse?" Jim's mouth felt like it was full of cotton balls. He shifted from side to side in his chair but could find no comfort.

Steinberg spoke softly, "I'm sure it will be fine, Jim. I saw in the note you wrote that you discussed her findings with Dr. Baker. But you didn't document that he said he'd come to see the patient. But it's too late to add that. For certain, don't, and I repeat, *do not* do anything to change the chart now. If you want to write things down at home to jog your memory later, by all means do so."

Jim was suddenly seeing things in a bleaker perspective than during his weekend ruminations. Then, he had simply felt bad for Edna Doyle and was beating himself up over the possibility that he could have done better. Now Dr. Steinberg was shifting Jim's thinking to an entirely different and much more ominous train of thought—the possibility of being blamed in a complaint to the Medical Licensing Authority, or worse, a lawsuit. And just in case there was any doubt in Jim's mind, Steinberg confirmed his nastiest fears.

He looked at Jim squarely, saying, "I hope you don't mind, but I might see if Dave Johansen could talk to you about this."

"Who is Dave Jo—"

"Don't take this wrong, Jimmy, but he's a lawyer friend of mine. He's an excellent bridge player—has an analytic mind. Does lots of medico-legal work—defense of course. He's been at it a long time and understands the perspective of a doctor trying to do his best in difficult circumstances."

"He what?" Jim wasn't sure he had heard properly. He could feel he was trying not to hyperventilate.

"It's okay, Jimmy. He's a good guy. A great squash player. He's only ten years younger than I am, so I should be able to beat the crap out of him. But I can't. I can beat most masters playing at the club but I cannot win against Dave for the life of me. And that's the kind of lawyer he is. He loves to win. Doesn't accept second place easily. Won't hurt to meet him anyway. Would that be okay, Jim? Can I put you two in touch?"

"Hmm?" Jim was making a conscious effort to regain his composure and was only half-listening.

Steinberg spoke louder. "Dave Johansen. Is it okay if I set up a meeting with you and Mr. Johansen to hash this out? Just in case there's more in store down the road?"

"Sure. Yes. Yes, thank you, Dr. Steinberg. I appreciate your support."

"Good. Consider it done. Well, that's all I wanted to say. Thanks for stopping by. What are you up to tonight, Jimmy?"

Jim was aware that his vacant eyes and his creased forehead betrayed the emotional state he was trying to hide. He tried to smile and said, "There's a man in emerg with belly pain. Hank just called me about him. Looks like it might be a busy night."

Steinberg suddenly stood up and offered his hand for Jim to shake. As Jim reciprocated, Steinberg said reassuringly, "Relax, Jim! It's just another belly pain! Something you've been dealing with for years. Get going and have a good night."

Jim's expression relaxed slightly, and then he said, "Well, I guess I'll see you later. You do know you're on staff call tonight?"

"Yes, Jim, I suppose you're right. Call me if you need my help."

Chapter 5 ~ Acute Abdomen

Jim wandered down the corridor toward the Emergency Department, munching on a sandwich that he had only half-eaten at lunchtime. Amanda had packed it for him the night before. Hastily leaving their apartment at 5:30 each morning, he never had time to prepare his own lunch. He rarely spoke to Amanda in the morning, just slipping out trying not to awaken her. He'd usually check quietly on Emily and when he was sure he could see her breathing, he'd be off to work. Sometimes he'd go three or four days in a row without actually seeing Emily awake, due to his early mornings and his nearly continuous on-call responsibilities. Jim was sorry he'd missed her roll over for the first time several weeks ago. She was an easy baby—at six months, she'd been sleeping through the night for half of her life.

Jim turned the corner toward the Emergency Department. He spotted Hank chatting to Rhani Praveen, a fourth-year medical student who had recently started on the general surgery service. Her black hair and dark complexion contrasted with Hank's pale features. Both wore white lab coats over surgical greens, in preparation for a long night of in-hospital call. *Rhani is very bright*, Jim thought as he contemplated Hank's intellect in comparison. As the junior surgical resident on the service, one of Hank's responsibilities was to teach the medical students. It just so happened that this particular student had been top in her class during the first two years of medical school. Rhani had previously told Jim she studied intensely and that success hadn't come easily at the start. She credited her hard-working immigrant parents for her achievements. It was probably not a bad thing for Hank to have an eager, capable medical student on the service. Hank would probably be okay, and likely was smarter than he appeared, but he had his work cut out for him over the next few years.

Jim sat down and said, "How's it going, Hank? Got everything under control?" Then to Rhani, "I hope he's teaching you something useful. We want you to learn all the surgery you can while you're with us, even if you don't want to become a surgeon."

"It's just that I don't think I could handle the residency," Rhani replied. "I love it so far, but I don't think the lifestyle is for me."

"Well, we'll see what we can do to change that," Jim smiled, then turned to Hank and said, "won't we, Hank?"

"Sure," Hank replied tentatively.

"So what's going on with this fellow?" Jim pointed over to the cubicle in Section B, where a man was moaning behind the partially drawn curtain. "Let's sit down, rest our feet and discuss this. Rhani, why don't you give me the history and tell me what you think? That's okay with you, isn't it Hank?"

"Oh, sure," Hank said.

Jim motioned to the others to sit down at a workstation, just out of earshot from their patient. Rhani seated her slender frame and brushed a few strands of hair from her forehead. Her hair converged into a bun at the back. Jim, sitting between them, noticed Hank's eyes fixed on Rhani. "So, what's the story, Rhani?" Jim spoke loudly, hoping to remind Hank of the reason for their gathering.

"Well," Rhani started cautiously, "Mr. McKiddie is seventy-two and lives in a nursing home. He has had three back operations in the past and takes oral morphine for chronic back pain. He has hypertension. He was sent in here by ambulance early this afternoon because the nursing staff noted he had been complaining of abdominal pain for two days. The history is a little bit vague, but apparently there has been no bowel movement in the past ten days, possibly more."

"Whoa!" Jim exclaimed. Hank remained silent.

"Oh, yes. He was also vomiting," Rhani continued. "On examination, he is tachycardic with a heart rate of 120 beats per minute. Blood pressure is 100 over 65 and his temperature is elevated at 38.9 degrees. His general exam is unremarkable, but he has a very tender abdomen, especially in the left lower quadrant."

"Is he guarding? Is there rebound tenderness?" Jim was especially interested in knowing whether there were signs of peritonitis.

"Yes, I was going to say that he has both," Rhani added.

"Tell me what these signs mean." Jim couldn't help noticing Hank looking bored, his eyes roving across the Emergency Department.

"Guarding is when pressing on the abdominal muscles causes them to tense involuntarily, protecting the peritoneum or abdominal inner lining from pressure from the outside. And rebound tenderness is when releasing pressure quickly from the abdominal wall incites sudden pain, probably from jiggling inflamed peritoneum."

"Very good. She's good, isn't she, Hank?"

"Yes, very good," Hank replied dutifully.

Jim continued, "So it's a little off topic, but since you are doing so well, how do these signs fit with appendicitis?"

Rhani blinked and then continued. "Well, when the pain starts with appendicitis, it's a visceral pain, felt like a cramp, often periumbilical. Then when the inflammation of the appendix spreads to involve the lining of the abdominal cavity, you get localized peritonitis. So at this stage, perhaps twelve hours into appendicitis, the patient will have localized guarding over McBurney's point in the right lower quadrant, or even rebound tenderness."

"Excellent. And what happens when you check for rebound tenderness on the left side in someone with appendicitis?" Jim's eyes widened as he awaited Rhani's response.

"If they have appendicitis, and you release quickly from deeply palpating the left lower quadrant, they will get a sharp pain on the right side. It's called Rovsing's sign," Rhani proclaimed proudly, looking at Hank.

"All right. Very good. Now what about this guy—what do you think is going on with him?"

"He's got tenderness on the left side, with features of peritonitis, so I think he has diverticulitis. And his white count is 22,000, which would fit."

"Hank, what d'you think? You've been keeping quiet so far," Jim said.

Hank cleared his throat and then said, "I agree. When Rhani and I examined him, we were very concerned about not only his tenderness, but also other signs of infection. We both think it's diverticulitis."

"So Hank, I know you know this, but why don't you tell me and Rhani about diverticulitis. What is it and who gets it?"

"As people get older," Hank began, "they develop little pockets in the colon, probably related to a low-fibre diet, chronic constipation, and perhaps it's also somewhat genetic. So if they have *diverticulosis*, they may not even know it. Until one day, one or more pocket gets plugged with stool and gets infected, becoming *diverticulitis*. Diverticulitis can settle with antibiotics, or it can require surgery, especially if the bowel perforates."

"Very good, Hank. In Mr. McKiddie's case, what did his X-rays show?"

"A lot of poop but no signs of obstruction. No free air."

Free air outside the bowel would be a sure sign of a perforation. "So you don't think he's perforated his colon?"

"No, not yet," Hank said with some hesitation.

"Do we need to operate?"

"Yes, I think so. Before he perforates."

"Rhani, are there any other tests we could do at this stage to decide whether or not we need to operate?"

"CAT scan?" Rhani's pitch escalated, accentuating her uncertainty. Hank smirked.

Jim shot Hank a cold stare and then said, "No, we've only got two scanners and most of the time one of them is down for repairs. We have to keep one available at all times for trauma. The scanner is too slow to handle every abdominal pain that comes in at night. Maybe some day, but not for a decade, and only if we're lucky.

"We could get a gastrograffin enema," Jim continued, "if we're worried about a perforated colon. The radiologist shoots some water-soluble contrast up Mr. McKiddie's butt, takes a few pictures and if there's a perf, next thing you know we see gastrograffin leaking outside the bowel, even though we can't see free air on the plain films. But that's chapter one in *How to Not Make Friends with the Radiologists*. Personally, I think they'd rather do a CAT scan, but until we get some quicker machines, we either decide with a gastrograffin enema, or we operate without. Well, how 'bout we go see Mr. McKiddie and make a plan."

Jim rose out of his chair and walked swiftly over to the cubicle. Above the usual clatter in the Emergency Department, Mr. McKiddie's occasional whimper could be heard from behind the curtain. Jim pulled it aside to reveal a curled up figure on the emergency room stretcher. He was lying on his side and was not moving. His open eyes were vacant and sunken. He was breathing rapidly. A worker from the nursing home sat at the bedside. She immediately stood up and backed away, allowing Jim to get in close to Mr. McKiddie. Jim took the patient's bony wrist between his thumb and index finger, eventually finding a weak radial pulse. He bent down and shouted, "Mr. McKiddie, I'm Dr. Smythe. Can you open your mouth and stick out your tongue?" No response. He then turned to Hank and said, "Can you help me turn him on his back?" The old man groaned as the two surgical residents gently picked up his arms and legs and shifted him onto his back. His greasy, dishevelled grey hair and the stubble on his sunken cheeks made him look ten years older than his stated age. "Open your mouth," Jim yelled as he gripped Mr. McKiddie's cheeks in his right hand and pulled downward on his jaw. Jim noticed not only the parched tongue but also the continued lack of a significant response. This patient was sicker than

Hank and Rhani had led him to believe. They may have gotten all the facts right, but they had missed the overriding general condition. Mr. McKiddie was floridly septic and was going to die unless they could do something for him. Jim proceeded to examine his abdomen. He placed his right hand gently over Mr. McKiddie's umbilicus and with minimal pressure elicited a wince and a yelp from the old man. He watched Mr. McKiddie grimace as he palpated around the abdomen, muscles guarding throughout. *There's no question*, Jim thought, *this man has an acute surgical abdomen*. Checking for rebound tenderness was always left to the end of the exam, as the sudden release of the hand was often the most torturous of maneuvers, causing the patient's trust of the examining doctor to instantly vanish. Jim didn't even bother checking for rebound, feeling sorry for Mr. McKiddie, his mind already made up about the need for surgery.

"Let's review the X-rays and the chart together outside," Jim announced. They excused themselves from the oblivious Mr. McKiddie and his accompanying worker, heading over to an X-ray view box.

As he looked at the films, Jim concurred with Hank and Rhani's findings, noting there was no obstruction or free air, but there did appear to be at least ten days' worth of stool. The three sat down side by side in front of the images as Jim thumbed through the old chart. He noted a barium enema report from six months ago, apparently done because Mr. McKiddie had had a change in bowel habits. What Jim found striking about this report was the absence of comment about diverticulosis. Just a redundant colon, nothing else. *Diverticula don't develop overnight*, Jim thought. So maybe something else was going on.

He looked squarely at Hank. "Diverticulitis—are you sure?"

"I think so," Hank said.

"Well, I'm not so sure. But I do agree with you that he needs an operation. I'll phone Steinberg while you call the O.R. And we'll need Intensive Care for this guy. He's not likely to breathe without help for at least a few days—and that's if he's lucky."

Chapter 6 ~ Amanda

Feeling a touch of sadness, Amanda Smythe hung up the telephone. Jim wouldn't be home until much later. She thought it sounded like he had a big bowel case with Dr. Steinberg this evening, and she never knew how late that type of thing could go. At 8:30 in the evening, she had just put Emily in her crib and was glad to hear from Jim, even though it was a short conversation. Jim had been miserable all weekend and at least he sounded a little excited about going to the operating room that evening. No matter how hard Amanda had tried all weekend, she couldn't seem to get Jim to relax. Yes, he'd had a tough case on Thursday night and yes, it was compounded by the fact that it had occurred when Herman Baker was on call. Amanda didn't know all the details, but from Jim's description it sounded like a pretty horrific evening, culminating in the death of a lady who had come in talking only hours before. Jim was usually pretty good at handling stress at work and detaching himself from the nasty outcomes. He was always one to see black or white, where many would see shades of grey. *I guess that's why he became a surgeon, and that's why I love him*, she thought. Jim had no problem making decisions and sticking to them. He wasn't always effective at identifying subtle nuances, but when it came to making a decision, Jim was reliable. *No, he's not the most complex of personalities*, she thought. *And he's not the deepest of thinkers. But he is smart, especially when it comes to practical issues. In a case like this, though, if he can't absolve himself of responsibility, then the only alternative is self-torture. Many others would see a reality that lies somewhere in the middle and move on, but not Jim.*

Amanda recognized that nurses at work found Jim attractive with his blond hair, fine features and blue eyes. She took pride in her own appearance and never took for granted that passersby on the street would prolong a glance at her. She stood in front of the full-length mirror. Using an elastic band, she gathered her dark brown hair in a ponytail and then turned to one side. She was feeling content that her pregnancy had not harmed her figure. In fact, although she was still breastfeeding, her body was better than ever. If only she had the energy and Jim had the time…

It was Jim's decisive manner that had led them to rent their small apartment just across the street from the University Hospital. Having plenty of cash left by his parents, Jim could have afforded any accommodation but was reluctant to have his financial situation become widely known. So when the modest abode in such a perfect location became available for rent, Jim convinced Amanda they needed to snap up the opportunity immediately. This, of course, was before Jim knew where he was going to spend the bulk of his chief year. As it turned out, for the first nine months, Jim was scheduled to be working at St. Joseph's Hospital, which was only an eight-minute drive away. He was scheduled at the University Hospital for the final three months. This suited Jim in large part because Dr. Steinberg did most of his operating at St. Joe's. Amanda was happy either way. Her nursing shifts had been few and far between and had ceased at least temporarily as she advanced through pregnancy with Emily.

With amusement, Amanda recalled the day she met Jim. She had just tossed a disaster of a boyfriend, so she wasn't feeling in the market for meeting anyone new. But as a young scrub nurse working with Dr. Steinberg that day, she couldn't help but notice the two new medical students on surgery. For some reason, she focused on Jim and took great delight in teaching the techniques necessary for sterility in the operating room. Dr. Steinberg, who had known Amanda for over a year and had just met Jim the same day, encouraged her with an occasional wink or nod but never gave any overt verbal support.

Amanda sat down with a cup of herbal tea at the small dining room table. She recalled how she had toyed with the idea of veterinary medicine and even medical school before eventually going into nursing. She knew she wanted to be in a helping profession, but she wasn't sure what time commitment she was willing to make. She never told Jim that she wrote the MCAT exam on a whim to see whether she could get into medical school. She found out much later that she had scored a lot higher than Jim did on his MCAT, but that was a small detail she could easily misplace to maintain a strong relationship with her husband. What Jim may have lacked in natural intellect he made up for in energy and his love of hard work.

Exhausted, Amanda stood up, rinsed her teacup and headed for bed with a good book.

Chapter 7 ~ Hank

Jim and Hank stood by the vending machine in the hospital basement. Jim had sent Rhani on ahead to the O.R. while he used the excuse of getting a snack so he and Hank could have a quick discussion. Mr. McKiddie's case was up next in about twenty minutes, they hoped.

Hank inserted his final coin, then pressed hard on the button. When the machine didn't respond immediately, he slammed it three times in quick succession with his closed fist. A clanking sound arose from deep inside and Hank's can of Coke tumbled out. He bent over and plucked it with his right hand, pulled the tab and was guzzling within seconds. Jim stood silently watching until Hank stopped for air.

"I wanted to give you some feedback on your rotation so far, Hank," Jim said, standing still.

"I thought you were getting a pop," Hank responded, uneasy.

"No. I guess I changed my mind. As I was saying, I usually like to tell people how they are doing after a few weeks, so they know where they stand and what to work on."

"Oh." Hank avoided Jim's gaze as he picked at a small scab on his chin.

"Don't worry, Hank. You'll be fine! But there are some things you need to think about."

"Such as?" Hank looked up tentatively.

Jim paused. He didn't know exactly where to start. "First of all, you need to keep up with your discharge summaries. When you fall behind, the staff surgeons crap on *me*. So I'd suggest you dictate the summary when the patient is discharged from the hospital. Don't wait for Medical Records to call you with a huge pile of charts."

"Okay. I know. I'll catch up this weekend and try that approach."

"Also Hank, you need to read. It may be early in your five years. But it will go by quickly. There are some things you know well, and other subjects that need work. It's normal to have gaps at this stage. But you need to get in the habit. It's especially important when surgery is booked ahead. We can't predict the emergency cases, but there's no excuse for not knowing all the ins and outs of an elective operation. Some staff surgeons are stricter than others, but there's one thing for sure: if you want to do the surgery on any given case, read ahead. All surgeons are happy to take away a case from the resident because he didn't read beforehand. If you don't read, they won't let you do much cutting."

"Okay, I knew that. It's just a matter of finding the time." Hank was now repeatedly dabbing his chin with the cuff of his lab coat. Each time, he'd stop and observe a fresh spot of blood.

As the constellation of bright red marks grew to six, Jim could finally stand it no longer and offered, "You know, if you just leave it alone, it will stop bleeding. You could keep doing that forever and it wouldn't stop."

"Oh, ya, right," Hank said, looking down as he rolled his cuff inward, hiding the evidence of his misguided attempts to stop his pimple's ongoing hemorrhage.

"Your operating skills are fine for this stage. That will come with time."

"Good. I always get so nervous when I'm given the chance to do something in the O.R."

"I know. That was the same for all of us. But some time in the first year that usually goes away. Then you've got the long road ahead to actually become proficient. You're on this rotation until Christmas. I expect by then you'll have much more knowledge depth and be well on your way." Jim resisted the temptation to point out Rhani's superior level in the knowledge department.

"Okay. Thanks, Jim."

Just as Hank turned to the elevator, Jim added, "And by the way, focus on you, not other people."

"Huh?"

"You shouldn't worry about other people. Just read. Don't be concerned if someone else seems better. Just make sure you improve every week."

"I'm not sure—"

"Okay, look. Rhani told me you were asking her about three ways to get into the lesser sac. The exact question Baker asked you in the O.R. last week. The one you didn't get."

Hank's face flushed deeply. "I—I was just trying to—"

"Never mind what you were trying. The thing is that it backfired on you, didn't it? She told me she got all three. Who the hell would've thought a medical student could answer that question?"

***

Dr. Steinberg sat in the surgeons' lounge across from Jim, Hank and Rhani. All were in their surgical greens and ready to start, but one delay after another had pushed Mr. McKiddie's operation late into the evening.

A nurse popped her head through the lounge doorway and said, "Dr. Steinberg, the fresh frozen plasma will take a few more minutes to unthaw. The anesthetist would prefer not to start until we have the plasma running."

"Fine, Gina. But let's get the patient ready to go. Let's not wait for the plasma and then take another twenty minutes to get the patient into the room." He rolled his eyes in Jim's direction.

"Okay, we'll take him around to the room as soon as we send a porter downstairs for the plasma." Gina disappeared into the hallway.

"Did you catch that, Jimmy?"

As usual, Jim didn't know whether Steinberg was referring to something that had occurred five minutes or five months ago. "I'm not sure," Jim said, slightly puzzled.

"Unthaw. Did you hear? Why would you want to *unthaw* fresh frozen plasma? If we're going to use it for surgery, I'd prefer they thaw it rather than unthaw it!" Steinberg gently slapped his knee and started to laugh, alternating glances at Jim, Hank and Rhani.

Jim chuckled politely and said, "No, I missed that one completely. Always a stickler for proper language aren't you, Dr. Steinberg?"

"Of course, Jimmy." He turned to Rhani and squinted. "And Rhani!"

"Yes?" Rhani's eyes opened wide and she sat bolt upright in her chair.

"I read your history on Mr. McKiddie. It was very good."

"Thank you, Dr. Steinberg."

Jim stood up and nodded as he walked into the hallway. He eyed Gina at the nursing desk, filling out some paperwork. Gina, about ten years older than Jim, was an attractive redhead who had worked in the O.R. for several years. She was divorced with two teenagers at home. Jim had heard a few tales about her sexual exploits with men who worked throughout the hospital. It was nothing one could be certain about, but even for a happily married man like Jim, the idea provided ample fodder for curiosity and even occasional gossip. Tonight, though, Gina's personal life was of no interest to Jim. He wondered whether there had been any fallout from Thursday night's case, Mrs. Doyle. Since she had been scrubbed in on the operation, any discussion by the nurses would come back to Gina. Although he knew he should let it go, Jim wondered whether there was any talk behind the scene about how he had dropped the ball. He had to talk to her.

As he approached the desk, Gina glanced up but avoided his eyes and busily resumed scribbling on her paper. Jim ignored her rebuff and said, "Gina, I was wondering if you had heard anything about that case the other night. The one that died? You remember that one that bled out?" *How could she forget?*

She looked up from her desk and said tersely, "I'd rather not talk about it now. But no, I've heard nothing. And by the way, your patient has just gone around to the room. I was just going to call Dr. Steinberg."

Jim could see why her deep brown eyes and freckled face might attract an occasional man, despite the potential to become the subject of hospital gossip. "Okay, let me know if you hear anything." He regretted the words as soon as he said them, realizing they sounded a tad desperate.

"Sure." She picked up the intercom and called into the surgeons' lounge, "Dr. Steinberg, we're ready for you."

Chapter 8 ~ Skid Marks

Mr. McKiddie was lying supine, asleep on the operating table. His abdomen was exposed and prepped with iodine solution. Green surgical drapes hid the rest of him from the surgical team, while the anesthetist and anesthetic resident were working behind a vertical curtain of drapes at the level of the patient's chest. Jim stood on the patient's right side, opposite Dr. Steinberg. Hank was next to Jim, and Rhani stood beside Steinberg. Gina, the circulating nurse, opened a sterile package for the scrub nurse while looking away from Jim.

"May we start?" Jim reached for the scalpel, which the scrub nurse carefully handed to him.

"Yes. Go ahead," came the response from one of the anesthetic team.

Jim could hear the frequent beeps of the pulse oximeter, indicating Mr. McKiddie's rapid heart rate. He pressed the scalpel into the midline and with a steady stroke cut downwards, around the umbilicus and toward the pubic bone. Dr. Steinberg retracted the skin with a surgical sponge under his gloved hands as the layers separated easily. Jim could think of nothing better than doing surgery with his mentor. He felt the freedom to do the operation as he would choose, yet he knew Dr. Steinberg was ready to jump in supportively in the rare instance that Jim needed a little extra help. He wondered what it would be like a year from now without the help of a staff surgeon, when Jim would be in charge, but he knew he'd be ready. A teacher like Dr. Steinberg had a way of imparting the necessary level of confidence to his residents.

Opening the final layer into the abdominal cavity, Jim immediately smelled a putrid odour, affirming the need to be in Mr. McKiddie's abdomen to fix a significant problem. Hank inserted suction into the abdomen, drawing out murky fluid. Not only did it smell, but wisps of whitish material floated in the fluid, confirming peritonitis. As the abdominal wound opened further, Jim placed his entire hand and forearm, nearly up to the elbow, into Mr. McKiddie's pelvic area. In the left lower quadrant, Jim could feel a mass in the region of the sigmoid colon. His hand felt significant warmth from the infection. As Hank sucked more fluid out, Jim noticed flecks of brown stool in the fluid coming up the suction tubing.

"There's obviously a perforation here somewhere," Jim said. He positioned a retractor under the abdominal wall in the left lower quadrant and gave the handle to Hank. "Here, pull hard, lean back if you have to." Hank nodded. "There it is!" Jim could see, on the front surface of the sigmoid colon, an opening the diameter of a nickel. Poking through the hole was a rock-hard piece of stool the size of Jim's fist. A maroon, two-centimetre rim of paper-thin colon surrounded the hole, indicating the area was devoid of its blood supply. The entire sigmoid colon was covered in stringy bits of exudate from infection.

Dr. Steinberg leaned forward, standing on his toes to see over the edge of the abdominal wall and get a view of what Jim was seeing from his side of the table. "When you phoned me, Jimmy—you were bang on! Looks like a perforated stercoral ulcer to me! How'd you know that anyway?"

"He had a barium enema X-ray six months ago showing no diverticulosis. And here's the thing—he's in a nursing home, on high doses of morphine for chronic back pain. If that's enough to shut down his bowel movements for ten days, it could have allowed a hard piece of stool to erode through his colon wall."

"You called it right, Jimmy! How many stercoral ulcers have you seen before?"

"That's my second. I saw one in first year at the University Hospital," Jim replied proudly.

"How about you, Hank? Ever seen one?"

"No. Don't believe that I have," Hank said.

"Tell me, Hank," Steinberg said, turning sideways to look into his eyes, "what is a stercoral ulcer and how does it occur?"

Hank froze and said nothing. Jim thought he could feel Rhani bobbing up and down beside him, as if she wanted to volunteer the answer Steinberg was seeking.

Before she had a chance, Steinberg explained. "It's pressure necrosis. You get such a huge load of hard pieces of shit, jam packed into the colon, that eventually one of them causes ischemia of the wall of the colon. The wall next to the hard piece of crap gets so thinned out that its blood supply is compromised. Next thing you know, there's a hole. Pretty scary, isn't it Jimmy-boy? Makes you want to get on some Metamucil right now to avoid poor Mr. McKiddie's fate."

“Yes, just about,” Jim said. He’d not read about or heard the pathophysiology of stercoral ulcers explained so eloquently before.

“And the thing of it is,” Steinberg rattled on, “the mortality rate for perforated stercoral ulcer is about 50 percent. He probably perf’d earlier today or even yesterday. Just ’cause his X-rays didn’t show free air when he came into emerg at noon doesn’t mean he hadn’t already perf’d. This guy is sick. Good thing you arranged Intensive Care, Jimmy. He definitely needs ICU. ”

Jim started to pour irrigation fluid into the abdominal cavity while Hank was enthusiastically waving the suction into the depths. As they continued, the fluid returns came clearer, no longer murky and with only an occasional fleck of stool in the suction tube.

“So what are we going to do, Jim?” Steinberg’s level of excitement was only slightly waning.

“Hartmann’s procedure. Take out the perforated section of sigmoid colon, staple off the distal end and bring out the upstream end as a colostomy.” Jim then turned to Rhani and asked, “Do you know why we do that?”

“Because it’s not safe to rejoin the colon when he’s so sick and infected?”

“Absolutely.”

With the abdomen as clean as it was going to get, Jim and Dr. Steinberg proceeded to free up the sigmoid colon, clamping, cutting and tying blood vessels supplying the section they were about to remove. Jim then applied a surgical stapler across the lower bowel and with one firm squeeze of the handle, the distal end was closed off with two rows of surgical staples. With a surgical clamp next to the staple line, Jim cut in between, thus freeing up one end of the bowel. As Jim prepared to clamp off the proximal end and cut out the damaged eight-inch segment of colon, Steinberg interjected, “Jim, you’re doing a fine job. But before we bring this end out as a colostomy, I think we’d better decompress it. It’s already dirty in here and I don’t want this fellow to spend the next eight weeks in ICU with ten pounds of cannonballs in his colon that can’t get out through his colostomy.”

Before Jim had a chance to respond, Steinberg cut away the piece of colon, handed it off to the scrub nurse and began to pull baseball-sized chunks of rock-hard stool from the open end of Mr. McKiddie’s colon. Jim counted nine as Steinberg launched them one by one toward a large metallic bucket on the floor. Lined with a green garbage bag, the bucket sounded a loud dull thud with a residual clang each time Steinberg’s missile landed on target. The final projectile missed, skidding across the operating room floor. The round brown lump halted in the corner, near the anesthetist. “Sorry about that,” Steinberg said sheepishly, then proclaimed, “I need some new gloves. And Jimmy, you’d better do some more irrigation. It's still a bit dirty in here. In fact, forget the gloves. I'm going home to bed. I've got a squash game I'd rather not miss tomorrow morning. Jimmy, let Hank close, then you mature the colostomy and get this fellow settled in the ICU. Call me if you need me."

"Thanks, Dr. Steinberg."

Steinberg looked over the screen in the direction of the anesthetic team and then back at his residents and said, "Oh and by the way, good job tonight, men!" Steinberg paused and then added, "You too, Rhani." He turned to the two nurses and while walking out the door he said, "You, too, of course. Thanks, ladies."

Gina scowled as she wiped skid marks off the floor from Steinberg's one bad toss.

With Hank's help, Jim proceeded to bring the end of the colon out through the abdominal wall in the left lower quadrant. Hank then sutured the long midline incision closed. From now on, Mr. McKiddie's bowel movements would exit his body into a bag attached to his skin by an adhesive ring. Most would not consider it pleasant, but a colostomy was a small price to pay for a saved life. Later, after months of recuperation, if the patient didn't mind the pain and inconvenience of elective surgery, the colostomy could be reversed. The open end of the colon could be taken down from the abdominal wall and joined to the stapled end in the pelvis when conditions were less risky. Jim knew from previous experience that most would choose to have the colostomy reversed, like an expectant mother forgetting the pain of previous childbirth.

As he placed sutures between the skin and the circular open end of colon to mature the colostomy, Jim could hear the anesthetic resident comment that the patient was more stable, with improved blood pressure and heart rate. Still requiring ICU, possibly for weeks, Mr. McKiddie just might survive. Jim thought about how much he loved surgery, to meet a man on death's door and within hours alter the direction of his future. Who cared if one lousy case from last week had gone bad? Amanda was right: you can only do so much. Mrs. Doyle might have died no matter who had been on call that night. He shouldn't feel guilty about such an inevitable outcome. He remembered his reasons for choosing surgery and sticking with it over the years. Mr. McKiddie had come at a good time, just when Jim needed a reminder of why he was willing to go through such an intense and drawn-out residency program. Jim realized how lousy he'd felt since Edna's death and hoped the exhilaration he was now experiencing would continue.

Chapter 9 ~ Outpatient Clinic

The next morning, Jim awoke ten minutes before his alarm was to go off at 5:15. He'd only been asleep since about 1:00 a.m. because it had taken a while to get Mr. McKiddie settled into the ICU. In the darkness, he reached for Amanda but she was gone. Wide awake, he quickly got out of bed and walked down the hall into Emily's dimly lit room to find Amanda sitting in the rocking chair, giving a rare early morning feed. He was glad she was up so he could tell her about the previous evening and his excitement about seeing his second perforated stercoral ulcer.

"Hello, sunshine," he said enthusiastically.

"Shhh!" Amanda whispered, putting her index finger up to her lips. "She's almost asleep!" Emily was barely visible, cradled amongst blankets on Amanda's chest.

"Sorry! I just had such a great night," he whispered.

Amanda's eyebrows raised and she smiled. "Oh, I'm so glad. I want to hear all about it later, but I've got to get back to bed." She stood up and carefully placed Emily back in her crib, kissed Jim and then sauntered down the hall to their bedroom.

Unperturbed, Jim went to the kitchen and planned his day while fixing himself a cup of coffee. The highlight would be with Dr. Ted O'Brien, doing a potentially difficult gastrectomy for stomach cancer. O'Brien, whose age lay perhaps midway between Jim's and Dr. Steinberg's, was an excellent staff surgeon for senior residents. He didn't offer much surgery to the juniors, but seemed willing to give free rein in the operating room to those in the final year of residency. As with most surgeons, his personality was intense at times, causing Jim to tread carefully. His scrawny frame and boyish face did not always project an appearance of authority, so occasionally he'd lash out in the operating room if he was not obtaining what he expected from the residents and nurses who surrounded him.

Before the gastrectomy with Dr. O'Brien, there was plenty of other work to do. First there would be rounds on all the surgical inpatients. A necessary part of surgical residency was addressing the patients' needs until they were sufficiently recovered from surgery to go home. To finish rounds before surgery started at 7:45, Jim would meet on the surgical ward at 6:00 a.m. sharp with his pack of EBUs. *Ego Boosting Units*, as he'd once heard them called, were students and junior residents who supported and followed their leader faithfully, usually in groups of six or more. They could be spotted from several stories up, ambulating in their white coats through the hospital atrium like a cloud of insects swarming around their chief resident. At other times, they followed Jim like a flock of goslings steadfastly trailing their mother across the street. With additional students and residents doing electives, the entourage under Jim's command currently numbered six. The trick was to organize them so they could provide useful service to the team in return for the privilege of spending time on surgery at St. Joe's. The better he trained his EBUs from the beginning, the less likely Jim would be stuck bailing them out of mistakes. It was also helpful if junior residents could do the bulk of teaching the medical students, leaving Jim to do what chief residents liked to do best—operate. It was a symbiotic relationship that had existed for many years before him, and Jim was personable and practical enough to make it work for him, now that he was chief.

After rounds, he'd normally go to the O.R., but he'd unfortunately promised to attend Dr. Steinberg's outpatient clinic that morning. There seemed to be a move afoot, from possibly the highest level of education administration, to require residents to spend more time seeing patients in an ambulatory setting. Regrettably, this meant less time in the operating room, and even worse for Jim, this new trend was being implemented only in his final residency year. Junior residents now could do their outpatient penance in the early years, whereas Jim had missed that opportunity. He now had to catch up, which he thought was a little unfair. How on earth was he going to get all the operating experience he needed? By osmosis? He could learn the outpatient stuff later, on the fly while in practice. After an obligatory three hours in the clinic, Jim hoped he'd get to the O.R. by 11:00 a.m., just in time to scrub on the gastrectomy with Dr. O'Brien.

Jim arrived in Dr. Steinberg's clinic promptly at 8:00. The morning would bring about twenty-five patients, mostly follow-ups with an occasional new consultation thrown in. The clinic started well with a handful of patients Jim knew from surgery a few weeks ago. He actually found himself enjoying the morning, chatting with Steinberg in between patients while getting closer to the gastrectomy. He phoned up to the O.R. twice to make sure they weren't running ahead of schedule and he'd firmly instructed Hank to page him if there was any chance the case could go early. Jim could not be late. It was better to not show up at all than to arrive late. Jim fretted about the possibility of Dr. O'Brien doing a gastrectomy with Hank as the first assistant while he toiled away downstairs in the outpatient clinic with Dr. Steinberg.

At 10:40, one consultation remained: a lady about a probable case of breast cancer. How hard could that be? Cancerous lump, make a plan to take it out along with a few lymph nodes. Ten minutes to see the patient, five minutes to review her with Dr. Steinberg. He'd then have five minutes to get to the operating room and change from his shirt and tie into greens.

He picked the folder out of the slot in the examining room door, adjusted the collar on his white lab coat and gently knocked on the door as he entered the room. To Jim's surprise, there were four people in the small room. The fifty-two-year-old patient, Mrs. Egemen, was sitting on the examination table with a blue hospital gown gaping at the front. A man about her age was sitting in the chair at the foot of the table. The chair at the desk where Jim planned to sit and take notes was vacant. Directly across from the examination table were two tall women, leaning up against the wall. Jim made his way between the people, introduced himself and sat down at the desk, at the far end of the room.

The eldest daughter spoke first. "I thought we were going to be seeing Dr. Steinberg. Isn't he the surgeon?"

"I'm Dr. Steinberg's chief resident. He'll be in momentarily but he asked me to get started." He glanced at the wall clock behind Mr. Egemen's head. *Eighteen minutes*, he thought. *Not off to a good start.* Mrs. Egemen had a narrow face that was heavily tanned and wrinkled somewhat beyond what one would expect for her age. Her blond hair was in a blunt cut, not quite to her shoulders and brownish grey at the roots.

The daughters looked like younger versions of their mother, likely in their early to midtwenties. Mr. Egemen was in work boots, jeans and a lumberjack shirt. He was balding on top and wore glasses. "Well, let's get the show on the road," he piped up. "My wife has a lump that her family doctor thinks is cancer. What are we going to do about it?"

Now we're talking, thought Jim. *A man of action.* "Where is it?"

"It's in her breast," Mr. Egemen responded.

"Yes I know. But which breast and what part," Jim replied, staring directly at Mrs. Egemen.

"My left breast, toward the outside," she said as she pointed with her right hand, the gown parting in the middle and exposing both breasts.

"How long ago did you first notice it?"

"About three weeks ago," her husband replied.

"And you are aware the mammogram says it's suspicious for cancer? We'll need to remove the lump surgically," Jim stated.

The younger daughter leaned in toward the middle of the room and said, "What about a needle biopsy?"

"Yes, that's true," Jim said, slightly taken aback. "They—We are starting to do those more frequently. Then plan an operation after the results are in. That way we can do surgery with a confirmed diagnosis in mind."

"When I had my hernia fixed," Mr. Egemen interjected. "I had a lot of trouble with the anesthetic afterwards." *A reasonable concern*, Jim thought, but before he could respond, Mr. Egemen continued, "First they tried a spinal. But they had a heck of a time getting the needle in because of my back surgery. So then they put me right out. But that was just the begin—"

"Well that's interesting, Mr. Egemen, but we are trying to sort out your wife's situation of possible breast cancer."

Mr. Egemen persisted, "The reason I mention it is my wife deserves better than the treatment I got."

Jim shifted his weight from one leg to another and noticed Mrs. Egemen looking up at the ceiling while both daughters simultaneously whispered, "Da—ad!"

"No, I'm serious," Mr. Egemen waved his hand in the air. "I want the best for my wife. It's like when I had my back surgery, the doctors didn't know what they were doing—"

"I'm not sure that's really relevant," Jim interrupted, "and although it's interesting, we need to make a plan for your wife." He glanced at the clock in disbelief as he could see a gastrectomy slipping through his fingers toward Hank.

It was the older daughter's turn to weigh in. "What if you put a needle in it, or even just take the lump out? If you let the air get at it, doesn't that make it spread? Can't you just do the surgery without a biopsy?"

Dumbfounded, Jim did not know how to respond. He hadn't even examined her and it was now 10:51 a.m. He figured his last hope was to get Dr. Steinberg in to sort through what was turning out to be a much more complicated situation than he'd anticipated. "I—I think what we should do is—is," Jim stammered, "I think we should get Dr. Steinberg in here to answer some of these questions and to examine you. He said he'd be ready about now," Jim lied as he looked at the clock once more. He quickly headed for the door, smiling and muttering something incomprehensible, even to himself, as he backed out into the hallway and closed the door.

He prayed that Dr. Steinberg would take pity on him and simply send him away to the operating room while taking care of the situation himself. Jim felt a hand on the back of his shoulder just as he sniffed Dr. Steinberg's hair gel.

"Well, did you get this lady sorted out?" Steinberg asked, nodding.

"Not exactly," Jim said, deflated, realizing the early escape to the O.R. was not going to happen.

"Let's sit down and talk about it, Jim. Then we can go in together, examine her and get this clinic wrapped up by 11:30, noon at the latest."

Jim's pager suddenly started beeping. He glanced at the number—the O.R. Probably Hank. Jim couldn't bring himself to ask Steinberg to excuse him, having barely started tackling this complex breast cancer problem. He was beginning to understand why the educational authorities were encouraging a modicum of outpatient experience for residents before releasing them on the population at large.

"Who's that? Anybody important?"

"No, it's okay," Jim said, trying to not look dejected. "I can call them in a few minutes."

Steinberg led him into the small coffee room, where they sat down at a round table. Steinberg smiled and asked, "Why so discouraged, Jimmy? We have good reason to want you to spend more time seeing outpatients."

"I know," Jim said, looking at the wall clock. "It's just that I was hoping to get upstairs to a gastrectomy with Dr. O'Brien."

"Don't worry about Dr. O'Brien. He'll be fine. I'm sure he's got lots of help," said Steinberg reassuringly.

It's not O'Brien, Jim thought, *it's me I'm worried about. And that slippery gastrectomy that's all but lost by now.* "I know he'll be fine," he said aloud.

"So what's with Mrs. Egemen?"

"First of all," Jim began, "her husband is a bit domineering. Won't let her—or me, for that matter—get a word in edgewise. And then her daughters are coming up with a bunch of crazy questions."

"Alternative therapy?"

"Huh? No, they didn't ask about that."

"Not yet, anyway," Steinberg stated calmly. "Letting the air touch the cancer? Causing it to spread? Was that one of their questions?"

Jim's eyes widened. "How did you know?"

"It's a common question," Dr. Steinberg was grinning. "And you have to be ready for it. Anticipate it. Preempt it."

Still incredulous, Jim added, "But how did you—"

"Look, Jimmy. It's not an unreasonable question. You have to see it from their perspective. Everyone knows someone who had a relative who had a biopsy and bingo! the cancer spread like wildfire. Ran right through them. In two months, the poor fellow was dead. You and I know that's just a timing issue. If we biopsy enough cancers, in an occasional one, the horse is already out of the barn with the door firmly closed behind. And that makes an interesting but sad story, so it gets repeated. The ones we biopsy and then cure are relegated to the annals of boring medicine and are forgotten. So everybody knows someone, if not directly then at least indirectly, who has had a cancer biopsied just before their unfortunate demise. You and I know that's not a cause and effect relationship. But they don't know. Especially if they're the fifth person who heard the story told, with a few modifications at each telling. And remember, Jimmy, these people are stressed to the max. They're not at their rational best when we see them before cancer surgery. So you need to anticipate and deal with these issues on a regular basis. Something you don't learn by operating on inpatients all the time. Aren't you glad you came here today, Jimmy?"

"Yes, I am," Jim admitted.

"And they often ask about alternative therapy—some as rational as a few vitamins, all the way to herbs, spices and magnets. And you know what I tell them, Jimmy?

"No, what?"

"As long as they take proven surgery, radiation or chemotherapy and as long as they don't go broke in the process, I don't care what magical cure they take. It's their right to do so. But they need to keep us informed and not substitute black magic for proven treatment. What really breaks my heart is that once a year, someone will walk out of here with a curable cancer, vowing to monitor it themselves and take some unproven remedy. I've seen a few real tragedies over the years. By the time they come back a year later, it's too late."

"Hmm," was all Jim could say in response.

"And the other thing you have to remember: you don't want to push them away from conventional therapy. When they start talking alternative treatment, you've got to listen, give them all the time they need and hope they at least stick with the proven stuff."

"Okay," Jim said softly.

"And about that husband," Steinberg continued, "Mr. Egemen mightn't be such a bad guy. Put yourself in his shoes. How would you deal with it if you were in his situation?"

"I guess you're right."

"Of course I'm right, Jimmy! Now let's go in together and get this lady sorted out!"

As Jim looked at the clock, he realized the tradeoff was not so bad. Another gastrectomy would come along soon enough.

Chapter 10 ~ Gastronomy

Dr. Steinberg and Hank walked through the noisy cafeteria, Jim following closely behind. They settled in at a table, each with coffee and a muffin courtesy of Dr. Steinberg. The loud drone grated on Jim's ears. He was nearing the end of another busy week in October. Although he was on call on the weekend, his staff surgeon for that particular weekend, Dr. O'Brien, had told Jim to take Friday night off. "We'll be okay without you for one night," he'd said. "Take your wife out for a change. Even have a glass of wine! Heaven knows, you hardly ever get a chance to do that these days!" Jim had gladly accepted the offer, secretly hoping that if any significant pathology was brewing in the community, it could delay coming in until Saturday morning. He'd hate to miss a rare or interesting surgical problem on his night off.

Hank was gobbling his muffin so rapidly that grease spots were appearing on his glasses and muffin crumbs were falling onto the table. He absently brushed them onto the floor as Dr. Steinberg spoke.

"Jimmy, what are your plans for next year?"

"Well, I know you said I should do more training." Jim took a deep breath. "But I'm actually thinking of going into practice."

Hank pushed the last fragment of muffin into his mouth and started crumpling his napkin into a tiny ball. The other two muffins sat virtually untouched as Steinberg responded. "I know you could get a job in most any community hospital, but if you want to work at a place like St. Joe's, or the University Hospital, then you'll need to do an extra year or two of training. I'm sure at the end of a five-year residency to become a specialist in general surgery, the last thing you want to think about is more formal education. Give it some thought though, Jim. You've got ability and can go far. A fellowship year in laparoscopic surgery, for instance—I think that's a field poised to expand. But it's getting late. By the end of October, all the good spots will be taken. You just say the word and I can put you in touch with the right people."

"Thanks, Dr. Steinberg," Jim said. "But I've actually been looking at Lakefield."

As he raised the muffin to take a bite, Steinberg suddenly paused and placed it back on the table, his mouth gaping. "You what?"

"I've been looking at Lakefield. Amanda grew up there."

"I heard what you said. I just thought..."

Jim had not seen Steinberg lost for words like this before. Feeling intense pangs of guilt, he added quickly, "It's just that—"

"I know. It's okay. I shouldn't be surprised. Should have perhaps worked on this a little harder, a little sooner."

"I know," said Jim. "But I'm not sure you could have said anything to change my mind. I think I want to go somewhere that I can be my own boss and do my own surgery." He then turned and said, "Somewhere without surgery residents—no offence, Hank. I'd rather just do my own thing without feeling obliged to give my surgery away to trainees. I love to teach, but I think I love to operate more. And with narrowing scopes of practice at the U, I'd miss out on the variety of surgery I'd get at a community hospital."

Steinberg sat chewing slowly while staring at Jim. After a long pause, he spoke. "Well Jim, I know you'll do well wherever you go, and Lakefield will be lucky to have you."

Polite conversation ensued while Hank watched Jim and Steinberg finishing their muffins. Silence followed until Steinberg added, "Jimmy, don't forget, I'll do whatever I can to help. And if you change your mind about further training, let me know as soon as you can."

He sensed some disappointment on Dr. Steinberg's part, but Jim decided to take it as a compliment.

***

As he hurried down the stairwell to the basement, Jim looked forward to returning to the residents' lounge after a long absence. Over the previous four years, he had spent many hours in residents' quarters throughout the city. Hank and other junior residents of all specialties would catch a few disjointed hours of sleep here while taking in-house call. Although call rooms were modest, a freshly made bed and a private shower were available for each of the residents on call for the night. The amount of sleep each house staff could obtain depended on the specialty rotation, time of year, phase of the moon and a host of other factors.

On surgery, junior residents averaged between two and four hours of sleep. Call was sandwiched between two regular twelve-hour workdays, resulting in a tired group of residents. The call cycle repeated every third or fourth night, just before recovery from the previous call could occur. Residency was packed with learning, experiences and even legendary feats without sleep. Most trainees accepted it as a rite of passage toward becoming a specialist physician.

In addition to the bare necessities, the lounge had a pool table, couches, chairs and cable TV. There was also a small kitchen with a microwave and a fridge. It was an ideal location for random encounters with fellow residents. The lounge occasionally even served to inaugurate a romantic affair. Circumstances permitting, a rare tryst sprouted into marriage. One or two times a year, violating official policy, a raucous bash with plenty of food and booze would erupt. But to some residents and medical students, the lounge was merely sleeping quarters on the way to achieving their educational goals.

In the final year, chief residents had the luxury of being on call from home. The downside was how much they needed to be available, often up to twenty-five nights a month. Amanda had become used to it. It wasn't like she hadn't known what she was in for when she married Jim. Due to home call, Jim spent far less time in the residents' lounge, and as he walked toward the entrance late this afternoon, he realized how much he missed the camaraderie.

Today, an educational session on geriatric medicine was scheduled in the lounge for 4:00 p.m. A drug company was sponsoring the event. The only reason Jim showed up was that Amanda's cousin was the drug rep attending and supplying the pizza. He figured he could drop by for a slice and yak with a few residents. Then he could report back to Amanda that yes, he had seen Deedra. After sitting through the first five minutes of a boring video about some new drug for the elderly population, Jim could self-activate his pager and then excuse himself to get back to work.

He negotiated his way around four medical students who were engaged in a loud game of solids and stripes while simultaneously munching on pizza. Jim waved at Deedra, a cute twenty-three-year-old with short brown hair who was leaning against her drug display while speaking to a fourth-year neurosurgery resident. Jim smiled and continued to search the room for familiar faces. About twenty people were milling about, devouring a massive supply of food. Jim couldn't help but marvel at the sheer amount of talent in the room. Some were headed for academic triumphs he couldn't imagine, while others would be dispersed across the country in various community hospital positions. Some had sacrificed a chance at a career in athletic, musical or business fields to pursue an often less celebrated but more secure and gruelling medical path.

A rotund cardiology resident balanced his Sprite in the crook of his arm while he stabilized a soggy piece of Hawaiian with two hands in front of his open mouth. He was bumped from behind by a medical student, which resulted in pizza topping tumbling onto the rug. The resident looked around and then kicked a couple of chunks of pineapple from the carpeted area into the tiled kitchen, where they would obviously do less harm.

As Jim stood in line awaiting his gustatory reward, he fleetingly considered the ethics of drug company sponsorship of educational events. He realized some people in higher places would analyze the subtle nuances that could influence physicians' drug prescribing practices. But for Jim, it was either fine or it was not. There was no in between. And he had long ago decided events like this were acceptable. Half the time he had no idea who was putting on the event, so that as far as he was concerned, it was okay. For most residents, the *educational* component of the presentation was of uncertain value. Like vultures consuming roadkill, uninterested in what kind of life the carcass had led before its demise, residents were just happy because there was food. And it was free.

Jim reached the front of the queue and grabbed a greasy slice of pepperoni with a can of Coke. He eyed Hank in the corner. Tomato sauce on both cheeks, Hank was inhaling two pieces at a time, one stacked on top of the other. Jim scanned the room and thought he should get down to the lounge more often. With the video about to start, he activated his pager, waved at Deedra and bolted, pizza and Coke in hand.

Chapter 11 ~ How to Save a Drowning Man

Jim sat in the second row of the small classroom, relieved that it was not his turn to be on the hot seat. He stared out the small window. Red and yellow leaves were blowing off the trees onto the street below. This time next year, his exams would be under his belt and he'd be doing surgery on his own, without the watchful eye of an attending surgeon. Directly in front of him sat Simon, the sole resident in the front row, who was soon to be examined by Dr. Steinberg. Simon fidgeted, awaiting his fate while Jim and four other residents watched from the second row.

Dr. Steinberg broke the silence, bursting through the door and closing it gently behind him. "Good morning, folks. I see Simon is in the hot seat today." Dr. Steinberg sat down at the front of the room, his right hand resting on a large oak desk. Perched at the front of the desk was an X-ray view box, holding two films that would be illuminated by flipping the backlight switch. He smiled, rubbing his chin. Simon nodded, then smoothed his rumpled red hair with his right hand until his glasses were crooked. He adjusted them back into place.

Jim was especially glad that he was not being examined today. This was the first of many practice oral exams for the chief residents. Every Sunday morning, from September until May, the chief residents from the four teaching hospitals across the city assembled to either observe or be the subject of a practice oral. By the time one had to sit the real exams to qualify as a fellowship surgeon in late June, each chief resident had heard nearly every possible question pertaining to general surgery. Passing multiple-choice exams in May was a necessary step prior to sitting the oral exams. A most stressful event, orals covered more practical general surgery questions compared to the written exam, which ensured a baseline of knowledge. The oral exams consisted of two one-hour sessions requiring verbal answers, mostly around surgical cases. They were much more intimidating than any written exam and could make or break an entire year. Anyone could have a bad day come exam time, so the six chief residents—half women, half men this year—assembled weekly to maximize the chances of success in June.

Dr. Steinberg and Dr. Herrick alternated Sundays, taking residents through an eight-month process of learning how to successfully sit the most important exam of their careers. Dr. Herrick had a reputation for being vicious in an exam setting. Having been an examiner on the national surgical exams for twenty years, he had a knack for determining whether a candidate would make a competent surgeon and he also had a sixth sense for identifying and exposing knowledge gaps and weaknesses. Like a cougar stealthily stalking its prey, if he chose to pounce, there was no escape. Dr. Steinberg was a little less intimidating but nonetheless just as skillful in identifying those potential surgeons whose judgment around patient care could be substandard. Jim recalled hearing about a terrifying practice oral exam given to a second-year resident four or five years previously by Dr. Herrick and Dr. Steinberg. The examining surgeons were sitting side-by-side across the desk from the victim, alternating taking potshots, when the resident came out with a response that clearly upset both professors. Herrick stood up, his voice escalating as he berated the resident ceaselessly. Despite his reputation, no one had seen Dr. Herrick get so angry over a practice oral exam. As he was foaming at the mouth and beating his fists on the desk, Dr. Herrick probably had no idea of the effect he was having on the resident, who quit the surgery program the following day.

Dr. Steinberg quickly reviewed some of the ground rules. "This will be like a real oral exam. It will last sixty minutes. All chief residents are here to observe. I expect you'll learn as much as Simon today. Next time, it will be someone else's turn. We will not only be teaching surgery during the sessions but more importantly, we will teach you how to sit an oral exam. You will learn how not to get dragged down a certain path you will regret. During the exam today, the only people who will speak are Simon and I. At the end, the rest of you will have the opportunity to make comments or ask questions, but you will otherwise remain silent. Okay, shall we start?"

Each resident quietly nodded in agreement. Jim could feel fluttering in his chest, vicariously nervous for Simon but thankful today was not his day.

"Okay, Simon," Dr. Steinberg started. "You have a twenty-five-year-old man who presents to the Emergency Department with acute abdominal pain. He is exquisitely tender with a rigid abdomen and has a low-grade fever. How do you proceed?"

"I would take a thorough history and do a physical exam. I would want to know how long the pain has been going on." He shifted his chair and looked around the room. "I would then order some blood tests and get some X-rays."

Jim immediately thought of the most likely possibilities: perforated ulcer, pancreatitis or acute gallbladder inflammation. General surgery appealed to Jim because there weren't usually many diagnostic possibilities in the list for acute surgical abdominal pain. The critical answer was often a choice between surgery or non-operative management. His thoughts were interrupted by Steinberg's incisive line of questioning.

"Okay, Simon, list three points in this young man's history you'd want to know."

"Whether he's had a history of ulcers, how much alcohol he drinks and what medication he takes, if any."

"Why?"

"Risk factors. If he drinks alcohol, he'd be at risk of pancreatitis and ulcers." Simon altered his position in his chair as he appeared to be searching intently for something more to say. Jim, behind and to his right, could see flushing on the right side of his face. Simon wiped beads of perspiration from his freckled forehead with his sleeve. Jim considered the pancreas, the organ that produces insulin for the blood and also digestive enzymes for the intestine. He thought back to the latest guy they'd had with pancreatitis. Under such circumstances, the vicious cycle of inflammation can result in the pancreas partially digesting itself. The man ended up in the Intensive Care Unit for a month. Jim made a mental note to think twice the next time he and Amanda were out at one of the resident parties. The last thing he'd need would be a bout of pancreatitis from too many beers. *It's disquieting when you know too much*, Jim thought. Life had been easier when he could drink in ignorant bliss.

"What about pancreatitis—what are the risk factors?"

"Alcohol, gallstones, and… and—"

"What about gallstones, Simon, how do they cause pancreatitis?" Steinberg was now pacing back and forth at the front of the room.

"Rarely, a stone can pass out of the gallbladder into the common bile duct, and in some people the pancreatic duct joins the bile duct before draining into the intestine. In these cases the stone can get stuck and cause backup of pancreatic enzymes into the pancreas, causing inflammation and auto-digestion."

"Back to our twenty-five-year-old. What blood tests would you order?"

"CBC, electrolytes, liver enzymes and lipase."

"What X-rays would you order?" Steinberg's cadence was increasing, giving Simon little time to think between questions.

"Three views of the abdomen," Simon answered confidently. Steinberg was facing Simon, standing to the right between the X-ray view box and the window. With his left hand, he pulled down the blinds to darken the room as he simultaneously lifted the toggle switch on the view box.

"What do you see?" Steinberg asked.

Simon started tentatively, "It's an upright chest X-ray."

"Good," Steinberg stated, with a touch of sarcasm.

To Jim, it wasn't as obvious as X-rays he'd seen before, but he was pretty sure the telltale sliver of a dark shadow below the right diaphragm muscle could only mean one thing: free air. Air outside the bowel meant a perforation until proven otherwise. Why wasn't Simon speaking up?

"Well, Simon, what do you see?" He was now sounding irritated, his pitch rising and his voice taking on a more nasal tone. As Simon stammered on, Jim started to feel sorry for him. If he couldn't recognize free air at this stage of his training, he was in big trouble. "Well, Simon. I know you know this!"

"Free air!" Simon let out a prolonged sigh of relief after the words exited his mouth, but Steinberg continued, depriving Simon of any time to revel in his correct answer or gain his footing for the next question.

"Okay. What does this twenty-five-year-old man have?"

"Perforated ulcer!" Simon blurted.

"What else could it be?" Steinberg continued.

"Perforated diverticulitis," Simon added.

"Is that likely in this age group, Simon?" Steinberg queried, his voice still racing as he now stood squarely in front of Simon, looking down through the top half of his bifocals, his hands on his hips.

"No?"

"Is that a question? Or an answer, Simon?"

"No! Diverticulitis is possible, but not likely in a twenty-five-year-old."

"What else could it be, Simon?"

"Perforated appendix?"

"Have you ever seen free air from a perforated appendix?"

"Well, no. But I suppose it's possible," Simon added, his voice shaking.

"Well then, Simon, what are you going to do next?" Steinberg stepped back and sat in the chair at the front of the room, not taking his eyes off Simon.

"Operate. I'm going to take him to the operating room, for what is most likely a perforated duodenal ulcer."

Good, thought Jim. As much as he liked to shine above his colleagues from time to time, he was uncomfortable watching Simon looking so tentative this early in a practice exam. At least now, Simon appeared to be gaining some control. This seemed like an easy oral exam question to Jim and he just wasn't sure why Simon had been faltering.

Steinberg stopped pacing and said, his tone mollifying, "Before you tell us about what operation you'd do, Simon, tell me a bit about ulcers. What causes duodenal ulcers?"

Simon's shoulders drooped. He paused and took in a deep breath. "Too much acid."

"What about diet? What about bacteria? Medication?" Steinberg was picking up the pace again.

"No, diet plays no role in ulcers. Not like we used to think. And bacteria—*H. pylori*—might play a role, but it's a little unclear at present."

"Medication?"

"You treat *H. pylori* with—"

"No, Simon, I know that. Do medications cause ulcers?"

"Yes, Aspirin or other NSAIDs can cause ulcers."

"Good, Simon, tell me about surgery for ulcers, what are the principles of ulcer surgery?"

"Vagotomy—cutting the vagus nerves shuts down acid production."

"What else do you have to do?"

Jim immediately thought about the two main options in uncomplicated ulcer surgery, either opening the outlet of the stomach—a pyloroplasty—or removing the bottom half of the stomach—antrectomy—to allow stomach emptying after the vagus nerves have been cut.

"If you cut the vagus nerves, the stomach will no longer propel food downstream, so you have to combine a vagotomy with a drainage procedure. Pyloroplasty or antrectomy."

"What about now? Do you see these operations very often in the nineties?"

"No, not so commonly any more," said Simon.

"And why not?" Dr. Steinberg asked. Jim could count on one hand how many elective ulcer operations he'd seen in the last year. But he knew Dr. Steinberg had probably done one or two vagotomies per week back in the seventies.

"Medication," Simon said. "Proton pump inhibitors such as Losec are a huge factor. And possibly *H. pylori* eradication."

"Okay, one more question before we get back to our case, Simon. What's the most important difference between gastric and duodenal ulcers?"

"Stomach—gastric—ulcers can be cancerous and therefore must be followed up, whereas duodenal ulcers are almost never malignant."

"Okay, good. Now back to our twenty-five-year-old male. He's had pain for a day and a half. He's been on Losec twice a day for dyspeptic symptoms for months. No history of ulcers. Not on any medications that might cause ulcers. You said you were going to operate, Simon. What are you going to do?" Dr. Steinberg was now leaning back in his chair with his legs crossed and his hands neatly folded in his lap.

"I'm going to take him to the operating room for a laparotomy."

"What incision?"

"Midline."

"Upper midline?"

"I'd start small, above the umbilicus, just in case it's a surprise, like diverticulitis. If I smell stool on entering the abdomen, I'll extend the incision downward, but if it's just bile and no smell, I'll convert it to an upper midline incision for a presumed perforated ulcer, most likely duodenal in this age group." Simon seemed more relaxed and confident again.

"Okay," Steinberg continued, "so you open him up and see a lot of bile and some pus, mostly in the upper abdomen. You put your hand in and feel an inflammatory mass around the duodenum. With some good retraction, you get a good look and you see a hole the size of a dime on the front wall of the duodenum. What are you going to do?"

"Wash him out and patch the ulcer with a piece of omentum."

Good, Jim thought. Simon was now finding his stride, rattling off answers at least as well as Jim would be doing. He thought back to the last time he had scrubbed on a perforated ulcer, about six weeks ago. After irrigating all of the murky, infected fluid from the upper abdomen, they simply laid a piece of greater omentum, the fatty apron attached to the stomach, over the hole and secured it with a few silk sutures.

"And what's the name of your patch?"

"Graham patch," Simon replied proudly.

"Yes. Now Simon," Steinberg continued, "you remember this man developed a perforated duodenal ulcer *while already taking* anti-ulcer medication."

"Yes?" Simon said tentatively. He cocked his head to one side.

"Well," Steinberg said pointedly, sitting more upright and staring directly into Simon's eyes, "if he gets a perforation while on medication for ulcers, what good are you doing by just patching this one? Aren't you worried about a recurrent ulcer?"

Jim could now see where this was going and he didn't like it. Steinberg was laying some tempting bait in front of Simon. Before Simon had a chance to respond, Steinberg added, "What's the chance of recurrence if you just patch it? Is there anything else you'd like to do for your patient?"

No, Jim thought, *don't touch that one Simon!*

"I'd like to do a definitive ulcer operation!" Simon blurted.

"But you just said you'd patch the ulcer," Steinberg said, kindness in his voice.

"I wouldn't just patch it. No, I take it back. I would do a definitive ulcer operation—either a vagotomy and pyloroplasty or a vagotomy and antrectomy. I'm just trying to think what would be best."

Jim had lost all hope. Simon was falling apart and possibly didn't even know it.

"Which will it be then? Pyloroplasty or antrectomy?" Steinberg was now smiling broadly, his prey firmly in his sights. "He's got many years in his life ahead of him in which to get a recurrent ulcer. Tell me, Simon, which operation would you do?"

"Vagotomy and antrectomy!" This time Simon shouted it out but was again flushing and perspiring heavily. Jim could see a host of calamities around the corner for Simon's mock patient.

"So then you'd patch the duodenal ulcer, cut the vagus nerves and remove the bottom segment of the stomach. How would you reattach him?"

Jim thought of the two different ways of reattaching after a partial gastrectomy, named after a nineteenth-century surgeon, Dr. Theodor Billroth.

"I'd hand sew it. A Billroth I."

"Would you leave a drain in?"

"No. Well, er, yes! Definitely I'd drain it!"

"Okey dokey. So the operation goes fine. You leave a drain in. Then four days after surgery, he spikes a high fever—39.5."

"Oh, well I'd get blood cultures," Simon paused. "And I'd—"

"He then starts to pour bile out his drain. What are you going to do now, Simon, reoperate?"

"No. I'd put him on antibiotics."

"He then goes into septic shock and gets intubated and transferred to the Intensive Care Unit. Would you operate now?"

"Yes! Yes!"

"Do you know what operation you would do for him this time?"

"No," Simon shook his head, "no, I don't." The other residents exchanged glances with each other and then with Jim, who was very happy not to be Simon right now.

"Do you want to go back and reconsider whether you'd do an ulcer operation? Or perhaps you would rather have simply patched the ulcer and gotten out?" Steinberg was grinning.

"I'd patch it and get out. No antrectomy. No pyloroplasty."

"That sounds better to me, Simon," Steinberg replied, beaming.

The next thirty minutes, Steinberg continued his barrage. Simon fared somewhat better than his disastrous attempt to save the twenty-five-year-old with the perforated duodenal ulcer but nonetheless was obviously feeling the heat while his resident colleagues looked on in consternation. After a series of short-answer questions that seemed to last forever, Steinberg stood up and smacked a yardstick on the nearby desk, startling everyone.

"Okay, what did you think of Simon's performance?" He looked over Simon's head to the residents in the second row.

Silence. Jim considered giving some lukewarm support for Simon and then thought better of it, remaining silent.

"Well, I'll tell you then," Steinberg continued. "It was not Simon's most shining hour but it's early in the year. And if any of you think you might have done better, I can stick around for another exam today. But Simon made a few errors. Number one: Don't back down. Pick your course and stick to it. Don't be swayed by temptation laid in front of you by the examiner. Which brings me to rule two: Don't be wrong. If you think you could be wrong, you will be more likely to screw up with rule number one and end up backing down. Say what you know and what you've seen before in surgery, and don't make up stuff on the fly based on something that sounds reasonable or you think you've read. And then there's rule three, which applies specifically to this ulcer patient but could come up in many other instances."

Steinberg looked over at Jim. When their eyes locked, Jim knew a question was coming his way. "Jim, what do you do when you see a drowning man?"

Puzzled, Jim sat for a moment and then said, "Throw him a lifejacket?"

"Exactly!" Steinberg scanned the group and then asked, "What did Simon do for his drowning man? Anyone? What did Simon do?"

The residents were alternating looking toward their feet and then at the ceiling. Simon appeared completely knackered.

"Simon did a much longer operation with higher risk. He tried to give the drowning man swimming lessons! Remember, throw the man a lifejacket, don't try to teach him how to swim."

Makes sense, Jim thought.

"Your man with the perforated ulcer would have been going home five days after his surgery, and by trying to teach him how to swim, you gave him infection and a leak and nearly killed him. And I bet you've never seen that done before quite like you described."

Simon was now nodding steadily, appearing grateful to be nearly done with today's ordeal.

"You'll all improve from these sessions. Next time I'll bring donuts and coffee. See you then," Steinberg said as he left the room, closing the door behind him. The residents sat quietly. Jim's head hurt and he was exhausted from observing the past hour. He wondered how Simon must feel right now.

Candace, one of two chiefs at the University Hospital, broke the silence. "I also heard they'll never let you leave the room on a correct answer."

"What?" asked Jim as he looked around at the others.

"No, she's right. I heard that, too," said Simon.

"What d'you mean?" Jim asked.

"When my brother did his fellowship exam three years ago," Candace continued, "he said everyone in his year was made to answer a question incorrectly before they were allowed to leave the room."

"How can they do that?" Jim had a hard time believing her. "What if you know all the answers?"

"I'm telling you, it's true." Candace turned in her chair, bestowing the advice on all of the residents, who were now listening intently. "They don't want you to leave the room thinking you know it all. So no matter how well you do, they will always find a tough enough question to send you packing. You know you've passed if they throw you an impossible question at the end of the hour. It's when they send you out after thirty minutes that you're in trouble."

Chapter 12 ~ Tracheostomy

At 7:25 a.m., Jim, with EBUs clinging closely behind, entered the Intensive Care Unit through the automatic double doors. All seven were dressed in yellow disposable gowns. They washed their hands and headed over to Mr. McKiddie's bed. Half of the ICU occupants were housed in one large, open room. Ten private, glassed-off rooms around the perimeter held the remaining beds, often occupied by patients who were vulnerable to infection or who carried transmissible diseases. Upon entering ICU, visitors were swamped with the loud, intermittent hissing of life-supporting ventilators. Occasional alarms, telephones and haphazard voices augmented the clatter. The ICU smell was immediately familiar to Jim, a pervasive combination of scents, alternating between medicinal and putrid.

The group in their yellow attire swarmed around Mr. McKiddie's bed in the open area, closest to the door. The EBUs stood open-mouthed, staring at the unconscious Mr. McKiddie. He was markedly swollen compared to the gaunt elderly man who had presented to Emergency nearly two weeks earlier with a perforated stercoral ulcer. The slits of his eyes were slathered with lubricant while his lips and cheeks were bulging from edema, a consequence of massive amounts of intravenous fluids administered during his most septic phase ten days ago. Jim picked up a binder from a small table and glanced inside, then snapped the chart closed and looked up at the group. "Mr. McKiddie needs a tracheostomy." Up to this point, the patient had been ventilated via an endotracheal tube through his mouth, but with no hope of extubation—removal of the tube—in the near future, it was time to surgically place a tube through the front of his neck into the trachea, for prolonged respiratory support. *With any luck, Mr. McKiddie will continue to improve and the tracheostomy will be only short-term, perhaps a month*, Jim thought. "We'll do it later today at the end of our elective list in the O.R." Jim reached with his right hand and while palpating the patient's neck, he added, "Short neck. It won't be the easiest one to get a tube in." He jotted down a few notes on the order sheet of the patient's chart.

A short, blond nurse dressed in greens sauntered in amongst the group and elbowed her way next to Jim. She was chewing gum, which Jim thought was against the rules for the ICU. She tilted her head to one side and with hands on hips, she looked at Jim and said, "It's about time you get this trach done. You know we want it by ten days and it's past that already."

"Yes, we know," Jim replied. "It's been kind of busy lately. We'll get it done today for sure." Looking up from the patient file, he said, "Let's go. No time to waste." As he made his way out of the nurse's earshot, he stopped with his group as they congregated at the exit. He announced to the assembly, "A quarter of the patients in this unit don't make it out alive. Think about it. These patients are sick. And speaking of making it out of the ICU alive, if you want to survive your ICU rotation, you need to listen to the nurses. They can make you or break you. They're almost as bad as obstetrical nurses."

One of the junior residents stood on his toes and interjected, "Hey, my wife's an obstetrical nurse!"

"Well, er…shall I say as strong-willed as obstetrical nurses," Jim stammered. "They have a territory to protect. Their area is highly specialized. The last thing they want is some smart-assed medical student or resident coming in and thinking he knows more than they do."

"Oh. I suppose…" the resident replied.

Having properly bailed himself out, Jim headed out the door toward the O.R., eagerly trailed by his pack of EBUs.

***

Mr. McKiddie was lying still on the operating table. His endotracheal tube, soon to be removed, was taped to the corner of his mouth. Jim was about to make a two-inch cut across his lower neck, find the trachea and make a hole in it. Standing opposite Dr. O'Brien, Jim paused with his scalpel poised above Mr. McKiddie's neck and asked the anesthetist if he could commence surgery.

"Just give me a second, Jim. He dropped his blood pressure here on induction. I just need a minute or two to correct that." The anesthetist injected a small syringe full of a clear solution into the intravenous line. Next to Jim and Dr. O'Brien on the sides of the patient's chest, a junior resident and Rhani leaned forward, trying to see the neck where Jim was about to cut. Iris, the scrub nurse, stood next to Rhani at Mr. McKiddie's waist. Two medical students stood on stools several feet back to catch a glimpse of whatever they could during the procedure. There was an air of anticipation and as Jim waited for the medication to take effect, he reviewed the impending operation. Once he made an opening in the trachea, he'd need to move smoothly and rapidly. There is a brief dangerous period of a few seconds after the anesthetist has withdrawn the existing endotracheal tube from the patient's mouth but before the new tube is inserted through the incision in the neck, when there is no tube in the windpipe and therefore no control over the airway or oxygenation of the body. The tube exchange must be done swiftly and successfully, as the patient's life is literally in the surgeon's hands. In heavy people with a thick neck, the hole can be deep and narrow, making it a challenge to see the target clearly. If the aperture is not big enough, or obscured by blood at the wrong time, the outcome could be catastrophic. Unlike an emergency or *slash trach*, there's no excuse here for not being successful. In an elective situation like this, everything is completely controlled. This experience may be lifesaving in the future if one is faced with an emergency airway obstruction outside of the operating room.

The anesthetist grunted and nodded at Jim, who then placed the fingers of his left hand on Mr. McKiddie's neck to stabilize the skin. With only a small area of neck exposed through a window in the surgical drapes, Dr. O'Brien used his left hand just at the top of the breastbone to provide counter traction to Jim's left hand. "He may be skinny," O'Brien said, "but he's got a short neck. With all this arthritis, we can't extend the neck much. You don't have a lot of room to work here, Jim."

Jim made a two-inch incision across Mr. McKiddie's neck, just above the sternal notch, then responded, "This could be trickier than expected." He suddenly became anxious about the possibility of complications.

As if reading Jim's mind, O'Brien spoke. "What are the complications of tracheostomy tube insertion?"

As Jim formulated his response, he handed back the scalpel and then deepened the incision with cautery. He said, "Complications that can occur in any surgery, such as heart and lung complications." He paused as he made a vertical cut with cautery between the muscles in the midline. He inserted a metal retractor into the separation and pulled, opening the muscles in the middle of the neck. He then handed the retractor to Rhani while Dr. O'Brien passed his retractor to the resident to hold. Jim continued, "Loss of airway, obviously, would be a disaster." As Jim and Dr. O'Brien both tugged on the retractors held by the assistants, the muscle layer parted, exposing a small, whitish area in the depths of the wound. Jim felt it with his index finger. "There's not a lot of room here, but I feel the tracheal rings." He then glanced at Iris and said, "Langenbeck retractor." As she handed the L-shaped instrument to him, Jim inserted it at the top of the wound and pulled gently toward the head. O'Brien took the instrument in his right hand. Jim continued, "We can see more of the trachea if you pull the thyroid isthmus upwards." He palpated again with his finger and added, "We still don't have lots of space here, but I can definitely feel the tracheal rings. Feel this," he said, looking at the resident, who hurriedly inserted his finger, his eyes widening above his surgical mask as he moved his finger gingerly in the small hole. Jim then directed Rhani to take a turn. As she eagerly introduced her finger into the neck, Jim continued, "Yes, complications. Infection, of course. And then damage to local structures such as the thyroid gland. And bleeding. You can have early bleeding at the time of surgery, or bleeding can be late—"

Suddenly, as Rhani pulled her finger up out of the wound, dark blood welled up from the operative field. Completely obscuring their view, blood was overflowing above the wound edges, dripping down onto Jim's shoes.

"Sponge! Suction!" Jim shouted as he thrust a white surgical sponge into the wound. Holding pressure to contain the hemorrhage, Jim felt fluttering in his chest. He continued to pack sponges as Dr. O'Brien deftly suctioned the blood. Loud gurgling was heard as blood made its way up the suction tubing. With Jim maintaining pressure in the neck, he could see the bleeding was at least temporarily staunched "We've had some bleeding, but it seems controlled for now," Jim said in the direction of the anesthetist. One at a time, he removed sopping wet, dark sponges while maintaining pressure on the wound with his left hand. As he lightened the pressure, Jim saw an instant gush of blood. "Mixter!" While reestablishing pressure, he took the Mixter forceps from the nurse and guided the tips around a large vein on his side of the wound. With two clicks, he clamped off the vein below a small hole. Without being asked, the nurse firmly placed a second Mixter in his outstretched right hand. As he clamped off the vein above the hole, Jim withdrew his left hand and said, "Scissors." He proceeded to cut through the clamped vein where it had been torn. He then tied both ends of the vein closed as, one by one, Dr. O'Brien removed the occluding forceps.

"I'm so sorry!" Rhani sounded like she was going to burst into tears.

"That's okay, Rhani," O'Brien said. "It's not your fault. Could've happened with anyone. Just goes to show how fragile veins can be. As opposed to arteries, which are much tougher." He then turned to Iris. "Is our tube ready?"

She held up the L-shaped tracheostomy tube in her left hand. The part she clutched would soon extend in a perpendicular direction out of Mr. McKiddie's trachea and neck to connect to the ventilator, while the segment below the bend would extend vertically downwards in his windpipe. A balloon at the bottom end of the tube would hold it in place, sealing off the trachea around the tube, preventing any air leaks while the ventilator moved air through the tube, in and out of the patient's lungs. She injected air through a tiny plastic hose to check for leaks in the protective sealing cuff. "It looks good to me, Dr. O'Brien," she said. She deflated the cuff and placed the tube, now ready for insertion, back on her instrument tray.

Jim concentrated as he cleared the trachea of any remaining blood. He dabbed his target with a fresh sponge. “Ready?”

“Anytime,” O’Brien replied. “You’re supposed to go at the second tracheal ring. Just go as high as you can.” Then to the anesthetist, “We’re about to open the trachea.”

Jim made a vertical cut in the trachea, exposing the endotracheal tube in the depths of the wound. “Tracheal hook,” Jim said to the nurse. As he inserted the small, hooked instrument into the slit in the trachea, he lifted upwards and said, “That’s much easier to see. Shouldn’t have a problem getting a tube in there.”

“As long as your hook stays firm and there’s no more bleeding,” O’Brien replied.

Jim said, “Okay, slowly pull back the endotracheal tube.” As the anesthetist gradually drew the ventilator end of the tube out of Mr. McKiddie’s mouth, Jim could see the tip moving upwards inside the trachea and disappearing toward the mouth. While he gazed at the empty windpipe through his surgical tracheal cut, Jim could now smell the distinct odour of anesthetic gases escaping from the wound, filling the room. He started to feel lightheaded, but retaining full control of his senses said, “Tripod!” Dr. O’Brien thrust a three-pronged instrument into the tracheal opening, and while he spread the hole wider, Jim popped the cuffed end of the L-shaped tracheostomy tube through the wound and into Mr. McKiddie’s trachea.

“There you go, Jim,” O’Brien said, “Smooth as silk!”

Jim inflated the cuff to secure the position of the tracheostomy tube and to create an airtight seal. The anesthetist handed the ventilator hose from above the patient’s head and Jim connected it to the fresh tracheostomy tube. Jim could see Mr. McKiddie’s chest rise and fall with rhythmic breaths of air from the ventilator. With a proper seal obtained and no more gases leaking into the room, Jim was relieved. He wondered whether anyone had ever passed out from inadvertent inhalation of escaped gaseous anesthetic drugs. With the potentially hazardous part of the procedure behind him and the airway again secured, Jim relaxed.

“Okay, let’s close and get out of here!” O’Brien’s loud voice startled Jim.

“Suture!” Despite the brief hemorrhage, Jim thought it had been an excellent operation. He was satisfied that he would no longer have to worry about Mr. McKiddie’s airway.

Chapter 13 ~ Jugular

Jim quietly pulled the door closed behind him and sat down in the residents' lounge, sinking deeply into the couch. He'd hoped to find more activity here to give his mood a lift. He longed for a rambunctious match of pool or a beer with fellow residents in front of a contentious football game. He'd just come from a Wednesday afternoon chat with Dr. Steinberg. It was all arranged. Tomorrow he was to meet with Steinberg's pal, the lawyer—just a precaution—to discuss the Edna Doyle case. "Johansen's a good guy," he'd told Jim. "A little quirky, mind you, but a fine lawyer. And he loves to win."

As program director and mentor, Dr. Steinberg had told Jim he just wanted the best for him and he'd heard through the grapevine that there might be a complaint around the corner. Apparently, Edna's husband had accepted administration's explanation that his wife's demise was an elusive presentation of a rare condition, but the son was not so sympathetic to their account. Steinberg had been informed the son was asking questions, such as, "Shouldn't you be able to detect internal bleeding promptly in this day and age?" Perhaps, but splenic artery aneurysm wasn't exactly the first thing that came to mind, even to a seasoned professional like Steinberg, when someone presented with vague belly pain. The son had been peppering administration with queries and accusations by mail and telephone from across the country. Although he'd not spoken directly to the family, Steinberg had been asked on several occasions to comment on the case. Dr. Steinberg had told Jim earlier this afternoon that he sensed a complaint to the Medical Licensing Authority was not out of the question. And for this reason alone, it made sense to do a little preemptive preparation. Hence, he'd arranged a meeting between Jim and the lawyer for the following day.

The residents' lounge was quiet and nearly empty. The TV was off for a change. Jim spotted Hank in the far corner of the room, staring in Jim's direction.

"Hey, Jim. You okay?"

"Yes. Well, no." Recently, Jim had discovered a few things about Hank, allowing him to feel easier about confiding in his younger resident. Four years his junior in training, yet only a year younger, Hank had been a field scientist for a couple of years before medical school. Few would have thought this somewhat disorganized glutton actually had life experience outside of university. Jim had also observed more reliability and consistency in Hank's work on the surgical team lately. He had a newfound respect for Hank and was willing to entrust him with his recent quandary.

Hank picked up his coffee cup and moved closer, seating himself directly across from Jim.

"What's going on?"

"That complaint seems to be moving forward. I'm meeting the lawyer tomorrow."

"What complaint?" Hank asked.

"Well, it's not a formal complaint—yet. But d'you remember that splenic artery aneurysm case several weeks ago—the one that died—when Baker was on call?"

"Of course I remember."

"Steinberg's set me up with a lawyer-friend squash-buddy of his for a little chat tomorrow."

"Hmm," Hank mused.

"This just sucks. This is supposed to be the time of my life: last eight months of chief resident year. All the operating I want. Jobs or fellowship positions next year, mine for the taking. And all I can do is think about this shitty case. And now it could turn into a complaint."

"Everybody gets complaints and lawsuits during their surgical career. It's just part of doing this type of business." Hank had finality in his voice, as if only reaffirming what Jim should already know.

Jim hadn't seriously considered the possibility of a lawsuit thus far. He was taken aback. He shrugged his shoulders, sitting taller in the couch. "I know, it's just that the timing couldn't be worse. The whole thing makes me want to pack it in. Quit, you know." Jim's voice cracked. He then cleared his throat and fabricated a weak cough to disguise his angst. He paused, gathering his composure. "After all this time, I just want to walk away."

Hank's brow furrowed. "Wow, that's bad." He then leaned forward and looked Jim straight in the eye. "Who's your lawyer?"

"Johnson. No, Johansen or something."

"*Jugular Johansen?*" Hank looked incredulous.

"I guess," Jim said, not sure what to make of Hank's expression.

"He's good."

"Do you know him?" Jim asked, eyes wide.

"No. But I've heard he's good."

"Just how do you know that?" Jim was skeptical. "Do you know anyone who's met him?"

Hank paused, his thumb and forefinger rubbing his chin. "Don't think so. But I'm not sure anyone would admit to knowing one of these guys. It's not the type of thing you advertise, getting sued or being on the bad end of a complaint. I don't know where I've heard it," he shifted in his chair, redirecting his eyes away from Jim. He continued hesitantly, "but I'm pretty sure having Jugular Johansen on your team is a good thing—if you have to be on one of these teams, that is."

Jim lifted out of the couch and stood up. *Jugular Johansen. Tomorrow may not be so bad after all.* "Thanks, Hank. I don't know how much you actually know about this guy. But it does give me something good about tomorrow. I wasn't looking forward to it." With no excitement in the lounge and no emergency surgical cases on the list, Jim suddenly decided he needed to be home with Amanda. "Thanks for listening, Hank. Have a good night on call. Give me a shout if you need anything. I'm going home."

***

The next day, Jim wandered into the downtown office-building lobby, slightly disoriented. He hadn't worn a suit for at least a year and he felt his neck being constricted by his tie. He scanned the lobby randomly, noting the high ceilings and angular, charcoal marble walls and benches. The atmosphere was cold and impersonal. His eyes locked on the directory. He walked over to it purposefully, feeling a little more at ease with his surroundings. There it was: Johansen, Wang, Somers. Twenty-third floor. It took another thirty seconds for Jim to realize there were three sets of elevators. The ones he wanted went to floors twenty-one to forty. He walked over slowly, lamenting the fact that he was missing another gastrectomy this afternoon. His guts roiled as he contemplated his destination on the twenty-third floor. He was relieved he'd skipped lunch as he realized a full stomach could be a hazardous condition while going to see his new lawyer for the first time.

He entered the elevator, following several men and women dressed in business suits. At least five others squeezed behind him. The return rush from lunch, Jim guessed. The elevator door closed. A tall man close to the door pushed number twenty-three and then pressed additional numbers as others called out their destination requests. The elevator was warm. He was touching shoulders with three other people. Jim looked up at the man who pressed elevator buttons and towered over everyone. It wasn't very often Jim encountered someone at least six inches taller than he was. The man's jaw was angular, chin dimpled and his grey brush cut portrayed the air of a military man. As the elevator accelerated upward, gnawing at Jim's stomach, he thought, *Could this be Jugular Johansen?* He gazed admiringly at this lofty, powerful man and considered the possibility of being represented by such a dominating figure. He pictured this specimen pounding the wiry Steinberg on the squash court and then decimating his prey in the courtroom. As the elevator ceased accelerating, reaching its terminal velocity, Jim was feeling confident. Two stops later, the man exited the elevator with Jim following close behind into the foyer of floor twenty-three. Grabbing his attention immediately was an ostentatious sign in block letters: Johansen, Wang, Somers. Beneath the sign stood two large, dark wood panel doors: the entrance to Jim's destination and, hopefully, the solution to his problem. The man strode ahead of Jim, swung one of the doors wide open and paused slightly, allowing Jim to follow into the law firm reception area. The man whisked past the receptionist, nodding as he went, and disappeared into a hallway behind her desk. *So far, so good*, Jim thought.

"I'm Jim Smythe," Jim heard himself speak tentatively to the receptionist. "I have an appointment with Dave Johansen."

Hardly looking up, she responded tersely, "Have a seat Mr. Smythe. Mr. Johansen will be with you shortly."

"Thank you," Jim mumbled and then he escaped to the waiting area, a huge open space in front of floor-to-ceiling windows overlooking the city. Despite it being a cold, cloudy day, the expansive view was impressive. The downtown buildings were tall, rectangular and grey, with only a hint of green amongst smaller structures far in the distance. Inside, plush off-white couches surrounded glass coffee tables. With matching wall-to-wall carpet, the space was eerily quiet. All Jim could hear was white noise from the air circulation system. He took a seat and glanced down at the reading material in front of him. *The Globe and Mail*, *Financial Post*, *The Economist* and *Business Week*. Jim hadn't read a newspaper or magazine, other than *Sports Illustrated*, in over a year. Sure, he'd read surgical journals and textbooks, but he suddenly felt out of touch with current events. Some day he'd have to find the time to learn a little about the world beyond bowel resections and gallstones. As he looked around at such unfamiliar surroundings, he became acutely aware of how nervous he was, simply awaiting a precautionary meeting with a lawyer to discuss a surgical case gone bad. How would he feel if this went further?

A voice boomed from behind, "Mr. Smythe!" Jim turned and to his relief, spotted chisel-chin towering over him.

He stood and, still looking up at the man, said, "Yes?"

The man simply replied, "Follow me."

Jim had to take large, rapid steps to keep up with the man, who now led him down the narrow, carpeted hallway behind the reception desk. Suddenly, the man stopped short, Jim almost slamming into him. Grabbing a handle to the right, he opened the door and then signaled Jim with his left hand to proceed ahead into the room. Jim tentatively walked into a large boardroom with a huge table surrounded by at least two-dozen robust leather chairs. At the far end, a water jug sat next to a tray of upside down glasses. Coasters were positioned in front of two chairs at that end. As he stared down the long table, Jim thought soberly, *Each of these chairs is worth more than my car!*

The man belted, "Sit at the far end—but not at the head of the table; that's Mr. Johansen's seat. He'll be with you shortly. Help yourself to some ice water. Or there's coffee or soft drinks on the cart in the corner." Without another word, the man left, closing the door softly behind him.

Jim walked slowly to the far end of the table, admiring the wood panel walls, original paintings and an occasional sculpture as he made his way there. He sat down and poured himself a glass of water. As he set the jug down, he was again cognizant of the silence. He rubbed his sweaty palms on his suit trousers just before he noticed napkins neatly set out on the drink cart. He could feel his heart pounding as he continued to wait for Mr. Johansen. He took a sip of water, soothing his parched tongue and lips.

Abruptly, the door burst open, and a brown haired man in a jacket and tie quickly entered, decisively closing the door behind him. He looked small to Jim, perhaps because he was so far away at the other end of the long boardroom table. As the man approached, Jim saw he clearly *was* a diminutive man. He was somewhat unkempt, with clumps of brown hair going in all directions. His tie was off-centre. As he smiled, moving closer, his bucked teeth protruded. He wore dark framed glasses that were slightly crooked on his face. He marched up to Jim, his hand outstretched as he said, "I'm Dave Johansen. It's a pleasure to meet you. Maurice Steinberg has told me a lot about you." The voice was high-pitched.

As Jim reached to shake Mr. Johansen's hand, he couldn't help but be reminded of a Jerry Lewis movie he'd seen in black and white many years ago on TV. As they shook hands, Johansen's grip was weak yet prolonged, rendering Jim uneasy. All he could think was, *How in hell can this guy beat Steinberg on the squash court? And what kind of a lawyer is he?* Jim noticed the lines on his face and greying at the temples. He placed the man at about fifty-five years old.

Mr. Johansen sat at the head of table, Jim not far to his right. Jim gazed at his lap and then took a sip of water. Johansen opened the conversation.

"Look, Jim, I know this is just an introductory meeting and there is no formal complaint yet, but I have to make a few things clear. Ground rules. Okay?"

"Yes," replied Jim.

"Dr. Steinberg has told me all about this case and it is a good idea we're meeting today. First of all, I do a lot of medico-legal work. It's just about all I do. Today this consultation is free. But if it goes to a complaint—*and I say if*—then you'll need some regular, paid-for legal help. That's when you get your national physicians' legal protection agency to hire you a lawyer. You can request me if you wish, but you will have someone assigned, so it may or may not be me. Understand so far?"

"Yes," Jim replied sullenly.

"And secondly, you should not discuss this case with anyone but your lawyer." Jim felt a pang of guilt as he pondered Amanda and the numerous residents with whom he'd commiserated repeatedly about the case. "From now on, anyway," Johansen continued, as if he'd read Jim's mind. "Anything you say—to anyone—can be questioned and used against you at a later time."

Jim decided to come clean on this one from the start. "I'm not going to lie to you—"

"Don't ever say that to me, Jim."

"What?"

"'I'm not going to lie to you.'"

"Yes?"

"Fine," Johansen said conclusively.

"What?" Jim asked pensively.

"Sorry?"

"What don't you want me to say?"

"'I'm not going to lie to you.' *Don't say 'I'm not going to lie to you'*. It doesn't instill a lot of confidence. In fact, the very assumption I make is that the next statement will be false. Never let me hear you use that expression again, Jim."

Jim shifted in his chair and said, "Yes, sir."

"Now this case," Johansen continued, "seems to hang on two issues. Number one: the possibility, and I repeat, possibility, that this lady should have been diagnosed with internal bleeding and had her splenic artery aneurysm treated earlier. And in that case, maybe she could have been saved. I know it's questionable whether anyone would have been able to do anything at all about her condition. That's the simple question, the one we can fight if you are challenged on this point."

The room was warm. Jim loosened his tie ever so slightly and said, "Okay…" He was about to ask for the second point when Johansen continued.

"The second point is, Jim—and this is the trickier one in my opinion—is whether you actually led Mrs. Doyle to believe she should go home. I know you didn't write a discharge order on the chart, but according to the husband, you said she could go home. So she lef—"

"I what? I never said that! Now I wouldn't lie to you Mr. Jo—"

"I just told you, Jim, never use that expression with me!"

"No, what I meant, sir, was—"

Jim abruptly stopped as he discerned Mr. Johansen wasn't breathing. His lips were pursed over his protuberant top two front teeth as his face reddened. Behind his glasses, Mr. Johansen's eyes were wide and fiery. *Breathe*, Jim wanted to say but didn't dare. As Johansen's ruddy complexion intensified, Jim noticed columns on either side of his neck, rising to the angles of his jaws. His jugular veins, fully distended like overinflated inner tubes, appeared about to burst. Finally, as if his head were unable to hold more pressure, he exhaled, gasping, "I don't care what you meant, Jim! Don't tell me you're not going to lie! When you do, I think the next thing you'll do is become economical with the truth! Don't say that!" His redness fading quickly and his jugular veins collapsing, Mr. Johansen continued panting, eyes fixed squarely on Jim.

"Wh—what I meant, sir," Jim began hesitantly, "is that I did not tell her or the husband she could go home. I don't know where you got that idea!"

"Okay, Jim," Johansen continued evenly, "it's not clear from the medical record, but apparently, according to Dr. Steinberg, the husband later said he went to the hospital cafeteria, and when he returned, his wife said that *you* told her she could go home. So, he takes her home. Next thing you know, she passes out unconscious in their kitchen and back they go, this time by ambulance, and this time she doesn't come out alive. And apparently, the son from down east is extremely unhappy about this and is making big noises about launching a formal complaint."

"But I didn't tell her she could go home. I told her she *might be able to go home*. And her husband was there when I told her that." Jim was beginning to feel persecuted, until he realized Mr. Johansen was just doing his job in relaying the information.

"That's not what he says, Jim. Like I said, this could be a tricky thing to sort out, when a seventy-four-year-old man with a dead wife says one thing, and you say another. Who should you believe? Who would you want to believe if you were looking in from the outside?"

Jim stared up at the ceiling, then back down on the table, only half-listening as Johansen continued, "The other item that concerns me, Jim, is Dr. Baker. I have this vague memory that I've met him before, but you know him much better than I do. How Dr. Baker perceives your role in all of this could be important. As your staff surgeon, is he going to stand up for you? Back you up?"

Jim thought back to his first week as a general surgery resident over four years previously, when he and Herman Baker had had their first run-in. Jim had been on call, unaware of Baker's disdain for inexperienced trainees. Late in the evening, Jim had seen a patient in the Emergency Department with abdominal pain. He remembered the details very clearly.

He had seen Mrs. Shively, an eighty-seven-year-old lady who had been vomiting for two days. She had abdominal pain and was dehydrated. She lived alone in her own house, the one she'd occupied for over fifty years. Her husband had passed away over ten years before. According to the only daughter, who was visiting from across the country, Mrs. Shively had been failing lately. More than once, she'd inadvertently left the stove turned on. She was inattentive to her hygiene and clearly hadn't bathed in weeks. She had an ulcerated area on her shin that wouldn't heal. When Jim asked her about it, she said she had banged her leg on a shopping cart five months ago and that no, she hadn't seen a doctor about it, she just needed more time to heal.

Mrs. Shively was no stranger to the operating room. She'd had a hysterectomy, an appendectomy and a cholecystectomy. With all of her surgical scars, her abdominal wall resembled an aerial view of a busy railroad station. The lines signified plenty of opportunity internally for adhesions, or scar tissue, to obstruct the bowel, causing pain and vomiting. When Jim pressed on her abdomen, he looked into her haggard eyes and could see her grimace. Wisps of grey hair projected in all directions. Jim could detect her pungent scent, a mixture of body odour and urine. "Does that hurt?" Jim asked as he pressed harder.

"Of course it hurts!" Her teeth had several gaps on the upper and lower rows.

Her daughter interjected, "She's been vomiting all day today. You have to do something! I'm flying back home tomorrow and she can't stay like this alone."

"I'm going to go and look at her X-rays," Jim said thoughtfully, "and then I'll call Dr. Baker, who is the staff surgeon on call tonight. I'll be back shortly and we'll make a plan."

Jim retrieved her films in the Emergency Department's X-ray viewing area. As he studied them, the emergency physician, a tall, middle-aged woman wearing a white lab coat with a stethoscope dangling around her neck, approached him from behind. "I know it's not the worst bowel obstruction I've seen," Dr. D'Angelo said, "but it's definitely not normal."

"But there's some air in the colon," Jim replied. "It couldn't be a complete obstruction. Perhaps early or incomplete."

"Oh, I don't know, there are lots of air fluid levels," Dr. D'Angelo countered.

Having only recently finished a rotating internship and being quite new at surgery, Jim acquiesced. "Okay, well I guess so. I'll call Dr. Baker and run it by him."

Jim stepped around the corner to a workstation, sat down and picked up the telephone. He looked up Dr. Baker's number on the on-call sheet. As he held the receiver to his ear, waiting for Dr. Baker to pick up, he pondered Mrs. Shively's situation. The poor lady really was in a bind. Living alone, unable to care for herself, and now her daughter flying back home. He thought about her alone in her house, vomiting, probably from a bowel obstruction from adhesions. No, her X-rays were not absolutely classic, but they were suspicious for a blockage that would require surgery.

Dr. Baker's nasal voice whined on the other end of the telephone, "Hello?"

Jim had never actually worked with Dr. Baker but had met him while still a medical student. He suddenly felt nervous as he was about to present Mrs. Shively's case over the telephone. He spoke, his voice halting. "Dr. Baker, it's Jim Smythe…I have an eighty-seven-year-old lady with a bowel obstruction in emerg." As he began to explain her situation, he emboldened the case for admitting her to hospital. He couldn't imagine facing the daughter, saying she'd have to take her mother home and see how she did overnight. Jim recognized later that he had sold Dr. Baker a bill of goods that night, but it was not without reasonable grounds, although it was perhaps wishful thinking that her problem was surgical and that they could do something to help her.

"Are you sure, Jim?" Baker asked. "Are the X-rays clearly showing a bowel obstruction? Do I need to come over there now and see her for myself?"

Baker's hint that Jim might not be up to the task simply was enough to tip the balance toward admitting Mrs. Shively into a surgical bed. "No, I'm sure," Jim said confidently.

"Okay," Baker said, "admit her to surgery for IV fluids, stick in a nasogastric tube and repeat her X-rays in the morning."

When Herman Baker caught up with Jim the next day, he was livid. Her repeat X-rays were fine, but it turned out both Baker and the radiologist interpreted the admission X-rays as showing a non-specific gas pattern. She'd never actually had a bowel obstruction.

"Look here, Jim, this is not a bowel obstruction!" Baker droned on at the nursing station in front of about eight residents, medical students and nursing students. "It never was an obstruction! The radiologist reported the gas pattern was non-specific and clinical correlation was required! Don't you have *any* clinical judgment by now? This lady's got the flu. And now she's blocking a surgical bed, possibly for weeks, because you admitted her and I was too stupid to come in and check her last night!"

Jim noticed the other residents and students trying to find other tasks, attempting to look busy at anything else to minimize the embarrassment Baker was already inflicting on him. "I just thought with all that previous surgery and those X-rays—"

"This lady, who can't take care of herself, could be awaiting a placement for weeks, stuck in a surgical bed because you admitted her to surgery! You know the wait for nursing home beds can be horrendous. I can't believe you would do that!"

The public mockery was bad enough. But Dr. Baker took it further, apparently at a staff meeting, recommending that Jim receive a stern warning, if not an outright fail, on his first rotation of his surgery residency. Of course, as Jim heard later, Steinberg had nipped that one in the bud, blasting Baker in front of the other surgeons for blaming a junior resident for a decision that was ultimately his to make as the staff surgeon on call. And why hadn't he come in to assess Mrs. Shively himself, if it was so important that she must have a surgical problem to be admitted into one of his beds?

As it turned out, Mrs. Shively was on the surgery ward for nine weeks while social workers, administrators and others tried to expedite her placement into a nursing home. And all the while, Herman Baker complained bitterly and publicly about how this lady would not be his problem had the junior resident actually known how to diagnose a bowel obstruction, or lack thereof, the night she came to hospital. His rants were so outrageous that some of the residents speculated he had a drinking problem, although it was never proven. Finally, as program director, Steinberg had put a stop to the fiasco, apparently ordering Baker to be silent on the issue. Jim only heard the details vaguely, and much later, but he was relieved by the détente that occurred due to Steinberg's insistence. Ever since those first few weeks of residency, Jim had treaded very cautiously around Herman Baker, reluctant to risk reigniting their earlier clash.

"Well?" Johansen's piercing voice startled Jim. "What d'you think? Is Herman Baker the type of staff who would back you up?"

Jim fumbled with his pen, twisting an elastic band around it, staring into his lap. He hesitated. Finally, not looking up, he quietly stated, "I'm not sure."

Chapter 14 ~ Appendicitis

Jim opened their apartment door to the uplifting scent of simmering pot roast. He hoped he would have time to enjoy it and wouldn't be called back to the hospital. He was exhausted.

The meeting at Johansen's office could have been worse. But Jim really didn't know what to make of him. If Steinberg recommended him, he had to be good, but on what basis was this suggestion being made? His squash game or his ability as a lawyer?

Amanda hurried toward Jim while he was still in the doorway and reached up, putting her arms around him.

"Well, how did it go?" she asked and then kissed him firmly on the lips.

"I'm not sure, really. Can we sit down first? Where's Emily?"

"Down for a nap, what did you think? Of course we can sit down. Can I get you a beer?"

"You know I can't drink when I might get called in, sunshine."

"Right. Maybe three or four nights a year," Amanda replied tersely.

"Only eight months to go. Then I'm done. After the oral exams in June, I'll make up for lost time." They walked over to the living room couch, Jim leading Amanda by the hand. They sat down, their thighs touching.

Amanda's eyes lit up as she faced Jim. "Emily's starting to crawl!"

"That's great. Maybe she'll perform for me tonight."

"It's so exciting," Amanda said, grinning. "I'm just sorry you're missing so much of it."

"I know, me too."

"Oh, honey, I'm worried about you. You work so hard!" Her eyes brightened. "How'd it go with the lawyer? I bet he looked it all over and said things will be fine, but he's there if you need him?"

"Well, not exactly," Jim said.

Amanda's body stiffened. "What did he say?"

"He said a lot of things, including that I shouldn't discuss the case with you—or anyone but him, for that matter. He thinks there may be some good arguments that it was a difficult case, but the fact is, she went home after seeing me, and that I could be held responsible."

"Jim! But that's not your fault!"

"I know, but it's still something that concerned him."

"So what did you think of him? D'you think he's any good?"

"Steinberg says he's good," Jim replied.

"That's not what I asked. What do *you* think?" Amanda took his hand in hers and rhythmically bounced it on her knee.

"I'm not sure what to think. He's a little creepy. But he seems to know his stuff."

"Well, I know you, Jim. He has to either be good enough, or he's not. There's no in between. You need to decide for yourself where you sit with this guy. And if he doesn't make the grade, get someone else," she said firmly.

"It's not that simple, sunshine. Dr. Steinberg recommended him. And there hasn't actually been a formal complaint, so I don't officially need a lawyer at this stage."

"Then it's perfect. It's not too late to dump him and get someone else, if that's what you decide. If he's not up to snuff in your books, then toast him. There should be no half measures here. If the time comes, get someone who's good enough for you."

"All right, you've made your point," Jim said as he stood up. "Are we eating soon? I'm going to check on Emily."

***

For some reason, November seemed to infuse more hope, energy and excitement in Jim. They'd had their first snowfall of the year and although it didn't last, the changing season reminded him of what little time he had left in his residency. He had fewer than five months to go at St. Joe's, followed by a three-month final push at the University Hospital before exams. With each day of additional experience, confidence in his surgical skills was blossoming.

It was a quiet Friday afternoon for a change. He hung up the telephone after agreeing to meet Hank for coffee. *Hank sounded so exhilarated*, Jim thought. He was continuing to grow on Jim. He seemed to be more on top of his reading these days. As his reward, Hank was beginning to witness his own achievements as a first-year resident. Last night, Jim had been out of town at a seminar so Hank was taking call with Herman Baker on his own. With no senior resident on call, Jim was a little concerned as to how Hank's night would unfold. But if Hank's ebullient voice was any indication, at least from his perspective the night on call went just fine. Hank had done three appendix operations. One of the most common surgeries for a junior resident to perform from start to finish, an appendectomy could range from one of the easiest to the most challenging of operations, depending on the position of the appendix, the degree of inflammation and the size of the patient. An opportunity to do three in a row, all in the same evening, was any junior's fantasy, providing a great opportunity to bolster self-assurance.

Jim remembered his first appendectomy with vivid clarity. He had been a junior resident only twelve hours. It was July 1, the new academic year ushering in a tender batch of residents throughout the city. Dr. Steinberg was on call. By this time, Jim had known him for a couple of years and it was Steinberg who had written one of Jim's references to get into the surgical residency program. Having admitted the twenty-one-year-old male with appendicitis, Jim was fully expecting the chief resident to demonstrate how to do an appendectomy. Just as the case was about to start, a motor vehicle accident victim came rolling into the Emergency Department. To Jim's delight, Steinberg sent the chief resident to assess the trauma patient, saying, "You go down and get that patient sorted out. Don't worry about us. Jimmy and I will be fine here with this appendix."

Although he couldn't recollect his first name, Jim could still recall the patient's surname, Nguyen. He had had abdominal pain since the previous evening. He threw up once and then noticed the pain had shifted to the right lower side of his abdomen. By the time he came into Emergency, he had a low-grade fever and was walking bent over, clutching his right side. Jim looked at his white-coated tongue and noticed his pungent breath. As Jim pressed into his abdomen, especially low on the right side, the patient winced, his abdominal muscles suddenly becoming board-like. As Jim suddenly released his hand, Nguyen let out a loud yelp, signifying rebound tenderness. Nguyen's white blood count was elevated to 16,000, as one would expect in a case of acute appendicitis.

When Steinberg quietly discussed the case with Jim and the chief resident, he proclaimed, "If that appendix is normal, I will eat it! And I don't say that very often, Jimmy. That's a classic textbook case."

At the scrub sink, Jim washed his hands with excitement, fully expecting Steinberg to do the case and perhaps let him close the incision. He suddenly considered the possibility that Mr. Nguyen did not have appendicitis. The appendix, a worm-shaped organ that is attached to the colon and has no known function, should be soft and no thicker than a pencil. If plugged with stool, it can swell, becoming inflamed and infected, changing to a rubbery texture and growing to twice its normal thickness. He dismissed the idea of a normal appendix because Steinberg seemed so certain, but then considered the possibility it could be ruptured. Perhaps Jim hadn't moved the process along quickly enough down in the Emergency Department. If it had ruptured, complications might ensue and Jim could be blamed.

Dr. Steinberg slammed the scrub sink button with his knee, turning off the tap. With Steinberg in the lead, they backed through the swing doors into the room. Nguyen was asleep, supine and being ventilated with inhalation gas. Now in full surgical garb, Dr. Steinberg was standing to the patient's right, the operating surgeon's side, with Jim on the left. They squared off a small window with sterile green towels in Nguyen's right lower quadrant. Just as draping was completed, without a word, Dr. Steinberg walked around to the patient's left, leaving Jim to trade places in a state of elation and trepidation.

Now on the patient's right, Jim was suddenly overtaken by panic. His hands rested on Nguyen's right lower quadrant while his knees started to shake. While Jim tried to hide his anxiety, Steinberg loudly said, "Scalpel!" He then pointed his finger toward Jim, leaving no doubt for the scrub nurse about where to pass the instrument. For a flash, Jim contemplated asking Dr. Steinberg to spare him from this impending surgical adventure. Just let him watch one more before he had the burden of doing a case. His breathing cadence increased, despite him trying to control it. As butterflies danced in his chest and a sudden wave of nausea washed through him, the scalpel was thrust into his right hand. With blunt forceps, Dr. Steinberg gently traced a two-inch angled incision over McBurney's point. *It's now or never*, Jim thought, his knees starting to buckle. As he pressed the knife into Nguyen's skin, Jim became less aware of his own physical discomfort. Scratching only partway through the skin, he heard Steinberg's booming voice: "Press harder, Jimmy, we haven't got all day!" As he applied more downward force with a second stroke of the scalpel, Jim saw the yellow fatty layer reveal itself like welcome springtime buds on trees. Steinberg practically threw a couple of metal retractors into the fat and as he pulled them apart, the white external oblique layer miraculously appeared in front of Jim's eyes. At Dr. Steinberg's direction, Jim cut along the fibres of this layer, exposing underlying muscle layers. "Now put this hemostat into the muscle so we can use the muscle splitting technique. We'll spread the muscle fibres apart instead of cutting them." As Jim inserted the tip of the instrument, Steinberg's retractors darted into the hole Jim had made and instantly the peritoneum, the final filmy layer, was clearly bulging out through the muscle. Jim wasn't quite sure how it had appeared in front of him so spontaneously. After Jim cut through the peritoneum with scissors, Dr. Steinberg, said, "Here, let me have a feel." He popped his index finger in through the hole in the right lower quadrant and within five seconds, pulled it back out, having hooked the thickened pus-laden appendix, pulling it out onto the abdominal wall. "Ha! What'd I tell you? I knew it was going to be a hot one!" Jim proceeded to clamp, cut and tie blood vessels to the appendix, freeing it up except for its junction to the cecum, the large bowel in the right lower quadrant. Jim tied off the base of the appendix firmly, securing four knots. Using a scalpel, he cut flush to the clamp on the appendix above his tie, completing the removal. He deposited the inflamed appendix and attached hemostat clamps into a K-basin, which clanged loudly.

Steinberg then proclaimed, "There, you've done it, Jimmy, your first appendix! Well done!" By now Jim was floating, reliving the last few steps in his mind, thinking how easy it had been and what a great job he'd done. As he was closing the incision, one layer at a time, he lamented the upcoming end of the operation. Like when he read a good book, he wished there were a few more chapters to enjoy. It had gone by so quickly. As he was putting in final skin stitches, Steinberg said, "So what would we have done if the appendix was normal? And don't say I would have eaten it. I don't say that type of thing if I'm not sure. But *theoretically*, what would we do?"

"Take it out regardless. After we look through the incision for alternate causes of the pain."

"Excellent. And what else could it be?"

"Sometimes it's a virus. Mesenteric adenitis," Jim responded and then added, "which would get better on its own anyway. But better to get the appendix out to prevent confusion in the future if he has further attacks."

"Right on, Jimmy." Dr. Steinberg looked into Jim's eyes and said, "Your first appendix! I'm so excited for you!"

Jim couldn't wait to tell Amanda and phoned her immediately after the operation was completed. Jim was on cloud nine for days. Now in retrospect, as a chief resident, Jim realized his mentor could have practically told him to hold the knife in one position while Steinberg moved the patient back and forth under the scalpel as if operating a band saw. But nonetheless, it was still a milestone Jim would never forget.

***

Jim spotted Hank in a corner of the cafeteria, chomping on a burger. He wandered over with his coffee and said, "Lunch?"

"I had an early lunch," Hank said. "This is just to keep me going until supper."

Jim sat down and then said, "So you had a good night with Baker?"

"Fantastic. Like I told you, I did three appendixes from start to finish!"

"All three, skin-to-skin?"

"All three," Hank said proudly.

"You know, Baker is pretty good at giving stuff away. I'll give him that. Compared to someone like O'Brien. As a junior, you can't expect to get a lot of cases from O'Brien." Jim paused. "So, were they hot?"

"The first two were hot. The third one, not so much," he said meekly. Hank screwed up his face and furrowed his brow.

"So? There's nothing wrong with a cold one now and then. Ten to 15 percent should be normal. Otherwise you're not taking enough out and may let some rupture. I'd rather take out ten normal appendixes than let one rupture."

"It's just that…"

"What?" Jim sensed Hank wanted to tell him something.

"It's just that…the first two went great—both hot. We finished at 10:30, but I had to call him back just before midnight about the third one."

"So?"

"I told Baker I wanted to admit the patient for observation. I just wasn't sure she had appendicitis. But he told me over the phone I had to decide: we either operated or sent her home."

"Okay, so how long had she had the pain?"

"Twenty hours," Hank shoved the last bite of his cheeseburger into his mouth.

"White count?"

"Twelve thousand—just a bit elevated," Hank said, his words garbled from chewing.

"Look, Hank, I'm kind of surprised I'm defending Baker, but I can sort of see where he's coming from. In my view, if someone has appendicitis, you should be able to decide one way or another after twenty hours of pain. You either operate or you don't. Fairly clear set of two different options. I could see waiting if it was six hours of pain. But after twenty, it doesn't seem unreasonable to me to take a stand. So then what?"

"I wasn't comfortable saying she *didn't* have appendicitis, so Baker just told me over the phone to book the case. He came in and we did it at one-thirty in the morning. And guess what? The appendix was normal. Probably an ovarian cyst that burst. All we found was a bit of blood-tinged fluid in the pelvis and a ruptured follicle on the right ovary. So that was it. Took out my third appendix in one night and went to bed. I just wish the first one had been normal, not the last one. You get some annoyed looks from the nurses and the anesthetist if the appendix is normal and it's almost two in the morning."

"What did Baker say? Was he upset?"

"It was no problem. He said 'just in time—at least she'll never get appendicitis down the road.' Then he made some comment about newly minted staff surgeons taking two hours to do appendectomies in the middle of the night with a laparoscope. At least we were in and out quick. And that was it. Baker was just fine."

"Well, that's great, Hank."

"I was happy."

"Just one other thing," Jim said, leaning forward. "Discharge summaries? Can you get caught up? I'm getting grief from some of the surgeons."

"Okay, I know. This weekend, for sure."

Jim looked at the wall clock and then said, "Gotta go, Hank. I've got a quick case in the O.R. with Baker starting in about ten minutes."

"You're going to see Baker? Can you take his I.D. badge up to him?" Hank began fishing in his lab coat pocket amongst some papers, sticks of gum and a chocolate bar. He pulled out the nametag and handed it to Jim. "He left it in the locker room last night."

"He's always leaving that somewhere," Jim said, scowling. "He thinks he's been here long enough that everyone should recognize him without it." His expression lightened as he continued. "Sure. I'll give it to him. And good job on those appys last night!"

Chapter 15 ~ McKiddie Revisited

Saturday morning, Jim and his EBUs made their way over to McKiddie's bed in the ICU, now at the end of the row furthest from the nursing desk. With one last patient to see on rounds, Jim was looking forward to the rest of the day off. He and Amanda were driving to Lakefield to spend the day with her parents. They were always anxious to see Jim and Amanda, especially since Emily's birth. And with Jim's parents both deceased, it was always a pleasure to have an afternoon and a home-cooked dinner with Amanda's mother and father.

With intensive care patients attended closely by ICU physicians, Jim had not paid Mr. McKiddie a visit for over a week now. Jim was pleasantly surprised to receive a page this morning. Over the phone, the nurse stated that her patient had been making great strides the past seven days. He was reportedly alert, smiling and writing notes. But Mr. McKiddie had briefly experienced some bleeding from his tracheostomy tube, and could Jim please come and take a look? Mr. McKiddie was still unable to talk, except for brief periods when his tracheostomy tube was plugged. During these succinct forays toward normality, he'd breathe and speak around his tracheostomy tube, which was temporarily disconnected from oxygen tubing and plugged at his neck. If prolonged, such an activity could result in a patient becoming short of breath. Yet trial plugging was the last test before removing the tracheostomy tube completely, restoring normal breathing and speech. If he could breathe around the plugged tube overnight, Mr. McKiddie's tube was ready for removal.

Jim and the EBU's congregated around the bedside. Mr. McKiddie was sitting up in bed, glasses on, reading the newspaper and looking nothing like the man with the perforated stercoral ulcer Jim had met weeks before. He folded his newspaper into his lap, grinned broadly and waved his arms at the group. Wheezing frantically through the tube in his neck, Mr. McKiddie raised his right hand and occluded the hole in an effort to speak. "Good morning," he rasped, his jovial eyes darting back and forth amongst Jim and the members of his squad.

"Hello, Mr. McKiddie. I'm Dr. Smythe and we're on Dr. Steinberg's surgical team. Dr. Steinberg is the surgeon who fixed your perforated bowel a couple of months ago. But you probably don't remember any of that."

Mr. McKiddie released his finger, shrugged his shoulders, turning his palms inward and toward the ceiling. He beamed, starting to wheeze and sputter through the tube.

This man has no clue who I am, Jim thought. Jim had never seen Mr. McKiddie in any state of coherence until today. Not even the day they had met. The old man probably had no idea just how sick he was, so close to death for several weeks. Yet here he sat, grinning, soon to recover sufficiently to return to his friends and staff at his nursing home. "Your nurse called me this morning to say you had some blood coming from around your tube." Jim spoke loudly, assuming his seventy-year-old patient would have some difficulty due to hearing impairment, especially in the noisy ICU environment. Mr. McKiddie nodded steadily, looking straight at Jim, who continued, "Do you mind if we lay your bed down and have a look?"

As Mr. McKiddie was nodding his head in agreement, his nurse stepped closer to the bedside and pressed a button, causing the bed to recline. She busily adjusted his pillow and spoke quickly to Jim. "He was coughing a few hours ago. We suctioned some blood up the tube. There was also a bit of oozing around the edge." She was pointing to some gauze at the margin of his tracheostomy tube as it exited the skin in Mr. McKiddie's lower neck, immediately above his sternum. He was now lying completely flat, without a pillow, staring at the ceiling.

Jim slipped a glove onto his right hand and then gently tugged at the gauze, freeing it from around the tube. As he yanked to release it from adherent dried blood, Mr. McKiddie winced. "Sorry about that, sir," Jim said. "It's just a little stuck and there's no easy way, other than to give it a quick pull."

Mr. McKiddie mouthed the words, "It's okay."

"There it is!" Jim declared. "There's just some granulation tissue at the wound edge. That's what was bleeding."

"It was quite a lot of blood," the nurse interjected. "And most of it was coming up inside the tube, not around it. Are you sure it's nothing more?"

Jim sighed and turned to his group of learners. "This is just granulation tissue. It's part of wound healing. It's very pink and it often bleeds to the touch." He looked over at the nurse and added, "Some of the older nurses refer to this as 'proud flesh'. It's just a buildup of prominent tissue during the post-operative phase. If it protrudes too much, we can fix it."

"Okay…" the nurse said expectantly.

"Do you have any silver nitrate?" Jim asked.

"Oh, for sure, I can get you some of that," the nurse responded as she started to walk away toward a supply cart across the room. Over her shoulder, she added, "I'll be right back."

Jim continued explaining to his team, "All we have to do is cauterize the granulation tissue with silver nitrate sticks. The granulation tissue will shrink and scar, with no more bleeding. Then Bob's your uncle!" Jim felt a slight inexplicable uneasiness as he awaited Mr. McKiddie's nurse, who was now returning, silver nitrate stick package in hand.

He reached out as she passed him the cylindrical container, which was wrapped in a plastic bag. He turned to Mr. McKiddie, who now already appeared to be sleeping flat on his hospital bed. Jim opened the plastic and took the cap off the container, which he tipped, allowing what looked like three long matchsticks with a brown coating of silver nitrate at each of the tips. "You have to be careful not to touch the tips or allow them to be exposed to the air too long, otherwise they get oxidized and lose effectiveness." He moved closer and then said to Mr. McKiddie, "This might sting a bit, but it will clear this up so it won't bleed anymore." Mr. McKiddie opened his eyes and nodded. Jim was trying to remember something he'd read about tracheostomy tubes and bleeding but he couldn't recall it. He took a silver nitrate stick in his right hand and touched the coated tip to the protuberant fleshy tissue at the lower edge of Mr. McKiddie's tracheostomy tube. He repeatedly rolled the balled tip over the tissue, which changed from pink to grey. Mr. McKiddie tensed his shoulders and Jim said loudly, "Sorry. I said that would sting a bit." He then turned to his right, where five team members were anxiously peering over Jim's shoulder, trying to obtain a clear view of the demonstration. He continued, "You see how the tissue is turning grey? That means it's working. I'm just going to see if I can touch it up deeper inside, in case that's where the bleeding was coming from."

Jim put the silver nitrate container on a nearby table, slid a glove on his left hand and gently held Mr. McKiddie's tracheostomy tube. He tipped it in one direction and then another, trying to maximize the gap between the tube and the skin at the lower edge. Jim gently poked a silver nitrate stick deep into the crevice next to the tube, hoping to cauterize any remaining unwanted granulation tissue, out of sight and deep to the skin.

As he angled the tube more acutely to obtain a better view, a gush of bright red blood spurted up inside the tube, precipitating a fit of coughing and sputtering. Mr. McKiddie gasped for air. As the next cough sprayed a fine mist of bloody sputum evenly over his face and lab coat, Jim reflexively squeezed his eyes tight shut, then wiped his face with his sleeve and opened his eyes. With each frenzied exhale, Mr. McKiddie continued to expel small amounts of bright red blood out his tube. His tracheostomy tube was now lightly covered by Jim's gloved right hand. His body was rigid, slightly flexed at the waist as each spasm of coughing prevented his head from relaxing onto the bed. His eyes, only minutes before exuding joy, now communicated only fear to Jim, who was also gripped with terror.

The nurse yelled, "Suction!" in the direction of a respiratory therapist who was already running toward the commotion.

While lightly shielding the orifice of the tracheostomy tube with his right hand, Jim pulled the base of the tube slightly toward Mr. McKiddie's chest. He tipped the exposed end in the direction the old man's chin. If he could alter the angle, perhaps the inside segment of the L-shaped tube would push against the front wall of Mr. McKiddie's trachea. In a torrent of recall, Jim's worst fears were coming true. He knew he'd read something bad about tracheostomies and bleeding, and it seemed to be unfolding in front of him. As he steadied the tube in the perfect position, a respiratory therapist darted a fine suction hose down the tube and cleared all the remaining blood. The nurse administered intravenous sedation to Mr. McKiddie, abruptly terminating his awareness, and with it his dread.

"Give me a syringe!" Jim said. "I need to inflate the cuff!" With the bleeding seemingly under control, if Jim's theory was correct, he now urgently needed to hyperinflate the balloon at the internal end of the tracheostomy tube. The increased pressure might more effectively hold back the potentially fatal exsanguination that lay in waiting.

He couldn't believe how he'd just zeroed in on such a benign cause of bleeding as superficial granulation tissue, when all along Jim had known about tracheo-innominate artery fistula. Jim pictured the innominate artery traversing the upper thorax, left to right from the aortic arch, in front of the trachea to where the artery splits into the right carotid and subclavian arteries. The critical point, where this large artery passes between the trachea and the sternum, can in the setting of previous tracheostomy surgery occasionally be a site of fatal hemorrhage. In rare instances where the tube is placed too low in the trachea, or where anatomic variations render the tip of the tube too close to the overlying innominate artery, repetitive movement can create a small connection, or *fistula*, between the artery and the windpipe high in the chest. Over time, pulsations can create a pinhole, which can leak small amounts of blood, heralding impending disaster. If the hole widens into a substantial opening, torrential bleeding can occur, leading to death within minutes. The hole usually occurs between the sternal notch and the carina, the point at which the trachea splits into two bronchi, one going to each lung.

With Mr. McKiddie's tracheostomy cuff overinflated, the hole will likely stay safely covered, Jim thought, *until we can demonstrate the problem and repair it.* In the direction of his stunned EBUs, Jim began hurling commands. "Hank, call Dr. Steinberg and tell him we've got to take this guy to the O.R. immediately. We'll need to do a bronchoscopy. We'll need cardiothoracics to come along. I think Mr. McKiddie has a tracheo-innominate artery fistula that is about to let go!"

Hank, pale and hyperventilating, pulled out a pen and paper. "One more time, Jim?"

"Steinberg—O.R.—cardiothoracics—tracheo-innominate artery fistula! Now!" He then turned to Rhani and said, "Phone my wife, Amanda, and tell her I won't be home for a few hours."

Rhani, her eyes like saucers, nodded, turned and ran without a saying a word.

Jim gripped the sedated Mr. McKiddie's tracheostomy tube firmly, hoping it wouldn't budge as they prepared to move him in his ICU bed over to the operating room.

***

While Emily slept in her car seat on the kitchen table, Amanda gently rocked her daughter back and forth with her left hand. She reached for her cup of tea with her right hand, not wanting to interrupt the placid motion. Emily had just fallen asleep. Jim was over an hour late. In a normal family, she thought, her child would be all bundled up, strapped in and ready to go when the husband said he was going to be home. But Amanda knew Jim—and his job, for that matter—and not to plan for punctuality. But she never knew *how late* he was going to be. If she could have predicted at what hour Jim was going to arrive home today, she might have made other plans. She could have gone to the gym or taken Emily out to visit a friend so Amanda could spend some adult time with another parent or two. But instead she continued to wait for Jim as they'd planned, to visit her parents in Lakefield.

Soon after Amanda became pregnant with Emily, she made an extra effort to connect with others her age. She'd heard of brain rot, as she called it, associated with pregnancy and raising small children. Several of her friends were well into that stage at the time, and Amanda feared falling into the same traps, compounded, of course, by the heavy demands of Jim's surgical training. As she scaled back her nursing shifts at the hospital through the pregnancy,

Amanda explored other options to keep her stimulated. In anticipation, she found a gym that provided child-care, and usually attended five days a week. And she joined a group of mothers who walked in the winter and cycled in the summer with their kids in tow.

She couldn't complain about being married to a guy as fun as Jim and having the financial security he brought into their lives. Although she hadn't known at the time they were married, Jim had received a significant amount of money when his father died, topped up when his mother passed away from cancer a few years later. When she found out, a few weeks after they were married, Amanda was appalled that Jim hadn't asked for a prenuptial agreement. He simply responded by joking he wanted to be sure Amanda didn't marry him for his money, so he simply neglected to tell her about it. In retrospect, Amanda was certain Jim was in their marriage for life. He was just that type of guy who made a decision and stuck with it. Even in an institution as emotional as marriage, Jim would find a way to make it work if there were bumps in the road. Sure, they'd had some arguments from time to time, but fortunately, neither seemed to hold a grudge and usually any hard feelings would settle down after a brief cooling-off period. Although Amanda had heard the statistics, she remained convinced that her marriage would last.

Another interest she pursued in her quest to spend time with other adults related to Jim's inheritance. He'd shown little attention to managing their money, so Amanda took it upon herself to study finance and investing, through courses at the local college. She was becoming quite conversant with the terminology, and had even discovered how to buy and sell investments from home using her computer. Although much of the studying was on her own, she'd made some friends who were always willing to meet to talk about the stock market. Care for Emily was sometimes a challenge, but Amanda was resourceful enough to have created a menu of options at her disposal. She smiled as she thought how it was a good thing she loved Jim; with his lack of attention to finances, she could really clean him out if she wanted.

As she continued to oscillate Emily's car seat, Amanda looked up at the clock and frowned. *How late is he going to be this time?*

She jerked in her chair as the telephone rang directly behind her. Turning, she picked up the receiver. "Hello?"

"Hello," the voice said, "is this Amanda?"

"Yes."

"Yes, this is Rhani. I'm one of the medical students working on Dr. Smythe's service. He wanted me to phone and tell you he's going to be late."

"He already is late," Amanda fumed.

"Well. Yes. I know. But what I mean is, he's going to be later than he is."

"How late?"

"An hour? Or two? Or maybe more," she said tentatively.

"Okay, well look. Rhani, is it?"

"Yes."

"Well, Rhani, you can tell Jim—" Reluctant to shoot the messenger, Amanda hesitated. "No. Just tell him fine, I'll leave him a note. Thanks for letting me know, Rhani."

"Okay, bye," the voice said meekly just before the line clicked.

"Shit!" Amanda peeked at Emily, who was still sleeping. "Good thing you didn't hear that, Em. So you and I are going on a trip to Grandma and Grandpa's place. I'm sure they'll be delighted to hear you babble. And Daddy will just have to decide for himself whether he cares to join us!"

Amanda wrote a note on a piece of paper, leaving it on the kitchen table. She and Emily were out the door within minutes.

***

Jim had not let go of Mr. McKiddie's tracheostomy since he inflated it in the ICU. Now, fifteen minutes later, he stood in the operating room. He continued to gently cradle the tube coming from his patient's neck, watching for any further signs of bleeding. The cardiothoracics resident and staff surgeon were milling about at the scrub sink, chatting with Dr. Steinberg. Jim could see Steinberg through the small window in the O.R. door, waving his arms in the air. The double doors swung open. Steinberg pushed his way through, followed by the cardiothoracics resident, Kalil, and his staff surgeon, Dr. Bloomfield. Kalil was tall and slim with a dark complexion. Bloomfield was portly and pale. Jim had always liked Kalil, who had been his chief resident in general surgery two years ago. One of the few separate specialties to take place after a five-year general surgery residency, cardiothoracic training consisted of two years mastering the craft of surgery in the chest, mostly heart surgery. Any emergency surgery, especially not specifically relating to the heart itself, often required some coaxing to entice interest in cardiothoracic surgeons. They just didn't seem inclined to become engrossed in cases outside their glamorous domain of elective cardiac bypass surgery. Hence their oft-used nickname, cardiotheatrics, and also a plausible reason for Dr. Steinberg's hand waving outside the operating room.

Steinberg continued gesturing at Dr. Bloomfield as Kalil watched on, appearing amused. "I don't care if it's not the heart! I don't care if it's not a fistula! This guy has had bleeding in his chest and it's not really my domain!

Why don't you guys have a look into his trachea, and we'll be around to help if we can."

"Look, Maurice," Bloomfield responded, "I'm not used to diagnosing this kind of thing. I've never used a flexible bronchoscope, and I haven't used a rigid one in five years! That's my only concern. Can't one of the ICU guys bronch him?"

"No," Steinberg continued, "the guy on ICU doesn't do bronchs. He's one of these low-tech older guys like us. Hell, I bet Kalil's done fifty in the last few years. Haven't you, Kalil?"

"Sure. I got no problem with that," Kalil said, his British accent not quite concealing a hint of Arabic enunciation. He was grinning under his mask.

"Okay, it's settled." Steinberg pointed to Mr. McKiddie's neck, which was still under Jim's close attention. Mr. McKiddie was under anesthetic now, being ventilated through his tracheostomy tube with the cuff overinflated to hold off further bleeding from inside the trachea, vitals stable, no signs of hemorrhage. Steinberg then turned squarely to Bloomfield and added, "Let's get started. We'll bronch him together with Kalil at the helm. If we find a fistula, I'm outta here and you take over. You guys should love to deal with a great case like that. And I'll tell you what, I'll throw in Jimmy as an assistant—I'm sure you'll need all the hands you can get on a case like this."

Jim immediately thought of Amanda and their trip to Lakefield, the plan to spend the day and evening with her parents. He was now already late. If they found something bad, he'd be hours. Why hadn't McKiddie decided to bleed about six hours later? Then Jim would have already been on his way and someone else would have had to deal with it and get cardiothoracics involved. But it was an interesting case. Jim had never actually seen a tracheo-innominate artery fistula before. He'd stay. Steinberg had told him he had to remain with the team. He'd explain to Amanda later.

"Okay, let's go, what are we waiting for?" Steinberg boomed.

Kalil was already at the head of the bed, quietly talking to the anesthetist. Jim, immediately next to Kalil, listened to their conversation. Kalil was going to pass a flexible bronchoscope through the patient's mouth, toward the trachea. He was already threading the thin, black, fibre-optic bronchoscope tube through a cuffed endotracheal tube. Once Kalil had seen what he needed to see with the bronchoscope deep in Mr. McKiddie's trachea, it would just be a matter of sliding the new endotracheal tube over the bronchoscope, positioning the new tube and inflating the cuff. The bronchoscope could then be removed and if necessary, surgery could commence to repair a fistula if, in fact, a connection between the innominate artery and the trachea had been proven. The tricky step, of course, would occur when they deflated the current tracheostomy cuff and removed the tracheostomy tube to slide the bronchoscope in its place and perform the diagnostic evaluation. If bleeding ensued from deflating the tracheostomy cuff, the case could become dicey in a hurry.

Surgeons, house staff and nurses huddled around the operating table as Kalil gently inserted the bronchoscope into Mr. McKiddie's mouth. With one eye looking into the eyepiece of the scope, his hands holding the dials that controlled the direction of the tip of the scope, Kalil cleared his throat and spoke to the anesthetist. "When I get down there, Jim is going to deflate the tracheostomy cuff and remove the trach tube. At that point, I'll have about thirty seconds to look down as far as the carina and then withdraw the bronchoscope, leaving the new trach tube in position." He glanced toward the students in the room and added, "During that time, Mr. McKiddie will have no respiratory support. And Jim, if I have troubles, you'll need to get that trach tube back in his neck right away—you're our backup."

"Okay." Jim took a few deep breaths and he could hear Kalil doing the same.

Above the monitors, the clatter from the ventilator and some background chatter by a couple of medical students, Kalil suddenly announced, "Everyone ready!" With his head bent over the eyepiece, his left hand guided the tube further into McKiddie's mouth while his right controlled its direction with the dials. "Okay, Jim, I can see the top of the trach tube. Are we ready to go? Is he well oxygenated?"

"One hundred percent," the anesthetist replied.

Jim proceeded to deflate the tracheostomy cuff and slide out the tube, clearing the way for Kalil to dart down with the bronchoscope.

"Okay, I'm heading down," Kalil announced. Then abruptly, "Yup! He's got it all right! There's a big clot on the wall of the trachea. I don't want to disturb it."

"Are you sure?" Bloomfield queried.

"Of course I'm sure," Kalil responded. "If I disturb it, he'll bleed to death!"

"No," Bloomfield added sarcastically as he grabbed the bronchoscope from Kalil's hand, pulling it toward him. "Are you sure it's a fistula?" His left eye closed, looking into the eyepiece with his right, Bloomfield continued, "All I can see is fresh blood!" He thrust the bronchoscope back to Kalil.

Kalil positioned the scope under his right eye and shouted, "That's new blood, all right! The clot must've been blown off." Jim could hear blood sucking up the bronchoscope as he watched Kalil press the suction button on the scope with his left hand. He steadily tweaked the dial with his right hand.

The rhythmic beeping from the pulse oximeter began to change pitch, dropping a semitone with every heartbeat. "His oxygen saturation is down to 90 percent!" Jim could hear fear in the anesthetist's voice. Ninety percent wasn't so terrible, in Jim's opinion, it was just the speed of the descent that bothered him. He looked down at the hole in Mr. McKiddie's neck. He could discern the smooth, black bronchoscope through the hole in the trachea, but he could not yet see the endotracheal tube sliding over the bronchoscope. He could see Kalil in his peripheral vision, vigorously trying to thread the endotracheal tube over the bronchoscope, but it seemed to be held up just outside the patient's mouth.

"It's not sliding," Kalil shouted. "Get me more lubricant!" A nurse hastily appeared, squeezing a tube of clear gel onto her left gloved hand. She slathered it over the bronchoscope, next to the patient's lips. As he anxiously awaited the passage of the tube beyond the tracheal opening, Jim observed bright red blood arising from deep in the neck. He could no longer see the bronchoscope, which was obscured by the ongoing hemorrhage. Suction!" he shouted. He snatched the suction wand from the scrub nurse and proceeded to clear blood from the depths of Mr. McKiddie's neck. He could hear Kalil sucking blood through the bronchoscope.

"Seventy-four percent! You've got to get a tube back in there, Jim," the anesthetist shouted. "Now!" Jim's chest tightened as he gazed at the small hole in Mr. McKiddie's neck, now partially hidden by blood. *There's no way I can find my way into the trachea from here*, he thought. With his left hand, he dashed the suction into the hole one more prolonged second. In his shaking right hand, he gripped the old tracheostomy tube. He held it up, poised in an attempt to plunk it back into position. Back where they had started, but better than nothing if they could once again control airway and bleeding by reinflating the cuff.

"Sixty-eight percent! Now, Jim!"

"No, hang on a second, it's okay, I've almost got it," Kalil responded.

Jim observed beads of sweat on Kalil's forehead, his surgical cap also darkened with blotches of perspiration. Without a word, Kalil completed sliding the endotracheal tube down over his bronchoscope while continuing to intently concentrate, hunched over the scope. He pushed hard on his left hand toward McKiddie's mouth and then barked, "Inflate the cuff!" Holding the endotracheal tube with his left hand while the anesthetist inflated the cuff with a syringe, Kalil took one more look down the bronchoscope, then swiftly pulled it out. The anesthetist connected the endotracheal tube to the ventilator.

Kalil then turned to the centre of the room, threw his gloves in the garbage and said, "That should do it! Now let's get scrubbed and fix this fistula, before it starts to bleed around the cuff. It's only going to last so long!"

Jim listened to the pulse oximeter move in a more encouraging direction and cross the 90 percent threshold. He followed Kalil and Dr. Bloomfield out to the scrub sink, excited to prepare for the most exhilarating part of this case: repair of the fistula.

Jim and Kalil stood next to Dr. Bloomfield, facing the scrub sink, silently washing their hands. Jim imagined Kalil was probably burning with anticipation and elation, while Bloomfield was somewhere between fear and boredom. Although Jim would never do a case like this in practice, he always found an opportunity to work in the chest both instructive and gratifying. Even though he'd be first assisting at best, he couldn't wait.

His thoughts were interrupted by Steinberg's loud voice from down the hall. Jim turned to see Steinberg's head emerging from the locker room doorway, angled at forty-five degrees. He'd already changed back into street clothes, which for Steinberg was always a jacket and tie, even on a Saturday. "Jimmy, let me know how it turns out!" he shouted.

"I will," Jim replied.

"Call me at home tonight!" Steinberg swiftly disappeared behind the door and was gone.

As they finished their scrub, Bloomfield, Kalil and Jim filed into the room. Rhani and two other students watched from the corner as the surgeons donned fresh operating garb.

Mr. McKiddie appeared more stable as they placed operating drapes over his brown iodine-painted skin, leaving a large window from his chin to his umbilicus.

Kalil, on the patient's right, was the first to speak. "May we start?"

"Of course, go ahead," Dr. Sanchez replied.

Jim was standing in the first assistant position, while Dr. Bloomfield positioned himself next to Kalil. Jim held a surgical sponge with his fingers tightly on the skin overlying Mr. McKiddie's breastbone while Kalil cut with a scalpel the entire length of his chest from the neck down to the abdomen. After cauterizing small bleeders, with the sternum fully exposed, Kalil said, "Sternal saw."

The nurse handed him a slightly unwieldy instrument with a serrated blade on one side. He adeptly tucked the blade under the top of the sternum. After carefully checking the instrument's position, he pressed the button starting its motor. The noise, like a chainsaw, was deafening. Kalil guided the instrument, lifting upwards the whole time, as it moved toward the abdomen. When it reached the end, the saw lifted up with a jolt and the sound cut out as Kalil released the button and handed the saw back to the nurse. Jim, his ears and heart both throbbing loudly, was now peering into the front of Mr. McKiddie's thorax through the vertically cut sternum. Without a request, the scrub nurse handed Kalil a metal retractor, which he proceeded to place into the gap. Turning a bolt with each hand, he opened the chest like a book. Jim could see the beating heart wrapped in pericardium. Other midline mediastinal structures were clearly visible, while the lungs were off to either side. Jim quickly spotted the carina, where the trachea splits into two bronchi, each supplying air to a lung. He followed it upward with more ease than expected and readily identified the innominate artery traversing over top of the trachea, angling upward from the patient's left to right. Jim was reminded of the relative simplicity of chest anatomy, compared to wading through abdominal fat to find anatomic structures.

"There it is," Kalil announced. "That's gotta be a fistula."

"How do you know just by looking at it?" Jim asked.

"It's easy. There should be a nice, friendly plane between the artery and the trachea. But you can see there's a lot of inflammation and scarring around here. Normally, I should be able to slip an instrument between the two." He took a Mixter forceps in his hand and slid the pointed end to where the artery seemed to be plastered onto the trachea.

"Don't show us," Bloomfield piped up.

"Of course not, Dr. Bloomfield," Kalil said. He looked up at Jim and continued. "If I could separate this now, we'd be looking at a hole in the front wall of the trachea and five units of blood coming out the back wall of the artery. The reason he doesn't bleed out in the first place is that the fistula forms gradually, starting as a pinhole. The intense surrounding inflammation confines the tract between the artery and the trachea. So what are we going to do, Jim?"

Recalling their previous relationship when Kalil had been chief resident on general surgery, Jim responded enthusiastically, "Get proximal and distal control first. Then repair the fistula."

"Good. We'll put two vessel loops around the artery. We'll wrap one on either side, but a good distance from the fistula, to get control of the artery. That way, we prevent a bleed when we attack the fistula. How are we going to repair it, Jim? Sutures? Interposition graft?"

Jim thought of the two miniscule holes in the trachea and the artery. He wondered whether they could just close them with sutures. The trachea might tolerate stitches, but Jim wasn't so sure about such a big artery. And if it had fistulized once, it would likely do so again unless a more definitive solution was obtained. A tube graft to reconstruct the artery didn't sound like a good idea to Jim as it was likely to get infected, since the fistula included the inside of Mr. McKiddie's trachea, a ready source of bacteria.

Without waiting for Jim's answer, Kalil deftly slid the tip of a Mixter forceps around the innominate artery, about two inches from the midline, close to the aortic arch. "Vessel loop," he said. As the tips of his instrument emerged on the other side of the artery, Jim passed him a red silicone vessel loop, a stretchy, smooth filament about the thickness of a shoelace. Kalil grasped it with the tips of his Mixter and pulled it back around the artery, thus encircling the artery with his vessel loop. "There's one side of the fistula controlled," Kalil proclaimed. They proceeded to surround the artery on the other side of the fistula in exactly the same manner. He then applied vascular clamps next to the vessel loops to totally occlude the artery on either side of the fistula.

"Now, you can separate the fistulous tract, Kalil," Dr. Bloomfield said. Kalil gently spread his Mixter forceps behind the innominate artery, insinuating the instrument between the artery and the trachea. As they separated completely, residual bright red blood drained out the artery's back wall.

After they had removed unhealthy tissue around the tracheal opening and closed the hole on the tracheal side of the fistula with four permanent sutures, Kalil repeated his question. "You never answered me, Jim. How are we going to fix the artery side of the fistula?"

"I don't think you'd want a graft," Jim began cautiously, "because foreign material is out due to risk of infection here."

"Right. Tell you what, Jim, how about we just chop out the bad segment and oversew both ends of the artery? Much less chance of recurrent fistula. And although, in theory, disrupting the innominate artery might result in lost circulation to the right side, our friend here is pretty sick and doesn't have the luxury of time while we piss around studying his circulation. Collateral flow should take care of things. My vote is we just take out the bad section and stitch the ends closed. Does that sound okay to you, Dr. Bloomfield?"

"That's exactly what I'd suggest, Kalil. It's simple and it's effective." Dr. Bloomfield was shifting back and forth on his feet. Jim thought he could hear him wheezing. "But make sure you bury the suture lines in some nearby muscle or other good tissue. There's a lot of pressure in the artery this close to the heart. The last thing you want is for him to blow your suture line and bleed to death ten days from now."

Kalil and Jim continued by cutting out a two-inch length of Mr. McKiddie's artery and oversewing each end with a permanent monofilament suture. Just as they were about to bury the closed ends, Bloomfield declared emphatically, "Well, you boys can take it from here. I think I'll let you finish. Good job, men!" Dr. Bloomfield was out the door before Kalil had finished thanking him for his help.

After they put the finishing touches on the closed ends of the artery, they wired his sternum together and closed the overlying skin with surgical staples.

Seated at a desk in the recovery room as he checked Rhani's post-operative note, Jim saw it was nearly 5:30. Worried he'd forget, he reached for the telephone and punched in the numbers he'd previously committed to memory.

"Hello, Dr. Steinberg? It's Jim."

Dr. Steinberg's friendly voice resonated on the end of the phone. "Well, Jimmy-boy, what did you find?"

"As expected, a fistula," Jim responded.

"So what did you do?" Steinberg sounded truly excited.

"We divided the fistula, repaired the trachea, cut out a section of the artery and oversewed both ends."

"Nothing fancy, Jimmy. No graft, no bypasses. You know why, Jimmy?"

"Well, I was a bit worried about stealing circulation from the right side by simply suturing both ends...but—"

"Of course you were, Jimmy. But in the end, do you know why you did what you did?"

"Well—"

"He needed a lifejacket, man, and you threw him one! Never give a drowning man swimming lessons! The simplest solution is often the best."

"Makes sense to me," Jim said.

"See you Monday, Jimmy."

Jim hung up the telephone and thought about Mr. McKiddie, who had come close to death for a second time in the past couple of months. What next?

He remembered Amanda and their planned trip to Lakefield to see her parents. He wracked his brain, grappling with what he should say, before picking up the phone again.

Chapter 16 ~ Reverse Turf Wars

On Tuesday evening, he arrived home after another exhausting day at work. It didn't surprise him in the slightest when, the moment he entered, he spotted on the hall table the envelope marked PRIVATE AND CONFIDENTIAL in bold lettering. Amanda said hello but continued to look down at Emily in her arms. She approached and then kissed and hugged him more firmly than usual. "Did you see the letter?" she asked, letting go.

"I noticed it the second I came in the door. Medical Licensing Authority." He paused and said thoughtfully, "It's not like I couldn't see it coming." Jim gave Emily a kiss on the forehead and tried to smile in response to her incomprehensible chatter.

"I almost opened it for you," Amanda said, "and then thought about calling you. But I left it. It was difficult. I've been staring at it on and off all day, hoping it's just some routine thing."

"Hard to imagine it being nothing," Jim said as he led Amanda to their living room couch. They sat down, Amanda placing Emily on the carpet amongst a collection of stuffed animals.

With resignation, he tore open the envelope and unfolded the paper. At the top of the letter, in boldface type, it read: "Complaint: Edna Doyle – deceased". As Jim read the substance of the complaint, he began to feel excessive warmth. His head began to spin as he mulled it over. The complainant was, in fact, the son, a Mr. Gavin Doyle who lived halfway across the country. The allegations were astonishing: Jim was being accused of discharging his patient with internal bleeding, although he knew, or ought to have known, that her situation was life-threatening. He had fallen short of his duties when investigating her symptoms and had demonstrated disregard for the condition for which she sought help. "They must be kidding!" Jim said, desperation in his voice. "I'm the only one named in the complaint! It says I 'failed to adequately inform my attending staff of relevant information necessary for proper care of the patient'! I can't believe it!"

"Now wait a second, Jim," Amanda started hesitantly. "I bet all of these letters go like this. They're not going to lodge a complaint and phrase it in a manner that suits you. Of course it's going to sound accusatory." She turned toward him on the couch and folded her arms across her chest. "It's coming from the patient's family. The Licensing Authority probably has no choice. They're just putting the complaint out there so you can respond to it."

"But I can't believe they're singling me out! As a resident, everything I do is under some degree of supervision. And I discussed it with Dr. Baker. I even wrote that on the chart! I didn't send her home! She left!" Jim's tone was escalating as the gravity of his predicament gripped him.

"Maybe it's good they aren't complaining about Baker. If you were both targets, perhaps Baker would be less willing to stick up for you. If he's off the hook, perhaps he'll actually support your position!" Amanda fixed her eyes on Jim, looking hopeful, he thought.

"Yes, I suppose you could be right," he said deliberately, then added, "You know, I've thought about this a lot. I want Johansen. I think he'll be the best for me."

"Are you sure? Absolutely certain? Remember what I said, Jim—he's got to be completely the right choice. You don't want to get into this partway and then realize you've made the wrong decision."

"One hundred percent. I want Johansen. I'll call him tomorrow."

***

It was a Saturday afternoon in mid-December and Jim was hoping to have a quiet day. With rounds on all the inpatients completed, he was just about to head home to see Amanda and Emily, when Hank Forsberg called him in a state of panic.

"Jim, it's Hank!" Jim held the telephone a few inches from his ear as Hank carried on. "You've got to settle this. There's an argument in the residents' lounge."

"What's it about?" Jim asked, his curiosity piqued.

"That guy I told you about earlier today. The one in ER. That idiot who messed up his leg snowboarding."

"What's the problem?"

"It's a little disagreement we're having. Cheung from plastics and Hunter from orthopedics. They're not exactly cooperating."

"Oh, one of those disputes," Jim said calmly. "I'll be there in a couple of minutes."

As Jim walked down the two flights of stairs to the main hospital level, he thought of the two other participants, both first-year residents. Of the two, Sam Cheung was his least favourite. Ever since the first day in his plastic surgery residency, he had made it clear he was only interested in cosmetic surgery. All the other elements of plastic surgery—burns, trauma, hand and facial reconstruction—were all just unfortunate stumbling blocks that stood between him and his ultimate goal: to be earning big bucks doing boob jobs in a major urban centre. Jeff Hunter was a little better. Jim liked him from the few interactions they'd had over multiple traumas in the Emergency Department, or an occasional word exchanged in the residents' lounge. He had curly blond hair, blue eyes and a muscular frame.

With a few details added afterward, Jim understood the patient, Jonathon, to be a twenty-year-old university student who'd been snowboarding with some buddies a few days previously. At lunch, he had had a few too many beers and then went out for more snowboarding fun on the hill. On a particularly steep run, he took a slightly divergent course from his pals. He found himself careening through a thicket of trees at high speed when he finally cut hard and wiped out, his front leg slamming into a spruce, the rest of him fortunately unscathed. With some help from his friends, he was transported down to the bottom of the hill, where he found his left leg to have a couple of small gashes just below the knee. The wounds appeared relatively clean apart from some small bits of embedded thread from his clothing. His shin was swollen and tender to the touch. His confreres packed him into his vehicle while one of the more sober of the bunch drove him back to the city. When the group of amateur medics converged at one of their downtown houses, they carefully examined and cleaned up his leg. Too embarrassed to present to hospital with seven or eight beers on board, he elected to stay put for a while. In too much pain to sleep, he decided to have a few more beers. Besides, he could now walk on the injured leg, albeit with some caution, so he felt it couldn't be broken. The following day, Jonathon's leg felt marginally better, and he had an exam on Friday, so he really didn't have time to have his leg checked out then. Jonathon hobbled to his exam the next day, vowing to go straight to the hospital for an X-ray on the way home. His plans were foiled, however, since he had to have the two or three obligatory après-exam beers to celebrate the halfway point of his first-year psychology course. Too drunk to attend the hospital Friday night, he had to settle, hung-over, for an early trip in at nine o'clock Saturday morning. By this time, Jonathon was having a lot more pain with weight-bearing and the swelling on his shin was shiny, reddish brown and warm to the touch. He felt feverish and had intermittent chills. The emergency physician was certain he'd need some surgery to clean up what was now a mess of infection in the soft tissues of Jonathon's lower leg. By noon, Jonathon had X-rays completed and had seen junior residents from general surgery, orthopedics and plastic surgery.

As Jim made his way down the final turns in the corridor to the residents' lounge, he could hear yelling.

"Like I said, we don't do feet!" Sam Cheung was pacing back and forth as Jim entered the room. With his lab coat tossed over a chair, Sam looked impressive in his pastel pink and purple-striped dress shirt, cufflinks, precisely pressed trousers and Gucci shoes. Jim wondered how a junior resident could afford to dress so well.

Jeff Hunter weighed in with equal enthusiasm. "Look, his feet are fine. His bones are good. It's soft tissue. That's the problem. That should be plastics. There's no fracture! What the hell is orthopedics going to do when there is no fracture?"

They both turned toward Hank, who was sitting at a round table, unwrapping a Caramilk bar. Jim smiled and pulled out a chair, sitting beside Hank while the two junior residents approached. "Jim," Sam pleaded, "Jeff's right. There's no fracture. So it probably shouldn't be for ortho. And you know plastics does not do feet—or anything in the leg, for that matter. Anything that might affect gait is not in our territory."

Jim could see where this alliance was headed. "Then what do you propose?" Jim had seen this dynamic so many times before that he now found it amusing. "You know Herman Baker is on call for general surgery and will not accept this patient in one of our beds if it means elective general surgery cancellations on Monday."

"But there's probably infected blood in there," Jeff countered. "In fact, it's probably pus. Stinky pus and lots of it. That's what general surgery does! You guys love that stuff!"

"Just because there's pus doesn't mean it has to go to general surgery," Hank said as he pushed the remaining square of the chocolate bar into his mouth, licking his lips and fingers.

"Okay guys, what do your staff say?" Jim asked, first looking squarely at Sam.

"My staff is Stavros. I called him once already, right after I assessed the patient, and he said we were only to be involved if he needs coverage with a muscle flap or a skin graft, which is not to occur until the infection is cleared. We're not to admit the patient."

"Well, perhaps you can call him back and say that Baker will take him to the surgical bed on condition that if there is a graft or a flap in the works, then we transfer him to a plastics bed. Baker won't be happy if a guy like this is in a general surgery bed as of Monday morning. General surgery elective cases would have to be cancelled Monday if our beds are full. And that's not acceptable if this dude is essentially under plastics, getting grafting or something. If that's the case, you take him in a plastics bed. Call Stavros."

"You kidding? I'm not calling Stavros back! It's Saturday afternoon and I've already disturbed him once about this patient." Sam folded his arms across his chest emphatically.

"And Jeff," Jim continued. "It's not exactly like we do a lot of elective surgery on the leg. Orthopedics would be much better at navigating through the muscles if the surgery goes deep. Do you think you guys could be there?"

"I'll be there if you need me, Jim. But if there are no broken bones, he's not coming to an ortho bed. Period." He then shrugged his shoulders and added, "That's what I've been told by my staff. I'm just following the rules."

Feeling a little fed up, Jim said, "Do you think your staff could call each other, perhaps speak to Baker?"

"No," Sam hastily responded.

"No, uh-uh," Jeff added quickly, shaking his head and looking at his feet.

Hank was carefully folding his Caramilk wrapper on the table and remained silent.

"I can't believe this! Your staff won't talk to each other," Jim said, shaking his head. "Why does the communication have to travel down through us and back to them? And where are your chief residents in all this?" Jim glared at both Sam and Jeff, who were standing side by side near the door, appearing ready to make an escape.

Jeff started, while Sam was vigorously nodding his head. "Oh, no. They don't do cases like this. That's what we're here for. We do these now so we can focus on the big stuff when we're chiefs."

"Okay," Jim said calmly. "You can leave. Tell your staff we'll take the patient. I want both of you to come to the O.R. if we call you. And if he needs to stay beyond eight o'clock Monday morning, we transfer him. If it's grafting he needs, then Sam, he goes to plastics. If he can't walk or his leg looks like it's going to fall off, then Jeff, he's yours. But we will not babysit him in a general surgery bed while you guys work on him from a distance."

"Okay," the two junior residents chimed as they bolted out the door.

Jim looked at Hank and simply said, "Unbelievable."

***

The four residents huddled around Jonathon, who was under anesthetic in the operating room. Baker was waiting in the lounge. Stavros and the orthopedic staff surgeon on call were each going to take a pass on this one and could have a look next time, should another operation be necessary. Baker had told Jim he wanted to attend briefly during surgery, to ensure Jonathon was not going to be unnecessarily admitted to a general surgery bed.

Sam Cheung held Jonathon's left foot up in the air, the leg at forty-five degrees, while Jim unwrapped the gauze dressing. Next, the circulating nurse proceeded to paint the entire leg with iodine while Hank, Jim and Jeff watched. Sam continued to suspend the leg. When it was completely prepped, they wrapped the thigh in surgical drapes. Sam gently placed the foot back on the operating table.

After the usual scrub, Jim stood silently, scalpel in hand, poised above the exposed swollen leg as the other residents observed. "If he goes into one of our beds, I get to do the case. Sorry, guys," Jim said without remorse. He pressed the blade onto the front of Jonathon's shin, just below the knee. The skin was taut from bulging underneath. He cut downwards, parallel to the tibia, over top of the anterior muscle compartment. A festering mixture of clot and pus burst through the incision, erupting closely behind Jim's knife blade. The smell was definitely foul. Jim felt a wave of satisfaction as he released the purulence. He then took his index finger and swept the wound from top to bottom under the skin, first left then right. As he cleared the wound, he said, "Always double glove on cases like this, Hank, otherwise you'll smell it on your fingers for hours after." He then turned to the scrub nurse and asked for some hydrogen peroxide. She handed him a bowl of clear liquid, which he poured into the wound. On contact with Jonathon's tissue, it immediately frothed out of the wound, spilling over the drapes, taking residual clot and pus from the depths of the surgical site with it. "I love this stuff," Jim said. "I have no idea if it does any good, but it sure is fun." He then irrigated under the skin, cleaning the underlying muscle of any residual blood and debris. "We'll just leave this wound open and let it heal from the bottom up. If we close it, another abscess is guaranteed."

"The muscle looks good, Jim," Baker startled him from behind. "Looks like this guy can be out of his surgical bed by tomorrow, with home care for dressing changes." He then turned to Sam and added, "Now, don't you guys wish you'd just taken him yourselves? I'm going to make sure Stavros follows him as an outpatient, not me. This is going to take weeks to heal in, but at least he doesn't need to be in hospital."

“I’ll tell Dr. Stavros all about it,” Sam replied. “And besides, it’ll probably be me seeing him in one of those massive clinics.”

Without suturing the skin closed, Jim covered the exposed muscle with moist gauze and then applied two layers of wrap, completely covering the leg from above the knee down to the ankle.

“See, all this bickering was for nothing,” Jim said.

Chapter 17 ~ Legal Aid

It was midafternoon on a frosty December day. Jim pressed the button for floor twenty-three and inhaled briskly. He recalled his first visit to Johansen, Wang, Somers several weeks ago, when the elevator had been crammed with people. Today, an elderly gentleman clutching a cane was the only other passenger when the doors closed. *Other people are Christmas shopping rather than visiting their lawyers*, Jim thought bitterly. This time, his trepidation was not so much over the unknown, as he'd already met Johansen and the surroundings were familiar, but rather the planned topic for discussion. He'd sent his summary of events to Mr. Johansen over a week ago. Jim had described his encounter with Edna Doyle with utmost attention to detail, resulting in a five-page narrative he'd faxed from Dr. Steinberg's office. Mr. Johansen had copies of hospital records and the letter of complaint. He'd apparently even obtained Dr. Baker's account, written for the preliminary inquiry directed by the hospital. Jim feared this document most vehemently, like a guillotine blade poised, biding its time until released. The elevator slowed and then halted abruptly at the twenty-first floor. The man hobbled off, leaving Jim alone, staring at the bare walls for the short trip up two more levels.

When Jim reported to the reception area, chisel-chin immediately appeared and led him to the familiar boardroom, where Jim seated himself in the same chair next to the end of the long table. The room was quiet and empty. Jim adjusted his tie, ensuring it was straight but not too tight around his neck. He blinked repeatedly as one of his contact lenses migrated and seemed reluctant to return to position due to the dry air. But he resisted the temptation to rub his eye, for fear of rendering it bloodshot for the next few hours. He held his eyes open widely and then fluttered his lids until the lens floated back into place.

Jim pulled a copy of his narrative out of his pocket and smoothed the crinkled papers on the table in front of him. He poured a glass of ice water and sipped several times, relieving the searing in his throat. A sudden ruckus made him look to the end of the room as Dave Johansen appeared in the doorway. Jim stood up. Mr. Johansen held a large briefcase in his left hand while cradling a stack of files between his elbow and his chest. He carried a laptop computer in his right hand. Turned at forty-five degrees, he awkwardly ambled as close to the wall as possible, yet still bashed his briefcase against the chair backs as he went. As he approached Jim, he grinned, exposing his top two front teeth. Snorting, he smashed the briefcase onto the table, then released the files from under his elbow, allowing them to fall into a disorganized pile to his left. He then carefully placed the laptop directly in front of him in a space he created between the briefcase and the files. Still standing, he smoothed the shiny black laptop with his fingers as if it were the hood of an expensive sports car. As Jim reached out for a handshake, Johansen held up his right hand, palm facing outward like a traffic cop. From his left tweed jacket pocket, he pulled a white computer mouse. He flipped a switch on the undersurface of the mouse and carefully set it down on the table in the narrow space to the left of the computer. "It's wireless. Have you ever seen one of these before?"

"Well, yes," Jim said standing with hands now by his sides.

"Good to see you again, Jim," he said, holding out his right hand.

Jim reached out and shook, reminded of Mr. Johansen's loose grip at their first meeting. Johansen's tie was crooked. As he awaited the release, Jim noticed chaotic tufts of brown hair on the top of Johansen's head. The dark brown arms of his cumbersome glasses disappeared into mats of grey hair above his ears. Johansen finally let go of his hand and said, "Have a seat," in his familiar shrill voice.

They both sat down, kitty-corner from each other with Johansen at the end of the table. Mr. Johansen opened his laptop and hastily shuffled the mouse on the table with his left hand. Mr. Johansen then slammed the laptop shut, picked up a file from the top of the pile and said, "So, I suppose you want to know where we're at?"

"Yes, sir."

"As you know, we now have a formal complaint from Mrs. Doyle's son to the Medical Licensing Authority. In parallel, the hospital is doing a yet-to-be-formalized review. In my opinion, it's only a matter of time until St. Joe's converts this to an official investigation."

Jim loosened his tie and unbuttoned the collar of his shirt. He took in a few slow, deep breaths.

Looking at the open file, Johansen continued. "It is my expectation that the MLA will await the results of the hospital investigation before drawing their own conclusions. But rest assured, the MLA is busy in the background, gathering information in order to bring this to a resolution as quickly as possible. It is a matter of significant importance that your situation with your license doesn't get delayed."

"I...I beg your pardon?" Jim slipped off his suit jacket and placed it over the chair back. He felt an ounce of relief as the sweat down the back of his shirt started to evaporate, cooling his skin.

"May I remind you, Jim, that you are working under an educational license. As of June 30th next year, you will no longer be able to work unless you have your license converted to a formal general license, or obtain another educational posting of some sort."

Jim fidgeted under the table with his narrative papers, which he was rolling lengthwise on his lap. "But—"

"The MLA no doubt finds this a troubling situation. This is not a complaint by an angry patient who was kept waiting too long or treated badly by an arrogant doctor. Those types of complaints can either be resolved quickly or, if not, the MLA have no problem issuing a general license while awaiting the findings. In serious cases, for example when there's an unexpected death or the physician displays sexual advances toward a patient, the MLA has to be absolutely certain before issuing a general license." Mr. Johansen cleared his throat and turned the page in the file in front of him.

Jim folded his paper and stuffed it into his shirt pocket, saying, "So I'm being lumped in with sexual offenders, am I?"

"No! That's not my point, Jim. From their perspective, the MLA has to get this right and we are under some time constraints to get this sorted out—if you want a job in July, that is. So my recommendation to you is that we try to move this thing along as quickly as possible."

"Okay..." Jim was feeling he'd nearly upset Mr. Johansen by his question. Vowing to be more careful with his choice of words, he continued. "So, where do we stand now?"

"I have all the hospital records and I've reviewed them thoroughly. Nothing new there. You saw Mrs. Doyle. There wasn't much to find but you weren't completely happy with her condition so you phoned your staff, Herman Baker. You spoke to him and according to your verbal statement, but not documented on the health record, he agreed to see Mrs. Doyle. Next thing we know, she's gone home and come back, but this time bleeds to death."

Jim grimaced slightly as recalled the events, and felt a burning in his chest, going up to his throat. "What about Dr. Baker? What did he say?"

"That's interesting, Jim," Johansen said, grinning triumphantly. "He wrote this at the request of the hospital. But it was not intended for us or anyone else at this time—it was just for the hospital's informal inquiry. Fortunately, someone in Medical Records mistakenly placed it on the chart, so when I requested an updated copy of the records on your behalf, they sent it all, including Dr. Baker's comments. We would have obtained it eventually, but getting it now was lucky!"

"Was it? Did he say anything bad?"

"Yes, it was lucky. And no, I wouldn't say there's anything terribly incriminating in it."

Jim exhaled and loosened his fingers, which were gripping his trouser legs at his knees.

"What he said was," Johansen continued, "and I quote—'Dr. Smythe described Mrs. Doyle's condition to me over the phone. She'd had vague abdominal pain and had visited emergency two days in a row. On Wednesday, she'd had an ultrasound showing sludge in her gallbladder. On Thursday evening, when Dr. Smythe saw Mrs. Doyle, her hemoglobin was slightly diminished, which in hindsight was likely significant. As a result of my discussion on the phone with Dr. Smythe, she was to be observed in the Emergency Department until I assessed her. In retrospect, she may well have been silently bleeding at the time from her splenic artery aneurysm. Splenic artery aneurysms are extremely rare and are much smaller than aortic aneurysms. They can easily be missed on a conventional ultrasound.' He then rambles on about mortality statistics of splenic artery aneurysms and the latest research papers. After that, he talks about when he first encountered her in the operating room, when you had already started the surgery with Dr. Hank Forsberg. Dr. Baker then states that by that time, there was not much hope of saving her—which, in fact, nobody did."

Jim gulped some water, placed his glass carefully on the coaster and leaned forward. His forearms were resting on the table with his hands flat, fingers spread apart. "That's not so bad then, is it?" His eyebrows arched in expectation of Johansen's response.

"Technically you are correct, Jim. He didn't say anything too terrible about you in his narrative. But it is a well-written note."

"Tell that to Medical Records," Jim sighed under his breath.

"Excuse me?"

"Well, it's not as if Dr. Baker has a reputation for being precise or on time when it comes to doing his hospital dictations."

"Hmm. Well, be that as it may, this wasn't something dictated to Medical Records. It appears to be a carefully crafted document, almost as if he's been through this process a few times before. He seems to have left many doors open. In the event he is questioned further, or has to provide more detailed information, he really could go either way if it suits him."

"You mean—"

"Yes. There's a lot he didn't say. Without contradicting anything he's said so far, but with additional commentary, he could hurt you inadvertently. Or deliberately, for that matter, if it pleases him."

"Whoa." Jim pushed against the back of his chair and raised his palms toward Johansen in a defensive gesture. "You don't think…"

"All Baker has to do is say he wasn't apprised of the situation properly—by you. He could say, 'Had my chief resident, Dr. Smythe, only described the situation more fully to me, I would have directed him over the phone to admit the patient. We might have even done a CAT scan and had her in the operating room before she had a chance to arrest.'"

Jim cringed at the thought and hunched his shoulders, remaining silent.

"You never know what to think in these situations, Jim. The best thing is to prepare for all possibilities. And as such…"

"Yes?"

"We'll need an expert to review the case and give an opinion in support of your actions." Mr. Johansen retrieved a file folder from the middle of the pile, opened it and scrutinized it intently.

"An expert?"

Johansen looked up at Jim. "You don't need to worry about that, Jim. I'll take care of it and your national legal protective association covers the cost. It's just that I've heard through my contacts at the hospital that the complainant has already obtained an expert witness for their side. I haven't seen anything concrete yet, but I imagine they will find someone with suitable qualifications to make a statement and testify if necessary. Lifesaver?" Johansen held up a cylindrical packet of Butter Rum Lifesaver candies.

Jim shook his head and mumbled "No, thank you."

With his left thumb, Mr. Johansen shelled out a candy onto his right palm, which he slapped up to his open mouth. He puckered his cheeks and smacked his lips as he vigorously sucked the candy. "You know Jim, normally we're in no hurry to move forward through this process. But with you, it's different. You've got this timeline to get your general license. If you had two years ahead of you in residency, you could carry on with your educational papers and we'd sit back and let things run their course. But the quicker we can move this along, the better."

With nothing to say, Jim sat silently and stared into his lap.

***

Wednesday in the early evening, Jim headed down to Emergency to review a fifty-six-year-old lady with abdominal pain whom Hank had seen. Dr. Steinberg was also on his way in to the hospital and had said he'd be dropping by to discuss the case.

Jim and Hank each took a chair on either side of Darlene, the latest medical student on the service. In a matter of minutes, Jim spotted Dr. Steinberg, who ambled down the hall toward them wearing his blue blazer and a flashy tie. The three sat in a semicircle. Hank swallowed the remaining chunk of his Crunchie bar and wiped the corner of his mouth carefully with his slightly off-white lab coat sleeve. As Steinberg arrived and leaned up against the counter, Jim jumped up, gesturing toward his chair with his hands.

"No, don't be silly, Jimmy! You guys have been on your feet all day. I just sat down for an hour-long supper at home. I'm fine to stand!"

"Hank just reviewed this lady," Jim said, looking up at Steinberg.

"Hang on a second, Jim. Did you talk to him?"

"Who?" Jim asked.

"Hank," Steinberg replied.

"Yes, we talked about the patient just now," Jim said, puzzled.

"No, Jimmy. Not today. Remember I asked you to have that chat with Hank last week?"

Jim paused, unable to recall any specific discussion.

"Discharge summaries?" Steinberg fixed his eyes on Hank.

"Oh, ya," Jim replied, recalling a discussion they'd had in the cafeteria. "Hank, you've got to get them done."

"It's not me, Hank," Steinberg interjected. "As you know, I do most of my own summaries. But the others, they're getting on my case because Medical Records is getting after them. And you know the rules—juniors do the discharge summaries."

"I will," said Hank. "Tomorrow after work."

"Good. Now tell me about this lady."

"We think it's just a gallbladder attack, but she's still throwing up, so she may need to come in," Hank said.

Steinberg smiled slightly and looked at Hank. "Okay. On the phone, Jim said this lady has had pain and vomiting for a couple of days. Lost a bit of weight too, I understand. Tell me more, Hank. And why do you think it's her gallbladder?"

"Well." Hank paused, sat up straight in his chair and took in a deep breath. Darlene looked on, gazing intently at Hank while her thumb and forefinger rubbed her chin. Hank continued. "She's had abdominal pain and vomiting for two days. A year ago she had an ultrasound, which showed she had stones, but she didn't want to do anything at the time because she wasn't having pain. She's a bit thin, but other than that there's not a lot to find on examination."

"What did the rectal exam show, Hank?" Steinberg placed his hands on his hips and contemplated Hank fixedly. Jim could see trouble on the horizon as he observed Hank's complexion suddenly turn ghostly pale.

Hank swallowed and then said, "I—I didn't actually do a rectal—yet."

"You what? You didn't do a rectal? In what circumstances would you *not* do a rectal? Hank, what are the *two contraindications* to a rectal exam?" Steinberg smiled slyly and winked at Jim, who knew what was coming next.

"Um, two contra—two contraindications to a rectal..." Hank stammered. "Uh, let me...Number one is immunosup—"

Steinberg screwed up his face and shook his head slightly, back and forth.

Darlene was vibrating in her seat, her right arm jolting upward slightly as if ready to unleash the correct answer to the astonishment of the entire class.

"Darlene?" Steinberg turned, taking the pressure off Hank. Jim tried to maintain a serious expression.

"Is it an abscess?" Darlene's voice peaked at the end of the question, displaying her perfect white teeth, her eyes opening widely. She then slumped down in her chair. Her mouth closed and her eyes returned to normal as Steinberg stared at her, stone-faced.

"Two contraindications to a rectal exam?" Steinberg eyed all three, his head slowly turning back and forth. He held up his right fist in front of his face. His index finger sprung to attention and he continued, "Number one: No rectum!" His middle finger immediately extended along side the other one. "Number two: No finger!" He then slapped his thigh and cackled uncontrollably. Jim rolled his eyes slightly and made an effort to join in the others' chuckles.

After a short lull, Steinberg explained to Hank and the others that he expected a more thorough evaluation of this lady and they were to call him when they were finished. Jim never ceased to be amazed by the experience and intuition of some of his teachers. Despite the joking about a rectal exam, sure enough, this patient turned out to have an abnormal palpable shelf at the fingertip on rectal exam, suggestive of a tumour. Further studies showed that she had an advanced stomach cancer with metastatic disease through her abdomen and pelvis. Of all the people he saw, how had Dr. Steinberg known to make a big deal about her and her rectal exam? Jim had no clue and respected his mentor all the more.

***

Dr. Steinberg and Jim were seated in the cafeteria, having a quick cup of coffee before going to the operating room. Jim was wiped, having done surgery the past three nights in a row.

"But you've got to be careful, Jimmy!"

"Huh?" For a moment, Jim didn't know whether he'd nodded off. He wondered whether Dr. Steinberg was talking about doing a surgical procedure, driving a car or something completely different. He tried to think back to any conversation they might have had in the past month that could have led to this statement.

"What you say. You've always got to watch your mouth around them. Never know what might be repeated and used against you."

Jim immediately thought of Edna Doyle, her splenic artery aneurysm and the advice Dave Johansen had given him about keeping silent on the subject. But he couldn't tie it to any discussion with Dr. Steinberg. "Are you referring—"

"Kids, Jimmy! You have to be careful what you say around them!"

"Oh, right." Jim suddenly recalled a conversation they had started a month ago, where Dr. Steinberg was offering up advice about child-rearing. "Can never be too careful, I suppose," Jim agreed tentatively.

"Take, for example, our daughter, Jennifer," Steinberg continued. "When she was eight years old, I was talking on the phone at suppertime to my junior resident. He wanted me to come in and take a sewing needle out of someone's foot. Those can be tricky, you know. Someone steps on a needle, it breaks off and all you have to go by is a tiny puncture site on the bottom of the foot and a one-inch needle on the X-ray. Much more difficult than they look, you know."

"Yes?" Jim rubbed his chin, trying to appear wide awake.

"So anyway, I tell my junior resident I don't do foreign bodies. What I don't say is that it should be orthopedics, that those can be tricky, and all the other things I should have said. I just said 'I don't do foreign bodies, that should be ortho!' and hung up the phone. Next think I know, our eight-year-old tells a Chinese student in her class that her daddy doesn't operate on foreigners. So guess what happens next?"

"What?" Jim was beginning to take more interest.

"Next thing I know, an administrator from the school comes banging on our door when I'm at work. They want to know all about the environment that our daughter is being raised in! It takes an hour for Liz and the school representative to figure out what's going on. That I'm not some kind of xenophobe. Course, I didn't hear anything about it until I got home." He guffawed, leaning back in his chair. “So watch what you say, Jimmy. And if you do screw up, wives are much better at sorting it out.”

Jim chuckled and said, “Our daughter is only nine months old, but I’ll keep that in mind for future reference.”

“Of course, Jimmy, but time moves along quickly. Before you know it, she’ll be nine *years* old.” He took a gulp of coffee and plunked the half-full ceramic cup onto the table, adding, “Let’s go, we don’t want to be late for the O.R.”

Steinberg stood up and sprang toward the exit with Jim trailing closely behind.

Chapter 18 ~ MVA

Jim was missing Hank already. The holidays had been fairly busy. Junior residents and students were scarce between Christmas and New Year's. Usually one junior was available for in-house call and the rest were off with their families. Jim had taken Christmas day off and spent Emily's first Christmas in Lakefield with Amanda's family. He was back to work the following day. Dr. O'Brien and Dr. Albano were on call over the holidays and Jim chose to stick around rather than take the flack for being absent. Besides, Jim always found Christmas a bit depressing, and his final push for June exams provided ample justification to be operating and studying at every opportunity. Being busy at the hospital also helped keep his mind off Edna Doyle and the complaint to the Medical Licensing Authority. Hank had finished his rotation with Jim and was now off-service doing plastic surgery. He was still at St. Joe's, so they could grab a bite together now and then. In exchange for Hank, Sam Cheung was doing his obligatory three months of general surgery.

Dr. Tabitha Haden, a second-year general surgery resident, was also new to the service. Jim figured she might keep Sam in line, as long as Sam didn't try to seduce her. From what Jim knew that was unlikely, as Tabitha had a boyfriend from the faculty of dentistry. She'd always brought him to residency functions, happy to cling to his arm an entire evening. It wasn't that Sam wouldn't be attracted to Tabitha. She had long, brown hair with a reddish tint, and wore more makeup than the typical surgery resident. But her self-confidence projected an air that she was off-limits, so hopefully Sam would read the vibes correctly and behave. Tabitha was sharply intelligent, which could only make Jim's job easier. Being in second year, she still was a junior resident and would share the same call rotation with Sam and two other juniors, so they'd never be on call at night together. But during the day, Tabitha could guide Sam, quiz him and essentially keep him out of Jim's hair.

Rhani Praveen was back doing an elective in general surgery at St. Joe's after a brief hiatus on pediatrics. There was still hope Jim might convert her to general surgery. With two other junior residents, an intern and two medical students, Jim had a full complement of EBUs to help him achieve his ultimate goal of spending maximal time in the operating room.

Jim climbed into bed at fifteen minutes before midnight on December 31st. With a young child and his current job, this was not a particularly special night. He and Amanda had seen in the New Year every other year they'd been together. But this year, he felt lucky to be in bed before midnight. As Amanda snored softly, Jim realized he was not far away from sleep himself. His body ached and the fatigue soon overwhelmed him.

Suddenly the shrill beeping of his pager roused him. He reached for it on the bedside table and tiptoed out of the bedroom to respond. The familiar four-digit number of the Emergency Department sapped his spirit as he realized he'd only been asleep for two hours. Jim called the number and was told a victim of blunt trauma from a motor vehicle accident had arrived by ambulance ten minutes earlier. The emergency physician and Tabitha were working on the sole survivor of the most badly damaged vehicle in the collision.

It wasn't until later that Jim pieced together the details of the events leading up to the accident. He imagined the trip that the victims, young sisters, had taken across the city. Not only did Jim gain experience in surgery that night, but he also reacquainted himself with a driving tip he'd long forgotten since lessons he had taken as a teenager.

Being New Year's Eve, the city was bustling. Shena Darlington, twenty years old, was excited to be spending one last night with her younger sister, Jenny, before heading back to university. They'd spent the evening partying with Jenny's friends. Only two years apart, they'd shared many pals at high school, so it was no chore for Shena to drive to her younger sister's friend's place for a New Year's Eve party. At about eleven-twenty, however, Jenny realized her most recent love interest was not showing up at the party and in fact was across town at another classmate's house. If they left immediately, Jenny said, they could arrive in plenty of time before midnight, positioning her perfectly to see in the New Year at the same soirée as Max Caselli. If her younger sister wanted a chance for a smooch with Max at midnight, who was Shena to stand in her way?

At 11:35 the two sisters slipped out quietly, not wanting to draw attention to the fact that they were departing so close to midnight. Shena squeezed in behind the wheel of the beat-up Pinto while Jenny excitedly piled into the passenger seat. After three drinks, Jenny giggled, fumbling with her seatbelt, which finally clicked into place while Shena looked on with amusement. Shena turned the key, put the car in drive and drove carefully along the icy street. Having had one drink, Shena did not want to push her luck by taking any chances. After Shena had driven about fifteen minutes along a busy street, Jenny shrieked to her sister to turn left at the next set of traffic lights. "And hurry, it's getting close to midnight," she slurred.

It seemed everybody was rushing from one destination to another, trying to arrive before the magical hour of midnight, Shena thought. As she approached the intersection at the bottom of the hill, she eyed a gap in traffic, an opportunity to turn left at the intersection. She thought it was her lucky night as the light stayed green and she pulled into the intersection. About to turn left, she hesitated and then pressed on the brake pedal. The car came to a stop in the middle of the intersection, the front wheels aiming left, ready to go at the next opportunity, be it a natural break in traffic or a yellow light. She glanced at the dashboard clock, reassured that they still had ten minutes to reach the party, which was only a block and a half away.

Everything that occurred afterward was either erased from her memory or never perceived in the first place. Shena explained to Jim, in a fit of panic, that she had been merely sitting in the intersection, awaiting an opportunity to move her right foot from the brake to the gas pedal, when her conscious world vanished. From the paramedic's description of the wreck, Jim figured he knew what had happened next.

A seventeen-year-old male, Justin Lippincott, careened down the hill in his parents' station wagon. Too drunk to notice the brown Pinto paused in the intersection for a left turn, his vehicle slammed into the smaller car from behind. Like a billiard ball decisively striking its unsuspecting target, Justin's vehicle torpedoed Shena and Jenny's car forward and to the left, into oncoming traffic. Had the Pinto's wheels remained aligned straight, as they should have been, Shena and Jenny might have been propelled forward through the intersection, only sustaining minor whiplash injuries. However, their car followed the direction of the front wheels and aimed at forty-five degrees into oncoming traffic. Their vehicle was T-boned by a pickup truck driven by a sober, middle-aged male. After the occupants of the Pinto were extricated, the semi-conscious Shena was taken to St. Joseph's Emergency Department. Jim heard that Jenny had been killed on impact. The driver of the pickup truck was shaken but unharmed. Justin Lippincott was receiving stitches in Emergency D under constant supervision by police, who were jumping through legal hoops to obtain a blood alcohol sample.

"How's my sister?" Shena shrieked, her neck encased in a hard collar that was securely taped down to a spine board. Her sandy brown hair was matted in clumps from dried blood. She grunted with each breath and her mouth was turned down at the corners, exposing her lower row of teeth. Jim gently brushed away some of the blood-encrusted hair from the right side of her head. Her right ear was torn with a full-thickness, jagged laceration extending from the apex of the pinna downward to where her ear disappeared behind the neck collar. Jim observed her agitated expression as she lay completely immobilized. Ignoring her question, he picked a few tiny cubes of glass from her hair with his right hand as he palpated, searching for scalp lacerations with his left. "How's my sister?" she repeated, her eyes opening wider at Jim's face directly above hers. The chaotic noise in the room ranged from constant jabber to regular beeps of the cardiac monitor.

"They must've taken her to the University Hospital," Jim lied. "She's not here anyway. But let's worry about you and fix some of these injuries. We're pretty sure you've got a fractured femur and we want to make sure there's no bleeding inside your abdomen." Jim was about to repeat the entire head-to-toe examination, which had already been performed by Tabitha, who looked on from just beyond Shena's feet. Turning, Jim looked at Tabitha. "Other than her ear and leg, did you find anything significant?"

"No. ABCs were fine. Airway, as you can see, is patent. She's breathing well, with good air entry bilaterally, and her circulation is okay. She had low blood pressure on arrival, but that has improved with a bag of saline. Last blood pressure was 106 over 70, and pulse, as you can see, is 95. There's no obvious neurologic disability. Exposing her, I've found nothing other than a slightly distended abdomen and the deformed left femur." Tabitha hesitated, then added, "Oh, and we haven't turned her yet. I haven't checked her back or done a rectal yet."

"X-rays?" Jim asked.

"Chest looks good to me—it's over there on the view box. No signs of an aortic arch injury. The lateral C-spine looks okay to C5. We thought we'd defer other X-rays until we're sure she's stable and has all the lines and tubes we need."

"C-spine?" Jim looked incredulous. "What's up with that? It's Airway, Breathing, Circulation. Not Airway, Breathing, C-spine! She's in a collar, for God's sake!"

Tabitha looked at her feet and said, "I know. But it was easy to do."

Jim shook his head and then raised the warm blanket, peering at Shena's exposed chest. He saw telltale abrasions and bruising from her driver's side seatbelt, angling down from her left shoulder and fading between her breasts before disappearing. Jim swept a few more bits of glass from the hollow under her left collarbone onto the spine board next to her. Shena's bra and other clothing remained underneath her, having been cut open at the front with scissors on arrival. He placed his stethoscope carefully on her chest. After listening for heart and breath sounds, Jim palpated for crunchy texture under the skin, a sign of subcutaneous emphysema or air in the tissues from a collapsed lung, possibly punctured by a broken rib. As expected from the X-ray, there was no sign of it. He pressed on her abdomen, which felt slightly doughy and distended.

Shena winced and then wailed, "Where's my sister? Where's Jenny?"

"Like I said," Jim replied with as much compassion as he could muster, "she's not here, but we'll let you know as soon as we get some firm details." Jim dreaded the conversation they would be having if the initial reports about her sister were true. He pressed again on her abdomen and asked, "Does this hurt?"

"Yes!" she sobbed.

Jim continued the examination and when he finished with her feet, he announced, "We're going to need to logroll her so we can check her back." Then to Tabitha he added, "I'll stand at the head when we roll her. You palpate her spine, then do the rectal exam." He turned to Marylou, one of the older, more experienced emergency nurses, and said, "Perhaps she should have something more for pain before we roll her. That leg is going to hurt."

"You bet," she said as she turned, reaching for a syringe of Demerol on the counter behind her. She swabbed the IV site with alcohol and slowly injected the pain medication into her line. "Now Shena, I'm going to top up your pain meds. We can't give you too much right now, so turning you might still be a little bit painful, but we'll try to take the edge off it."

"Okay," Shena cried out.

Four nurses and a respiratory therapist lined up along Shena's left side, ready to roll her toward them, carefully maintaining alignment of her body to protect her spinal cord in case of any undiagnosed spine fractures. The orthopedic resident, a tall, muscular fellow with a crew cut and green scrubs, cradled her deformed right leg.

"Okay," Jim commanded loudly. "On three! One, two, three!" The team turned Shena to her left side, carefully and slowly.

"Ooowww!" she shrieked.

Tabitha carefully palpated her spinal column and nodded to Jim. She then deftly slipped her lubricated gloved finger into Shena's rectum, while stating loudly, "I just have to check for injuries in your pelvis, through your rectum. It'll be just a second and perhaps a little uncomfortable."

"Ooowww! No kidding! Ow!"

The task completed, Jim slipped the spine board out from underneath her, and on his count they rolled Shena onto her back on the stretcher.

"We've removed the board, Shena, but you still can't move until we've done all the X-rays we need to do. Okay?"

"Okay," she replied feebly.

In the corner of the room, Jim spotted Hank, who must have been called in to assess Shena's ear as he was the resident on call for plastic surgery. Jim walked to the exit and motioned to Hank and Tabitha to come out to the hallway with him. "While they get more X-rays and ortho makes a plan about this young lady's femur, we on general surgery need to coordinate the overall plan. Particularly, we have to decide what to do, if anything, about her abdomen." As he walked with Tabitha by his right side, Jim turned his head back to the left and said, "C'mon, Hank. You're still one of us. You can check the ear out in a few minutes. But let's talk about her belly."

They sat down in chairs at the workstation, Jim in the middle. "Okay, Tabitha, what about her abdomen?"

"Well, I guess she is a bit tender. So we need to decide if she's bleeding internally."

"From what?" Jim's eyes darted between Tabitha and Hank.

"Liver, spleen, bowel," Tabitha responded without delay.

"What would make you suspect one over another?" Jim asked.

"Fractured ribs on the left would make me concerned about the spleen, while on the right it could indicate a liver injury."

"And the seatbelt?"

"A lap belt is sometimes associated with a small bowel injury or a tear of the mesentery low in the abdomen. But really we have no idea, so we have to decide what to do." Tabitha fastened the top button of her lab coat over her greens while smiling smugly at Hank.

"Okay," Jim said. "What are our options to decide about internal bleeding?"

"DPL—diagnostic peritoneal lavage—or minilap. If there's blood in her belly here in Emergency, then we do a full laparotomy upstairs. Or obvious bowel content in any amount would warrant surgery." Jim was beginning to think he'd prefer Tabitha to be on call if he ever got in a car accident. As much as Jim liked Hank, his answers were not flowing forth as effortlessly.

"How do you do a minilap?" Jim turned away from Tabitha and said, "Hank?"

"Okay," Hank started, fidgeting with his stethoscope in his lap. "Inject some freezing and then make a small, vertical cut below the umbilicus. When you get into the peritoneal cavity, pour a litre of saline in and then let it drain back into the bag by gravity. A little blood is acceptable, but if the fluid draining out has so much blood in it you can't read a newspaper through it, then she probably needs an open exploration in the operating room."

"Very good, Hank," Jim said. "Tell me, who needs a minilap?" His eyes remained fixed on Hank.

"Someone who is unconscious and can't be properly examined for tenderness. Someone who is going to be having extensive orthopedic procedures and who might decompensate if intra-abdominal bleeding goes undiagnosed."

"Who doesn't get a minilap?"

Hank looked blank. Tabitha seized the opportunity and said, "Someone who clearly has intra-abdominal bleeding or shock that needs exploration anyway. No point in wasting time with a minilap down here."

"What might you miss with a minilap and what other tests could you do?" Jim looked at Tabitha, who continued speaking.

"Minilap won't pick up retroperitoneal bleeding from a pelvic fracture or a smashed kidney. If it's contained bleeding outside the peritoneal cavity, it could be missed with a minilap. So a CAT scan is better in that instance. But it takes longer and is especially risky in an unstable patient who is not safe to be in the CAT scan suite for a half hour."

"Wait 'til we get our next generation CAT scanner," Jim added. "Then we might find it quick and accurate enough to scan more frequently, and do fewer minilaps."

Tabitha squared her shoulders back. She looked at Hank and then at Jim, stating, "It sounds like increasing technology makes our work easier. With all these fancy scanners."

"No," Jim said thoughtfully, "it just raises the bar—the expectations. With increasing availability of advanced technology, we are expected to use it more often. Fewer excuses to screw up." Jim suddenly felt a wave of nausea. He was uncomfortably warm and could feel his heart racing. He thought back to September 26th and why he hadn't done a CAT scan on Edna Doyle: it had never crossed his mind. His mouth was dry. "Why don't you guys go see how our patient is doing and decide whether she needs a minilap. I'm going to grab a drink of water." Jim stared into the distance, consumed by speculation about September, unable to rise out of his chair.

***

At five o'clock in the morning, Jim sat on the bench, alone in the O.R. men's locker room. Tabitha had done a minilap on Shena in the Emergency Department, and due to some blood in her abdomen, they'd opened her up in the operating room to see what they could find. There was no active bleeding, just a small torn vessel that had already stopped bleeding. Having sutured her abdomen closed, Jim was going home. The orthopedic surgeons were now placing a long intramedullary nail down her femur to stabilize the fracture, while Hank was working on her torn ear. Jim was exhausted but making a plan for how and when to tell Shena about her deceased sister. He pictured her sitting in the intersection, waiting to turn left. If only she'd kept the front wheels straight. *And it always seems to be the drunk driver that walks away from accidents like these*, Jim thought bitterly. He couldn't wait to get home and climb into bed with Amanda, to fall asleep and forget about the horrible first day of the year.

***

Dr. Steinberg sat at a small table hidden in a far corner of the noisy hospital cafeteria. He sipped his coffee and carefully placed the mug in front of him. "Of course not. Jim, you need to separate what's good and what's bad in your life these days and allow them to coexist side by side. I'd suggest to you that 95 percent of your life is perfect right now, and when this complaint is over it will all seem miniscule in hindsight. And in some ways, you should be thankful they're accelerating the process. If the MLA clears you, I think the chance of a lawsuit will be very small. Which is a good thing because those can drag on for years!"

Jim couldn't imagine the prospect. "I'll quit if it comes to that."

"No, you won't."

"It's just that I can't stand feeling constantly under attack."

"You have to realize, Jimmy, patients and their families need a few different options if they think there's been a medical error or they've been wronged. So eventually, we all end up facing a complaint to the MLA or a lawsuit." Steinberg hesitated. "What I'm trying to say is that it's part of being a doctor, having to face up to challenges like this. That's why they pay us the big bucks, or so they say."

"But as a resident, I don't even make big bucks yet. And I'd gladly trade some income for a better system. And Mr. Johansen tells me a lawsuit can go on for ten years...or longer! Isn't that a bit late for corrective action?"

"Who said lawsuits have anything to do with corrective action? And yes, it *is* too long. But patients and families need something. Although a complaint to the Medical Licensing Authority is sometimes a testing ground for a potential lawsuit, the MLA is sometimes viewed—incorrectly, I might add—as a bunch of old boys protecting each other. But on the whole, the MLA is fair."

"That's good to hear," said Jim.

"They don't like doctors who are repeat offenders, mind you."

"This is my first incident. I'm just worried about what other doctors might say about my role in the Doyle case." Jim's face tightened.

"You needn't worry excessively," Steinberg replied. "Oh sure, you can always find an expert witness somewhere to be critical of another doctor's care, but by and large, doctors stand up for each other. It's because we understand the pressures of the job and know that it's not always as easy as it looks from the outside, in hindsight."

"Yes, but would a doctor stand up to protect another doctor if it meant his own reputation could be smeared?"

"That I don't know, Jimmy. That's a good question."

"It's just too bad there's nothing in between—a system to give something to those hit by medical disaster. Quickly. And without *having* to find someone to blame."

"So tell me, how's that going to work? What will prevent patients from pursuing all three avenues at the same time?"

Jim had never considered the question but continued on the fly. "Make it quick and simple to access the no-fault option—set some strict criteria of course—but if it's relatively easy to tap that source, people will use it. And if they use it, they must opt out of the other channels."

Steinberg nodded. "Okay, I get it. They'll follow the path of least resistance—water flows downhill type of thing. So patients subject to medical disaster will access your middle-of-the-road option rather than playing the blame game. Sounds interesting."

Jim thought of Dave Johansen and how he seemed to relish a good fight. "The lawyers mightn't like it, but it would be better for us and for our patients."

"How perceptive of you, Jimmy-boy. My young friend who usually only sees black or white, good or bad, picking out a nice shade of grey! And by the way, don't you worry about the lawyers. They'll be okay."

Jim, feeling buoyed by the discussion, sat up straight and said, "Maybe it's something someone should work on."

"Sounds like a great idea. Only one problem."

"What?"

"You're not the first person to think of it. Mobilizing the forces to put it into action is the hard part."

"Oh."

Chapter 19 ~ Small Bowel Obstruction

Jim glanced out the window at the snowy street as he approached Emergency Section B. The late afternoon sun was beginning to set. He looked straight ahead and spotted Sam leaning against the wall, chatting up one of the young nurses. Jim was in no mood to waste time assisting Sam with his romantic goals. At least he was staying clear of Rhani and Tabitha—Jim would draw the line there if either of them became one of Sam's targets.

Jim cleared his throat and said, "Well, Sam, should we get to this lady who's been vomiting?"

"I'd better go," Sam said to the blond. "Talk to you later." As the nurse scurried away, he stood up straight and said, "Sure, I'll grab her chart."

As Sam returned with the chart, Rhani appeared from examining the patient in her cubicle. The three sat down to discuss the patient and, without difficulty, Jim was able to obtain a clear picture of this lady's history from Sam and Rhani.

Mrs. Klumpar was a seventy-nine year-old lady with diabetes, on insulin for the past four years. She was neither slim nor overweight. She lived with her husband of forty-five years and had three grown children who were all living within a few hours of her home. She had presented to the Emergency Department with a two-day history of nausea and vomiting. Originally, she had thought it was the flu, but in the past twenty-four hours, she began experiencing abdominal cramps, so she made a trip to the hospital. She'd had a mastectomy for cancer nine years previously but had no history of abdominal surgery.

"When was her last bowel movement?" Jim asked.

"I'm not sure," Sam replied.

"Two days ago," Rhani said.

"Has she passed gas?"

Sam looked at Rhani, who shrugged her shoulders.

“C’mon you guys,” Jim said. “It’s one of the most important questions you can ask on general surgery. Rhani, you know that.”

“Yes, I know,” she said.

“Okay, never mind,” Jim said, “let’s look at her X-rays and then go see her.”

Sam flipped the toggle switch on the X-ray viewer, the backlight illuminating the images.

Jim watched as Sam and Rhani studied the films, then asked, “Okay, Sam, what do you see?” Jim could identify unmistakable dilated small intestine, mostly full of air, laddering back and forth across the abdomen. There was no air beyond the small bowel, in either the colon or the rectum. The findings were not subtle. It was an unmistakable, high-grade small bowel obstruction. He also noticed air-fluid levels, supporting the diagnosis of a blockage.

Sam straightened his tie underneath his crisp white lab coat and said, “Well, she’s obviously got a lot of gas. Does she have a bowel obstruction?”

“You tell me, Sam. Is it large or small bowel, and what’s wrong with it?”

“I think it’s small bowel, and it’s awfully dilated. Yes, she’s got a small bowel obstruction.”

“See,” Jim said, glancing back and forth between Sam and Rhani, “general surgery isn’t so difficult, is it?”

“No,” they chimed.

Jim looked at the X-rays. “And look, here in the right upper quadrant. Totally unrelated to today’s problem. But she’s got gallstones. You don’t always see those on plain X-rays. In fact, they’re a little unclear ’cause of some random bits of gas up here but yes, those are gallstones.”

“Cool!” Rhani exclaimed.

“Okay,” Jim said. “Let’s go see her.”

He held the curtain open as Rhani and Sam went ahead into Mrs. Klumpar’s cubicle. Lying flat on the bed, she appeared to be of medium height and had grey hair, framing her wrinkled face. Her eyes brightened as the three entered. A short, skinny man with a full head of grey hair, whom Jim took to be her husband, sat in the corner on a small chair.

“Mrs. Klumpar, I’m Dr. Smythe. I’m the chief resident on surgery here. Dr. Albano is on call and we’ll be speaking to him soon, but do you mind if I ask you a few questions and press on your tummy?”

“Not at all. Most certainly.” Then to her husband, “They sure make doctors young these days, don’t they, Ivan?” Back to Jim, she added, “How old are you, anyway?”

"Old enough," Jim responded. He blushed while continuing his line of questioning. "Now how long have you had this pain?"

"It's not so much pain, young man. It started with throwing up two days ago, and then probably twenty times yesterday. I started getting a few cramps today. They really weren't that bad. But Ivan said I should come in because I couldn't keep anything down. I feel much better now that you've given me some liquid," she said, pointing to the intravenous line in her left hand.

"Have you passed any gas?"

"I beg your pardon?" Her voice lilted such that Jim didn't know whether it was due to incomprehension or indignation.

Jim spoke louder. "Have you broken wind? Farted?"

"I don't generally do that. But no. Nothing in the last day and a half."

"Open your mouth, please. I want to look at your tongue." It was only slightly dry. After listening to her chest with her sitting up, Jim had her lie flat again and expose her abdomen. "I want to press on your tummy. Are you bloated?"

"I haven't been this big since I had my last baby thirty-seven years ago."

Jim pressed on her abdomen, expecting some significant tenderness. He watched her eyes carefully as he palpated her taut abdomen throughout. He didn't seem to be eliciting any reaction. He checked low down for any lumps, looking for hernias, but found none. "Isn't this sore?" he asked, now pushing firmly across her abdomen with both hands.

"Oh, perhaps a little bit. But it's really not too bad. Do you think I could go home and come back tomorrow if it isn't getting better?"

"I don't think so. Your X-rays look worse than you do. I think you are generally not a complainer. You have a blockage of your bowel. And you're sure you've never had surgery on your abdomen?"

"Of course I'm sure. Had all my babies naturally. You'd think I'd remember if I had an operation before!"

"Okay," Jim said, alternating glances between Mrs. Klumpar and her husband. "I think you should be admitted to hospital to get this sorted out. Bowel obstructions like this usually need surgery, but we could put a tube through your nose, down into your stomach to drain it. If you aren't improved and passing gas by tomorrow, you might need an operation."

"*Bozhe mii!*" She then looked at her husband and said, "Ivan? What do you think?"

"He's the doctor," Ivan said, his palm turned upward, fingers pointing toward Jim.

"You're the doctor," she repeated. "Whatever you say."

"I'm going to call Dr. Albano and confirm that's good with him, and we'll be right back." Jim left the cubicle with Sam and Rhani following at his heels. He sat down at the table right in front of the X-rays, then pulled a wrinkled index card from his pocket, looked up Dr. Albano's home phone number and pressed the digits into the telephone.

"Hello, Dr. Albano? It's Jim."

"Hi Jim," Dr. Albano replied. "What's up?"

"We've got a seventy-nine-year-old lady with a small bowel obstruction. Diabetic. On insulin. No previous abdominal surgery. She's really not that tender on exam. Her pulse is 76, she's not febrile and her abdomen is really benign. Her white count's normal. I was thinking of admitting her, sucking and dripping, and if she's no better by tomorrow, she may need a look in the O.R."

"No previous surgery? No hernias?"

"That's right," Jim responded.

"And you're sure it's a bowel obstruction on X-ray? Not incomplete or iffy?"

"No. It's high-grade."

"Sounds like this lady needs an operation tonight," Albano said, certainty in his voice and a slight accent clearly transmitted over the phone.

"But she's not sore at all," Jim countered. "If you don't mind waiting, I'm sure she'd be okay until tomorrow."

"You know, Jim, I think we should just get to this tonight, rather than be trying to get her in tomorrow. You never know how busy the O.R. will be another day. How about you get things lined up and I'll come in and have a look at her. We can always cancel it if I think it should wait, but if she's got a high-grade obstruction with no previous surgery, we should just get 'er done tonight."

"Okay, I'll see you in a while," Jim said sheepishly into the phone as he looked at Sam and Rhani.

***

Amanda Smythe checked in with the receptionist at the window and then seated herself in Dr. Steinberg's empty office waiting room. She looked at her wristwatch. It was 4:55. *Jim will probably be working at least another hour*, she thought, *even if it's an unusually quiet day.* Amanda had spent the better part of Monday on the phone setting up this meeting and she did not want Jim to find out about it. After arranging a sitter, she parked two blocks away and headed to the hospital. She was fairly certain Jim hadn't spotted her as she stealthily made her way up the back stairwell to the floor of surgeons' offices.

Amanda scanned the wall, admiring the framed diplomas. *A year from now, Jim will have a waiting room like this. Although it will be a lot nicer than Dr. Steinberg's, if I have anything to say about the décor*, she thought. It was all but confirmed that Jim would be joining the surgical group in her hometown, Lakefield. Amanda was looking forward to living close to her parents in a situation where Jim would not have to work all the time.

Dr. Steinberg appeared in the doorway, beaming, with his arms held wide. He wore a blue blazer with a white shirt and a splashy tie. "Mandy-doll! How are you?" He walked forward and as Amanda stood, he embraced her enthusiastically.

He bent down, peering into the reception window, and said, "Diane, you remember Jim Smythe's wife, Amanda, don't you?"

"Of course I do," she said, expressionless. "We spent quite a bit of time on the phone the other day setting this up."

"Well that's just fine. Diane, you don't need to stay. Amanda and I are just going to have a brief chat in my office." He then turned to Amanda and said, "After you, young lady."

Steinberg walked behind Amanda down the hallway and directed her into his small office, where she sat in a chair facing his desk. Behind him, he left the door ajar and parked himself in his large swivel armchair. Amanda took off her winter coat and folded it on her lap. Steinberg jumped out of his chair and said, "Allow me to hang that up for you!" He took it and hung it on a hook on the back of the door, then walked back to his chair and sat down. He smiled and tilted his head forward, looking through the upper half of his lenses. "You look good, Amanda. I bet you're the perfect mother! How's Emily these days?"

"Oh, she's great. We can't slow her down. She can even stand for a second or two. Holding on to something, of course."

"Wonderful," Steinberg said enthusiastically. "You don't want to miss any of that, do you? Say, when was the last time I saw you?"

"The barbeque?"

"That's right, the July barbeque. I always love that one. It's great to see all the residents with their families outside the hospital. You know, I've felt bad about that ever since."

"Pardon?"

"It was undercooked."

"What?"

"Your burger. I thought it might be. I was just glad to hear you didn't get sick."

"Oh, that!" Amanda recalled that a hamburger, cooked by Steinberg himself, had been slightly pink on the inside. She'd forgotten. "It was fine."

"Now let's cut to the chase. What was it Diane said you wanted to talk about? Something about Jimmy-boy?"

Amanda took in a deep breath and clutched the arms of her chair. "I'm sure you know there's a complaint in the works."

"Oh, that. I wondered if that's why you're here. What's the problem?"

Amanda was taken aback, not realizing she had to explain why it was a problem. "It's just that…Jim seems to be pretty stressed out by the situation. I'm worried what's going to come of all this."

"Jimmy? He'll be fine! This type of thing happens and you just need to let it run its course."

"But he's acting rather strangely."

"Jimmy? He's doing great! One of the best residents that's come through here in a long time."

"I know he's good at work. But I don't think you understand, Dr. Steinberg. At home. He gets home and doesn't pay much attention to me or Emily. And he doesn't sleep. He spends hours on the Internet. He says it's all related to studying for his surgery exams, but I'm not sure I believe him."

"Okay," Steinberg said. "I'll keep an eye out for him. You know I always have. But if you think I should have a chat—"

"No! You can't let him know I was here. In fact, I don't know why I'm here." Amanda could feel tears welling up. "It's just that…"

Steinberg pushed a Kleenex box across the desk, placing it within Amanda's reach. She took one and dabbed the corner of each eye.

"I've known you longer than I've known Jimmy. Sure, I'll do whatever I can to help the two of you."

"I just wanted you to be aware of what's going on at home. Perhaps you can encourage him to think positively. No matter what I say to him, it doesn't seem to help. He's so negative. He just seems so depressed lately. And I know that's normal to some extent in a situation like this. I'm just worried it could turn into something worse. And I don't know what to do about it." Amanda could feel she was on the precipice of utter sobbing but concentrated, staring at the tip of Steinberg's chin. She smiled weakly and said, "Anything you can do is appreciated." She hesitated. "Can I call you again if there's anything more specific?"

"Of course you can, Amanda!" He pulled a pen from his blazer pocket and scribbled on a scrap of paper, which he folded and placed in her outstretched hand. "Here's my home number. Call me anytime."

"Thank you so much, Dr. Steinberg." She placed the paper in her purse.

They continued to chat for several minutes. Dr. Steinberg advised Amanda on various people she could speak to, in order to further address her concerns. Amanda was thankful for Dr. Steinberg's encouraging tone, yet still felt troubled when she left the office.

***

Dr. Albano studied the X-rays. He smoothed his thinning black hair and with his head tilted forward, stood back and studied the films silently. He wore a navy blue suit with light blue shirt and dark striped tie. Sam and Rhani looked on from his right side, with Jim on his left, trying to discern what interested Albano so much about this bowel obstruction.

"It's a classic case," Albano said, folding his hands across his chest.

"Small bowel obstruction?" Jim asked.

"No. Well, yes, that too," Dr. Albano replied. "But look at the right upper quadrant."

"Gallstones," Jim said evenly.

"Yes, but look harder," the professor added.

Jim peered at one of the X-rays, hoping the revelation would arrive. He felt like he was searching one of those 3-D posters, changing his focus, hoping for the image to materialize but only seeing random lines. Blinking, he was feeling the severe fatigue that weighed on him, having been at the hospital until midnight four nights in a row. For what seemed like an eternity, Albano did not speak, the silence unsettling to Jim. Finally, he saw it. The outline of branching shadows in Mrs. Klumpar's right upper quadrant coalesced into something meaningful for Jim.

"Of course!" Jim couldn't believe he had missed it. He'd never seen a case before, but he'd certainly read about it. "I should've seen that."

"You've got to at least think of it when there's no previous surgery, Jim." He then turned to his right and said, "Either of you see it?" Sam and Rhani continued to stare blankly at the X-ray.

"Air in the biliary tree in the setting of a small bowel obstruction," Jim began, "has to be a gallstone ileus."

"Oh, I read about that," Rhani exclaimed.

"You bet," said Jim. "If a person has ongoing gallbladder inflammation, over a long period of time, it's possible for a large gallstone to erode, or fistulize, from the gallbladder to the duodenum. It's incredibly rare, but if it escapes into the small bowel through a fistula, the stone, usually the size of a golf ball, can get stuck at the distal end of the small bowel, causing an obstruction. And air in the biliary tree is not normal. Unless they've had some sort of surgical procedure to allow air to get from the intestine into the bile ducts, pneumobilia, as it's called, in the setting of a bowel obstruction equals gallstone ileus until proven otherwise." Jim could hardly contain his excitement. "But I should've seen it!"

"You will next time, Jim," Dr. Albano said reassuringly.

"But there may not be a next time for ten years!" Jim said.

"Yes, you're right, but you never know. Could be tomorrow, could be never or somewhere in between. Let's get her to the O.R. and see if we're right. Even if it isn't a gallstone ileus, something is going on with this lady and in the absence of scar tissue from previous surgery to explain her obstruction, she needs an operation."

"How many cases have you seen?" Jim asked.

"Probably about five or six. But they were somewhat more common when I was a resident, when people tended to suffer from gallstones longer before getting treatment. When it occurs, it's often in elderly people, often diabetics. But I haven't seen a case for five years, maybe longer."

***

Exhilarated, Jim stood on Mrs. Klumpar's right side with a scalpel in his right hand.

"Make a lower midline incision, Jim," Albano said. "You can get to most pathology in the small bowel from the lower abdomen and it's an incision she'll find less painful."

Jim cut vertically downward from Mrs. Klumpar's umbilicus. As he entered the abdomen, dilated loops of small intestine bulged out through the incision.

When Jim started pulling out more loops of small bowel onto the abdominal wall, Albano said, "Just put your hand in, Jim." Then to Rhani he added, "Jim should be able to feel the stone. If not, he can start looking for a junction between collapsed distal bowel and dilated proximal bowel—that will always lead to the obstruction. But in this case, he might just find the stone right off the bat."

Jim squeezed his hand in through the lower midline incision, taking care not to damage the small bowel between his hand and the abdominal wall. Within seconds, he found the three-centimetre stone that, as expected, had migrated all the way through the small bowel into the right lower quadrant. He clutched it in his hand and pulled the segment of small intestine out through the incision. Like a snake bulging from recently consumed prey, the bowel was stretched by the large, round stone. Jammed into the far end of the small bowel, it was unmovable, with litres of fluid and partially digested food accumulated upstream of the impasse.

As Jim was about to make an opening in the bowel with cautery over top of the stone, Albano uttered, "I wouldn't do that. If you open the bowel where the stone has been stuck for two days, your suture line won't heal. You either have to milk it back to a more healthy area and make your enterotomy there, or you have to do a bowel resection, joining two ends of healthy bowel."

"I'll see if I can get the stone to budge." Jim tried to gently manipulate the solidly stuck stone along the intestine. It eventually broke free and Jim moved it backwards into a segment of intestine that was full of fluid. He squeezed it backwards a bit further and said, "There, that should work." Then to the nurse he added, "Bowel clamps."

Jim proceeded to occlude the intestine on either side of the stone with non-crushing bowel clamps to minimize spillage once he opened the small intestine. He then made a transverse cut in the bowel overlying the stone, which was bathed in intestinal contents, despite their efforts to exclude fluid to either side of the clamps. Sam held the suction over the bowel, as some foul material would inevitably spill out. Greenish brown fluid carrying a few unrecognizable particles teemed out of the hole until a few unmistakable kernels of corn gushed just before the stone blocked the opening. Jim was reminded how small bowel contents, normally without smell, can become rather rank if allowed to stagnate for two days. He'd ask Amanda to lay off serving corn for a week or two. They placed sponges around the leaking small bowel, controlling spillage. With gentle pressure on the bowel, Jim popped the gallstone out through the hole. He picked it up with amazement and plunked it into a metal K-basin, producing a dull clang.

"Wow!" Rhani exclaimed.

"See, Sam," Jim said with a slight sneer, "general surgery is far more gratifying than boring cosmetic procedures."

"That was cool!" Sam agreed.

As Jim sewed the opening in the bowel with interrupted dissolving sutures, Albano asked, "Well what about the gallbladder, Jim? Shall we deal with it tonight?"

"I'm not sure we sh—"

“You’re right. It would be a very big incision if we extended this upward to reach the gallbladder. This lady’s probably sicker than she looks. Perhaps we should consider coming back another day to deal with her gallbladder and fistula then—when she’s in a little better shape for it.”

“Sounds good to me,” Jim said. He couldn’t wait to get home to tell Amanda all about his first case of gallstone ileus.

Chapter 20 ~ Complications

As Jim strolled from one patient room to the next, EBUs in tow, he could hardly contain his excitement about his chosen career in surgery. He'd had another great day in the operating room with Dr. Steinberg and was finishing up evening rounds, about to go home for supper, just after six o'clock. He hoped for a quiet evening and a rare chance to play with Emily.

It was now ten days since Mrs. Klumpar had had her gallstone ileus operation. Her recuperation was stupendous: she'd been discharged from hospital on the fourth post-operative day. Operations like Mrs. Klumpar's, like an adept drive on the fairway, could bolster Jim's enthusiasm to return to the hospital. He would relive the triumphant moments repeatedly in his mind for days. When Jim discharged her, he requested a follow-up appointment to see Dr. Albano in a month, at which time they'd discuss what to do about the underlying culprit, her gallbladder. Jim was hoping she'd get back to St. Joe's for more surgery before the end of March, when he'd switch over to the University Hospital for his final three months of residency. He wanted to be present to remove her gallbladder, which would likely still be fused to her duodenum, probably with a retained connection that would require an open surgical repair of the hole in her duodenum.

As Jim and his white-coated followers entered the final room on the surgical unit, he immediately recognized something was amiss. His frail, elderly patient, Mrs. Schoonraad, lay sideways across her bed, covered only by a sheet. At eighty-seven, she'd presented with a large mass in the centre of her left breast, which she'd likely ignored for months, if not over a year. This afternoon, Jim and Dr. Steinberg had taken her for a quick mastectomy to remove the offending breast, as the cancer had ulcerated through the skin and was beginning to smell. As she lived alone, no one had noticed her problem until her daughter, who lived in town and visited frequently, began to smell it. Despite trying to conceal it with bulkier clothing, Mrs. Schoonraad's private issue became a family matter, ultimately resulting in a visit to the operating room with Dr. Steinberg.

As they moved closer, Jim noticed bright red blotches of blood soaking through the sheet over her chest, her blank eyes fixed on the ceiling. Her pale, spindly limbs protruded from under the sheet in all directions. She mumbled incomprehensible sounds. As Jim pulled back the sheet, revealing the dressing to be completely saturated with blood, his fears were confirmed. She'd likely been bleeding since soon after surgery, perhaps a slow trickle from a vessel perforating through the pectoralis muscle, which should have been tied off rather than cauterized. He felt a wave of guilt as he thought back to the operation, then turned to his flock and ordered, "Someone get a nurse! This lady needs some help and is going to have to go back to the operating room!"

"I'll go," Sam chirped—too late, as Rhani was already bolting out the door toward the nursing station.

The remaining EBUs watched wide-eyed as Jim peeled the dressing back. She looked like she'd grown back her breast, only it was now twice the size of the other side. It was bulging like a football, but blood was seeping between the stitches on her chest wall. Jim pressed gently with his fingers onto the spongy swelling and then exclaimed, "There has to be close to two units of blood in here!" With his left hand, he palpated her wrist, eventually detecting a thready pulse. "Where's that nurse? This lady is in shock!"

Rhani ran back into the room with a nurse on her heels. Jim and two EBUs straightened Mrs. Schoonraad in the bed and then he shouted at the nurse, "What's going on here? Everyone at coffee? This lady's bleeding!"

"I'm sorry, Dr.—"

"There's no time for apologies. Just give her five hundred cc's of Ringer's Lactate right away and get me some vitals!"

As Jim spoke, the nurse was already turning up the IV pump. She then began repeatedly squeezing the bulb, inflating the blood pressure cuff on the patient's right arm. Jim was pacing back and forth, huffing to himself.

"Blood pressure is 85 over 50," the nurse stated. She paused while following her stopwatch, gently holding Mrs. Schoonraad's wrist. "And her heart rate is 120."

"See what I told you? She's in shock! Get a CBC, lytes and two units of blood for her now! I'm going to call Dr. Steinberg and get the O.R. ready." Jim stormed out the door, heading toward the nursing station with his followers tentatively walking behind.

In the operating room, they opened Mrs. Schoonraad's entire mastectomy wound, exposing a huge mound of clotted blood. With his fingers, Jim scooped it out, exposing the underlying pectoralis muscle. Using suction and surgical sponges, they cleaned out a few hundred cc's of liquid blood. Jim then dabbed numerous candidate vessels, searching for the offending bleeder, cauterizing and oversewing any vessel that could have possibly been responsible for the bleeding.

When Jim was running out of potential bleeding points, Steinberg stated, "You know, Jim, it's often a little unsatisfying. We usually don't find an actual bleeder. So we just do what you've been doing the last twenty minutes, put in some new drains and close. We'll put a pressure dressing on, keep her flat in bed overnight and she'll be fine."

Jim thought back to the mastectomy earlier that day. Mrs. Schoonraad was the second to last operation in a great list of operations with Dr. Steinberg. The mastectomy went well enough that Dr. Steinberg left the operating room immediately when the breast was detached and said, "I'm going to run away for a few minutes. Close her up quickly, Jimmy. I don't want our last case to be cancelled." In the midafternoon, if there did not appear to be enough time to complete the surgical list before the end of the nursing shift at 4:00, the last operation would be put on hold or possibly cancelled outright. Jim remembered rushing the final steps of Mrs. Schoonraad's operation. His fear of missing the chance to do the final case, a laparoscopic cholecystectomy, was compounded by knowing Dr. Steinberg would be dismayed if it had to be rescheduled for another day. The more Jim recalled his hurried state over Mrs. Schoonraad, all in the attempt to accommodate another patient and satisfy his own appetite for surgery, the more guilt he experienced.

Steinberg leaned over her open wound and said, "It's okay, Jimmy. We all get complications from time to time. As a resident, you probably don't see half of them because they come back to us in the office when you're not around or have moved on to another rotation. But here's one for you to experience. It's all part of being a surgeon. You've got to have a bit of a thick skin and learn to live with complications."

When they finished up Mrs. Schoonraad's second operation for the day, Jim sent Sam Cheung down to the Emergency Department to see someone with abdominal pain while Jim and Dr. Steinberg went to the family room to talk to Mrs. Schoonraad's daughter.

"Everything's all right," Dr. Steinberg said as he gently placed his hand on her shoulder. "She did have a big collection of blood, which we cleaned out. There's no more bleeding now. We had to give her a couple of units of blood, and I apologize for that, but she'll be fine."

"I know you did the best you could, doctors. I'm just thankful you were able to get her in so soon and get rid of this cancer."

Dr. Steinberg said good night while Jim nodded, and they both left the daughter to wait for her mother to emerge from the recovery room.

Tilting his head toward the surgeons' lounge, Dr. Steinberg said to Jim, "Let's grab a quick cup of coffee."

Jim was puzzled as Dr. Steinberg was normally in such a hurry to leave, especially in the evening.

As he poured coffee into the two Styrofoam cups, Jim wondered how many hours this pot had been sitting, awaiting its victims. With a brown plastic stir stick, he mixed a package of Coffee-mate into each cup and handed one to his mentor. They were both still wearing surgical greens. Jim noticed how fit Steinberg appeared, despite being somewhere in his midsixties. Jim sat down opposite Dr. Steinberg, who spoke first. "You know, Jimmy, surgery isn't easy. And it's not the surgery part—that bit actually isn't too bad. It's all the rest that can get to you—that is, if you let it."

"You mean like this post-op bleed?" Jim sipped his coffee, trying to hide the bitterness. He wondered where Steinberg was going with this.

"Yes, like this post-op bleed. But there's more than that. Bad things are always happening in surgery. And then sometimes everything seems good. You think you can do no wrong. And when that happens, you know you've got to worry. There's always something bad lurking around the corner. If it's not a complication, perhaps it's a horrible diagnosis you dread discussing with a patient. And for some reason, you feel awful about giving the news of terminal cancer, as if it was your own fault that they have it."

"Hmm," Jim said as he stared intently at Dr. Steinberg.

"Sometimes we get short with people and want to blame someone else as a means of deflecting the bad feelings." Jim immediately thought of the nurse he had chewed out when he discovered Mrs. Schoonraad lying on her bed, bleeding. "And when we make mistakes," Steinberg continued, "we often feel terrible. The funny thing is, those are the patients who are most likely to forgive us. And then sometimes, when we do everything we think is right, someone shits on us." Dr. Steinberg nodded, his eyes fixed on Jim's.

"You mean like Edna Doyle?" Jim's voiced cracked slightly.

"Well, now that you mention it, Jimmy, that might be a good example of where you tried to do what was right, and now it's coming back at you. I heard there's a complaint through the Medical Licensing Authority. But you shouldn't worry constantly. I know it's impossible not to fret a little, but it will play itself out. And in the end—no matter what the outcome—you'll be fine."

"But it's like they're saying I deliberately killed her! That son is all fired up and wants me to take the blame."

"Look, Jim. See it from his angle. His mother died suddenly after going home from the Emergency Department. Of course he wants someone to take the blame. But perhaps he actually just wants to find out what happened and why. Don't take it personally. He has no idea who you are. But I'm sure when all the facts come out, you'll be fine." Steinberg gulped the remainder of his coffee and tossed the cup into the garbage can beside him. "And I'm the first to acknowledge, we don't handle bad outcomes very well in medicine. Especially in surgery, from adverse events to outright errors, if blame is always lurking just beneath the surface, that doesn't foster a culture of quality improvement. And the problem is, we're good at finding someone to blame but not so good at understanding the ramifications."

"Sorry?" Jim was puzzled.

"We have no idea how many subsequent patients are affected when a doctor or nurse is blamed for something. How many more unnecessary tests does a fearful physician order? How many nurses—or doctors, for that matter—leave the profession entirely due to these pressures? We simply don't have the answers to these questions."

Jim cleared his throat and said, "I just can't seem to put it out of my mind."

"I know you can't, Jim. But I've said it before: we all get complaints. You can't change the system overnight, so you have to learn to adapt. Over time, if you aren't sued as a surgeon, I'll be very surprised. And often lawsuits arise from cases like Doyle—a bad outcome—even though you might have done everything properly. But you will no doubt stress over mistakes—or simply over instances where you might have done better—on a regular basis. It's part of the job. The key, though, is to try not to let it get to you. Keep doing your good work, enjoy the high points but never get too complacent. Remember, there's always something bad on the horizon, even if you don't see it yet. It's just the way it is for us surgeons."

Sam suddenly ran through the doorway, panting, his dark black hair loosely parted in the middle as if blown in a strong wind. His stethoscope dangled from his lab coat pocket. "Excuse me," he said, looking at Dr. Steinberg, then turned. "Jim, that girl you did a bowel resection on—the one with Crohn's disease, from last week—I think she's leaked!"

"What?" Jim could scarcely believe what he was hearing. "She couldn't! That case went perfectly," he complained, glancing at Steinberg.

"What'd I tell you, Jimmy?"

"But that's impossible," he continued, looking back at Sam. "Are you sure? How do you know?"

"She was doing okay until yesterday but then started getting abdominal pain. She's now got a fever and has free air on the X-ray."

"We just operated on her last week," Jim exclaimed, standing up and starting to pace. "She's supposed to have free air this soon after surgery!"

"No, she's got a ton of it, Jim. And she's really tender. Her white count is 27,000."

"Shit." Jim looked at the ceiling and then at Dr. Steinberg. "I wondered whether we should have hooked her up. She was on prednisone right up until surgery. Dr. O'Brien and I talked about doing a temporary ileostomy instead of joining her. But everything looked so good. And she really didn't want to get an ileostomy."

"Well, it sounds like she might get one now," Steinberg said with a slight smile. "I'm sorry, Jimmy, but that's exactly what I mean about surgery. And you just have to go with it. Fix the problem and move on. If it's O'Brien's case, you'd better call him up after you've seen the patient. If you can't get him then call Dr. Baker—he's on call. Sounds like this lady might need to be back here in the operating room tonight. And remember, don't feel bad. Just fix it. Have a good night, boys." Steinberg glanced at the digital wall clock, which said 7:59. "I'm done here for today!" He stood up and with three giant steps was out the door.

Jim took in a deep breath. "Thanks, Sam. I'd better phone Amanda and tell her I'll be late—again. I'll meet you in emerg in five minutes."

***

Sure enough, Melissa appeared nothing like the woman Jim had discharged a few days ago. He recalled the twenty-one-year-old, whose smile was infectious. She now lay in the emergency room bed, her expression blank and her shoulder-length blond hair hanging in clumps. "How are *you*?" he asked, knowing the answer was not good.

"Fine?" she said. Her lips were dry and cracked. Her eyes were slightly receded and she wore no makeup.

Jim scowled faintly and said, "I don't think you're fine, from what Sam has told me. When did you start feeling unwell?"

She raised her head off the stretcher and winced, stating, "I felt perfect for a day when I got home. Then I started getting bloated. The pain came on last night. Then chills this morning."

"Where's your pain?" Jim asked

"All over," she said, waving her right hand above her abdomen. "And in my neck and shoulder," she added, rubbing the right side of her neck with her left hand.

"I'm afraid that might be referred pain, coming from irritation under your diaphragm." Jim stood with his right hand held out, approaching her abdomen. Her eyes narrowed and both hands hovered over her tummy, blocking Jim's attempt to pull the sheet off her. "I need to press on your abdomen briefly, just to help us get to the bottom of this."

"Okay," Melissa said, resignation in her voice.

Jim peeled back the bed sheet and then lifted her blue hospital gown, exposing her abdomen. She was now bloated, without the flat tummy Jim had admired on the day of her hospital discharge. Her recent midline incision, a thin, intense pink line extending vertically from her belly button downwards, appeared to be healing well. As Jim gently pressed on her rounded abdomen, Melissa briefly shrieked and pulled his hand away with hers. "I'll be very quick. I just need to feel what's going on here." As Jim made a second attempt at palpating, he could see the pained expression on her face while feeling her muscles tense suddenly. It was the same wherever he pushed. "Melissa, I think your anastomosis has leaked. I'm sorry but you've got peritonitis. Your X-rays and your blood count are also pointing in the same direction. You're going to need surgery tonight."

"Not a bag!" Melissa wailed. "I don't want a bag!"

"If we give you an ileostomy, it will be temporary. Once you've had a chance to heal, we can join the bowel back up. But for now, your bowel movements will go into a bag."

"For a couple of weeks?"

"At least three months," Jim replied without emotion. He was thinking back to her operation last week and how he and Dr. O'Brien had discussed the possibility of giving her an ileostomy right then, to prevent a leak. He recalled how he'd stitched her bowel together and wondered whether stapling it would have been better. Jim felt deflated and exhausted. He wished they'd done an ileostomy last week—then he would not be dealing with her anguish or his own right now.

"Three months!" she protested. Her eyes glistening, a couple of tears appeared at the top of each cheek.

"We have no choice. I'm going to call Dr. O'Brien right now. We'll get the operating room ready and it'll be tonight." Jim slid out past the curtain silently with Sam following close behind.

Chapter 21 ~ Despondency

"Jim?"

He did an about-face, surprised that anyone was standing behind him in the operating room hallway. Her straight red hair was mostly tucked under her surgical cap. She wore a touch of makeup around her eyes. Freckles dotted her olive-brown face, perhaps enhanced by a recent vacation south or a tanning booth. A strategically placed safety pin tightened the V-neck of her surgical greens, obscuring her cleavage. Ten years older than Jim, she tantalized him, whether she intended it or not.

"Oh hi, Gina, how are you?"

"I'm okay," she said rather hesitantly. "I wonder if I could talk to you, perhaps after this case?"

"Oh, sure." Jim immediately thought of Edna Doyle, and how Gina had been there that night, part of the fruitless effort to save her. He wondered whether she wanted to speak to him about Edna's unfortunate death. After all, he had asked her about it soon after and she'd never responded. He'd hardly seen her throughout the fall, perhaps just by chance not operating when she was on shift.

"You guys are normally pretty quick with a case like this, right? I'm off at eleven. You and Dr. O'Brien should be done in plenty of time. I just wanted to discuss something with you briefly, if that's okay." She placed her hands on her hips, her curves readily discernible, despite the surgical greens.

"What did you want to talk about?"

"I'd rather not say here. I'm not sure I should mention it…I should scrub."

"No problem," he replied. As the words left his mouth, he was startled by the acute shift in his thinking, as Jim considered her motivation just might be more personal, perhaps even amorous. He felt flattered but then thought of Amanda, steadfastly minding the home front. "We should be finished before eleven. And by the way, it's Baker tonight. I tried to reach O'Brien but he's out for the evening. So it's Dr. Baker." Jim wondered whether feeling a little curious, even excited, about meeting Gina at the end of her shift was breaching a boundary he shouldn't cross.

"Oh, okay," Gina responded hastily, her eyes directed toward the floor. "I'd better go." She disappeared around the corner while Jim walked in the opposite direction toward the surgeons' lounge to find Dr. Baker.

As he sat down opposite Dr. Baker, Jim became submerged in despondency again over Melissa with her failed anastomosis and her upcoming surgery. Sam was sitting beside Dr. Baker while Darlene was close by, her nose buried in a thick, yellow surgical textbook.

"Why'd you hook her up anyway, Jim?" Dr. Baker sneered, scratching his belly under his green top while looking provokingly at Jim.

"We talked about a stoma," Jim glumly stated. "But everything looked so good."

"But she was on prednisone," he whined. "Anyone on steroids for Crohn's is at higher risk of a leak."

Darlene looked up from her book, appearing interested in the conversation.

"That was really the only factor that went against reattaching her bowel. Everything else was okay. She's young and healthy. Her bowel was otherwise in good shape, with no tension on the anastomosis. It really looked like a reasonable thing to do at the time."

"Well, she's here tonight with a leak, Jim. Perhaps you'll think twice next time."

Jim wondered why Dr. Baker was chastising him over this. Would Baker pose the same questions to Dr. O'Brien if he were sitting here? Like any typical tormenter, Baker selected his prey wisely and would never tangle with an equal over such a decision. Jim found it not only depressing but also humiliating to be badgered in front of his house staff.

"Dr. Baker," the voice blared over the intercom. "There's been a slight delay getting your patient up from emerg. She's in holding right now, so it shouldn't be too much longer."

"Fine!" Dr. Baker looked up at the ceiling as he responded. Then to Jim he added, "This is just great. Not only am I stuck here dealing with someone else's leak, but I have to sit around waiting to get into the O.R."

Baker drivelled on. Jim tuned out the whining, thinking about all of the places he'd rather be instead of at work. He pictured Amanda climbing into bed. He wished he could be there to join her, perhaps with Emily lying between them, which didn't seem to happen often enough.

"Dr. Baker, we're ready." The intercom startled Jim. He shifted in his chair, relieved to escape the lounge and get started with surgery.

***

The operating room was no better as the bellyaching continued. When they started the case, Baker was complaining about the delays: it was already ten o'clock—they should have started an hour ago if anyone had any competence. Gina handed a scalpel to Jim. He made a cut through the recent midline scar. As he reached the tough fascial layer, he pressed the knife on to the yet undissolved sutures from last week. As each stitch gave way Dr. Baker pulled embedded suture fragments from the abdominal wall with a hemostat clamp. When Jim cut through the final layer into Melissa's peritoneal cavity, an audible puff of air was released from her abdomen. The smell followed instantaneously. Jim sucked up about a litre of murky brownish fluid, confirming the diagnosis.

As they moved through each step of the surgery, Baker transitioned to another target. The government had no idea how to fund health care. Medical students weren't well enough prepared by the time they entered their clinical years. Gina passed a sponge to Jim, rolling her eyes at Jim when Baker made an outrageous remark about nurses. Otherwise, she kept her head down, appearing to concentrate deeply on the job of fixing Melissa's leaking bowel.

When they finally found the leak, Baker said, "No wonder she's so sore and has so much contamination. That hole's got to be a half inch wide! So we give her an ileostomy, Jim. No point in trying to repair that sucker. And you make sure this lady goes back under Dr. O'Brien. The last thing I need is to be pestered about her by the nurses over the next week."

"I'll make sure."

Jim spent the next ten minutes removing the leaking segment of bowel. He doubly tied off blood vessels to the section, cutting tissue in between his ties. Sam cut each suture that Jim held up, while Dr. Baker and Darlene looked on. After stapling off the segment of large bowel to be left in her abdomen, Jim attached two long, blue Prolene sutures to the end, to make it easier to find in three months when Melissa might have her ileostomy reversed. Jim brought out the end of small intestine through an opening he made in the right lower quadrant of her abdominal wall. After closing the midline incision, he'd suture the end of the small bowel to Melissa's skin, creating her ileostomy. Finally, as they washed out the abdominal cavity and removed the remaining sponges, Jim looked over his shoulder, only to see Philip at his side, Gina's replacement. The two nurses counted instruments, in preparation for the end of Gina's shift. Jim glanced at the wall clock, which displayed 10:58 in bright red digits. He then looked over at Gina, who subtly shrugged her shoulders. Her eyes glistened and then she looked away. With half an hour left to complete Melissa's surgery, Jim guessed he wouldn't be having his little chat with Gina this evening. *Perhaps for the better*, he thought.

"You finish up, Jim," Dr. Baker said, his tone somewhat more conciliatory. "I'll be on my pager if you need me." He stepped back as the circulating nurse untied his gown from behind. Removing his gown, he turned it inside out and stuffed it in the laundry hamper in the corner, then tugged off one glove, enfolded it in the other and tossed both into the garbage bin.

"Thanks, Dr. Baker," Jim replied, glad to be left to finish up without supervision. He added, "I'll make sure Dr. O'Brien takes over in the morning." Dr. Baker disappeared out the door into the hallway.

After closing the midline incision, Jim matured the ileostomy by meticulously placing sutures around the perimeter of the end of the small intestine and then into the surrounding skin. As Jim tied the sutures, the bowel end turned inside out and mushroomed above the skin, creating an ileostomy bud. Philip handed Jim an adhesive ring, which he placed on the abdominal wall encircling the ileostomy bud. Like snapping a lid on a Tupperware container, Jim then secured the bag.

By the time Jim's helpers had written the post-operative orders and he had dismissed them, it was 11:45. He scanned the hallways and then poked his nose into the nurses' lounge in case Gina had remained after all, but she was nowhere to be found. As Jim retreated to the locker room, his legs were burdened by fatigue from standing practically all day, several days in a row. Today had started out so well with Dr. Steinberg in the O.R., but then went from bad to worse with Mrs. Schoonraad's and Melissa's complications. He thought about his next day off, which was not for ten days, the first weekend in February. He had no interest in coming to work tomorrow, let alone for the next ten days.

Jim stepped off the elevator on the main floor and buttoned his winter coat, wondering whether his car would start in the cold tonight. *Wouldn't that be enough to finish off what has already turned out to be a crappy day?* As he headed toward the exit, Jim took a short detour to check his mail in the residents' lounge. He entered the narrow alcove and reached up to the familiar box, third one from the end, top row. He couldn't quite see into the slot, but with one sweep of his hand, he gathered the only envelope it contained. He held it in anguish as he read the return address. Johansen, Wang, Somers. Below the address line it stated, "PERSONAL AND CONFIDENTIAL" in boldface type. *Shit. Why did I have to retrieve mail at this hour anyway?* He stood for thirty seconds, debating whether to open it or leave it for the morning. He considered the possibilities and although no option was good, he decided to open the letter. His hands shaking, he turned over the envelope and peeled back a corner, inserting his finger. Using it like a letter opener, he carefully pulled his finger along, trying to open the envelope as quickly as possible without tearing the contents. Jim was pacing as he slid out the letter. He felt his knees buckle, then continued around the corner and plunked himself into an armchair in the lounge, looking around to confirm the room was empty. He unfolded the letter. Suddenly sweltering, he unbuttoned his coat and then blinked as he held the page in front of him. He first looked to the bottom of the page, where he confirmed the correspondence was from Dave Johansen.

"Dear Dr. Smythe:

Re: Edna Doyle – deceased"

Another dagger. I know she's deceased.

"Further to our conversation several weeks ago, it appears the complaint is proceeding on at least two levels. In addition to the Medical Licensing Authority complaint, the hospital is also launching its own formal investigation. In order to deal with this as effectively as possible, it is important that we meet in the near future. Please make arrangements through my staff to meet at my office as soon as practicable."

Jim closed his eyes and shuddered. He felt paralyzed. He didn't know whether to get up out of the chair or to remain sitting. He was exhausted but knew he wouldn't be able to sleep. He folded the letter and stuffed it into his coat pocket, carefully closing the zipper. After a couple of minutes of fitful deliberation, he decided to go home if his car started. If not, he'd sleep at the hospital. In that event, at least he wouldn't have to decide what to tell Amanda tonight.

As he put the key in the ignition and turned it, his car immediately came to life, despite the freezing cold. Jim sat, waiting for the car to warm up, wondering when he could arrange to see Dave Johansen. Twenty-four hours ago, he would have dreaded missing a few hours of surgery. Now, he couldn't care less about an absence from work, except for the fact that it was going to take some finesse to arrange the time off so no one knew the reason. He'd have to try to pick a day that Steinberg would be operating. Dr. Steinberg knew what was going on and would be supportive.

He put the car into gear and slowly drove home.

After quietly changing into shorts and a t-shirt, Jim climbed into their warm bed next to Amanda. From her breathing pattern, he surmised she was asleep. He lay on his side, facing her, taking comfort in the familiar smell. After a few minutes, he turned onto his back, waiting to fall asleep. He thought about tonight's surgery. He brooded about Edna Doyle. Next, he shifted onto his left side, facing away from Amanda.

"What?" she said quietly.

"You awake?"

"I am now," Amanda responded. "So?"

"So what?"

Amanda turned on her bedside lamp and squinted. She brushed her hair away from her eyes while she sat facing Jim, who turned onto his back again, and was staring at the ceiling. "Look, normally you're asleep within seconds. You've been tossing and fidgeting for the last five minutes with no sign of settling. What's going on?"

Jim could feel a searing pain originating somewhere between the back of his nose and his throat. His eyes started to water. "I had an awful day. Oh, it started out fine. I was with Steinberg all day. Then, when I phoned you? That was the first of two of my complications I had to take back to the O.R."

"Are they okay?"

"Oh they're fine. I'm not so good though. The second case, Baker was riding me the whole time, as if it was all my fault."

"But that's Baker. You know that's the way he is."

"I know. But he was worse than ever. I don't know what's eating at him these days. He even snapped at Gina a couple of times."

"Well, that's not your problem, Jim. You know he's like that. When he gives you the gears, make sure you consider the source."

Jim sat up and turned sideways in the bed to face Amanda. "It's just that... it wasn't like I didn't feel bad about it already. And then…" he said, his voice weakening.

"What?"

"I got a letter from Dave Johansen. The hospital is launching their own formal investigation into Edna Doyle."

"Oh, honey!"

"He wants me to meet him at his office." Jim stood up and paced at the foot of the bed. "Yesterday I loved surgery. And now I hate it! How can you love something so much one minute and then on the turn of a dime, despise it?"

Amanda climbed out of bed and approached Jim, who continued to tread back and forth at the end of the bed. When he reached her side she took him in her arms and said, "You really feel you hate surgery?"

"I do. I fucking hate it right now."

"You really are naïve, aren't you?"

"Huh?"

“You have no idea, do you?” Her expression was incredulous.

“What?”

“What’s the opposite of love?”

“Hate,” he quipped.

“Of course not,” Amanda said as she squeezed him tight to her chest. “What’s the opposite of love?” she repeated.

“What?”

“It’s so obvious, but you just don’t know, do you? The opposite of love is indifference. If you love something and hate it the next moment, there’s nothing wrong with that. That’s not as strange as you might think. There’s a lot of similarity between love and hate. But if you suddenly didn’t care—became totally indifferent toward surgery—that’s when I’d get worried. Now let’s get back to bed. You’ve got to get up in about four hours.” She led him by the hand around to his side of the bed.

Jim slid under the covers while Amanda walked back and climbed in on her side. As Jim wondered when he might fall asleep, he cuddled close to Amanda and said, “You know, I’ve never thought of it that way.”

***

In her pajamas, Amanda sat in the plush armchair of their apartment living room. She’d put Emily to bed only minutes before and took solace in the silence. Jim hadn’t been home before midnight once in the last week. She didn’t know how he could stay awake, let alone function as a chief surgical resident. Amanda hoped February would bring better days for Jim and his outlook on life. He seemed to find any excuse to spend endless hours at work. Amanda wondered whether this was his one and only way of taking his mind off the Doyle case and the developing complaint. She was surprised Jim couldn’t compartmentalize his life better—it seemed the only way to alleviate his stress was to throw himself into his work. What little time he was at home he’d spend planted in front of the television or the computer, tuning out his family. Any efforts she made to engage him were met with complete disinterest.

This morning, on the way out the door, Jim had told Amanda about operating on an abscessed appendix and a perforated ulcer last night with Dr. Steinberg. That would almost certainly mean Dr. Steinberg would be at home tonight. She’d been carrying around the piece of paper ever since their meeting, and now she pulled it from her purse and unfolded it, staring at the phone number. Amanda picked the telephone from the cradle and pressed Dr. Steinberg’s home number into the keys. Her sweaty hand clutched the telephone and pressed it to her ear.

Before it rang, she clicked the line dead with her thumb and gently placed the phone on the table beside her. Was she imagining this was a problem? Was she being unreasonable? Alarmist? She picked up the telephone again and hit redial, determined to speak to Dr. Steinberg, hoping he'd be home. She counted four rings.

"Hello?" Dr. Steinberg's voice was unmistakable.

Amanda drew in a deep breath. "Dr. Steinberg? It's Amanda Smythe calling."

"Mandy! Great to hear from you."

"Is it okay to call you at home? You said it would be all right."

"Of course it's fine! Did Jimmy tell you, we had some great cases the past couple of days!"

"Yes, he did mention it," she said.

"And I meant what I said."

"About what?"

"Jimmy—he really is one of the best residents that's come through here in a long time."

Amanda smiled slightly. "I'm glad to hear that, Dr. Steinberg. But remember the last time we talked, I said he didn't seem to be handling the stress so well?"

"I do. Yes. And I've been watching for signs of that at work, but haven't seen any problems."

"I'm just worried, he's taking this complaint so personally. There's going to be a hearing at the hospital soon—and frankly, I don't know if he can keep it together until then." Amanda paused. Hearing no response, she continued, "I know he seems invincible when he's at the hospital, but he's not. And I don't know what to do about it."

"Listen, Mandy. Jim's going to be just fine. But do you know what might be the problem?"

"No, what?" Amanda crossed her legs in the armchair and sat up straight.

"Jim likes certainty. And this whole complaint thing is anything but certain. And I'm not saying anyone else would find it any easier, but when Jimmy is being told, or worse accused, that he didn't provide the best care to someone who ended up dying, he has a problem with that. Some people can recognize that this constant cloud will blow over some day. They can reconcile two seemingly incompatible situations. Most good surgeons can be accused of making mistakes and will still continue to provide excellent care to their patients. And Jimmy's doing just that—he's top notch. But he doesn't handle ambiguity well, so he's throwing himself into his work to compensate. Which is all very well and good, unless it causes him to screw up. He may think this Doyle thing is the worst scenario he could imagine, but it's not. And the last thing he wants is another bad case on his hands, perhaps from an unwise decision because he's over-tired and stressed out."

"I never thought of that," Amanda replied. "I was more looking at it from my own personal perspective."

"Oh, there's that, too. I've seen more surgeons get div—I've seen surgeons get into trouble at home and I'd hate to see that for you and Jimmy, believe me."

"What can I do?"

"As I've said, Amanda, when this whole thing is behind him, it will be like a bad dream. Jimmy will be back to his old self, overnight. But in the meantime, I'll talk to him. I won't tell him you called, but I'll see if I can steer him in the right direction."

"I'd really appreciate that, Dr. Steinberg."

"We've got practice oral exams on Sunday. I'll make a point of speaking with him afterward. And call me again if you need to, will you?"

"I will. And thank you."

Chapter 22 ~ Taking Over

Head down, Jim walked into the empty classroom and took a seat in the front row. He'd come to work earlier than usual for a Sunday, to get rounds completed before the practice oral exam session. He slipped off his lab coat and placed it on the chair back, then scratched his chin and realized he'd forgotten to shave this morning. Normally practice orals were a high point of the week. The group of six chief residents was becoming polished, not only from a knowledge perspective, but also in organization and ability to articulate like an experienced surgeon. Although anything could happen on exam day in June, the effort was beginning to pay off. *Except for me*, Jim thought. Today was his turn again. In early January, Dr. O'Brien had demolished Jim to the point of utter humiliation. It seemed every time Jim picked a course of action, it was wrong. The more backpedalling he had to do, the more he second-guessed himself. Today was his day for redemption—except he was ailing with a cold. He was exhausted and didn't have a shred of enthusiasm for being here.

One by one, other chief residents entered the room and sat down. Candace Sparks selected the chair next to Jim at the front, while the other four took places in the row immediately behind. She was fidgeting with her black ponytail, slipping an elastic band around the end. With one toss, it came to rest on the back of her white lab coat. No one seemed to pay much attention to Jim. He wondered whether they all knew about his inescapable torment. Simon started up a conversation with the others in the row behind about a recent case of a pancreatic abscess. Normally such a topic would entice Jim into the discussion, however he continued to stare blankly at the white board at the front of the room, dreading his role on the hot seat during the next hour.

The door opened and Dr. Steinberg appeared, beaming. He hung his blazer on the hook behind the door and announced, "Good morning, ladies and gentlemen! Are you ready? You're over halfway through the year. Soon you should be gearing up for the written exams in May, which I assume you'll all pass. Then we can focus on the orals in June."

Jim felt a throbbing behind his eyes. He took a Kleenex from his pocket and blew his nose, then carefully folded it up and clenched it in his lap.

"So I think today is Jimmy's turn, is it not?"

"Yes," Jim replied with little enthusiasm.

"I haven't had much chance to interact with those of you who aren't at St. Joe's." His eyes fixed on Jim, he continued. "Would you mind if one of your colleagues did the exam today, Jimmy, and you take a rain check?"

"That would be fine with me," he said quietly, trying not to sound relieved.

"Well then, how about you, Candace? Would you mind?"

Candace flushed and looked around at the other residents. She adjusted her glasses and looked back at Dr. Steinberg. "No problem."

"Okay, Candace," Steinberg said, pacing back and forth across the front of the room. "Let's get started. A fifty-five-year-old man is referred to you with a lump in the thyroid gland. When you examine him, he has a two-centimetre mass just off the midline in the right side of his neck that moves with swallowing. You cannot palpate any associated enlarged lymph nodes. He has experienced some mild pressure in his throat. He has no symptoms of thyroid dysfunction and his thyroid hormone levels are normal. What tests are you going to do?"

"I'd do an ultrasound to get the exact size, see if it's solid or cystic—because if it's fluid, perhaps all he needs is to have it drained with a needle. The ultrasound would also identify smaller nodules, too tiny to feel. Either way, I'd stick a needle into the lump and send what I get to cytology, looking for thyroid cancer," she said with confidence. Jim was thankful he was listening and not being questioned.

"Okay." Dr. Steinberg. "There are no other nodules. The lump is solid. The fine needle aspirate shows a follicular lesion. What would you do next?"

"I'd discuss the possibility of removing the right thyroid lobe to take out the lump. Statistically, a follicular lesion is less likely to be a cancer, but it *could be*."

"What types of thyroid cancer are there? Can you classify them for me?" Steinberg sat down and crossed his legs while leaning back.

"Papillary, follicular, medullary, anaplastic and of course, lymphoma."

"Very good. Now describe to me how you would do a right hemithyroidectomy." Dr. Steinberg stroked his chin with thumb and forefinger and smiled.

Jim's head was pounding.

"I'd make a transverse incision across the lower neck, two finger-breadths above the sternal notch..."

Jim pulled a fresh Kleenex from his pocket, carefully folded it and placed it squarely across his nose. Blowing hard, he evacuated a substantial load from each nostril. He tried not to look into the Kleenex as Candace droned on about thyroid surgery. He could hear her talking about parathyroid glands and nerves she wanted to avoid damaging, but Jim's thoughts were swirling about a Thursday evening in September, when he could have been—in fact should have been—more forceful with Dr. Baker. If only he'd insisted they admit Mrs. Doyle to the surgical service, then Jim would not be suffering today over her demise. Whether or not she'd survived, at least the responsibility for her fate would have been shared with Dr. Baker. If only he could go back to that night and alter his actions. He felt culpable for the fact that he now cared more for his own outcome than that of Mrs. Doyle, but he pondered the unfairness if he was forced to bear the burden of her death, while Dr. Baker's reputation remained unscathed. Surely those at the Medical Licensing Authority would know that Jim's discussion on the phone with Dr. Baker should have resulted in some shared responsibility. Unless, of course, Baker minimized his involvement. If he decided to be critical of Jim, while distancing himself in the process, then the MLA might have no sympathy for Jim. Without the ability to upgrade beyond his educational license, he might find himself out of a job by the time July rolled around. Too late to be accepted into additional training, yet unable to land an independent position as a surgeon, Jim could find himself mired in a huge predicament.

His headache was accompanied by nausea. He gazed at a tile on the floor as he could feel his eyes crossing. Jim tried desperately to stay awake, but Candace's dissertation on implanting a damaged parathyroid gland into the sternomastoid muscle did not revitalize his waning concentration. His head nodded forward and then suddenly jerked upwards. He narrowly avoided falling forward out of his chair. Jim continued to look at the floor, but he was sure Dr. Steinberg was watching him. Candace continued, talking about radioactive iodine treatment in the setting of thyroid cancer.

As the examination progressed, Jim heard very little of what transpired. Steinberg guided Candace through a series of questions ranging from hemorrhoids to hernias to rectal cancer, and although Jim was vaguely aware of the discussion, he perceived little and in fact learned nothing. A total waste of his time, in his view. As Candace gushed on about everything she knew of surgery, Jim brooded over what he despised most about it.

"Well, that's it for today, folks. How do you think Candace did?" Dr. Steinberg was beaming as he took his blazer from the hook on the door.

Everyone nodded while providing accolades for Candace's performance. Even Jim mumbled some positive words. Although he hadn't heard much of what she'd said, he was certain she'd done well.

"I agree. Good job, Candace. If you perform like this on exam day, then you've got nothing to worry about. Keep it up." He fastened the middle button and then added, "See you next time, gang. Continue to work hard and enjoy your last few months. You'll never have a time in your life again when you do so much operating."

As the other residents filed out, Jim remained seated, motionless. Dr. Steinberg reached for the door and closed it. He sat down facing Jim and said, "I'm glad you didn't hightail it out of here, Jimmy. I was hoping to talk to you."

Sullen-faced, Jim looked up and wiped his nose. "I've got this awful cold. I'm sorry. I wasn't paying close attention today."

"Jimmy, how do you think you are doing?"

"To be honest, I was happy you passed me over today and had Candace do the exam."

"I know."

"I just didn't think I had it in me today."

"Yes, I know that. Why do you think I called upon Candace?"

"I thought you said—"

"Of course that's what I said. But I just didn't think today was your day." Steinberg sat up straight in his chair, honing his eyes in on Jim's.

"But last time, with Dr. O'Brien, I crashed and burned during the exam. I didn't want a repeat performance today." Jim looked down at the familiar tile on the floor.

"What? You kidding? Dr. O'Brien spoke to me after that one. He said you did great! Said it was the toughest practice exam he'd ever given. And every time he tried to trap you, somehow you'd gracefully navigate your way out of trouble. Are you sure we're talking about the same exam?"

"Well, he said I did okay. I thought he was being sarcastic."

"Whoa, Jimmy! Get some perspective here! I know you're stressed, but you're going to be fine."

Jim didn't want to burden Dr. Steinberg any more than necessary, but he had to say something.

"It's this complaint. It's taking over my life. I can't stop thinking about it. One lousy evening, and I'm being attacked over it."

"Jimmy! Relax for a minute! You do know that you can't change the past. You also should be aware that this will turn out fine."

"That's what you say. But I'm not really allowed to talk about it, according to Mr. Johansen. So I don't know how much I can tell you. But it's just...I'm being accused...It's like they're saying I show up to work intending to hurt people. It's not like that!"

"I know that. And don't *you* forget it."

"I'll never forget splenic artery aneurysm, ever, in my life."

"Of course you won't. In fact, for the next ten years, everyone who has an unexplained blip in heart rate or drop in blood pressure, you'll think splenic artery aneurysm. And of course that's ridiculous, but that's how it works. We make decisions based on our recent experience. You'll even put people through a bunch of useless tests because you can't put this case out of your mind. And it's even worse when fear of lawyers, complaints and lawsuits are part of it. But eventually, after a few years, this case will have receded in your memory sufficiently that you'll remember it, but won't put the diagnosis disproportionately high on your list. And guess what? You may never see one again! Or perhaps you'll come across one or two in your entire career. And d'you know what really seems unfair? The next one still has a 50 percent chance of dying even if you think of the diagnosis! So get used to it. This is all part of being a surgeon. You need to be comfortable with the fact that you will not always know the answers and even if you do, your patients won't always have a good outcome."

"I know that, and that's something I've heard since medical school. But try living with the concept. That's what's nearly impossible."

Steinberg looked incredulous. "What do you mean, Jimmy? I've been living with it for the past thirty-five years! You can learn the attitudes you need. I'm sure you know surgery is not just chopping out organs and putting things back together. There's more outside the operating room you have to learn than inside. But you knew that, Jim."

"Yes, you're right, Dr. Steinberg."

"Of course I'm right!" Steinberg reached for the door handle, turned it decisively and swung open the door.

Jim remained seated. "If I can just get past Mrs. Doyle..."

***

"Jim, it's Tabitha. I've got an unusual case down here in Emergency D." She was breathing hard and speaking quickly on the end of the phone.

Jim pressed the receiver to his ear as he leaned back in his chair in the residents' lounge. "Wait a minute," he said. "Is it the one with the sunflower seeds? I think I heard Dr. Wong going on about that case over an hour ago."

"That's the one. Anyway, I nearly cut my finger!" Her voice quivered as she spoke.

"Slow down. I need more detail. And are you okay?"

"I'm fine. But here's the deal..."

***

Jim sauntered through the cafeteria to grab a muffin on his way down to the Emergency Department. As much as he wanted to help Tabitha with her quandary, as a matter of principle he was in no hurry. On a Saturday morning, Tabitha could wait while Jim contemplated the therapeutic options. He paid the cashier and sat down, peeling the wrapper off the sides of his muffin. He took a bite while he pieced together Dr. Wong's earlier version and Tabitha's more personal, animated account of the events.

Mr. Zack Wharwood, a thirty-seven-year-old, unemployed roofer, loved his sunflower seeds. He couldn't pin down the exact time or reason that he began to eat them regularly, but he'd probably purchased a bag once a week for the past five years. He enjoyed their salty taste. He found he could eat them slowly, shells and all, which allowed him to nibble throughout the day. It seemed to help reduce his intake of junk food, which was important, since he'd dropped fifty pounds and was now carrying only two hundred pounds on his five foot ten inch frame. Sunflower seeds had never seemed to bother his system until the past week. The previous Saturday, however, he was drinking with some buddies and, over a bet, consumed an entire two-kilogram bag in one sitting. He thought nothing of it at the time, thanks to the several beers that rendered such statistics unimportant. Now, a week later, he couldn't remember his last bowel movement but it might have been Sunday or Monday. He had had no clear reason to seek medical attention during the week, but as the weekend approached, he experienced increasing discomfort in his lower abdomen and pelvic area. "If only I could have a good shit!" he said to his friends, the ones who'd made him five bucks richer for the Herculean feat of sunflower seed ingestion. But by Saturday, he was in constant pain in the lower abdomen and rectal area, so he quietly set off to St. Joe's Emergency Department to see whether anything could be done for his predicament.

Dr. Wong was one of two emergency room doctors on duty Saturday morning. She picked Zack's chart from the top of the pile. After a cursory assessment, she requested some initial tests. Dr. Wong ordered X-rays, which demonstrated a pattern she initially didn't recognize, resembling a gigantic blowfish lodged in the centre of Zack's pelvis. After discussing his history in more detail, she figured the fuzzy grey ball most likely represented a huge conglomerate of sunflower husks and stool, impacted in his lower rectum.

By the time Tabitha saw him, Zack had a very tender anus from all of the examinations and enemas that had occurred under Dr. Wong's direction. Had she known the extent of the situation, Dr. Wong might have referred Zack to the surgical service sooner, but who knew her efforts to clean him out from below would fail? When Tabitha saw Zack, it was a challenge to convince him to roll over, but she needed to examine his rectum before reporting her findings to Jim. She drew the curtain of Zack's cubicle closed, ensuring not even the smallest crack was open for passersby to see inside. Tabitha always went to great lengths to explain what she was doing when anxious patients were involved. She carefully squeezed an ample supply of lubricant on her gloved finger, as one would prepare a toothbrush with a healthy dose of Colgate. With Zack curled on his side, she lifted the sheet, exposing his buttocks. "Just pull your right cheek up a bit so I can see the opening," she said dispassionately. She'd done it a hundred times before, but this time Tabitha got it backwards. "I'm just going to check your finger with my rectum." Horrified, she quickly added, "Well, you know what I mean!"

Zack faced away from Tabitha, so he must have missed the deep shade of crimson that her face instantly assumed. Gently yet rapidly, she inserted her index finger through his anal canal to assess the extent of the impaction. "OW!" Zach yelled as she passed her finger through the sphincter.

"Sorry," she said. "This won't take much longer." Unexpectedly, she encountered a rigid ball with protuberant sunflower husks, resembling shards of glass. "OW!" she screamed.

As she quickly withdrew her finger, Zack hollered in return, "OW? OW? What's going on down there?"

Dodging the question, Tabitha excused herself and disappeared to a private area where she yanked off her gloves and threw them in the garbage. She then examined her sore finger, squeezing it with her other hand to see if she could express any blood. Fortunately, the injury was more startling than real. When she stopped hyperventilating, she picked up the phone and called Jim, whom she knew was in the residents' lounge.

***

When Jim arrived in the Emergency Department, Tabitha looked flustered. She was hurriedly stacking papers at the workstation, her hair drawn into a ponytail and tucked into her white lab coat, which was buttoned from top to bottom. Jim sat down in a chair next to her. She looked away as she spoke. "Jim, don't make me go back in there! I can't see him! I'm so embarrassed."

Jim chuckled as he observed her cheeks fluctuate in hue by the second. "Look, Tabitha. I'll make it easy on you. You don't have to see him."

She gazed directly into his eyes and whispered, "Thank you!"

"But perhaps we should discuss the treatment options in case you encounter a similar situation in the near future." Jim was smiling.

"Anything you say!"

"Why don't I put you out of your misery and tell you what I think, and then you can go?"

"Fine."

"The way I see it," Jim began, "is we have two basic questions. Number one, do we clean him out from above or below? And number two, do we do it here in the Emergency Department or in endoscopy under sedation with the help of a colonoscope? Or do we disimpact him manually with him asleep in the operating room?"

"Whatever you say, Jim, I'm okay with it."

"Without going into a lot of detail, I think we should try from above, in the Emergency Department. It's early yet. We can give him a couple of litres of Golytely to purge his bowel from above. And then we run. No one can get near his rectum without him being under heavy sedation. Yet Dr. Baker is on call today, so I'm not keen on admitting the patient to a surgical bed with a problem like this. I'll go see Zack and order the bowel prep to flush him out. Then we try to avoid the Emergency Department until after shift-change. To be honest, I don't think the nurses here will like our plan. But personally, I worry more about pushback from Dr. Baker than I do about the nurses here in emerg. We'll give this a few hours, and if it doesn't work, I guess I'll have to call Dr. Baker. But you can go."

"Thank you!" Tabitha bounced out of her chair and sprinted down the hall, disappearing around the corner.

Jim spent the next fifteen minutes assessing Zack and writing up the plan, which included a heavy dose of morphine when needed. Jim then sought out the most agreeable nurse in the department and quickly explained the situation. He deposited Zack's chart at the front desk and went upstairs.

It was six hours later when Jim got a page from an emergency nurse on the evening shift. She informed Jim that his plan had worked. After a brief warning from Zack that he was about to deliver, a hefty dose of intramuscular morphine quelled the episode to a mere five minutes of shrieking. The initial bowel movement, while crowning with all those sharp husks, must have been torture, but the problem was now solved. After several subsequent sloppy explosions, Zack was on his way. He was reportedly extremely appreciative and told the nurses he'd learned a valuable lesson about sunflower seeds.

Best of all for Jim, a phone call to Dr. Baker had been avoided.

Chapter 23 ~ The Hottest Technology

"That's right, Jim. The hospital has launched their own inquiry into the Doyle case." Johansen smacked his lips, looked up from his open folder and blinked through his thick glasses.

Jim was perched in the familiar leather chair, his hands resting aimlessly on the boardroom table as he awaited a further explanation from Johansen. Unable to endure the prolonged silence any longer, Jim responded, "That can't be good."

"It's not necessarily bad. It's just possible it could work to your advantage."

"How could that be?" Jim leaned forward, eager to hear something positive for a change.

"It seems that the hospital doesn't have a lot of experience with these things. They're caving to pressure from Edna Doyle's family without really knowing what they are doing."

"And that's good for us?" Jim watched as Mr. Johansen breathed heavily.

"The good news is the timing. They want to nip this in the bud, which can surely work to your advantage. It takes the heat off the Medical Licensing Authority and you never know, if you come out of this looking good, it might be just what you need to make the family and the MLA back off. If they get the sense that you did your best in difficult circumstances, there could be a change of heart on all sides."

Jim sighed and said, "I could live with that."

"On the other hand," Johansen added, his voice booming, "it is entirely possible the family might want to go the distance, no matter what the hospital concludes from their inquiry."

Jim's body was rigid and he remained silent.

"And the big issue for you, as I am sure you are aware, is your license. As we've already discussed, we are under some time constraints. Even if you pass your fellowship exams, you must obtain an upgraded license. So in my opinion, moving forward quickly is in your best interest."

"How quickly?" Jim asked.

"We have a date," Johansen continued. "It's Thursday, February 20th."

"Seriously? That's two weeks away! I don't know that I'll be ready!"

"Jim, there's nothing you have to do to be ready. *I'm the one* who has to be ready. You just show up, wear nice clothing—like today—and be polite. We'll go over some strategies for your testimony closer to the date. In the meantime, I'm still awaiting the expert opinions."

"They're not ready yet, and we're going to trial in two weeks?"

"It's not trial, Jim, for goodness' sake! It's just an inquiry!" He slipped off his glasses, placed them on the table and continued. "I know for a fact the family has an expert witness and I have been assured I will have a copy of the written opinion early next week. And our expert, I expected his report a month ago. But it is coming. Sent by courier today."

"What do the experts say? Do they support my position?"

"Well of course, the expert from the family's side is not exactly going to shower you with compliments, Jim. Otherwise they wouldn't be bringing this forward. As for our expert, I'm assuming he'll back you up. If not, I'll seek an extension—delay it until we have a chance to assess the situation further. I think the key to all of this is Herman Baker. If he supports your actions, in my opinion, they'd have a tough time bringing both of you down together." He pulled a roll of Lifesavers from his jacket pocket and added, "Candy?"

Jim shook his head silently and belatedly added, "No, thank you."

Johansen popped a Lifesaver in his mouth and began sucking briskly. His cheeks indented rhythmically, accentuating his bulging upper teeth.

Jim looked away, his optimism sinking yet again as he contemplated Herman Baker.

Johansen droned on about process, precedent and other legal issues, while Jim continued to ruminate upon the events of September 26th.

***

"I have to meet him again in ten days," Jim said, sitting next to Amanda on the couch. "Tuesday the 18th. Two days before the hearing."

Leaning against his chest, she said, "Hm. At least it won't interfere with our annual Valentine's Day dinner out."

"I'm not sure I can do it this year, sunshine." Jim could see the disappointment in Amanda's eyes and then added, "But I'll try. I'll see what I can do."

***

Like statues, Jim and Tabitha stood in front of the X-ray viewer in Emergency C, staring silently. Finally, Jim spoke. "I have no idea."

"It looks odd there, just below the diaphragm," Tabitha said, pointing with her index finger.

"I know," Jim replied. It just doesn't add up to me, unless she's got cancer of the lower esophagus. Which would be pretty unusual, not to mention unfortunate, in a forty-seven-year-old."

The patient was a married mother of two teenagers who had recently moved with her family across the country due to a promotion at her husband's company. Glenna Raveling explained she wasn't very happy about the transfer, but it meant more money and prestige for her husband, so she'd acquiesced. When Jim first entered the cubicle to review her with Tabitha, he saw she was a gaunt woman with stringy black hair. Her large glasses dominated the upper half of her face, while her cheeks were sunken and pale. The first thing that came to Jim's mind was cancer, likely advanced.

She was previously healthy, apart from some kind of antireflux surgery twelve years previously. Used to treat intractable heartburn from stomach acid migrating up the esophagus, the operation could be of great benefit to carefully selected individuals whose lower esophageal sphincter was no longer working as a functional barrier to reflux. When medication ceased being effective in treating the symptoms, surgery was sometimes a good option. Usually such an operation involved a fundoplication, or wrapping a small portion of upper stomach three hundred and sixty degrees around the lower esophagus. Once sutures were placed between the two bits of stomach where they met at the front, the lower esophagus was gently encased for a distance of a few inches. Normally, a sudden increase in pressure in the abdomen would cause heartburn from acid moving upwards. After a fundoplication, the wrap would prevent this from occurring. The end result was usually no more acid reflux, no more symptoms and a happy patient. Occasionally, the wrap could be too tight, resulting in difficulty swallowing, which would sometimes be remedied by a gentle stretch with a dilator advanced through the mouth sometime after surgery. More commonly, surgery resulted in only minor side effects—a satisfactory tradeoff if the heartburn was gone.

In Glenna Raveling's case, the operation had turned out to be somewhat disappointing. Her surgeon had promised her the latest in technology: a device that would ensure the barrier to reflux was effective while allowing a simpler operation and quicker recovery. Mrs. Raveling could not provide any more details except that her reflux was improved for only about a year and then it seemed to recur, although it was admittedly not as severe as before surgery. She carried on with medication but was too busy raising her boys to pursue the issue extensively, apart from a consultation with her surgeon two years after surgery. When her complaint seemed to fall on deaf ears, she let it go.

But there had been a definite change over the last six months, which she noticed just before the move. Swallowing became much more difficult, such that she had to wash down every meal with water. More recently, the symptoms became much more difficult for her to conceal, so she gradually transitioned to serving her family omelets and pasta because they were "easier". When she started vomiting after nearly every meal three weeks ago, her husband insisted she see a doctor, but as she had been unable to find a family physician since the move, she ultimately came to the Emergency Department.

Jim observed her faint upper midline scar on her emaciated abdomen. Although smaller than usual, the scar was not as subtle as those from laparoscopic surgery. The burgeoning field of laparoscopy was, however, increasingly being embraced by many surgeons who performed advanced operations, including antireflux surgery. Her abdomen was non-tender, her face expressionless as Jim pressed firmly.

"Is it cancer?" She spoke meekly as her husband looked on from a small chair in the corner of the cubicle.

"It could be," Jim replied. "But more importantly, it might not be." He shifted on his feet and then added, "We are going to review your X-rays and call Dr. Steinberg, the staff surgeon on call tonight. We'll come back with him and speak with you shortly."

***

Standing by the X-ray view box next to Tabitha, he said, "It's probably cancer. Dysphagia and weight loss is cancer of the esophagus until proven otherwise. Except I can't figure how her previous surgery might fit in."

***

"Put 'er up there, Jimmy!"

Jim slipped the films back onto the X-ray viewer. The three stood shoulder to shoulder, with Steinberg in the middle.

Steinberg took a step back, all the while studying the X-rays. "She's got an Angelchik!"

"A what?" Jim asked.

"An Angelchik!" Steinberg raised his right hand, his finger pointing in the air. "I haven't seen one of those little fellas for at least ten years! Last time I had to dig one out of the pelvis. It was wrapped around the left tube and ovary!"

"Come to think of it," Jim said, "I think I've heard the name."

"Of course, you have. They were big in the eighties, although they didn't catch on around here as much as in some places. An Angelchik is a silicone ring or donut. It opens like a dog collar and they used to attach it around the lower esophagus through the upper abdomen. It was supposed to be as good as a fundoplication for preventing reflux, without the hassle of doing a wrap. A good surgeon could pop one in and be done in thirty minutes, skin-to-skin!"

"So why'd they stop using them, then?" Tabitha asked.

"They seemed pretty good at first. But like with any new technology that sounds too good to be true, after a while they started having problems. The most common complication was migration. They were being found anywhere in the abdomen, after a few years. Then some were actually eroding into the lower esophagus or upper stomach. And some could even cause obstruction. That's most likely this lady's problem."

"That's good news for her," Tabitha said. "Better than cancer."

"You bet it is. So Jimmy, I think we should admit this lady and arrange a gastroscopy for tomorrow. Just to make sure there isn't a cancer lurking there. Or a benign stricture that we could dilate. But if it's the Angelchik up to no good, we should take her to the operating room, get rid of the damn thing and just do a proper fundoplication."

"Okay, we'll get that organized," Jim said, relieved the news might not be as bad as expected for Mrs. Raveling.

"This is a good learning experience for both of you. I've seen new technologies come and go over the years. They often don't turn out to be as good as expected in the beginning. And although it's hard to resist, you rarely regret holding back, just a little, to see how the newer techniques pan out. That's why I don't do laparoscopic inguinal hernias or appendectomies yet. I'm just not convinced they're any better. And the fancy new ways often come with huge costs attached, driven either by industry, patients or well-meaning but overenthusiastic surgeons. Don't get me wrong, I'm no Luddite. I do lap choles because I know they're better and are here to stay, but it never hurts to be careful."

The next day, Steinberg's predictions proved to be correct. Mrs. Raveling's gastroscopy showed nothing wrong on the inside of the esophagus, but there was impingement from the outside. Later, they took her to the operating room, where again Steinberg's hypothesis was shown to be flawless. The Angelchik had ruptured and twisted in such a way that it obstructed the esophagus. By the time Jim got it untangled, he had a difficult time picturing how it had contorted, but he was sure it was the problem.

They finished the operation with a fundoplication that went smoothly.

"You watch, Jimmy. She'll be home in three days and never look back."

***

Jim stood up in the dictation booth, having completed his description of an anterior resection for rectal cancer he'd just done with Dr. O'Brien. With a fifteen-minute break until their next case, Jim's mouth watered as he pictured a fresh cinnamon bun. Only available on Tuesday mornings, it was the one treat per week he allowed himself. He stopped by the familiar cart outside the O.R. lounge and nodded at the lady dressed in greens and an O.R. cap.

"Could I have a coffee with one cream and sugar?" he asked.

She smiled and replied, "Certainly Dr. Smythe. Cinnamon buns are fresh, too."

Jim surveyed the golden, fluffy buns, seeking one with the largest amount of brown sugar clumped around the edges. He carefully detached one, ensuring he maximized the quantity of solidified sugar that adhered to his pastry, then slipped a five-dollar bill from his pocket to the lady, who handed him his change and coffee.

"Thank you, Enid," he said over his shoulder as he headed into the lounge.

He walked through the doorway into the crowded room and was instantly engulfed in noise. Jim stood for a few seconds, listening. The group struck him as comical, jabbering loudly while dressed in greens and a variety of colourful caps. Three spirited conversations transpired simultaneously, filling the room with a verbal cacaphony. In the far corner to his left, the plastic surgeons and their house staff appeared to be discussing sports. One of them pointed to a hockey replay on the television. Hank was in their group, stuffing a cinnamon bun into his mouth. A second one was doomed to the same fate, cradled on a small paper plate in his lap. Orthopedic surgeons in the other corner argued with gynecologists about efficient use of operating room time. Nearest to Jim, his own general surgeons chatted cheerfully while a few of their residents and medical students struggled to listen intently. Dr. Maurice Steinberg, Dr. Ted O'Brien and Dr. Giuseppe Albano were all seated near the entrance to the room, each waiting for his own surgical case to be called. *Not a bad cohort of general surgeons*, Jim reflected. He walked between their two rows of chairs and sat down next to Steinberg, facing the other surgeons.

Jim placed his coffee on the small table to his left as he settled into the uncomfortable, vinyl hard-backed chair. He took a bite from his cinnamon bun and stared straight ahead, trying to shut out the multitude of discussions in the room.

"I don't remember him, Maurice," O'Brien said, as he leaned back in his chair.

"No, I'm sure you would," Steinberg replied. "He finished residency here about eight or nine years ago. He moved down east right after exams. What was his name…"

Snapping his fingers, Albano pointed across at Steinberg and blurted, "Bellow—Terry Bellow!"

"That's it," Steinberg exclaimed while O'Brien nodded in agreement. "Anyway, he's out in practice for five years and then for no obvious reason, he runs for mayor! And poof! He gets elected! All that training gone! No more surgery. Can you believe it?"

"Come to think of it, I'd heard about that," O'Brien added. Jim had heard the story too and he remembered being astounded that anyone would give up ten or fifteen years of education to become a mayor. Jim smiled and nodded.

"You think that's bad," O'Brien continued, "I did my exams with four other surgeons and guess what? I'm the only one actually still doing surgery. After only fifteen years. Four have quit!"

"Quit?" Albano asked, his eyebrows raised.

"Well, they haven't all stopped completely." He counted fingers on his left hand and said, "The first guy to drop out lasted only two years. He got sued and decided it wasn't for him. He's done all that training and now he only assists. Damn good assistant, I'm sure, but not like he needed to get through a whole residency and exams for that. And secondly—"

"Now hang on here, Ted," Steinberg jumped in. "Jimmy doesn't need to hear about these guys." Jim shifted in his seat, took another bite from his bun and washed it down with a slug of coffee, relieved that Steinberg was trying to redirect the conversation.

"Ah, Jim's a big boy. He can speak for himself," O'Brien said, nodding across at Jim. "And it's not like this is a big secret. Everyone seems to want an out these days. Especially the younger guys. All the night work…the lawsuits…I bet half the surgeons would quit if a well-paying but less stressful opportunity came along." O'Brien shifted in his seat and faced Steinberg. "Anyway, so the second guy…One day he just up and left to do hair transplants after only four years of general surgery. Can you believe it? They said the stress got to him, too. That was his reason for leaving."

"Oh my God," Albano said, shaking his head. "What a waste!"

"No, I'm serious, guys. Jimmy doesn't need to hear this!" Steinberg's voice was rising in volume and pitch. Jim could feel his heart pounding and his palms sweating. Other conversations in the room were trailing off.

"Ah, c'mon, Maurice! Ted's just about done," Albano said. "Besides, I'd like to hear what he has to say. It never hurts to get a dose of reality, does it, Jim?"

Breathing hard, Jim said meekly, "Sure."

Raising a third finger, O'Brien continued. "So the third guy lasted less than ten years. He got into trouble with the Medical Licensing Authority over who knows what. Next thing you know, he's done! And no one has heard from him since!" He threw his hands up in the air and shrugged his shoulders.

Steinberg stood up and started pacing.

"And the fourth one, he quit so he could just do colonoscopies. No surgery. Can you believe it? Until he committed—"

"Whoa, stop!" Steinberg yelled. The room went silent. Jim gazed at the floor. "You do colonoscopies, don't you Ted?"

"Yes. Of course I do. You know that." Dr. O'Brien's eyes darted back and forth.

Jim gripped the sides of his chair and squeezed until his fingers hurt.

Steinberg, towering over O'Brien, continued. "Then tell me, Ted, what's the definition of a colonoscope?" He glanced around the entire room, all of its occupants silent.

"Huh? I dunno."

"A colonoscope," Steinberg continued, "is a six-foot tube with an asshole at both ends! Ha! I love to tell that to some of my favourite patients just before I stick a tube up their butt!" Steinberg plunked down into his chair, slapping his knee, and emitted a roar of laughter that reanimated the hushed crowd, causing guffaws amongst the most timid of students. Even O'Brien grinned. Jim loosened his grip on his chair and let out a deep breath, thankful for the reprieve Steinberg had granted him from having to listen to O'Brien's rant about the fates of previous surgical trainees.

Chapter 24 ~ Tuesday, February 18, 1997

"After the experts are questioned, it will probably be a nurse's turn." Johansen squinted as the afternoon sun shone through cracks in the blinds.

Jim could hardly believe he was sitting in the familiar boardroom for the final time before the inquiry. In two short days, the process would be underway, totally beyond his control. There was still a chance this whole messy affair could be fixed—or he might find himself sinking in quicksand. Returning to the moment, he asked, almost as an afterthought, "Which nurse?"

"We have a couple of nurses but one in particular, a Marylou Breckenridge, could help us. But her charting does not establish the circumstances of Mrs. Doyle's departure from the Emergency Department clearly enough."

Jim thought about Marylou, an experienced ER nurse who could normally smell trouble if a sick patient went unnoticed by a physician. She'd saved Jim on one or two occasions when he was a junior resident. Obviously, she hadn't been overly concerned about Mrs. Doyle's condition, otherwise she would have said something at the time.

Johansen leaned back in his chair and, holding the folder at arm's length, he snorted. "It would be really helpful," he continued, "if someone—anyone—had either documented or could state that Mrs. Doyle left the hospital against your wishes. Presently, we are being told that in some vague way you gave her the impression that she could go home—that nothing was wrong."

"But I didn't tell her that!" Jim experienced the all too familiar burning in his throat and sweating, as if he were sitting in the middle of a desert. He loosened his tie slightly and undid the top button of his collar. He was growing weary of being told something that simply hadn't happened. "What about the husband—what does he say?"

"Mr. Doyle has always been a bit unclear about the circumstances. At first he said you told Mrs. Doyle to go home. Then, when asked to put his thoughts in writing, he said he went to get a muffin at the cafeteria. When he returned, his wife said she could go home. The problem is, if he was vague then, he's worse right now. At the time, he was in the early stages of Alzheimer's disease and apparently he's declining. Our best hope right now might be his written statement, which obviously contains second-hand information and doesn't identify you by name."

Jim recalled September 26th and tried to picture Mr. Doyle. All Jim could remember was that Mr. Doyle hadn't said a lot.

"The big challenge, in my mind," Johansen continued, "is going to be their expert witness. A Dr. Cannon. Heard of her?"

Jim shook his head.

"She comes across quite clearly in her written opinion about what she thought you should have done. She said you should have had Mrs. Doyle in the CAT scanner right after you saw her."

Jim shuddered at the thought of an unknown expert clearly expressing such a damning opinion about what action he should have taken. "She wasn't there! How does she know what I should or shouldn't have done?"

"How is not the pertinent question for me. That's her view. It's my job, with the help of our expert, to cast doubt on her opinion."

"What does our expert have to say?"

"He accepts your actions as reasonable. I think he sees it more from your perspective at the time, not in hindsight."

"And others? Is there anyone else we can call to support me?" Jim asked hopefully.

"There is another nurse," Johansen began. "I've been playing telephone tag with her the last few days." He pulled a pink slip of paper from the front folder at the top of his pile. He held it up and read the name. "A Ms. Gina Connelly. Know her?"

"Yes," Jim said, his voice descending in disappointment. "She's an O.R. nurse. By the time she was involved, Mrs. Doyle was pretty much dead. It was too late. Besides, I don't think Gina likes me. I don't think she'd go out of her way to help me."

"Well, that's it then. And of course, Dr. Baker and you will both be called upon to answer questions. Dr. Baker is a bit of a wildcard. I'm not sure I know exactly how to handle him. And remember, Jim, no matter what anyone says, don't get riled. You need to be calm and rational. State only facts you are certain about. And I know you've reviewed the medical record thoroughly, but go over it a few more times so you won't be caught out unexpectedly."

Jim's mind wandered as Mr. Johansen rambled on about questions that might arise. Jim could feel he was staring blankly, having to dig deep to ensure he wasn't nodding off.

If only Mrs. Doyle had attended one of the other hospitals in town, Jim would not be sitting here with his lawyer. He'd be closing in on final exams, unburdened and excited. He'd been tethered for so many years by surgical training that the end of June should mark an accomplishment and a release of unprecedented proportions. Instead, he might have nowhere to work and no place to do further training, all because of the unfortunate set of circumstances that embroiled him. His mind swirled as he imagined being jobless with a wife who had been planning to live near her parents in Lakefield. He couldn't fathom the prospect of such a quagmire.

"Is that clear?" Johansen's chirpy voice startled Jim.

"Yes," Jim lied. "But can you go over that one more time to be sure?"

"I want you to read over the document I gave you last time, about being a witness. You still have it don't you?"

"Yes."

"Much of what you say will make a larger impact if you present yourself as who you are—a good doctor who was faced with a complex problem that did not appear as such at the time."

"I've read it over a few times. But I'll definitely go over it again. I'm taking tomorrow night off so I'll have time to review everything and still be well rested."

"Good, Jim. Because that's exactly what I was going to suggest." Johansen stood up at attention and shot out his right hand. "Anything else between now and then, call me, day or night. You've got my numbers."

Standing to shake hands, Jim replied, "Yes I do." As he was clasped by Johansen's moist, limp palm, he couldn't help hoping that his lawyer had a better grip on his case than on his hand.

***

Jim left Mr. Johansen's office building just after 5:00 p.m. Deflated, he was in no mood to go home. The tone of the meeting had been depressing. The only way he could keep his mind off everything Johansen had said was to go straight back to the hospital. Tabitha was not happy that Jim decided to scrub in on a couple of gallbladders, pushing her into an assistant position. Jim knew that this late in the year, chief residents should not steal gallbladders from juniors, but he didn't care. He wasn't sure what to tell Amanda and he wanted to wait until

Emily was off to sleep before returning home, so why not spend a few hours doing cholecystectomies?

He glanced at the dashboard clock as he drove toward home. A quarter after nine should ensure Emily was asleep yet Amanda still up. After robbing Tabitha of two gallbladders, he'd then told her he wanted the rest of the evening off, and not to call him except under the most extreme of circumstances. She was to deal directly with the attending surgeon tonight. Again, she didn't look happy, but so what? He had more important issues on his mind. As he navigated the Civic around the last few corners before arriving at their apartment, Jim wondered how he was going to break the news to Amanda. He couldn't bear the isolation and despair any longer. The torment of the last few months had weighed on him long enough, and he knew he had to end it. He was certain he'd be relieved when he finally told her. He turned into his parking space a little too fast and then with his right hand firmly cranked up on the parking brake, jerking the car to an abrupt halt.

He climbed the stairs to their second-floor apartment and took a deep breath before inserting the key into the lock. As he let himself in, he heard Amanda turn off the tap in the kitchen. He closed the door loudly. "Where were you?" Amanda called out from the kitchen. "I thought you were going to be done a few hours ago."

Jim stood in the entryway as Amanda glided around the corner to face him.

"What's the matter, honey?"

He hadn't even opened his mouth and she already knew something was wrong.

"I think we'd better sit down," Jim said, leading her to the couch in the living room. When they were seated touching each other, he spoke first. "I can't do this anymore."

"Do what?" Amanda's face was inches from Jim's, her green eyes locked with his.

"If they find me guilty in this complaint, I'm quitting surgery. In fact, I'm not even sure I can go to the hearing. I'm seriously thinking I'm done!"

"You can't do that," Amanda scolded, her eyes squinting in disbelief.

"I can. I've thought about it. And I will. I just haven't decided whether it's worth giving the hearing a shot." Jim crossed his arms decisively in front of his chest.

"Now wait just a minute," Amanda stated emphatically. "First of all, you aren't going to lose, or as you put it, be found guilty. Secondly, I don't care what you want to do, you're just one half of this team, and you will not be quitting anytime soon. You're too good a surgeon to think about quitting!"

He took her left hand in his right and continued, "If this complaint isn't settled soon, I'm going to have trouble getting a license. They mightn't let me do my exams, for that matter. My sights have been set on June for so long, and if I have to wait another year to do the exams, I'll quit! If I can't do exams or get a license, then that means no moving to Lakefield. And I have no backup plan! It's too late to arrange any more training for next year. And I'm sure as hell not going to move to Lakefield as an unemployed surgeon just to live close to your parents. I couldn't stand the humiliation!"

"Okay then," Amanda said in a hushed tone, "what do you propose to do—that is, if you lose at the hearing?" Her nostrils flared as she breathed heavily.

"I'm not sure yet. But not surgery. I don't want any part of a career that treats me like a villain! And you know we've got enough. I can find something else to do and not worry about money right now."

"Oh, right," Amanda continued sarcastically. "Are you going to sit around all day and watch CNN? I know you've been enjoying that type of activity a lot lately when you're not at the hospital. And you might think it's a great hobby, but it's not a career. I'm happy for your recent interest in world events, but this hearing has absolutely disconnected you from your family. Your daughter needs you, but when you're not working, all you can do is watch TV or surf the Internet. Do you think quitting is going to change any of that? You need to do surgery so you can maintain passion about the rest of your life. Quitting will just give you more time on your hands to be apathetic. And if you want to know, it sucks to be me and Emily lately, when that's all you do at home. I'll wait for you to get your shit together. But no, you're not quitting surgery. I won't allow it!"

"*Won't allow it?*" Jim shrieked. Incredulous, he continued, "What do you mean, won't allow it? What say do *you* have in the matter? *I've been the one* busting my butt the last nine years to get this far!" He then gasped and blurted, "I'm sorry, that's not what I—"

"Don't you *dare* speak to me that way, James Alexander Smythe!" Red-faced, Amanda stood up, looking down on Jim as he wilted into the couch. "You may have worked hard, but I haven't exactly been on vacation the whole time since we got married. Sometimes I feel like a single mom, but you know what? Sometimes I think being a single mom would have more certainty about it. I work hard all the time, only to be teased now and then. Just when I think I'll have some time to spend with my husband, it gets snatched away at the last minute by a bowel obstruction. How d'you think that makes me feel? Huh?" Without awaiting a response, she continued, yelling, "You know what your problem is?

Do you? You can only see black or white! There's nothing in between! But I'll tell you! There is a third option. You can let the chips fall as they may, and if you lose, and I repeat, *IF*, then you find something to do for a year and get your exams next year. And if you want to quit then, I'll allow it. You can quit because you make a rational choice not to remain a surgeon, not just because you're cowering under a lousy system, just like you're cowering on that couch right now! And you know what else I'm going to tell you? I could have been a doctor! As a matter of fact, I scored higher—I—I showed aptitude for—for many professions! It just so happened that I wanted to raise a family. I know some women can do both these days. But I knew I wanted the option to stay home for a few years. I chose nursing because I like taking care of people and I also knew it would give me the most flexibility to stay home with children. And speaking of choices, why do you think I chose you? In part, because I wanted to be with someone who could do what I wasn't going to do. I loved seeing you rise in your chosen profession as a surgeon. Sometimes, I've even been a little jealous of you. But in the end, I'm happy for you. So you're not going to bail out on me now. You *will* go to that hearing on Thursday! And win or lose, unless they won't let you, you *will* be taking your oral exams in June! I can't believe you'd throw it all away just because you can only see black or white. Except you're not so good with black and white anymore, you're becoming blind! Blinded by despair! You're talking about doing something you'll regret, and I want no part of it! I'm so fucking angry right now—no—*fucking pissed at you, Jim!* You can try to sleep right here on this shitty little couch and think about it!" Panting, she paused and placed her hands firmly on her hips. "And remember what I told you, the opposite of love is indifference. It's not like I don't give a shit."

Jim looked up at Amanda. His eyes watered as she towered over him. He cocked his head as he heard a cry from Emily's room.

"Do you hear your daughter crying? Do you want to look after her for a change? If she needs me, I'll be in bed!" Amanda stomped down the hall, slamming the bedroom door behind her.

***

Jim rose groggily from the couch and limped to the bathroom. After their fight, he hadn't slept well, but Jim was grateful Amanda never held a grudge. He knew she was right and he'd apologize at the next opportunity.

It was still dark outside. His body ached from turning throughout the night. The sofa had provided little support for his sore back. He turned on the shower, waited and then stepped in. Although the hot water soothed his muscles, it did nothing to alleviate his overwhelming sense of lethargy. Both physically and emotionally, Jim felt like he had little energy left to keep going. In twenty-four hours, he would be getting dressed for the hearing, and within a day or two after that, it could all be over. Unless the hospital simply punted it to a higher level, such as the MLA. Jim didn't want to think about that. He wondered whether he could get some rest today, but even if he called in sick, he wouldn't be able to sleep. Wouldn't that be funny if he phoned the hospital, claiming to be ill? His staff surgeons would think he was dying or something. As far as Jim knew, they were totally oblivious to the torture that he was undergoing over the Doyle case. Except perhaps Steinberg and Baker, who Jim was certain were aware of the hearing. Jim had asked Steinberg to grant him Thursday and possibly Friday off work. When Jim tried to explain the reason, Steinberg simply waved his hand and said, "I don't have to know, Jimmy. Take all the time you need." Jim hadn't spoken to Baker about the hearing, and in fact had avoided him as much as possible for weeks.

Jim stepped out of the shower and dried himself off. He was determined to work the full day. It was easier to be at work than to remain at home. He'd go through the motions and then try to escape at suppertime, hoping to have a quiet night and possibly even get some sleep.

Most of the day was routine. Jim scrubbed on a few cases but when possible, he dashed away to the residents' lounge to sit in front of the television, although seeing nothing. He snatched a few opportunities to inform his staff surgeons and his team of EBUs that he'd be away the next couple of days, trying to imply he was going to be at a conference, without actually saying anything substantive.

At 5:45, when Jim was about to go home, Tabitha called him down to the Emergency Department about a man in his early thirties with a self-inflicted gunshot wound to the abdomen. She and Sam were downstairs, frantically trying to stabilize the patient, but they needed Jim's help immediately. Tabitha also told Jim they'd need to call the staff surgeon and get the O.R. ready right away.

Suicide attempts would occasionally be referred to the surgical service and they could often be challenging. Jim had heard the statistics about suicide. It was most common in the early hours of the morning, when loneliness, despair, drugs and alcohol are likely to be at their peak. Women, who were more likely to resort to pills, tried more often but succeeded less frequently than men. One did not need to be a surgeon or a statistician to realize gunshot wounds were serious. A suicide attempt could tragically become a permanent solution to a temporary problem. Therefore, quick action to reverse the physical damage was of utmost importance and urgency. Despite his aversion to facing today's heartrending situation, Jim could not walk away.

As he jogged toward Emergency A, Jim contemplated this young man in his thirties. According to Tabitha, he was brought in by ambulance from the financial district about an hour after he fired a solitary .22 slug into his upper abdomen. Apparently there were no eyewitnesses, however coworkers heard a shot and gained access to the man's office fairly promptly. The triage nurse in Emergency was told that financial ruin had precipitated the event. Whether this referred to monetary devastation of others or of the patient himself was not clear. Details would likely come forth eventually.

The resuscitation room was chaotic. The man was already intubated and a respiratory therapist ventilated his lungs with a hand-held bag. A nurse was starting a third line while two other IVs were rapidly infusing crystalloid solution to compensate for lost blood volume. Tabitha stood next to the patient's head with Sam at her side.

"Jim, we're going to give him unmatched blood," Tabitha exclaimed. "He was quite hypotensive on arrival. The entry site is in the right upper quadrant. We couldn't see an exit wound on his back. Not surprising, as the bullet showed up on the abdominal X-ray. He's very bloated. I think he's lost a lot of blood."

Jim glanced at the blood pressure reading of 105 over 56. "Pressure's not too bad now and a pulse rate of 115 isn't terrible. Looks like your IV fluids have helped." Jim looked at the patient, who appeared pale. There was straw-coloured urine trickling through tubing between his Foley catheter and a drainage bag. Jim pulled back the sheet, exposing the patient's abdomen. It was distended. A small patch of greyish-blue skin surrounding a tiny hole in the right upper quadrant marked the bullet's entrance site. Depending on the trajectory, the bullet could have hit any number of organs, from the heart or lungs to structures deep in the pelvis. Internal bleeding was a near certainty. Due to the position of the entrance wound, the liver was the organ most likely damaged. An exit wound would be helpful in determining trajectory, but if Tabitha had checked and not located one, they had to find out in the operating room.

"Sam, do admission orders. Tabitha, can you write up his history?"

"Sure," she replied.

"Have you called Albano? Called the O.R. yet?"

"No. I was just about to when you arrived."

"Portable chest X-ray?"

"Done," Tabitha said decisively. "It's on the viewer. Looks okay to me. The abdominal X-ray shows the bullet lodged in his mid-abdomen, to the right."

"Hemoglobin?"

"Not back yet. It should be done soon. Blood was drawn close to a half hour ago."

"Okay, let's get this guy ready for the O.R. now!" Jim was speaking loudly, feeling full of energy. "Someone put in a nasogastric tube. I want unmatched blood running before we move him to surgery. And give him two grams of cefazolin and a tetanus shot if he hasn't had one yet. I'll call the O.R. We'll start with a laparotomy but be prepared for a thoracotomy. He looks okay at the moment, but if he decompensates and arrests before transport, we crack his chest here in emerg."

Jim quickly ran out toward the workstation to phone the O.R. with the details. Then he stopped short and doubled back, realizing he didn't even know the man's name.

Chapter 25 ~ Penetrating Abdominal Trauma

Beads of sweat formed on Dr. Albano's forehead, just below his O.R. cap. With the abdomen now opened and fully packed with sponges, Jim took in a deep breath. He glanced over at the heart rate monitor: 105. Not bad.

"That was a lot of blood," Jim said calmly.

"You're telling me," Dr. Albano replied. Then to the anesthetic resident, "Can we take these sponges out anytime soon? Have you caught up yet?"

"I think we're okay," Dr. Gossett replied. "There's two litres in the suction and probably a couple more soaking the sponges in the abdomen. He had two units of unmatched blood before you opened and I'm just running in the second unit of crossmatched blood right now. So he's probably still behind, but he's young and seems to be holding his own. Where's the injury? Was it only the liver?"

"I don't think so," Jim replied. "It looks like the gun was aimed downward slightly. The bullet entered the top of the liver and exited it just beside the gallbladder. Those two openings don't seem to be bleeding now. I'm worried the vena cava could have been bleeding, a little further down."

One by one, Jim removed blood-soaked sponges, leaving a few untouched where he suspected the bleeding source to be located. With Tabitha, Sam and Darlene holding retractors, Jim felt slightly crowded, but he could see clearly where he needed to work. He firmly pressed his left hand onto a small remaining clump of sponges that seemed to be controlling bleeding at the back of the peritoneal cavity. With the colon retracted downward, it appeared the bullet had continued between the undersurface of the liver and the transverse mesocolon, where it had then entered the retroperitoneum. They were lucky to be operating on such a thin person, with minimal fat to obscure the operative field. Jim focused directly over top of where he would expect the inferior vena cava to be. A hole in the largest vessel draining venous blood upwards toward the heart could be catastrophic.

"Sam, hold this bit of small bowel off to the side. It looks like it keeps wanting to get in our way. Cover it with a moist sponge and we'll check for damage later."

Jim returned his attention to finding the bleeding source. "Sponge stick!" He held out his hand, awaiting the long ring forceps clamp with a four-by-four sponge folded in its jaws. *The perfect simple solution to apply localized pressure to an area of hemorrhage*, he thought as he looked up at Gina.

"Sponge stick!" Gina replied as she slapped the instrument into his right hand, skirting his gaze.

"I'm going to get rid of these sponges and apply pressure with the sponge stick, okay?"

"Sounds good, Jim," Dr. Albano replied. "Your exposure is excellent." He framed the area with his hands as Jim was about to remove the sponges. "Tabitha, you be ready with the suction."

"Ready."

"Okay, here we go," Jim said as he pulled all the sponges away with his left hand in one blood-soaked clump. With it, a clot pulled away and dark venous blood welled up instantly. "There it is!" Jim swiftly pressed the end of the sponge stick into the midpoint of the hemorrhage, arresting it immediately.

"You've got it!" Albano said with excitement in his voice.

Tabitha suctioned the blood away, allowing Jim to focus on a small area directly beneath the sponge stick, as soon as he was ready to remove it.

"Four-O vascular Prolene, please." Jim held out his right hand and took the needle driver without looking at Gina. Holding the sponge stick in his left hand, he rolled it away from the point of maximum pressure, one millimetre at a time, until some dark blood escaped from under the base. He placed a Prolene suture through the vein wall and then said to Albano, "Can you hold the sponge stick while I tie this suture?"

"Certainly."

Jim tied six knots on the Prolene suture and then held the two ends firmly upwards, placing a mild degree of tension at the bleeding site. "Now you roll away the sponge stick gradually while I run this stitch until the hole is sealed."

Albano rolled the end of the sponge stick miniscule amounts at a time while Jim placed three more bites in the suture line.

"That's it! I'm tying it here."

"That's fantastic, Jim. You're a genius!" Dr. Albano pulled away the sponge stick as Jim tied six knots at the other end of his suture line.

"Incredible," Jim said. "It looks like he grazed the side of the vena cava. I don't even think we need to worry about a hole in the back wall. It just caught the edge."

"Lucky he hit the vena cava beneath, and not directly behind the liver, Jim. In that case he'd be dead by now. A few inches higher and we'd have found it impossible to expose it in time to save him."

"I bet the bullet is lodged somewhere behind here in the paraspinal muscles. I don't think we need to go looking for it. We're done this part. Now we'll just have a look for other injuries and get out. I think he just might make it."

Jim suddenly felt relaxed, all tension in the room lifting. They spent the next half hour looking for other injuries and closing the abdomen. By the time they were done, the patient looked fit for extubation in a recovery room and likely would not need the Intensive Care Unit.

Jim sent Tabitha home, reassuring her that he and Sam and Darlene would take care of the paperwork.

The three sat together at the recovery room workstation, their patient in full view a few stretcher bays away. He lay peacefully, receiving oxygen by nasal prongs while his recovery room nurse attended closely at his side. As Jim shifted in his seat, he could feel the warm, sticky sensation of blood that had soaked through his greens onto his underwear and upper right thigh. Dr. Albano walked through the sliding door, dressed in a suit and tie with his briefcase in hand. "How's our patient?" he whispered.

"He's good," Jim replied. "Breathing on his own, but still fairly sedated."

"Can you make sure he's under constant observation overnight and ask psychiatry to see him in the morning?" He continued to speak quietly.

"For sure. We'll put it in the orders," looking to his right at Darlene. Then to Sam he added, "Can you check over her orders?"

"Sure," Sam replied.

"You did really well today, Jim. Thanks."

Jim smiled weakly and said, "Thank you, Dr. Albano."

"We'll see you tomorrow then."

"Actually not, I'm—"

"Right, I almost forgot. You're going to a conference. What's the topic?"

Jim blushed and started to sweat. "Uh…it's, uh…medico-legal issues."

"Ah, good. Well have fun and learn lots! You deserve a couple of days away from this place."

"I'll try," Jim said evenly.

"See you on the weekend then, Jim."

"Probably."

In the locker room, Jim told Sam he did not feel like working tonight, so if there were any problems, he could call Dr. Albano directly. Or perhaps Tabitha would be willing to help, if needed. Sam agreed and thanked Jim for including him in such an interesting case.

Exhausted, Jim climbed into his Civic and fastened his seatbelt. The euphoria of the surgery kept him awake, if not alert. His thoughts drifted to the young man who had shot himself over money problems. Leaving the hospital, a nurse had told Jim something about hundreds of people losing their retirement savings. Jim wasn't sure the problem was temporary, nor would there be any easy solution for his patient. A surgical triumph, but still a human disaster.

As he approached home, Jim's mood continued to wane, his own problems emerging at the forefront of his mind. The hearing for the next one or two days could break his spirit and he just wasn't sure he was up to the challenge.

Sitting at the kitchen table, Jim opened a can of beer and took a swig. He could hear Amanda coming down the hallway from Emily's room.

"I'm sorry about last night," he said. "You were right."

"It's okay. I know what you're going through." She leaned over, kissed him on the lips and sat down. Smiling, she whispered, "I think Emily is going to walk soon!"

"Everybody walks eventually," he replied sullenly.

Amanda's mouth turned down at the corners and she gripped her chair, digging her fingernails into its sides.

Before she had a chance to respond, Jim reached over and took one of her hands, adding quickly, "I'm sorry, sunshine. That's great. Really and truly wonderful. I'm just stressed to the max these days."

"Let's just get the hearing behind us and then things will be all right. Or if not, we'll make them right. I know it's still early, but you need your sleep for the hearing tomorrow. Finish your beer and get to bed."

As Jim's head sank into his pillow, he wondered whether he would fall asleep or be tormented by thoughts about tomorrow's hearing. His body ached. By the dim light of the clock, he could see his hand on Amanda but he could not feel her warmth. All he could sense was his pain and isolation. Fatigue prevailed. He slipped into a deep sleep.

***

Jim looked over at the clock's red digits: 3:54. He was grateful for the six hours of uninterrupted sleep he'd just had. More than he'd had in months. He could feel and hear the regular pulsations from his temporal arteries. Turning over, he listened to the rhythmic soft breathing next to him. Amanda was sound asleep. Jim turned over a few times during the next ten minutes. The hearing was fewer than five hours away. He realized he would not be falling asleep again, so he climbed out of bed.

Jim walked quietly to the kitchen and pushed the button on the coffee maker. Taking a pad of lined paper and a pen from the drawer, he sat down and stared at the pad, hearing the sporadic sounds of steam and drips as the coffee neared its completion. He sniffed the warm air of the kitchen and savoured the aroma, wondering what to write. The coffee maker gasped and then was silent. He stood up and opened the refrigerator door, picked up the cream carton and turned toward the table, then poured the cream, filling the bottom of his mug, which sat next to his pad of paper. He then picked up the heavy pot of coffee and poured, stirring it into the cream. Jim observed the change both underwent as they mixed in the cup. The turbulence settled and the coffee arrived at the final colour, the two components irreversibly altered by their interaction. The mixture continued to swirl while he added sugar and then replaced the coffee pot. Water briefly sizzled on the element. He sat down. In the silence, he took a sip, picked up his pen and started to write.

Dear Dr. Steinberg,

Of all the people I need to thank, you are at the top of my list. Not only have you taught me more about surgery than any other person, but I have learned more about life from you as well. I also credit you for directing Amanda and me together, or at least not standing in our way when we met in your operating room over six years ago.

I don't know what this hearing will bring, but I've dreaded it more than anything I can remember. If it turns out badly, I'm not sure what I will do, but clearly surgery and I will not have a future together, or at least not in the near term. I may need to get away for a while and I hope you will understand. I can no longer stand the criticism I am undergoing merely for being in the wrong place at the wrong time and for trying to help. If I choose to disappear temporarily, I hope that you will understand and respect my decision. As much as I trust you and those around me who are encouraging me, I cannot reconcile the other side that says I did not meet the standard of care. I entered medicine to help people and cannot understand why anyone could think my actions were anything but intended to help.

Thank you for everything.

Jim.

Unsure of what to do with the letter, he licked the envelope and sealed it. Then he wrote Dr. Steinberg's name and office address on the front and placed it on the table.

He looked up at the clock. Five minutes to five. Jim couldn't go back to sleep. But he had nothing left to do here, so he showered and then quietly dressed in his familiar suit and tie. He kissed Amanda and whispered, "I'll call you at the lunch break."

"Good luck," she replied, her voice slurred while half asleep.

He went into Emily's room and took a final peek at her before leaving the apartment and climbing into his Civic.

***

Down the hall from the main hospital boardroom, Jim sat in a small conference room, awaiting Mr. Johansen's arrival. He swept his tongue in front of his upper and then lower teeth, trying to moisten the inside of his mouth. He then swallowed what little saliva he could, which felt more like dust.

Jim heard a light rap at the door before it opened tentatively. Mr. Johansen slid through the partially opened door and then closed it gently behind him. He smiled, proudly displaying his two top front teeth. He looked different, Jim thought. Mr. Johansen's normally rumpled hair was in perfect position. His glasses were different—broader arms, with a white strip along the top. He wore an orange and yellow paisley bowtie. "Good morning, Jim," he beamed, sitting down in the chair opposite Jim.

"Hi." Jim could barely get the word out of his parched mouth.

"Relax, Jim. I have a good feeling about today. I think it will go well. And I've gathered a few more details about the process this morning." He set his briefcase on the table and continued smiling.

"Why? Why do you think it will go well?"

"It all comes down to what people have to say."

That's a cryptic answer, Jim thought.

"Just remember," Johansen continued, "to relax, state only what you know, and say it with confidence."

"Will I be talking this morning?" Jim could feel a searing in his chest.

"Quite possibly, but more likely this afternoon. From what I understand, lawyers from both sides will have the opportunity to question the two expert witnesses first. As I've mentioned before, the hospital is a little inexperienced with this type of process. But due to the persistence of the family and the gravity of this situation, they're proceeding with this quasi-hearing as quickly as they can. I think they want to get to the bottom of this soon, even if it is in a bit of an ad hoc manner. Everything is going out of order, since Dr. Cannon, their expert witness, has to catch a flight home at one o'clock. They're allowing the Doyle family lawyer to examine witnesses. The hospital has its own lawyer present, ready to intervene. A retired judge, a Mr. Justice Ripley, will be presiding over the events. As I told you Tuesday, this will likely be wrapped up by Friday at the latest, and with any luck it will be done today. The findings of this hearing will likely give some guidance to the MLA as to whether further action on their part is necessary. And of course, nothing today precludes the possibility of a lawsuit, which could go on for a long time. But we need to approach this one step at a time. Understood?"

Jim's thoughts were snagged on the possibility of a lawsuit, even though he knew Johansen was advising him to think otherwise. "Okay," he replied as his palms continued to sweat.

"Well, I'd say it's just about time," Johansen said, looking at his wristwatch.

A sharp pain penetrated his chest as Jim contemplated the prospect of heading down the hall into the hearing. Feeling like a lamb being led to slaughter, Jim reluctantly stood up and followed his lawyer on the short trip to the boardroom down the hall.

Chapter 26 ~ Hearing Difficulties

Jim had never previously set foot in the second-floor hospital boardroom, which seemed to be reserved for administrative meetings. For resident academic sessions, they would always meet in the much larger auditorium down in the basement. In contrast, this room was bright, with tall windows. About the size of Mr. Johansen's boardroom, a long central table stretched the length of the room. Surrounding chairs, although high backed, were smaller, upholstered with dark teal fabric and less opulent than those at the law firm. About half of the chairs had an occupant, many unrecognizable to Jim. He settled into his seat close to the entrance, in relative security sitting next to Mr. Johansen. The one missing familiar face was that of Dr. Herman Baker.

A pudgy man in a dark striped suit, wearing a hospital photo I.D. badge, stood surveying the room. His ruddy complexion and receding hairline probably added a few years to his appearance, but Jim pegged him to be about fifty-five. "Good morning, ladies and gentlemen. I am Harold Grifton and I thank you all for attending today."

As if I had a choice, Jim thought.

"I am administrative head of the patient care division of the affiliated hospitals of the university. Although I spend some time at St. Joe's, I divide my time equally among the three other teaching hospitals in the city. Before introductions, let me state outright that although this process will take the general format of a hearing, it is more a proceeding to establish facts, and in this case the circumstances surrounding the death of Mrs. Edna Doyle. No useful information is off limits. Our aim is to improve patient care and not necessarily attribute blame."

You leave blame to the other organizations, but you're essentially providing the groundwork for them.

Mr. Grifton held a paper close to his face and proceeded to introduce those at the table, starting next to him, working his way down toward Jim on the opposite side. As Jim gazed to his left, trying to place the individuals, Grifton's voice oscillated at the edge of Jim's consciousness. The retired judge, Mr. Ripley, nodded at Grifton's introduction and then scratched his bald head while smiling at all who sat around the table. Next was Marylou Breckenridge, whose attention Jim attempted to attract by raising his eyebrows. Without acknowledging Jim, she merely gave a subtle wave of her hand to the entire room while staring straight ahead. The hospital lawyer looked like he was possibly the youngest in the room. He fidgeted with a laptop computer, only briefly looking up from the screen when his name was called.

"And next is Ms. Estrada," Grifton droned on, "counsel to Dr. Herman Baker. I'm told Dr. Baker will be here after lunch, or before if we need him earlier, is that correct?"

Ms. Estrada nodded.

Jim could feel his body twitch at the thought of Baker, which was only augmented by the fact that he was going to have a lawyer present, a possibility Jim hadn't even considered.

Directly across from Jim sat Dr. Cannon, expert on behalf of the patient and her family.

"And returning to this end of the table, going down the other side, we have Mr. Kensington Briggs, counsel for the Doyle family." Mr. Briggs scratched his goatee. With his jet black hair and young features, Jim thought he couldn't be much over forty.

Mr. Grifton continued. "Gavin Doyle, son of Mrs. Doyle. And I understand your father is not well enough to attend today's session, is that correct?"

"Yes, that's true," Gavin Doyle said barely audibly, eyes fixed upon his fingernails. Next to Gavin was a tall, big-boned woman in a business suit, her gender confirmed by shoulder-length, brown, curly hair and large hooped earrings. She furiously took notes, consistent with Mr. Grifton's explanation of her role as the record keeper. Next to another two empty chairs sat Dr. Fredrick Chui, expert retained by Mr. Johansen. Jim leaned forward and turning his head leftward, scrutinizing the expert witness who he hoped was going to vigorously defend his position. Dr. Chui was slim and clean-shaven and wore gold wire-framed glasses. He nodded around the table, avoiding eye contact with Jim.

"So without further delay," Mr. Grifton continued, "we will begin by questioning our two expert witnesses. I assume everyone in the room has had the opportunity to review their reports. Questions will be directed at clarifying, supporting or refuting their opinions, rather than simply reiterating them. After

Mr. Briggs and Mr. Johansen have had the opportunity to question both experts, we will hear from Marylou Breckenridge, emergency room nurse. And if time permits today, Drs. Baker and Smythe have been kind enough to agree to answer questions this afternoon. I would ask that those responding to questions please sit at this end of the table." He gestured to the empty chair next to him with his hand, "while legal counsel can please take the seat opposite me. Although this is not a court of law, we will have an informal swearing in, if you will, prior to each witness being questioned. So I would now call upon Dr. Cannon to please take the seat at this end. Mr. Briggs, perhaps you could be seated here."

Mr. Ripley and the recorder huddled around Dr. Cannon, taking her oath while Jim's mind wandered. He eyed Dr. Cannon with a degree of skepticism. He didn't know who he hated more, Mr. Briggs or Dr. Cannon. Jim examined Dr. Cannon's features: her grey hair in a bun, the grey plastic reading glasses perched on her pointy nose. She appeared to be reading from a folder of papers. She refused to make eye contact with Jim. *What the hell could she know about bleeding, on a practical level?* To Jim she looked more like a grandmother than a trauma surgeon. He was relieved that at this point he could watch and listen rather than be the subject of interrogation, as he would no doubt be experiencing later.

Mr. Briggs turned his chair to the left, facing Dr. Cannon and revealing his back to Jim. "Dr. Cannon, could you state your qualifications for the record?"

"I have been a general surgeon for the past thirty-five years and I have a practice at a major university centre, participating in direct patient contact, teaching and research." *This seems more about regurgitating a rehearsed speech than meaningful interaction*, Jim thought.

"I have your curriculum vitae, Dr. Cannon, which outlines your qualifications, including 225 published articles in peer-reviewed journals."

She shifted in her chair, becoming two inches taller as her lips pursed, the closest she'd come to smiling so far. "Yes, that's correct," Dr. Cannon stated, looking around the room briefly at each participant.

"You qualified in general surgery after a four-year residency finishing in 1961, followed by a year of extra training at Cornell on surgical diseases of the spleen and portal hypertension, among other areas?"

"Yes."

"Can I conclude from your background that you are well qualified as an expert in general surgery for the purposes of giving testimony in this case?"

"Yes, that would be a fair statement."

"Thank you, Dr. Cannon. Let me begin by referring to your expert written opinion on this case. What material did you review in forming this opinion?"

"I reviewed the entire medical record from September 25th to 27th, including the post-mortem report, which of course was completed in October."

"Of course. Now, Dr. Cannon, I would like to take the participants in this hearing through some of the facts that helped you form your opinion. Edna Doyle presented to the Emergency Department on September 26th. Can you tell me something about her condition at that time?"

"She had two days of abdominal pain. Although her vital signs were stable, there were some evident features characteristic of internal bleeding. Her hemoglobin was significantly reduced at 102. The red cell indices did not indicate this was a chronic blood loss; rather, it was acute."

"Was there anything else in the record that indicated the possibility of internal bleeding?" Jim shifted in his chair, bristling at what might come next in this scripted conversation.

"Yes. In the nursing notes, it clearly states that the patient had felt faint and dizzy on the day of presentation." A waft of guilt overcame Jim as Dr. Cannon continued her assault. "In this scenario—abdominal pain, feeling faint and a low hemoglobin—it is my opinion that this is internal bleeding until proven otherwise."

"How do you know the low hemoglobin wasn't due to a chronic condition, such as iron deficiency?"

"If you look at the blood count more closely, you will note that the MCV—*mean corpuscular volume*, or size of the red blood cells—is normal."

"Yes?"

"Although not 100 percent true, normal sized red blood cells, as in Mrs. Doyle's case, would be more compatible with an acute blood loss rather than a chronic condition, such as anemia from low iron."

"Thank you, Dr. Cannon. Now what would you or any reasonable surgeon or surgical resident do in a case of suspected internal bleeding? Would you send the patient home?" Jim felt like a Band-aid had just been torn off an open wound, painfully exposing it for the world to see.

"Objection!" Mr. Johansen's voice cracked with the first and only word he had managed to blurt out this morning. He continued, "My client, Dr. Smythe, did not discharge this patient. The question is not only irrelevant to this case, it is giving a false impression of what actually occurred."

"Mr. Briggs, please retract or rephrase your question," Mr. Ripley said.

"Yes, of course. Dr. Cannon, what would you, or any reasonable physician do in a case of suspected internal bleeding?"

"It would be appropriate to admit the patient, find out where the bleeding is occurring and take measures to stop it."

"And in this case, where do you think the bleeding would be coming from, based on what was known at the time?"

"We know she'd had an ultrasound the previous day that essentially excluded an aneurysm of a large vessel such as the aorta. This leaves us with more subtle causes of internal bleeding, such as bleeding from a smaller vessel, or from the gastrointestinal tract. In cases of gastrointestinal bleeding, usually the blood comes out one end or the other such—"

"Do you mean vomiting blood or bloody diarrhea?"

"Yes, it will manifest itself in one way or another. And even if bleeding is coming from high up, say from an ulcer, if not through vomiting, it will make its way out as melena—black, tarry, bloody bowel movements—in relatively short order. Within hours."

"So if you are thinking internal bleeding but there are no manifestations of gastrointestinal bleeding, what would you conclude?"

"This woman was suffering from a rare cause of internal bleeding until proven otherwise. And splenic artery aneurysm is top of the list." Jim felt a warm wave of nausea overcome him and found it difficult to sit quietly without interjecting.

"So if you were concerned about rare causes of internal bleeding, are there any tests that might have been ordered that evening?"

"There were three investigations that might reasonably have been requested by Dr. Smythe that evening. A repeat ultrasound of the abdomen may have been helpful. Although no aneurysm showed up the previous day—just sludge in the gallbladder—an ultrasound on Thursday evening surely would have shown free fluid, which in this case would be blood until proven otherwise. And of course, if Dr. Smythe chose not to repeat the ultrasound, a CAT scan most certainly would have shown not only free fluid but possibly active bleeding and might have demonstrated the splenic artery aneurysm itself."

"Thank you, Dr. Cannon. And you said there was a third test Dr. Smythe might have performed?"

"Yes, an angiogram. This would have been a definitive means of diagnosing a splenic artery aneurysm as well as a means of treating it."

"Can you explain?"

"A radiologist can inject dye through a catheter inserted into a major blood vessel in the groin. The X-ray image can outline such subtle abnormalities as a splenic artery aneurysm, and in addition, a radiologist with skilled hands can release coils that float to the problematic area—the aneurysm—plugging it and therefore stopping the bleeding without surgery. Such a procedure could have been lifesaving in this case, had it been performed."

"But not one of these tests was done, was it Dr. Cannon?" Mr. Briggs looked up from his papers and then scanned the room, his eyes finally honing in on Jim.

"No. That is correct. No tests were done."

"Can you reiterate for us what you said earlier, Dr. Cannon, that this lady had signs and symptoms of internal bleeding?"

"Yes, that's correct."

"And in such a case? What would you suspect?"

"In the absence of overt visible causes of bleeding, if I were to suspect internal bleeding, I would focus on subtle or rare causes. In this case, since we know from the previous day's ultrasound that there was no abdominal aortic aneurysm, such bleeding should have been attributed to rare causes, such as splenic artery aneurysm."

"And in fact, that was what the autopsy confirmed—fatal blood loss from a ruptured splenic artery aneurysm, correct?"

"Yes, that's correct."

"No further questions." Mr. Briggs sat down abruptly and shot a glance at Mr. Johansen, then at Jim.

Mr. Johansen stood up, took a deep breath and straightened his bowtie. Facing the judge, he queried, "May I begin?" Mr. Ripley nodded while Johansen took his seat at the far end of the table, kitty-corner to Dr. Cannon. Johansen stared intently at her.

"Dr. Cannon," he began, "would you consider yourself an expert witness in general surgery?"

"Yes," she answered, her voice somewhat hesitating.

"And I understand you have done quite a bit of research in the areas of splenic artery aneurysms, spleens and portal hypertension, is that correct?"

"I've done my share," she said more confidently.

"I note here one of your research papers, entitled, "Burst Pressures of Splenic Artery Aneurysms". I understand that was a seminal article—excuse me, *the* seminal article—about ruptured splenic artery aneurysms. Is that correct?"

"Well, yes, some would consider it a defining paper on our understanding of when and why splenic artery aneurysms rupture."

"Tell me, Dr. Cannon, how common are splenic artery aneurysms?"

"They are not common."

"How prevalent are they?"

"It's possible that one in a thousand people have a splenic artery aneurysm. But the vast majority of those are not clinically significant. Perhaps 1 percent of those demonstrate some degree of clinical significance."

"So is it fair to say that during a surgical career, one might see only a handful of such cases? Or even less?"

"Yes, that's possible."

"Is it also fair to say that you possibly know more about splenic artery aneurysms than any surgeon—*any person*—in the country?"

"Oh, well, maybe. But, no, I wouldn't go quite as far as saying that," she stammered.

"I suppose with research, teaching and clinical practice, you probably think about spleens or splenic artery aneurysms perhaps every working day of your life?"

"Perhaps fleetingly, I suppose."

"And it's probably not an outrageous statement that you might think about splenic artery aneurysms even while you're on holidays—if only fleetingly, to use your word?"

"I really must query the relevance of these questions," Mr. Briggs interjected.

"I am trying to establish Dr. Cannon's credibility as an expert witness. I hope you will allow me this latitude, as her expertise is critical to interpretation of this case."

"Go on," Mr. Ripley said with a subtle wave of his hand.

Mr. Johansen nodded and continued. "Do you think of splenic aneurysms when you are on holidays?"

"Occasionally."

"On every holiday?"

"Yes, probably."

"Dr. Cannon, when was the last time you did a hemorrhoidectomy?"

"Pardon?" she said, her shoulders square as she moved backwards, increasing her distance from Mr. Johansen.

"Hemorrhoids. When was the last time you took out someone's hemorrhoids?"

"Oh my goodness," she stated, her eyebrows elevated. "I suppose it was twenty-five years ago. I have a very specialized elective practice."

"How about a hernia repair? When was the last time you fixed someone's hernia?"

"Excuse, me," Mr. Briggs interrupted. "Again, I am wondering where counsel is taking us with this. Is this really relevant?"

"Mr. Briggs," Johansen squawked, "with all due respect, I am trying to understand what kind of an expert we are dealing with in Dr. Cannon." Johansen fixed his eyes squarely on Dr. Cannon for a half second longer, then glared at Mr. Ripley. Jim had never heard Johansen raise his voice like this before.

Mr. Ripley turned to Mr. Briggs and then calmly stated, "It is Mr. Johansen's prerogative to pursue this line of questioning."

"Thank you," Mr. Johansen stated emphatically. "Now, when is the last time you did a hernia repair?"

"Twenty-five years ago."

"And what about on call, when was the last time you took emergency call at your hospital?"

"Five years ago. In recognition of years of service, our institution allows us at age sixty to go off the call schedule and focus on our elective practice, along with teaching and research."

"And when did you perform your most recent appendectomy? And I don't mean the chief resident doing one on your behalf while you are in the surgeons' lounge, but when did *you* actually last remove an appendix?"

"I'm sure I've done an appendectomy within the last fifteen years."

"That would be about when Dr. Smythe was halfway through high school. That's a long time ago, isn't it?"

"Yes."

"I suppose you haven't done any appendix operations laparoscopically then, have you?"

"No, I haven't."

"Now Dr. Cannon, should I go through the entire list of elective operations you do, or is it safe to assume you haven't performed many of them for ten to twenty-five years? Or perhaps before you answer that, maybe you could tell me what operations you *have done* in the last twenty-five years."

"I have a small elective practice that's relevant to my research. I primarily do splenectomies for non-urgent splenic artery aneurysms, for splenic vein thrombosis and for occasional malignancy."

Mr. Johansen gazed wide-eyed at Dr. Cannon. Standing up from his chair, his face tightened and flushed. *Breathe, c'mon, breathe*, Jim pleaded as he watched Mr. Johansen become more red-faced by the second. As Dr. Cannon started shifting in her seat, her eyes darting sporadically around the table, Mr.

Johansen let out a gasp of air, blurting, "Tell me then, Dr. Cannon, how many operations *do you do*—" His voice cracked and he took in a deep breath, "—in a month?"

"I do one day of elective surgery most months, so perhaps two or three operations a month."

"And how many splenic artery aneurysms do you remove in a year?"

"Probably one—every year or two."

"And when was the last time you operated on someone with a *ruptured* splenic artery aneurysm, with bleeding, as an emergency?"

"Probably at least ten years ago."

"And did the patient survive?"

"I don't recall."

"Dr. Cannon, tell me, what is the percent mortality of people treated for splenic artery aneurysm when the operation is done as an emergency—meaning a ruptured splenic artery aneurysm?"

"It's probably about 50 percent mortality."

"And why is that?"

"Probably delay in diagnosis."

"Dr. Cannon, you said in this case that abdominal pain with low hemoglobin is internal bleeding until proven otherwise and splenic artery aneurysm would be at the top of the list."

"Yes."

"Is that the top of the list for a general surgeon or senior general surgery resident, or the top of *your* list? With the benefit of hindsight, I might add."

She shifted in her chair, her face tightening. "Anyone's list," Dr. Cannon said meekly.

"I beg your pardon. I didn't hear that."

"Anyone's list," she stated more emphatically.

"And given what we've talked about today, when was the last time you performed an emergency operation—of any kind?"

"I told you, I haven't done emergency call for five years."

"Dr. Cannon, you are representing yourself as an expert in general surgery, is that correct?"

"Yes."

"But really, it seems to me that you *were* an expert in general surgery, but you are now an authority on spleens and splenic artery aneurysms. You can't really be both at the same time, can you?"

"I am now more an expert on diseases of the spleen and splenic artery aneurysms, but with my background in general surgery, I feel qualified to comment on both domains."

"Dr. Cannon, when was the last time you personally—and I don't mean your resident, I mean you—when was the last time you managed someone in hypovolemic shock, bleeding from *any* cause, in the Emergency Department?"

"Probably fifteen years ago."

"Thank you, Dr. Cannon. I have no further questions."

A brief silence fell upon the room until Mr. Johansen stood bolt upright from his chair and stumbled around behind it. He swiftly walked behind occupants on his side of the table and seated himself beside Jim.

"Well, I think we should take a short break to stretch our legs," Mr. Grifton announced. "Can we resume, shall we say, back here at ten o'clock?"

Jim followed Mr. Johansen quickly out of the boardroom, into the hallway. He could hardly contain his excitement as he strode down the hall behind Mr. Johansen, whose short steps had double the frequency of Jim's. They reached the small conference room where they had met earlier this morning. Johansen opened the door, shuffled into the room and sat down. He plunked down his briefcase while Jim seated himself across the table.

"I can't believe it," Johansen broke the silence.

"What?" Jim asked pensively.

"That Dr. Cannon. Her opinion is based on hindsight. It wouldn't have surprised me if she'd suggested a fourth test you should have ordered."

"Another test I missed?" Jim's heart sank.

"Yes. I'm surprised that with all that hindsight, she didn't suggest you order an autopsy the minute you met Mrs. Doyle." Johansen didn't crack a smile.

"Oh," Jim replied with relief. "But really, your questions to Dr. Cannon were good. I almost enjoyed that," Jim exclaimed.

"Whoa, Jim!" Johansen said quickly. "Not so fast. That whole session means nothing—nothing at all."

"What?" Jim's brow, initially elevated, gradually furrowed as he studied Mr. Johansen's features. "What do you mean, *nothing at all*?"

Mr. Johansen was stone-faced. "I don't mean to deflate your balloon, Jim, but what you saw there was an attempt to shed doubt upon this expert, who is most troubling to you and your position in this case. Yes, we made some progress, but we are still stuck with the fact that you saw a lady with internal bleeding and now she's dead. There's a significant mountain of facts, anxiety and fiction you need to overcome before you are totally off the hook. And if Baker holds firm, giving you no support whatsoever, then it could mean trouble. Baker is probably more important than we realize."

Jim slumped in his chair.

"But cheer up. It's not over yet. And remember, I hate to lose."

"Okay," Jim muttered.

"And with Baker, I have a plan if I need it, but it would be much simpler for all concerned if he just supports you—says you're a good resident, that he trusted your judgment. If you told him over the phone this lady didn't look like she needed any urgent tests, then he was satisfied. That would be the best scenario."

"I wouldn't count on that," Jim replied sullenly.

Chapter 27 ~ Experts Divided

The quiet murmur of voices speaking in hushed tones settled as Mr. Grifton closed the door and took his seat. Dr. Chui, the expert retained by Mr. Johansen, was already sitting in the witness chair at the end of the table. Mr. Briggs was seated in close proximity, separated from the witness only by the corner of the table.

Jim's mind wandered again as the swearing in took place. He wondered whether Dr. Chui was going to be as steadfastly supportive of Jim as Dr. Cannon was critical. He'd never met Dr. Chui prior to the hearing, but Jim knew him vaguely by reputation and had heard good things.

Mr. Briggs cleared his throat and when the room was silent, he began. "Dr. Chui, we've all read your curriculum vitae and your written opinion. I understand you have been in the practice of general surgery for about five years now?"

"That's correct," Dr. Chui said with a slight accent.

"I'd like to start from the operating room on September 26th and work backwards. Dr. Chui, is it fair to say that by the time Mrs. Doyle was in the operating room, she had little chance of survival?"

"Yes. I think by the time she was taken to the operating room, her chances were slim."

"Would you say the probability of saving her at that time was close to zero?"

"Not zero. But yes, very low. After a cardiac arrest from internal bleeding, it's very unlikely anything will reverse the course of events successfully. But that doesn't mean it was wrong to take her to the surgery. I think the decision was entirely appropriate."

"I understand. Do you think that the only chance Mrs. Doyle had that night was if the internal bleeding had been diagnosed and treated before she arrested?"

"Yes. Splenic artery aneurysm is often fatal because the diagnosis is not made soon enough."

"Would sending Mrs. Doyle home have been a contributing factor in her demise?"

"Mr. Ripley," Johansen interrupted, "I would ask counsel to rephrase the question, as we have not established that Mrs. Doyle was in fact *sent* home, and if she wasn't then the question is irrelevant."

"I apologize," Mr. Briggs said, holding his right hand in the air while he continued to stare intently at Dr. Chui. "Do you think if Mrs. Doyle had remained at the hospital and had testing done, that her condition might have been diagnosed before going to the operating room, instead of when it was too late?"

"I think I would be speculating..." Dr. Chui folded his arms in front of his chest.

"Okay. Perhaps we'll take a different tack. In your written opinion, you suggest that you would not have expected Dr. Smythe to order imaging that evening, such as a CAT scan or angiogram."

Jim could feel his cheeks warming. He glanced down at his hands under the table.

"Yes, that's correct," Dr. Chui replied.

"And why is that? Would not a CAT scan or an angiogram have been an excellent test to diagnose Mrs. Doyle's condition in a timely manner?"

"Yes, they might have been. But you are basing your question on knowing the diagnosis already." Dr. Chui folded his hands on the table in front of him, awaiting the next question.

"Let's put it another way. Dr. Cannon has said that Dr. Smythe had three possible tests—three to choose from, yet he didn't order any tests. Can you justify that lack of attention on Dr. Smythe's part?"

"Objection, Mr. Ripley." Mr. Johansen was wringing his hands.

"Mr. Briggs..." Mr. Ripley raised his eyebrows. "Would you be so kind as to rephrase your question for us please?"

"Yes, sir." Mr. Briggs turned back to Dr. Chui and asked, "Why would an attentive surgeon or resident *not* order a CAT scan or angiogram in Mrs. Doyle's circumstances?"

"First of all," Dr. Chui began, "an angiogram would only be requested if there was a high index of suspicion for a vascular problem. It is a technically challenging and time-consuming test that looks for very specific problems. You simply wouldn't order it unless you were drawn in that direction by another test—such as a CAT scan, for example."

"Then why not a CAT scan?"

"I was going to answer that," Dr. Chui responded firmly. "CAT scans take time and are not always easy to arrange at nighttime. They—"

"How long does a CAT scan take?"

"They can take a half hour or more, but they're not so easy to organize at night due to staffing and other factors. We just can't be ordering scans on everyone who comes into Emergency at night with abdominal pain. They can only be done selectively."

"Do you think a half hour might have been worth it, in Mrs. Doyle's case, if it might have saved her life?"

Dr. Chui stroked his chin and looked thoughtfully first at Mr. Briggs and then at Mr. Ripley. "Every night, many people come in to Emergency with abdominal pain. You simply wouldn't scan everyone. And there was no convincing evidence at the time in Mrs. Doyle's case to suggest a CAT scan was warranted. With all due respect, Mr. Briggs, you are suggesting a scan would have been a good idea because you know what it would have found. But we don't know the result when we order a test. I'm sure if Dr. Smythe had known the diagnosis, he would have considered further tests or treatment. But at the time, there were few clinical signs to suggest the gravity of Mrs. Doyle's situation."

Mr. Briggs paused and then shuffled papers in front of him. "Dr. Chui, given Mrs. Doyle's vital signs and low hemoglobin, do you not think Dr. Smythe should have at least done a repeat ultrasound?"

"No, I don't."

"Thank you. I have no further questions." He then turned to the far end of the table and said, "Mr. Johansen?"

Mr. Johansen calmly assumed the inquisitor position, nodded politely to the judge and began his oral examination of the doctor.

"Dr. Chui, I take it from your written opinion and recent discussion with Mr. Briggs that you think saving Mrs. Doyle with an angiogram or rescuing her later in the operating room were both highly unlikely?"

"That's correct."

"So really, the only way she might have been saved is if her clinical condition had led to prompt investigations that evening?"

"Yes. And in my opinion, it is doubtful that anything could have saved her that night."

"Yes, of course. So the crux of the matter is whether a senior surgical resident could have been expected to identify Mrs. Doyle's condition as serious enough to investigate further on the evening of September 26th. Is that correct?"

"Yes."

"In your opinion, did the symptoms, vital signs and blood test results warrant additional investigations that night?"

"No."

"No?"

"No. Her symptoms were mild and non-specific. Her abdominal pain and tenderness were both vague and of uncertain significance. Her vitals and hemoglobin were all borderline abnormal. At the time, the constellation of information available did not warrant further investigations, despite the fact that now in hindsight we know otherwise."

"One more question. Do you think it was reasonable of Dr. Smythe to hold on to the patient and request his staff surgeon on call, Dr. Baker, to assess Mrs. Doyle before any further decisions were made?"

"Yes, I think that was reasonable."

"Thank you Dr. Chui."

***

Amanda sat at the kitchen table, hardly able to contain her excitement. She put the video camera down on the table, safely out of reach of the baby. Emily was restrained in her highchair, giggling while gorging on lunch. As she swallowed, much of her food stuck to her cheeks or dropped onto the tray in front of her.

"Do you want to see the video again? Do you?" Amanda tried not to speak in a high voice reserved for small children, but it was not easy, especially given her level of excitement. She positioned the camera in front of Emily and pressed the button. Emily became silent, the sounds replaced by similar squawking on the camera. "See, there you are, walking across the living room. Oops! Emily fell down!"

Emily squealed and clapped her hands together, flinging food onto the floor.

"Your first day walking! Daddy will be very proud of you!" Amanda's jubilation waned slightly as she thought of Jim and his hearing at the hospital. Amanda was determined to wait patiently for the outcome rather than dwell on the hearing and be plagued with anxiety all day. There was really nothing she could do anyway and she needed to take pleasure in Emily's first steps, even if Jim was not there to share in the joy. All morning, Emily had walked throughout their apartment, stumbling and laughing all the while. Amanda had taken a short break to phone her parents with the news and couldn't wait to tell Jim. She stood up and reached for a cassette tape from the drawer. Peeling off the cellophane, she smiled while preparing to load a fresh tape into the video camera.

The phone rang.

Amanda bypassed the wall phone and picked up the cordless handset around the corner in the living room. Peeking her head back into the kitchen doorway, she eyed Emily in her highchair and placed the receiver to her ear. "Hello?" Amanda said tentatively.

"Sunshine, it's me." The monotone voice was unmistakable.

"Sweetheart, how are you?" She then mouthed, "It's Daddy," to Emily.

"Not good," Jim replied.

"What do you mean? How's everything going? You're not done yet, are you?"

"No. Just taking a lunch break. But I have to win this today and I'm not winning."

"What's happening?" Amanda leaned up against the doorway between the living room and the kitchen.

"It's close. The experts seem to be divided on whether I did the right things that night."

"So, that's okay, isn't it? If they can't agree, then clearly you didn't do anything that was obviously wrong."

"In the end, it might be okay. But it has to be settled soon." Jim sounded dejected.

"Just be calm, Jim. Wait and see. Don't make conclusions on your own." Amanda tried to achieve a balance of sounding both hopeful and rational.

"It's just…I'm not sure I can go back in there. I don't know if I can stand up to questioning by the other side. I can't stand being accused—"

"Jim, you'll be fine. You—"

"And the other thing," Jim continued, "it may be all over before I get a chance to defend myself."

"What do you mean?"

"This afternoon there's the ER nurse, Marylou, and Dr. Baker. The two people who could hurt me the most. If they criticize my actions that night, then I'm toast!"

"They wouldn't do that. Just wait to hear what they have to say!"

"Oh ya? When I asked Mr. Johansen if I'd be having to answer questions later this afternoon, and what to say, you know what he said?"

"No, what?"

"He said, 'That may not be necessary.'"

"So?"

"So, it may be all over by then. They may find me guilty and not even give me a chance!"

"Jim! He couldn't have meant that. He probably was saying it might end up being tomorrow morning or something. Are you sure he didn't say it mightn't be necessary this afternoon?"

"I'm sure. And I just don't know if I can go back in there and face those people."

"Listen here. You go back in. And whatever happens, I'll be here for you when you are done. Promise me? Go back in and do your best."

Neither spoke for several seconds.

"I promise. I gotta go."

"You okay?"

"Yes. I just gotta go. I have to drop off a note at Dr. Steinberg's office. And I'm doing my damnedest to make sure nobody sees me here at the hospital. They all think I'm away at a conference."

"Okay, Jim. Good luck. And I love you. See you after."

"Love you too. Bye." The phone line clicked dead.

Amanda placed the telephone back in the cradle and sat down on the living room couch. She'd not heard Jim sound so bleak before. He couldn't be thinking rationally. It couldn't be all that bad. She sniffed and wiped a tear from her right cheek with her sleeve. Without the opportunity to tell Jim about Emily, Amanda felt empty. It was such a good day, except for this hearing. She wondered what she could do but could think of no options. She hated the lack of control. It was totally out of her hands—she simply had to wait. At least they should go out for dinner. That's what married couples do, she reminded herself. They'd go out and celebrate Emily's first steps. After spending an hour together as a family, she and Jim would go out for a late supper to revel in Emily's accomplishment, no matter what the outcome of the hearing.

A loud, playful screech came from the kitchen. Life went on.

Chapter 28 ~ Average

Jim sat quietly next to Mr. Johansen and scanned the room as Marylou Breckenridge was being sworn in. Although he had skipped lunch, Jim was not hungry. The gnawing pain in the pit of his stomach returned. The expert witnesses had departed, replaced by Herman Baker, who sat beside Ms. Estrada.

They sat adjacent to one another, diagonally across the table from Jim. Ms. Estrada appeared to be about fifty. Her brownish grey hair was gathered in a bun at the back, apart from a few stray strands, which projected randomly at the sides. She wore a navy blue business suit and a stern expression. As Dr. Baker was leaning back in his chair, he smoothed his silvery hair and grinned while chomping on a piece of gum. He sported a tweed jacket with an open neck shirt. His eyes seemed too close together and Jim thought it made him look untrustworthy, but perhaps the feelings were merely because of their history together.

Mr. Briggs cleared his throat while he sat at the far end of the table, ready to question Marylou Breckenridge. She had shortly cropped grey hair and was dressed in her light blue nursing uniform.

"Can you tell me, Ms. Breckenridge, when you first met Mrs. Edna Doyle?" Mr. Briggs smiled as he awaited her response.

"She came into the Emergency Department in the late afternoon—at 5:45." Marylou looked up from her papers and over her reading glasses. "I started my shift at seven in the evening, so I met her soon after that. She was initially assessed in Emergency C, because the triage nurse thought she looked unwell. But when she appeared to be stable, she was transferred over to our side in Emergency E. I remember because she was the first patient I assessed coming on shift, soon after 7:00."

"And what was her condition at that time?"

"She seemed fine to me." Marylou looked down at her papers. Pointing with her index finger, she continued. "Her vitals were good—blood pressure was 112 over 66 and her pulse rate was 92 per minute. These numbers were improved from when she arrived. But I guess the IV fluids they started on arrival probably helped."

"So can you tell me when Mrs. Doyle was first seen by a physician?" Mr. Briggs rubbed his goatee between his thumb and forefinger, resting his elbow on the table.

"She was seen by Dr. Everitt before I came on shift. He didn't reassess her until after blood test results were back. Oh, yes, we also ended up waiting to get the ultrasound report from the previous day—that took close to an hour to track down. So I think Dr. Everitt didn't actually reassess Mrs. Doyle until about 8:15."

"What happened next?"

"Let me see..." she said, examining her papers. "I think Dr. Everitt asked me to call surgery to see Mrs. Doyle in consultation. I remember, they were all in the O.R.—the operating room—so no one actually came for at least another hour or hour and a half. I was expecting the junior resident to attend, but instead, Dr. Smythe showed up at...let me see...9:37 p.m."

"And how was Mrs. Doyle during that time, awaiting Dr. Smythe's arrival?"

Marylou's eyes darted back and forth and she blushed. "We have so many patients to cover in three different sections of Emergency E. I didn't actually have a chance to assess her for an hour and a half. But there were no voiced concerns, until she rang her call bell and asked for Gravol at 9:15. I gave her twenty-five milligrams in the intravenous at 9:35, just before Dr. Smythe arrived."

"And her vital signs through the evening? How were they?"

"Like I said, I was busy with other patients. But right before I gave her the Gravol, her vitals were unchanged."

"And after that?"

"I'm afraid...it's just that...I actually didn't see her from then until she left. Dr. Smythe assessed her and when I returned at 10:55, she was pulling on her coat. Her husband said the doctor told them she could go home."

"Did they say which doctor?"

Jim loosened his tie and undid the top button on his shirt. He shifted in his chair, awaiting her response.

"Well, it wouldn't have been Dr. Everitt, as he went off shift at 9:00 p.m. Although he would've informed another emergency doctor about the patient, he left the decision up to Dr. Smythe." Marylou looked up sheepishly and shrugged her shoulders slightly while staring at Jim.

"And what were her vital signs the last time you measured them?"

"She and her husband seemed to be in such a hurry. I convinced her to slide her arm out of her coat on the way out. Her pulse was elevated to 114, but I assumed that was because she'd just climbed out of bed."

"And her blood pressure?"

"105 over 55. Not abnormal for an elderly lady of slim build."

"Thank you. I have no further questions." Mr. Briggs stood up and returned to his place at the table, one seat over, next to Mr. Doyle.

Marylou glanced around the room and quickly rose from her chair.

"Excuse me!" Heads in the room turned toward Mr. Johansen. "I believe I might now have the opportunity to ask Ms. Breckenridge a few questions?"

"Yes, of course," Mr. Ripley said. "Ms. Breckenridge, would you be so kind as to remain for a few more minutes while Mr. Johansen asks you some questions?"

"I won't be long," Johansen promised as he clumsily slammed his briefcase onto the table next to Marylou.

Startled, she retreated slightly and then resumed her place, sitting at the end of the table, next to Mr. Johansen.

"Now, Ms. Breckenridge," Mr. Johansen began. "I just have a few questions. Did Mr. or Mrs. Doyle actually state that a doctor told Mrs. Doyle she could go home, or is it possible that they were simply under the impression that she might be let home later that evening?"

"I don't remember exactly. May I refer to my notes?"

"Yes, of course." Johansen replied softly.

"It says here, Mr. Doyle had just returned from the cafeteria. When he was away, the doctor told Mrs. Doyle she could go home."

"Did you see him returning from the cafeteria?"

"No. Like I said, Mrs. Doyle was pulling on her coat. They were in the process of leaving." Marylou was pressing her hands quietly on the chart, which lay on the table.

"And from your notes, or from your memory for that matter, do you know which of Mr. or Mrs. Doyle said the doctor told them they could go home?"

"No. I'm sorry. I don't know which one of them said that initially."

"Did either of them mention Dr. Smythe by name?"

"I don't remember."

"Do you have a discharge order written in the hospital record?"

She looked down at the chart. “No, I don’t.”

“Is that standard protocol? For someone to go home without a discharge order?”

“Normally, no. If there is no discharge order, we usually get them to sign a form saying they are leaving against medical advice.”

“And why, in this situation, did they not sign such a form?”

“I mentioned it. But they seemed like they were in a big hurry and I think one of them said they wouldn’t sign the form. Because the doctor said they could go home. So I simply wrote on the chart, ‘Client states she is leaving as physician said she could go home.’ And at that point, I had many other patients to attend to, so I let her go home and documented it on the chart.” Marylou placed her hands on the table and looked down.

“Thank you, Ms. Breckenridge. I have no further questions.”

Mr. Johansen picked up his briefcase and walked the length of the room, resuming his position sitting next to Jim.

Jim leaned over close to his lawyer and whispered quietly, “I never thought Marylou might be in a bit of hot water over this. But she doesn’t look too happy with your questions.

“It’s not about Marylou, Jim. This is about you. But anything I can deflect to others could be helpful to you. But here comes the most important witness now. Baker’s up. And then you, of course.”

Jim experienced a cramp in his lower abdomen. He didn’t know whether he could hold on. He felt like he was going to have an episode of explosive diarrhea. Clenching his cheeks together, he tried to concentrate. As Dr. Baker seated himself at the end of the table, Jim’s physical discomfort eased. Ms. Estrada sat next to Baker, directly across from Mr. Briggs. Jim looked straight ahead, listening to the swearing in process in the background while trying to ignore his abdominal pains.

“And do you promise to answer truthfully today?”

“Yes, of course,” Dr. Baker responded, resting his forearms on the table in front of him.

Mr. Briggs began, speaking softly. “Dr. Baker, please tell us when you first became aware of Mrs. Edna Doyle.”

“Jim—Dr. Smythe—called me at about ten o’clock in the evening on Thursday, September 26th.”

“And can you describe the content of this telephone conversation?”

"Dr. Smythe had seen Mrs. Doyle earlier for some vague complaints of abdominal pain. He wasn't entirely happy that her symptoms were benign in nature, so I offered to stop by the Emergency Department and see her myself."

"When you say he wasn't happy, what do you mean?"

"Well, as I'm sure you know, Mrs. Doyle was not a young woman and abdominal pain can be serious at times. But there was nothing really we could hang our hat on, if you know what I mean."

"Not exactly. Can you explain?"

"Sure. Her pain wasn't too bad. And she'd had an ultrasound the day before, which showed only some sludge in the gallbladder—a fairly non-specific finding. And although her hemoglobin was somewhat low, it wasn't alarming. But nevertheless, when one of my residents has concerns, I'm always willing to go and see the patient myself."

Jim shot a glance at Johansen, who subtly raised his flat hand toward Jim and nodded slightly.

"Was there any other discussion on the phone? Did you and Dr. Smythe discuss doing any other tests?"

"I do recall we talked about the ultrasound result from the day before. We were sure there was no aneurysm of the aorta. So with that information in mind, we didn't really discuss doing any more tests. But as you know, the patient showed up later with bleeding from a splenic artery aneurysm. And that would be too small to show up on an ultrasound."

"Was it reasonable that Dr. Smythe did not suggest admitting the patient or ordering any other tests?"

"Excuse me!" Mr. Johansen interjected. "I believe counsel is asking Dr. Baker to act as an expert witness in this case. Clearly, Dr. Baker cannot give an impartial, independent opinion about a case that he is personally involved in."

"Mr. Briggs," Mr. Ripley agreed, "I would concur that Dr. Baker cannot be expected to comment objectively as an independent expert. Can you retract or rephrase the question?"

"Yes, of course," Mr. Briggs said. Turning to Dr. Baker, he added, "At the time, did you agree with Dr. Smythe's plan as discussed over the phone?"

"Yes, based on the information Dr. Smythe gave me, I had no significant concerns."

"Okay."

"And as you know," Baker continued, "I had told Dr. Smythe that I would see the patient in an hour. But as Ms. Breckenridge has told you, the patient left the department at 10:55. So how could I see her if she'd already left? You can imagine my surprise when I encountered the patient in the operating room at 2:30 in the morning, bleeding out."

"Can you explain?"

"Well, you just don't expect a relatively well woman who has left the Emergency Department under her own steam to be brought back to hospital so soon in such a dire condition."

"Yes. Now Dr. Baker, do you think there was any chance of saving Mrs. Doyle by the time she was in the operating room?"

"No. Absolutely not."

"Okay. I'm going to shift gears here a little. Is it possible for a resident to discharge a patient? Or do all surgical consults have to be reviewed personally by the staff surgeon?"

"Most certainly, residents can discharge patients on their own. As long as they feel comfortable with the decision and as long as they provide the staff surgeon with sufficient information to back up the plan."

"In this case, did Dr. Smythe relay sufficient information to you over the phone to support his plan for this patient?"

Jim shifted in his chair, awaiting Dr. Baker's response.

"At the time, I figured he told me everything I wanted to know." Baker glanced at Ms. Estrada and then looked back at Mr. Briggs.

"Yes?"

"You see, there's always judgment involved and sometimes over the phone it's difficult to know how things are, compared to if you were face to face with a patient."

"Well," Mr. Briggs continued, "did Dr. Smythe provide you with the information you would expect?"

"I think so."

"Thank you. I have no more questions."

Dr. Baker reached to the tip of his protruded tongue and plucked out his gum with his fingers. He positioned it on a piece of paper and then rolled it into a ball and placed it on the table in front of him. Ms. Estrada leaned over toward Dr. Baker, covered her mouth with her hand and breathed a few incomprehensible sounds. Dr. Baker nodded and responded with his own whispered dialogue. After further quiet discussion, Baker slid his hand onto the table to retrieve the gum wrapped in paper and returned his hands to his lap. Baker leaned back in his chair, grinning.

Jim looked away and gazed blankly ahead. He couldn't help but think that Dr. Baker had given him only lukewarm support. He feared that no matter what the outcome of this hospital hearing, it wasn't going to be decisive enough to get him off the hook with the MLA.

Mr. Johansen was making his way, briefcase in hand, back down to the far end of the table. He sat down and opened his briefcase, pulling out a stack of papers, then closed the case and placed it under the table. Johansen stared intently through his thick glasses at Dr. Baker, who quietly coughed while slipping a fresh stick of gum into his mouth.

"Dr. Baker." Johansen adjusted his bowtie and quietly smacked his lips.

"Yes?" Dr. Baker stopped chewing.

"I know we've gone through much of this already this afternoon and I have seen your written statement, but I wonder if you would indulge me by reviewing some of the important points?"

"Certainly."

"I understand you first became aware of Mrs. Edna Doyle when Dr. Smythe phoned you at about 10:00 p.m."

"That's correct," he replied confidently.

"And what did Dr. Smythe ask you when he phoned? Did he propose a particular plan?"

"I don't recall exactly, but I think he was calling for advice. He didn't know what to do with Mrs. Doyle, so he wanted to bounce some ideas off me."

"Did he want to admit Mrs. Doyle to the surgical service?"

"No, he never said that, as far as I recall."

"Did he express any uneasiness about her condition?"

"I don't think so."

"Did he have any specific questions for you?"

"Like I said, he wanted to know my thoughts on the issue. So I said I would take a look at her myself."

"If he had asked your permission to admit the patient under your care, would you have agreed to do so?"

"Don't answer that," Ms. Estrada jumped in. She looked at Mr. Ripley and then continued, "My client does not need to speculate on what he might or might not have done."

"Mr. Johansen?" Mr. Ripley said, shrugging his shoulders.

"Yes of course, Your Honour, I withdraw the question." Mr. Johansen turned abruptly back at Dr. Baker and added, "Is Dr. Smythe a good resident?"

“I object,” Ms. Estrada said, sighing. “It’s not relevant.”

“Ms. Estrada, I think it is important to know whether Dr. Smythe had the trust of his staff surgeon. After all, it is my client whose actions are definitely in question today. I think it’s only fair to help determine how the decision-making process was shared between the staff surgeon and his resident.”

“Go ahead, Dr. Baker. I believe the question is relevant,” Mr. Ripley said evenly.

Ms. Estrada nodded at Dr. Baker. “I’m sorry,” Baker said, “what was the question?”

“Is Dr. Smythe a good resident?” Johansen’s pitch escalated and his nostrils flared.

“Honestly…I’d say he’s average. I’ve seen better. But I’ve also seen worse.” He folded his arms across his chest and leaned back in his chair.

From the far end of the table Jim could see Mr. Johansen’s body stiffen.

“Well, if he’s only average,” Johansen continued, “when Dr. Smythe said he wasn’t happy with the condition of Mrs. Doyle, would it not have been prudent to admit her?”

“I object. Speculation.”

“Sorry, I withdraw the question,” Johansen said without prompting from Mr. Ripley. “Let me put it this way, Dr. Baker. Do you recall Dr. Smythe saying he wasn’t happy sending this lady home?”

“No, I don’t recall that,” Dr. Baker replied, leaning forward and chewing.

“Why did you not simply agree to have Mrs. Doyle admitted to the surgical service when you spoke to Dr. Smythe on the phone?”

“Look, the lady didn’t sound too bad to me. But over the phone, you never know.” His voice trailed off as he continued, “Especially with someone like Jim.”

“Pardon? What did you say?” Johansen was beginning to hyperventilate.

“You just can’t always tell over the phone.”

“No, after that. What was it you said?”

“Sometimes certain residents, Dr. Smythe being one of them, give a picture over the phone that doesn’t turn out to be exactly as advertised when the patient is assessed by the staff surgeon.”

“Are you suggesting that Dr. Smythe could have done things differently?”

“Well he could have ordered—”

“You don’t have to answer—” Ms. Estrada interjected.

"No, I want to," Baker continued indignantly. "He could have ordered an ultrasound or a CAT scan."

"Don't answer anything more," Ms. Estrada said quietly to Dr. Baker, and then to Mr. Ripley, "I think this line of questioning is speculation and we have already established this is not relevant."

While the others were discussing the last point, Jim noticed Mr. Johansen was rapidly turning red. His lips were pursed and he did not appear to be breathing. And then Jim saw it—two unmistakable vertical columns—bulging jugular veins on either side of Johansen's neck, framing his reddening face.

"Fine!" Johansen exclaimed, exhaling as his neck veins suddenly collapsed. His colour returning to normal, he continued. "Okay, tell me then, Dr. Baker, when do you normally do surgery?"

"All the time," Baker replied. "After all, I am a surgeon."

"No, I think you misunderstand my question. Which day is normally your elective operating room day?"

"Fridays, usually. But I sometimes pick up extra time other days during the week."

"Have you ever had elective surgery cancelled because surgical beds are too full?"

"I suppose. Administration never seems to give us what we need."

"Why do you prefer to take call on Thursday nights?"

"I object. This is irrelevant," Ms. Estrada interjected.

"I think you will see the relevance soon, Mr. Ripley."

"Continue. Answer the question, Dr. Baker."

"Sorry, what was the question?"

"Why do you prefer to take call on Thursday nights?"

"Oh, I don't know. It just seems to work out that way."

"Aren't you tired on your regular O.R. day—Friday? After being on call the night before?"

"Sometimes, but at least…"

"At least you are less likely to have surgery cancelled on Friday if you are in control of who gets admitted to surgical beds Thursday night, isn't that true?"

"That has nothing to do with it."

"Isn't it possible that if Edna Doyle had been admitted to a surgical bed Thursday night, and happened to survive, that you might have had some of your Friday surgery cancelled? Isn't that possible?"

"I object!" Ms. Estrada shot Baker a cold stare.

"Never mind, Mr. Ripley. I will not continue this line of questioning." Mr. Johansen leaned back in his chair and smiled. "Dr. Baker, do you know a Ms. Gina Connelly, by any chance?"

Baker's rhythmic chewing ceased. Blood drained from his face instantly.

"If you can't recall, Dr. Baker, she's an O.R. nurse. But perhaps you know her not only in the O.R. but from outside?"

"I object. This is not relevant."

"Perhaps I could make it relevant, Ms. Estrada. Perchance you and I should have a little chat, off the record, before I continue?" Johansen shrugged his shoulders while turning his palms upward. He smiled, exposing his entire upper row of front teeth.

"Yes, that would be fine," she replied tersely.

Johansen stood up and scurried the short distance over to Ms. Estrada. He leaned over to her and mumbled some inaudible words. She responded while Baker sat close by, his forehead wrinkled and his body frozen. Jim yearned to hear the quiet conversation at the end of the table. Johansen motioned for Mr. Ripley and Mr. Grifton to join the discussion. Huddled together, they continued for another thirty seconds, at which point Mr. Grifton broke away from the group and announced, "We will take a short break. Dr. Smythe, perhaps you could wait in the hallway? Someone will be out to notify you when we require your presence again."

Jim nodded and slipped out into the hallway, closing the door behind him. He glanced around. Good. No people who might recognize him. He couldn't quite understand what was happening. He sensed tension and it seemed Baker was in some sort of trouble, but Jim was unable to piece it together. Jim suddenly recalled he was to be questioned next. His abdominal churning and cramping returned. He wouldn't be able to stand it if he had to undergo a grilling like Baker had just gone through. He glanced at the wall clock. It was getting late in the afternoon. If they recessed until tomorrow, he couldn't endure another night of waiting. He wasn't sure which he feared more—being peppered with questions, or a postponement until tomorrow. He decided: waiting would be impossible, simply intolerable.

Suddenly, the door opened and Baker emerged first. Head down, he walked right past Jim without a word. Ms. Estrada followed closely behind. Mr. Grifton, in passing, said to Jim, "Dr. Smythe, Mr. Johansen will be waiting for you inside." Single file, they continued. Next came the young hospital lawyer, who had said nothing but had taken notes all day. The recorder swiftly followed, with Mr. Ripley, Mr. Briggs and Gavin Doyle at each other's heels. Gavin nodded subtly at Jim on his way past, offering his first eye contact or morsel of recognition all day. Jim looked into the room. Like the sudden exodus after an encore at a rock concert, the room's occupants had evacuated quickly, except for Mr. Johansen. A few strewn bits of paper remained and chairs were out of place. Johansen sat close to the door with a mountain of folders in front of him on the table.

Chapter 29 ~ Retirement Plans

"It's over, Jim." Johansen's eyes tracked Jim as he sat down in the next chair.

"What do you mean, it's over? It can't be over! I have to prove my innocence!"

"That won't be necessary," Johansen replied, smiling.

"But I must!"

"Baker's in trouble, Jim. That means you're off the hook."

"What do you mean?" Although he couldn't quite comprehend the details, Jim could feel a heavy weight being lifted off his shoulders.

"Dr. Baker saw Mrs. Doyle."

"What?"

"And I don't mean in the operating room. We knew that. But he saw her in Emergency."

"Seriously?"

"Baker was the one the Doyles referred to when they indicated 'the doctor' said she could go home." Johansen was grinning broadly. "It's over, Jim."

"How do you know that?" Jim's knees started to shake. In a daze, he reached to his neck, loosened his tie and pulled it over his head, placing the tie on the table.

"Baker hasn't said a whole lot, but he did say enough for Mr. Ripley and Mr. Grifton to abandon you as the target of this investigation. What happens to Baker from here is of no importance to us."

"What do you mean? How much do you know?" Jim slipped off his jacket and tossed it on the chair beside him.

"Remember Gina Connelly?"

"Yes, the O.R. nurse. But she was in the operating room that night, not Emergency," Jim said, puzzled.

"True, she went on shift at 11:00 in the O.R. But she was with Baker when you phoned him."

"Huh?"

"That's right. She's been playing telephone tag with me. But two nights ago, she finally got hold of me. She wanted to get this off her chest. In fact, she almost told you in the operating room a month ago, after she broke up with Baker."

"Broke up?"

"That's right, Jim. They were having an affair. She knew that Baker saw Mrs. Doyle in Emergency because he left Gina to go see Mrs. Doyle. After he said she could go home, he called Gina and complained that you had troubled him over this useless consult, not realizing Mrs. Doyle was silently bleeding as she left the hospital."

"But there's no record that he saw her? Nurses always chart when we see patients."

"Well, this is where my information is a little sketchy. And by the way, much of what Gina told me was second-hand information. Plus, she'd washed her hands of Baker and didn't want to participate in any hearings, if at all possible. This being what I considered 'round number one', I figured we just might be able to convince Baker to come clean. Unless, of course, he supported you unreservedly. But since today wasn't decisively going in your direction—the experts were divided and witnesses weren't staunchly defending you—I had to pull out all the stops."

"But I still don't understand..."

"Oh, yes. How did he see Mrs. Doyle and not have it documented?"

"Yes." Jim leaned forward, listening intently.

"Baker didn't actually plan it that way. He also complained to Gina that you had his patient in Emergency E—he told her you could shoot a cannon through there and no nurses would notice."

"That's right!" Jim exclaimed, slapping his thigh. "He told me to never have any of his patients in E again."

"Well, that's how he felt at the time, but when he realized the lady who bled to death in the operating room was the same one he'd sent home hours earlier, he wondered if he could use it to his advantage. I'm only speculating now, but he'd probably seen her for only a couple of minutes. Who knows? Maybe he had a touch of alcohol on his breath and wanted to get in and out quickly, encountering as few people as possible. Whether he intended on dictating a note later isn't clear, but at the time, he made no record on the chart. He just told her she could go home. Perhaps if he'd previously had trouble with the MLA, he welcomed the opportunity to stay under their radar. So later, when he realized his predicament, he decided to let the dust settle. When he scrutinized the record the next week and didn't find his name recorded once in the chart, he decided he'd remain silent on the issue and see what happened. As time went on, he figured he was more in the clear each day. And although Baker saw Mrs. Doyle when her husband was in the cafeteria, he probably delighted in the fact that Mr. Doyle had a touch of dementia. He just didn't realize Gina would say something."

"But the lying. How could he?"

"First of all, Jim, you know him better than I do. Baker's probably not above lying once in a while. And as far as I know, he only lied twice."

"When?"

"Until today, the only person he lied to was you, at the end of Mrs. Doyle's operation."

"That's right. He told me he didn't realize it was the same lady that we'd spoken about on the phone, and he also told me that when he went to Emergency, she'd already left."

"Exactly. That was the first time he lied. The second time was today."

"When was that?"

"He said you were an average resident. I knew that was a boldfaced lie the second it came out of his mouth. Maurice Steinberg and others have told me otherwise. When Baker said that, I knew he was hostile toward you and I had no choice but to push him. And of course, the whole reason in the first place that he was resistant to admitting Mrs. Doyle to hospital was that he didn't want elective surgery cancelled on Friday due to lack of beds. But you know that—you've had enough of a history with him to understand the way he operates."

"Boy, is he in trouble!"

"Yes and no, Jim. It's going to take a long time for him to sort this thing out. But remember, he only lied to you. Yes, he sent this lady home, but our expert said it was not unreasonable. And yes, he can be in hot water for not documenting his encounter with the patient. But he was very careful about what he said and what he wrote for the inquiry. Still, I was suspicious of Baker from early on."

"Why's that?" Jim stretched his arms over his head and carefully placed his feet on the boardroom table.

"Two things. It wasn't so much what Dr. Baker said in his statement, it was what he *didn't* say. It was a very well-crafted document. He never denied seeing the patient. In his statement, he said you talked to him about Mrs. Doyle on the phone and that he'd go and see her. Then he starts trying to look like the independent expert on a case that he was personally involved in—something, of course, he can't really do. But he never actually denied seeing the patient. I thought it was strange he didn't find a nurse to ask why Mrs. Doyle had left. But he didn't. He just skipped over the Emergency bit and then went on and on, pontificating like an outside expert on splenic artery aneurysms. And then he bounced right over to the O.R. and babbled on about how he didn't realize it was the same patient you had discussed with him on the phone, and by that time there was no chance of saving her. But today, apart from calling you an average resident, he chose not to lie. When you were out of the room, he admitted he saw Mrs. Doyle and sent her home without documenting it. But that's all he acknowledged. Now he and his lawyer will have to deal with the fallout. But it's not your problem, Jim. You both missed the diagnosis of internal bleeding, but you're the resident. He's the staff surgeon and he sent her home. So you are totally in the clear. I expect the MLA will drop this complaint against you by the end of the month. You can get your license in July after all."

Jim could hardly believe how good he was feeling and how vastly his mood had transformed in a matter of minutes. Only now did he realize the extent of the load he had carried over the last few months. "Wait a minute," Jim said, his eyes narrowing on Johansen. "You said two things. What was the second thing that made you suspicious of Baker?"

"Oh yes, that. Well, he probably wouldn't remember it, but I played duplicate bridge against him in a tournament about ten years ago. I was sure he was sending signals to his partner the whole game. I hadn't seen him since, but I remember thinking he was a cheat." Johansen began to snort and turn red, then laughed uncontrollably.

Jim smiled broadly and, picking up his jacket from the chair, he stood and reached out to shake his lawyer's hand.

***

Having said good-bye and left the boardroom, Jim closed the door behind, leaving Mr. Johansen with his laptop and reams of papers spread on his corner of the table. Jim was sure the others had all left by now. In reality, he wanted to avoid only Dr. Baker. The others—the lawyers and administrators—they could all go to hell as far as Jim was concerned. But Jim would find it awkward to face Herman Baker, whose faltering in the boardroom today had resulted in an unceremonious plunge from which he might never recover. Jim could identify with the criticism Baker would no doubt endure for sending Mrs. Doyle home. That, as far as Jim was concerned, was not the worst error one could commit, despite the dreadful outcome. But Baker's overall credibility had suffered a severe blow today. Perhaps he deserved it. Jim had never had a good relationship with Baker. But despite their locking horns on multiple occasions over the years, he had performed many operations under Dr. Baker's supervision. Although Jim had to this point never considered it, they shared a bond. Their tumultuous relationship was forever altered today and for that, Jim would have no remorse. But for an instant, he felt sorry for Dr. Baker.

Jim looked into the distance down the hallway. A beaming Amanda was approaching, clutching Emily in her arms. As they came closer, Jim asked, "How did you know? You must have known something!"

"I was in Dr. Steinberg's office. Went to meet him for a little chat. He got a phone call five minutes ago from the hospital lawyer. Emily and I were sitting in his office when he took the call."

"Wait a minute! What were you—"

"Long story, Jim. Let's just say I was concerned about you so I arranged to meet Dr. Steinberg this afternoon." Still holding Emily, Amanda smiled and gave Jim a hug, her soft, shiny hair cascading over his face. Jim didn't think she'd let go. As Emily started to squirm, Amanda took a few steps back and placed her standing on the floor. Emily teetered and then walked steadily toward Jim, who crouched down, open-mouthed. She went straight into his arms.

Amanda put her hand on Jim's shoulder and said proudly, "See, what'd I tell you? Walking today!"

"I know. You're right. It's a fantastic day. Write down the date so we'll never forget."

Amanda laughed and then said, "How could we forget today? As much as you'll want to put all this behind you, this whole event is going to stay with you longer than you'll care to remember."

"No, it's good from all sides. I don't want to forget. Except September 26th—I'd be happy to obliterate that day from my mind."

As they walked down the hall, Jim carrying Emily close to his chest, her head resting against his, Amanda said, "Let's go to the cafeteria. Dr. Steinberg wants to meet us for coffee. Later, you and I are going out for dinner. You've got the night off. I arranged a sitter and we're going to celebrate."

"Where?"

"I really don't care. We'll think of something."

***

Dr. Steinberg smiled across the cafeteria table at Jim and Amanda. Despite the cacophony while workers dove into early supper, Emily lay across Amanda's lap in peaceful slumber. Her recently acquired skill of ambulating had apparently tired Emily to the point of sheer exhaustion. Jim was revelling in his newfound freedom from torment, and now realized he hadn't been his rational best lately. He inched his chair closer to Amanda so their thighs were touching.

Steinberg straightened his tie and spoke first. "Well, what'd I tell you?" His steely grey eyes darted between Amanda and Jim.

"Huh?" Jim was gazing off into the distance, unfocused.

Turning to Jim, Amanda said cheerfully, "I think he's talking to me, sweetie." She then looked back at Dr. Steinberg and added, "It's not that I doubted you, but it has been a period of uncertainty, to say the least."

"What?" Jim still wasn't sure what they were talking about.

"Let's just say, Jim, that Dr. Steinberg has been an invaluable source of reassurance for me lately, when I've needed a little outside support."

"When have you..." Jim hesitated as he could see Amanda rolling her eyes in his peripheral vision.

"Uncertainty, Jimmy. You've got to learn to be comfortable with uncertainty. I know you like to know the score. You're pretty up-front that way. But sometimes you've just got to carry on, not knowing all the answers. Be content just being. Take pleasure in the moment. You know what I mean?" Steinberg sipped his coffee and scowled. He reached for the sugar and poured it onto a teaspoon, stopping only after it overflowed into his cup. He stirred it in and grinned.

Jim wasn't sure how anything about the last few months could be enjoyed but he was in no mood to contradict Dr. Steinberg, so he remained silent.

"C'mon, Jimmy! We've had some great cases the past few months! You simply need to realize it hasn't been all bad just because of some minor complaint." He winked at Amanda.

"You're right, Dr. Steinberg," Jim responded. "If only I'd been in the mood to appreciate them a little more. But from now on, I'll try to be more appreciative of what I've got." He turned to Amanda and squeezed her hand.

Jim noticed the letter amongst some papers on the table in front of Steinberg. "I dropped a letter off for you earlier," he said, flinching.

"I know, I've got it right here, Jimmy. I was just going to open it," he said, picking it up.

"No! Can I have it back? I need to change it up a bit."

"Sure," Steinberg replied. He handed the letter to Jim and then continued. "Only six weeks left at St. Joe's and then you're into the last three months at the University Hospital. How does that feel?"

"It's good. And I don't know how to thank you for all the teaching..."

"That's easy. Teach others. And on another note," Steinberg continued, "I'm retiring this summer."

"You're what?" Amanda's mouth remained open as she looked straight at Dr. Steinberg.

"You heard me, Mandy. To be honest, I was hoping Jimmy would take over my practice some day. I'd even hold out for another year or two if you needed to go and get some additional training to bring back a special skill here," he said, turning his eyes on Jim. "Last fall, when you said you were going to Lakefield, I realized it probably wasn't going to happen, but there was still a chance. I didn't mention retiring the last few months because I knew you were preoccupied. But now that your burden has been lifted, Jimmy, I can tell you. I'm retiring this summer, unless you have a fantastic scheme to take over my practice. I could hold on a little longer."

"Well, that's a great compliment," Jim said, "but I don't think I could arrange any training this late in the year. And besides, I'm just looking forward to moving to Lakefield and spending more time with my family." He clutched Amanda's hand tightly.

"And I'm okay with that, too," Amanda said, not taking her eyes off Jim. "It'll be good to be close to my parents and get back to a semi-normal life."

"I'll tell you what, Jimmy—you remember Mr. McKiddie?"

"Of course." Jim turned to Amanda and added, "The one with the perforated stercoral ulcer who later nearly bled to death from his tracheostomy?"

"I remember. The one when Emily and I had to go visit my parents without you." She frowned and then patted his thigh.

"Well, he actually went home a few weeks ago," Steinberg said nonchalantly.

"Seriously? I wasn't sure he'd ever get home," Jim responded.

"Yup. I didn't want to bother you, so I went over to the cardiothoracics ward myself. They wanted to send him back to us on the surgery ward, but since he only needed a few more days in hospital, I suggested they send him home directly when he was ready."

"That's great," Jim said as he thought back to McKiddie and the number of days he had been on the brink of death.

"Anyway, Jimmy, he probably won't be ready to have his colostomy reversed until after I've retired. Perhaps I should tell him to see you in Lakefield to get it done when he's ready."

"Yes, I could handle that."

"Just get your year completed and exams done first and then worry about that," Amanda said. She then turned to Dr. Steinberg and continued, "You know, you were absolutely right when you said this would turn out fine. I think I can see the cloud has lifted already. You told me Jim would feel better instantly when this complaint was resolved and I think you predicted it flawlessly."

Dr. Steinberg slammed his ceramic coffee cup on the table and leaned forward. "Of course I was right!"

Epilogue

Halfway across the country, Jim sat in the hallway on a stiff wooden chair, awaiting his final obstacle to freedom. He straightened his tie and looked through the window, thankful he wasn't enduring the sweltering temperature outside. Any moment, the door to his left would open and he'd be called to his final one-hour oral exam in surgery. The morning exam had gone well, he thought, as he reviewed some of the questions he'd been asked. It seemed the only ones he had had trouble with were patient problems with controversial answers. Heeding Dr. Steinberg's advice and relying on many hours of practical exam experience, he felt comfortable with the uncertainty that arose from some of the cases he was asked to discuss. He simply spoke from his experience and when unsure of a course of action, Jim raised the pertinent opposing issues and then took a stand. When pushed by the examiners, Jim held firm. *If only I can repeat this morning's performance*, he thought.

With five minutes before his scheduled exam time, Jim allowed his mind to wander back over the past year. Five months of it had been tainted by the stress he was feeling over the Doyle case, yet he realized not a week had gone by without a terrific experience either in or outside the operating room.

At the beginning of the year, he had had his doubts about Hank, but his junior resident turned out to be a loyal colleague and friend. Tabitha, of course, was probably the smartest resident he had worked with all year and he took pride in knowing that he contributed significantly to her progress as a surgical resident. Even Sam, with all his self-interested quirks, made Jim smile from time to time. Rhani, the brightest medical student he'd had in a long time, had finally decided to pursue surgery. Jim wasn't surprised; it had just taken her a while to wrap her head around the possibility of a long, arduous residency program.

He'd had some great cases—from McKiddie to Klumpar and many others along the way, he'd not forget them for a long time. There were also some emotionally draining cases, those he'd rather consign to oblivion but likely could not.

Herman Baker was still at work, although in a reduced capacity, and he was keeping a low profile. He'd spoken fewer than five sentences to Jim since the hearing. Jim had no idea about Baker's situation with the Doyle case. The MLA had dropped the complaint against Jim before the end of the month, just as Johansen had predicted. Whether they were pursuing the issue with Baker was totally unknown to Jim. As far as Baker's professional and personal issues were concerned, Jim was now indifferent.

Many surgeons had contributed to Jim's surgical education, especially during the final year. Albano and O'Brien were standouts. He'd never be able to thank them enough. But well above them all was Dr. Steinberg. Not only was he a gifted teacher, but he was also like a second father to Jim.

The door rattled and then opened, startling Jim. A short man in a navy blue suit leaned around the doorway and said, "Dr. Smythe? Would you care to come in now?"

"Yes, sir," Jim replied.

Seated across the desk, the two examining surgeons took turns questioning Jim. They began with short, easy questions, likely to take away his nerves, just like the morning exam. The funny thing was that he didn't feel anxious. He only had the nervous excitement that accompanies competing in a championship hockey game. Or operating on a sick patient. It was nothing like the gut-wrenching anxiety he had experienced leading up to the hearing.

The questions were becoming more complicated, but each time, he thought back to a similar situation in residency.

"Okay," the taller examiner began, "you have a seventy-nine-year-old man who presents to your Emergency Department with three days of vomiting. He's had a previous appendectomy but is otherwise healthy. His abdomen is very distended but is only mildly tender. His white count is normal. Here are his X-rays." He reached over and flipped the toggle switch on the X-ray box. "You can move a little closer, Dr. Smythe, if that helps you."

From a distance, it was as clear to Jim as if he were staring at his street on a map of his hometown. Still, he thought it would be wise to accept the offer and move closer. As Jim approached the view box, then slightly bent over to examine the X-rays at eye level, nothing changed. It was obvious.

"Small bowel obstruction with air in the biliary tree," Jim stated calmly.

The two examiners turned their heads and looked at one another.

"Has he had any surgical or endoscopic procedure on his bile duct?" Jim asked.

"No."

"Then I would say this man has a gallstone ileus until proven otherwise. He needs to go to surgery."

"Would you not at least try a nasogastric tube overnight?" the short one queried, attempting to set an inviting trap.

"No, I would take him to surgery," Jim replied.

"Before you go to the operating room, can you tell me about the pathophysiology of gallstone ileus?"

Jim spent the next five minutes explaining cholecystoduodenal fistula as if he were explaining to a friend how to line up a difficult golf shot.

"Okay, now the surgery. What incision would you make?"

"Lower midline."

"Okay, you get in there and find a gallstone impacted in the distal small bowel. What do you do next?"

Jim explained what they had done with Mrs. Klumpar. He described removing the stone in great detail, as if it had happened yesterday.

"All right," the shorter examiner continued. "Would you take out the gallbladder?"

"No."

"No? I thought you just explained this was a gallstone ileus and that the stone eroded from the gallbladder into the small bowel through a fistula. There are likely more stones. Why wouldn't you take out the gallbladder? Are you sure?"

Jim's mind drifted briefly to the drowning man who needed a lifejacket, not swimming lessons. "No. I'd leave the gallbladder. We can always come back another day when it's less risky."

The examiners looked at each other and the tall one asked a question about treatment of breast cancer.

The other wanted Jim to explain how to do a hemorrhoidectomy, to which he responded in great detail.

They asked him about classification of colon cancer, hernia repairs and obstructive liver disease.

Jim was feeling fatigue as they continued to lob one question after another in his direction. He was sure the exam was nearing the end, but didn't want them to see him looking at the clock.

"Okay, what's the most common type of thyroid cancer?"

"Papillary," Jim replied instantly.

"Most deadly thyroid cancer?"

"Anaplastic."

"What's the most common salivary gland tumour?"

"Pleomorphic adenoma."

"What salivary gland tumours tend to be bilateral?"

"Warthin's tumour."

"What's a popcorn tumour?"

"I don't know," Jim replied without hesitation.

"Thank you, Dr. Smythe. That will be all."

Jim stood up, looked at the clock and smiled. He reached out to shake the examiners' hands, thinking he couldn't wait to phone Amanda.

ISBN 978-1-77084-239-7